FIRE WALKING

Marguérite Turnley

Published by
Shrubs Publishing
Armindale Road Baxland's Creek NSW Australia
info@shrubspublishing.com

Firewalking, Copyright 2022, by Marguérite Turnley
ISBN: 978-0-6453262-2-2

Shrubs Publishing

Quin is a target for killers. Sherry needs to escape from her life. Each answers an advertisement that leads to them working at an isolated homestead with armed guards watching their every move. People are filmed in intimate situations. The situation becomes deadly, and once again they try to escape.

Table of **Contents**

CHAPTER ONE

HAVE YOU EVER WANTED TO DISAPPEAR?

The question ate through to Quin's fragile inner peace. Yes! He desperately needed to find a way to disappear, to create a new life for himself. He was sick of looking over his shoulder every minute of the day in case a knife found its way between his shoulder blades.

Without warning, his newspaper was ripped out of his hands and replaced with a bundle of brown and white striped flannel. A woman's firm deep voice curled around his nerve ends like an echo from a mine shaft. 'We really must wear pyjamas, Mr. Jameson.' Quin scowled ferociously at her use of the royal 'we'. 'This is a hospital, not a holiday resort or a nudist colony. We can't have visitors complaining about the state of the ward now can we?'

The nurse flicked blue curtains around his bed, stuck a thermometer in his mouth and grilled him about bodily functions while noting his resentfully muffled answers on his chart. He tried not to bite the thermometer in half and was only partially successful. It was removed and its measure taken.

Quin tried to find words to describe his resentment at his lack of privacy and failed. The only course of action was to put his pyjamas on and try to retain some dignity. He failed at that too when his feet got caught up in the sheets and he had to fall out of bed to dress. Quickly he climbed back under the sheets. As camouflage they didn't quite make the grade.

One extremely intimate question was asked and the answer was greeted with, 'Speak up please. How am I supposed to write the correct answers if you whisper.' She laughed and his discomfiture became a volcano about to erupt when she consoled him with, 'Don't be embarrassed about other patients listening in. Everyone functions in the same basic way. Even you, Mr. Jameson.'

His head might be aching, his bruised and lacerated right arm bandaged in a sling, but he was still a man. He was sick of being treated like a schoolboy by women younger than himself, women he might have been dating in better days. He looked at the nurse's no-nonsense expression and thought, no, maybe not. She'd lay me out with one punch if I got too close. A masochist I'm not.

He also wished she would stop shouting. At the rate she was going the whole hospital would know when he went to the bathroom and what he did in there. Smoothing his expression into a smile, he lay back on the bed, one long leg bent at the knee, and, stretched one muscled bare arm over his head. He hooked his long fingers onto the metal bed frame and looked the nurse in the eye, saying softly, 'We're wearing pyjamas now, Nurse. The bottom half anyway. Check it out,' he offered.

Grinning wickedly, he slowly edged the sheet down below his waist and stroked the material with caressing fingers. 'It's hot in this room isn't it? Maybe I should get rid of some bedclothes.'

'Don't push your luck,' she replied in a firm but slightly over-loud voice, trying to regain her authority by straightening an already tidy locker and glaring at his chart as if it was a piece of evidence in a criminal trial. 'I can see you're a dangerous man, even when you're stuck in a hospital bed. Already you've got our nurses in a feeding frenzy. They're fighting over who's going to give you a shower tomorrow morning. I'm just grateful I'm on afternoon shift.'

Quin suddenly lost his sense of humour. 'I can shower myself,' he asserted, sitting up, his arm and chest muscles flexing restlessly. The inertia of being in a hospital bed was making him long for the freedom to exercise as he pleased, maybe go to the gym and play a few games of squash. Hitting something sounded like good idea.

'No way can you shower on your own,' the nurse said, grinning too as her control was reinstated. 'You need to be watched. If you fall you'd be in real trouble. So would we. Insurance is a blessing and a curse.'

'Watched! That's just great.' Quin's brow darkened with frustration, then a small feral grin appeared on his mouth. 'And after they've finished watching me take a shower I can take a turn and watch them. It's only fair.'

'Sorreee,' she sang. 'This is purely a one way street. We get to watch. You get to perform. That's the way it goes around here. And guess what? We like it that way.' Confident once more, she grinned as his dark scowl reappeared.

'It's being stuck in here that's eating me. And,' he gave her a sulphurous look, 'I hate being treated like a snotty nosed kid. "You don't look like one and that's half the problem,' she returned drily as her eyes roved over his smooth tanned skin and firmly muscled chest, the width of his shoulders which could never be mistaken for that of a boy and the thick waves of seal brown hair curling down to his shoulders. His face was classically handsome with just a touch of decadence around the eyes and mouth to make it irresistible. 'You're a man, that's a basic fact of life, but if you think we treat you like a kid then all you have to do is follow the rules and behave like a grown up. Cooperate and your life will be an easy ride. Buck the system and your stay will be rough. It's up to you.'

'I can get dressed and get out of your hair right now. That would suit me just fine.' He made to get out of bed and she pushed him back with a firm hand, tucking the sheets in around him tightly as if he was a fractious child.

'You know you can't do that,' she said, briskly pushing a pile of pillows into a wedge behind his back. 'You've had severe concussion. The hospital won't be responsible if you leave before being officially released. Anyway, you've got test results to come back. We'll see what your doctor says tomorrow morning.'

She pulled the curtains open and once more he was in a ward with three other men, none of whom were in any condition to provide coherent conversation. No question about it, hospital was boring the hell out of him. 'Perhaps now you'd like a drink,' the nurse asked from the doorway.

'Yeah. That sounds great.I'll have a rum and coke. Plenty of ice thanks.'

'Tough luck,' she returned with a grin. 'I'd have one with you if I could.'

'Okay, then I'll have Scotch, straight up.'

The nurse was still chuckling when she returned a few minutes later with his coffee. 'What's this?' he asked, mock severely, his sense of humour struggling to stay on top.

'Use your imagination. It can be anything you want it to be.' She gave him a slumberous look from eyes that promised, that goes for me too. 'I've got to bed down the ward for the night, Mr. Jameson. Do you need anything else?'

He shook his head. Seconds later she was gone, leaving him him alone with his suddenly morbid thoughts. Listening as the nursing staff swished curtains, doled out bedpans plus medication and thumped pillows into shape, Quin remembered another hospital, another ward full of patients with numerous visitors.

He had watched his father lie unresponsive in bed, not speaking or moving as his life ebbed away, the yellowish cast to his skin an indication of a liver that had lost its battle to survive. And he wished he'd taken the chance to say something, anything, to his father, to tell him he understood why he had deserted his only son for pleasure only to be found in a bottle, even if he didn't really understand. But it was all too little, too late for them both. Neither had spoken and the moment had gone. A day later his father had also gone, never to return.

The ward was finally quiet, the patient's visitors having left in a flurry of tears and 'see you tomorrows'. Instead of staying in the ward to listen to another comforting wife or cheerful relative saying goodbye, Quin took himself slowly and shakily down to the television room. His own visitors were non-existent and if he'd remained in bed listening, he knew it wouldn't have taken much to make him pack his kit and take off, regardless of what any nurse or doctor had to say.

Back in the ward, returning to his abused newspaper, he was attempting to hold it down with his left hand when it slipped and separated on the shiny blue cotton bedcover. It was a losing battle so he grabbed the section he had been holding and let the rest fall to the floor. Quin smoothed out the page and began to read from where he'd been interrupted:

HAVE YOU EVER WANTED TO DISAPPEAR?

Get rid of your problems. Start a new life in a different place, cash-in-hand.

FREE yourself from debt. Make your own decisions. Change your name and appearance if you wish. Write to the address below and include an up-to-date photograph. Only people in good health need apply. Applications kept completely confidential. Guaranteed employment for 12 months.

Tormented by possibilities, Quin tore the piece out of the newspaper, folded it, and thrust it into his wallet, chewing the words of the ad over in his mind until he finally fell into a restless sleep.

Quin was in serious trouble. He'd narrowly escaped with his life when someone driving a grey and black tray truck ran him off the road one night. His car was wrecked. He survived because of his seat belt and the fact that he hit the curb, rolling his car into a ditch instead of hitting a nearby power pole. No witnesses came forward.

The truck vanished into a maze of side streets straight after the incident occurred. Quin had no chance to see the number plate and, thinking about it later, felt sure it was deliberate, a direct result of another incident a few weeks previously. He knew then that he must think about leaving the city for a while.

Since coming to Melbourne to live at age twenty five, he'd tried to abide by the law. Sure he had parking tickets and the occasional one drink too many on a Saturday night but most of the time he was too busy to look for trouble.

While his sign writing and art supply business took up his weekdays, painting mountain landscapes covered his weekends. A woman or two along the way provided some distraction but there was no-one serious in his life. Not that he wanted to be alone forever. It just seemed as if he was waiting for the right one to come along and so far she had eluded him.

Maybe he wasn't a choir boy but he sure didn't deserve to be labelled a troublemaker. Not that he couldn't make trouble if he wanted to, he just couldn't be bothered any more. At thirty years old, he figured he'd grown out of that sort of mindless stupidity.

It was entirely by chance that he took a short cut in his car through an inner city side street early one morning, around two am. As Quin negotiated a speed bump, he saw a man lying inside a steel fence surrounding a floodlighted warehouse yard, his head covered in what looked like blood.

A police officer was bent over the man holding a pistol. The sign on the gate said 'Hammersmith Import Export Pty. Ltd. - Fine Art and Antiques - Authorised Personnel Only'.

Must be a robbery thought Quin as he slowed to observe the scene. I wonder what the guy could have been stealing?

A man loading crates into a truck with a fork lift also wore a police uniform. Another man in a security guard uniform was standing back holding a mobile phone to his ear. Several others moving to and from the building were dressed in khaki. Quin saw a couple of them shout and break away to race toward him. He began to realise his mistake. The robbery was still in progress. The blood covered man was a victim, not the criminal.

The police raised their guns but the shots they fired at his rapidly departing vehicle went wide of the mark. He escaped unharmed. Not even the car was marked. Speeding through deserted streets, hoping to elude anyone in pursuit, he found a manned police station in the city and reported the incident.

After being questioned at length as to his reason for being out so late in an industrial area, and having his driver's licence checked as if he was the criminal, Quin wished he'd kept his mouth shut. Also, that unsolicited report had been the start of an investigation into his private life that had escalated his trouble to boiling point.

The police began an examination of the warehouse but by the time they arrived any evidence of theft and murder had been covered up. There was no sign of breaking and entering and the guard who was posted on the gate at the time denied any knowledge of criminal activity.

Circumstances had been rapidly altered to make it look like he was making the whole thing up.

Threatening him with a fine or jail for making a false report, the police let him off with a warning. Quin suspected the robbery had been engineered from within the company but without extensive investigation and a search warrant, such a thing was impossible to prove. And there was the matter of police being present at the crime scene, before they were contacted. The whole thing was beginning to look like a cover-up.

When Quin reported the hit run incident that landed him in hospital a few days later, the police suggested he had been drinking and caused the crash through his own criminal negligence. Even though he was angry at their assumptions, he realised they had been influenced by negative newspaper articles about him after the Hammersmith robbery. They probably wouldn't listen to anything he had to say now or in the future unless he had hard evidence, like a dead body or photographs of an empty warehouse.

Hiring a private investigator to find out if any Hammersmith security guards had gone missing was way too expensive, and probably a waste of time since it would be impossible to get into company records unless he was a computer hacker.

Quin could do a lot of things, but computers were not his field and right then he didn't have time to learn. Unfortunately, the crooks involved in the robbery, whoever they were, seemed to think he might be able to recognise them. They had tried to get rid of him by running him off the road and he knew nothing would be allowed to stand in their way. It was only a matter of time before they achieved their final objective. His complete silence.

Quin was unable to give a detailed description of the men involved in the warehouse incident. All he could say was that some of them wore police or security guard uniforms. Some could have been military. The police department closed ranks against him, stating that the uniforms were obviously fake.

He agreed, they probably were fake, because if the thieves were real police gone renegade, they would know he was unable to identify anyone. And if that was the case, why was someone still trying to kill him. He couldn't think of anyone else who would want him dead. Unless he'd irritated the hell out of one of his clients. He decided to check just in case he'd forgotten someone with a gripe against him. Hard to imagine what kind of sign writing could make someone want to kill.

What concerned him most was the realisation that the warehouse thieves must have taken down his car registration number and traced him but, he wondered, how had they done that unless they had access to that kind of information through official channels, like the police data base.

Maybe they weren't the law but there had to be some connection. Possibly the leak came through the files being accessed illegally, in which case anyone could find out anything, anytime. It was too bad he had no way of finding out. It might have solved his immediate problems and allowed him to reclaim his life.

Lying awake in his hospital bed, depressed and brooding, Quin thought cynically, maybe I should let the bastards kill me and prove my innocence that way. It'd probably save everyone a lot of trouble in the long run. Or, I could put my own ad in the paper. 'To the guys who ripped off Hammersmith's Warehouse, I didn't see your faces, I can't pick you out in a lineup, so you can stop trying to kill me.' Hell, they probably wouldn't believe me either.

It was almost impossible for Quin to stay in business after the robbery was reported. The newspapers had dined out on the incident for days with splashy biased headlines. When they had found he'd blown a fuse and accused police officers of a cover up they had a field day, including in their colourful narrative several minor incidents from his mis-spent youth in Sydney and a few lines about his alcoholic father who had died when Quin was fifteen.

Quin had been born in Phoenix, Arizona. His artist mother, part Cherokee, part white American, had fallen in love with and married an Australian of Irish descent who was working for a time in the Arizona Desert as a geologist.

She died in an automobile accident when he was six years old and his father brought him back to Australia, to a strange world of broad Australian accents and gum trees, untamed

Australian bush, kangaroos, wild red and green parrots and kookaburras whose raucous laugh seemed to mock his every effort to understand and speak in Aussie slang.

Her legacies to him were a few landscape paintings she had done of the deserts outside Phoenix and Tombstone and a talent for art. She also left him a written history of her people and their perilous journey across America on the 'Trail of Tears' before they settled in North Carolina. An account of her own family members and their life in the North Carolina town of 'Cherokee' was included in the papers which he kept and cherished, planning and hoping one day to make his own journey to see the home of his ancestors.

An American child in an alien environment, Quin found it hard to adjust to school, his accent especially set him apart. He was bigger than most kids and had learnt to fight for his rights at an early age. Quin was eleven when his father lost his job and they moved from Melbourne to Sydney. Bitter at the curves life had thrown him, Tom Jameson began drinking heavily and Quin's life became even more unbearable.

He began dropping out of classes and running with a wild crowd, gaining a reputation for daredevil acts and handling problems with his fists. When Tom died of liver failure, an understanding foster family reclaimed Quin from the oblivion of the streets.

They recognised his need for stability, helping him to finish his education. Fortunately, his father had an insurance policy which enabled his son to go on to university where he gained a degree in business administration, plus a second degree in art and design.

All of his success in business and his clean slate since he was a rebellious teenager made no difference to people who could only see one side of the coin. Since the city was well stocked with those who believed everything they read in the newspapers as if it were gospel, ranks were closed against him after the Hammersmith robbery. His business slowed to a trickle of sightseeing, non-paying, tourists.

His picture had been taken by a news photographer outside the police station and was on the front page of the Melbourne 'Herald'. At the time he'd shouted at the reporter to 'get the hell away from me'. It wasn't a bad likeness he mused, trying to look at it objectively. It showed his Cherokee heritage in fierce dark brown eyes, olive skin, high cheekbones and firm blade of a nose.

His beautifully formed mouth was curved with disdain. Shoulder length seal brown hair was tied back with a leather thong and a fine silver chain clung to his tanned throat. The chain might have made him look effeminate if it wasn't for the faint shadow of a beard and the totally masculine shape of his body beneath his silky white shirt and tight fitting black denim jeans.

You still look like what you are he'd said to himself scornfully. A renegade trying to fit in with civilised society. But he knew that so called civilised society was really a pool of sharks vibrating with anticipation at the scent of blood.

His Irish grandmother on his father's side had always said that what really mattered was how you lived your life and how you treated other people. She had died when he was ten but he had never forgotten those words. He'd glared at his photograph in the newspaper, seeing an answering glare coming from the page and had known it was going to take a long time to forget his humiliation at the hands of the journalists and the law.

Sherry Delaney drew a line around the ad in the month old newspaper. It asked the question, 'Have you ever wanted to disappear?' Every day of my life for the past ten years she silently answered. Australia was her home. She didn't want to go to another country but maybe it was the only way. This could be the answer to a prayer, if only it wasn't too late for her to send a reply.

She fulfilled the requirement of good health. Hard work digging tailings out of a mine did tend to make a person fit. If only she had the chance, she'd shake the dust of Archer's Creek off her well worn boots and never look back. It would be worth it, not to have to look into the cold blue eyes of her tormentor ever again. He seemed to see into her tormented soul and enjoy the pain he caused.

This could be her chance to make a life for herself, independent of the man who called himself her guardian. At twenty she was legally an adult so Ralph had no right to tell her what to do, even if he did control her inheritance until she was twenty five. She thought back through the years to when she had first met him and shuddered to think of what those years contained.

Twelve years previously Ralph Marley, a widower, had come to Archer's Creek from Portland in the Western District of Victoria. Sherry remembered the day he'd arrived as if it were yesterday.

'Sylvia's dead,' Ralph had announced starkly to Sherry's parents, Michael and Rose Delaney. Ralph stood outside the door, hat in hand, looking like a desperate man.

'What happened, Ralph?' asked Michael, sympathy in his voice as he shook Ralph's hand to welcome him to their home.

'Took her own life. Probably because our daughter Susan ran off a few years ago. Sylvia couldn't accept it.' He appeared on the verge of tears as he stood there, twisting his felt hat in shaky hands and looking as if a good meal would be welcome.

'It was those damn pills,' he continued. 'The doc gave her sleeping pills and she took the whole bottle. It was about a month ago now. I've lost track a bit. Had to get away from there so I thought I'd come to Archer's Creek, to you. You always said there were plenty of jobs around here, Mike. I hope I haven't made a mistake. I couldn't think of anywhere else to go.'

'You're welcome, any time. You look like you could use a drink.' Michael took him by the shoulder and drew him into the living room. Ralph hesitated a moment and looked around before accepting the offer of hospitality.

'Thanks, Mike. I really appreciate this. It's been a bad time. Rose, it's good to see you.'

'Ralph , I'm so sorry about Syvia. You must be devastated. Make yourself at home.You'll stay of course? Rose smiled and gave Ralph a hug of welcome.

'Are you sure I won't put you out, Rose? I can go to the hotel.'

'Don't even think of it. Sylvia was our cousin and we look upon you as part of the family.' 'Thanks, Rose. You don't know what that means to me.'

Michael said, 'Come on, Ralph, I'll help you get your bags. I see you've still got your Landrover.'

'Yeah. It's getting old now, but it still goes like a bomb.'

The two men disappeared outside and Rose went into the kitchen to brew a pot of tea leaving eight year old Sherry to creep out from under the stairs where she had been listening to every word. Who was this man she wondered? And who was Sylvia? Why had someone named Susan run away?

At the table that evening Ralph said, 'I wanted to get away from Portland after the shock of Sylvia's death. It's terrible to mourn someone and have people comment on what I do and how I'm handling it, like I'm some sort of monster if I go to the hotel for a drink.'

'We don't think that, Ralph.' Rose patted his hand.

'Thank you for that, Rose. People loved Sylvia and they seemed to blame me for everything, as if I had something to do with her death. They even saw it as being a traitor when I talked to a young woman in the hotel bar. They said I was being unfaithful to her memory. Much as I miss my wife I have to accept that she's gone. Nothing can bring her back and I have to live my life as best I can. Anyway, I couldn't take any more so I packed my things and left town.'

As an impressionable child, Sherry had listened to her parents and Ralph discussing the inquest and how, on the night she died, Sylvia Marley had gone to bed with a glass of wine and helped herself to sleep with a bottle of sleeping tablets. The inquest had ruled the death a suicide. No questions had been asked.

At the time Sherry's young eyes hadn't seen through the falseness of Ralph's grief and the haste with which he disposed of Sylvia's possessions, including the small house in which they lived. She only knew he frightened her somehow when he looked at her and that her father had offered him a job plus a farm workers bungalow on their property for a low rent.

He insisted Sherry call him Uncle Ralph.

There was a disused gold mine on their land with a bit of money to be made out of sifting tailings for gold dust. Ralph worked at the mine and did jobs around the farm for extra cash. He also took most of his meals with the family which involved him in almost every aspect of their lives. If Sherry's parents needed to go out at night they usually left Ralph in charge. They trusted him completely.

Unfortunately, Michael and Rose Delaney were injured in a car accident when Sherry was ten, two years after Ralph had come to Archer's Creek.

There was some speculation at the time as to the cause of the accident which occurred on an open road in the late evening, but it was generally accepted that Michael had ploughed into the oncoming farm truck because he had fallen asleep at the wheel. The driver of the truck died at the impact of the vehicles.

Neither driver had consumed alcohol and there was no call for an inquiry.

Neither Rose nor Michael regained consciousness. In the few short days Michael outlived his wife, he rallied enough to add a codicil to his will giving Ralph the guardianship of his daughter and the job of administrator over her inheritance until she was twenty five.

The Delaneys had looked upon Ralph as a cousin and friend, especially since he had come to live on the farm and begun working for them. He gave all the appearance of a staunch church goer and a good worker, a member of the family who could be trusted with the care of a young girl.

Straight after the double funeral, Ralph moved into the large brick farmhouse Sherry's family had owned for generations and her life gradually began to take on the qualities of an interminable nightmare. Like gritty sand on a sheet of glass, he began to wear away any resistance anyone in the community might have shown to him as he took over every aspect of Sherry's life.

Ralph was a thickset man, of medium height, ginger hair fading into grey. He had gained weight over the years since he had become Sherry's guardian. His almost white eyelashes covered pale sharp eyes with an overlay of goodwill and friendliness. His shoulder and arm muscles had been well developed from his work on fishing trawlers along the coast, but as he'd grown older and stopped physical labour his condition was deteriorating.

Sherry had discovered from a letter she'd found recently, that Sylvia had led a terrible life with him. Shoved into the back of an outside storeroom, the large box containing Sylvia's things had been brought with Ralph when he'd moved into the main farmhouse. The letter was enclosed with a birthday card and written in a spidery feminine hand. It was addressed to 'Dear Linda' with a box number at a post office in Sydney.

Unmailed and placed in a plain undirected envelope, it catalogued a life of unrelenting violence and oppression. Amidst pleas for prayer and guidance there was also an ambiguous reference to Ralph's unnatural treatment of his daughter Susan which Sherry found extremely disturbing. The letter also said her daughter Susan had run away from home three years ago at sixteen and hadn't been seen by her family since. The date on it was a week before Sylvia died but nothing about the letter indicated her slide toward suicide.

Sherry wondered why Ralph hadn't opened the letter and destroyed it. He must have thrown the pile of papers into a box and tossed them into his car before he left home? Or maybe he had read it and as the contents were highly incriminating to him had decided to destroy it later and then forgotten about it. He could have resealed the envelope before putting it with the other papers? One thing for sure, she wasn't about to ask. She simply took the letter and hid it where he wouldn't find it, ever. Ralph was a very strange and complex man and it could have been his way of insuring the situation didn't get out of hand.

In many ways Ralph treated Sherry the same harsh way he had treated his wife and daughter. Sherry suspected he'd left Portland because he had needed to escape the rumours surrounding the tragedy of his wife's death. Susan was very lucky thought Sherry. She escaped. Now it's my turn.

She scythed through the newspaper to remove the advertisement before she could change her mind. Did she want to disappear? The answer had to be Yes! ASAP.

When she came downstairs, Ralph was standing by the front door, his sunburnt face tight with displeasure, hands flexing impatiently around the brim of his hat. 'I'm off now, girlie. They'll be waiting for me. Make sure you behave yourself, no using the phone. And get them chooks fed. I swear I have to do everything around here you lazy little cow. I don't know why I put up with you.'

Turning to look in the hall mirror, he preened before adjusting the wide brimmed Akubra hat, his fondness for his own nondescript appearance incomprehensible to Sherry. She opened her mouth to speak but before a sound was heard his stinging words drilled their way through her heart. 'Your parents would have been ashamed of the way you keep this house. It's a tip and a damn good thing it is they're not here to see it.'

The pain was like an old friend. She had felt it often and knew it would pass as did all things, even Ralph, eventually.

The thought that, one day, she might never see him again, never listen to his lying voice or hear the constant threat of abandonment, was the one thing that made life bearable, except for her tiny Yorkshire Terrier pup, Scrappy. The pup was still young but he was the best thing in her life, the only thing she loved. Ralph had threatened to get rid of Scrappy on a few occasions but since he hadn't done anything as yet, she could only conclude the man still had a fragment of humanity to his name. Or perhaps he was just too lazy to do the deed?

Having reminded his ward of her obligations, Ralph wrenched open the door, pausing in the doorway to say, 'Don't look like such a tragedy queen. I could send you out to work on your back and then you'd know what the real world is like.'

He slammed the door in his usual vicious style as he walked out, leaving Sherry standing silently in the hall, her slight body tense, resentful tears burning behind closed eyelids. How she hated that man and all he stood for.

If only she could get a job. Move away. It was unfortunate there weren't any jobs to be had in the area, and even if there were, she had no experience except housework, and no-one she knew wanted to pay when they could do the work themselves for nothing or get council help for almost nothing. She'd have to go to the city, but without money for a rental bond that wasn't a viable option.

Anyway, this is was still her home, and if she left, Ralph would win. He would have everything. Sherry would walk through fire before she would let that happen.

She heard his truck fire up and roar away, gravel spitting as he took the turn out onto the road too fast and knew if she'd spoken a word he'd have started again about how much she owed him and how she should be grateful to him for keeping her off the streets. How no man would want to marry a plain girl like her, a girl who had nothing going for her except a body and even that wasn't much to write home about. He might have taken her wrist in his large hand and squeezed the fragile bones until they felt like they would snap under the strain. The bruises would sometimes take weeks to heal.

Each time she happened to be in the same room with him she felt his eyes roaming over her body, dissecting and probing through the flimsy covering of her clothes even though she wore jeans and men's shirts. She sensed it was only a matter of time before his basic urges overcame any decency he might still have.

Somehow that line in Sylvia's letter about his unnatural treatment of his daughter Susan kept coming to mind and she knew she had to get away from him before it was too late, as far away as possible and as fast as she could go!

CHAPTER TWO

Sherry sank to the wooden floor, emotionally exhausted. So relieved Ralph had finally gone, she sat comatose for half an hour before getting shakily to her feet. The house felt cold and unfamiliar in the aftermath of his departure, as if he had exuded a trail of slime like a slug marking its territory.

When he went out at night it was often to conduct business of some sort, sometimes he said it was a Church or Council meeting and other times she knew by the clothes he wore that it was another kind of meeting altogether.

If it was the latter kind she knew from experience he would be very late home and probably reeking of alcohol. Sometimes she had even covered him up after he had fallen fully clothed into bed, hoping desperately he wouldn't wake up before she was able to sneak back to her own room and secure her door.

Strangely, in a self-protective move, he rarely overindulged in alcohol within the boundaries of Archer's Creek. Very few of the townspeople knew he had such a weakness. It was a miracle to Sherry that he hadn't been arrested for drunk driving or had his licence taken away. Maybe that was due to his friendship with Sergeant Burns more than anything else.

It was another miracle he hadn't crashed his car. She felt sure it wasn't anything good he'd done that saved his hide. It was probably more animal cunning and instinctive driving ability, one of the few worthwhile things about him.

She'd taken a screwdriver from the shed one day and taken money from the house keeping tin in the kitchen to buy a simple metal latch for her bedroom door, attaching it up high inside so it wouldn't be noticed. Ralph hadn't said a word, even after he'd tried to open her door on several occasions when he was drunk.

Tonight he'd put on a dark grey suit, white shirt and patterned tie with his black shoes gleaming like a mirror. She'd watched him clean them before they had eaten their evening meal, anointing the shoes with black polish and buffing them energetically, humming snatches of an old love song. He peered into the shiny black surface and smiled as if he liked what he saw.

Sherry knew when he hummed anything but hymns he was on the prowl like a tomcat. Hymns were a pretence of righteousness but she wondered how many people were fooled by them. On tomcat nights, she knew he wouldn't be home until dawn because he never went hunting in his own back yard. He always went farther afield, sometimes even as far as Bendigo or Melbourne. That way he could play his games in secret and the Archer's Creek townsfolk wouldn't be able to point accusing fingers at him.

He liked to maintain the facade of respected member of the Town Council, Mayor, businessman and devoted church Deacon. She wondered sometimes how he managed to juggle such a large amount of hats.

Tonight, she'd be able to write her letter in peace and sneak out to mail it before he returned. The paper she wrote on was cut carefully from an old exercise book. The words were much harder to come by. After many attempts, and many discarded pieces of paper littering the floor, she wrote the letter she hoped would change her life.

Dear Mr. Jones.

I'd like to apply for the job advertised in the Melbourne Herald on the 3rd of September. I know I am late applying but I have been unable to write until now. I would like to start a new life and this job seems like my opportunity to do so. I am twenty years old and in good health. I can cook and sew. I work as a housekeeper, type letters and am good at maths. I would do any job you ask of me to the best of my ability. Please consider my application.

Yours truly, Sherry Hunter.p.s. please address any reply to S. Hunter care of the above box number. Thank you.

Sherry worried for a while about giving her age as twenty and not twenty two or more which may have been more acceptable for a prospective employer. She was also concerned about signing a false name. Her father's late great aunt's name was Penelope Hunter and she had been a wonderful woman, working as a Missionary among the people of the Congo and Uganda in harsh conditions that would have broken a less strong and courageous woman than she. Sherry had always longed to be like her so she had chosen to use her name.

No, she thought fiercely, I am a hunter, a hunter seeking a new life. It would do. Besides, the woman in the post office was an eternal gossip and, if she used her own name, before Ralph even noticed she was gone, he'd be in possession of all the facts and come looking for her.

He'd know everything, when, where, how and why. He had ways to make her obey him; threats to Scrappy, fear based on years of intimidation from when she was a young girl. He'd probably get a lot of pleasure out of making a up a few more ways to inflict pain since he seemed to thrive on her fear and desperation.

Wondering what he would do if one day he realised how much she knew about his secret life, she shuddered with premonitory fear. It was too terrible a thing to think about.

She went ahead and signed the name Sherry Hunter with a flourish at the end of the letter. It was the first step into her new life and, hopefully, it was goodbye to Ralph Marley, forever. She gathered up her discarded attempts and burned them in the fireplace. An old school photograph was the closest she could supply that was up-to-date. She slipped it and her letter into an envelope before addressing it carefully.

The picture showed her standing alone, a small, thin teenager, expressionless and pale with fair hair scraped back into two long plaits which hung over her shoulders in the front, large eyes dominating her small face. Skinny legs in short white socks and black sandals showed under a short-sleeved, shapeless blue check school uniform. The photo was the only one she had and she hoped it would do. At least she had developed a little and looked older now. If she managed to get an interview, Mr. Jones seeing her in person would make all the difference.

If only she could get some money from somewhere without having to steal it. She remembered the times she had been forced to sneak change from Ralph's desk. He'd rejected her pleas for pocket money and refused to pay for anything but the most basic of female necessities. What clothes she had were sent by mail order through a catalogue, underwear, jeans and shirts suitable for working in and one cotton dress for church, shoes, the bare minimum of winter clothing.

Sherry knew that keeping her short of money was one of the ways Ralph used to control her but she was working on a way out of the situation. Getting out of the house and finding a job was the first step to freedom. Keeping the move secret was essential.

Quietly, moving as if Ralph could turn up at any moment, Sherry slipped upstairs and crept into the large bedroom which had once belonged to her parents. There was a certain anguish to being in this room where she had laughed and played pillow fights and where she had seen the great love her parents had in the little things they did for each other.

She remembered how they had always hugged and kissed her and shared their closeness with her even while she knew there were times they needed to be alone. Many times she had crept into their bed with them in the mornings and they had played games and told stories to each other while they ate toast and dropped marmalade on the sheets.

Memories of those lovely days were frozen at the point when the police came to tell Sherry about the accident. Ralph was looking after her that night while her parents had gone to a meeting in Beaufort, a nearby town.

He made a pretence of grief, of comforting Sherry through her shock and despair, but even then she sensed the falseness of it all. He took her to the hospital to see her father who was still alive. He was unconscious at the time, drifting in and out of awareness as the days passed.

When Ralph brought her into the hospital again three days after the accident Michael Delaney had lapsed into a coma and nothing could be done. Her beloved mother was dead, her father dying. Five days later at the double funeral Sherry and the whole town knew that Ralph had taken over. Her whole life was altered at that moment. From then on his lies and deception filtered through her life like coarse sand on glass and it took all of her courage to survive day to day.

Her parents room was different with Ralph in possession of it. He hadn't changed the wallpaper or the furnishings but his personality overlaid the memories with a cold mist, sharpening the constant agony of loss for Sherry.

She forced herself to ignore the pain and open the bedside drawer in which she knew Ralph kept personal things. She found a stamp for her letter and then noticed a bank book which lay under some envelopes.

As she picked it up money fell out, at least a hundred dollars in notes. It gave her a fright; so much money just lying there as if waiting for her to see it. A test of some kind? What would he do if she took it? Sherry looked around the room as if waiting for her nemesis to leap out from the wardrobe and seize her.

The silence was beginning to give her goose bumps but she made no sound and no move to leave. Her breath locked in her throat as she looked back at the drawer. The notes taunted her and seemed to call out, 'Come on. Pick me up. Hide me. You can use me to get away.'

Her fingers tingled and her eyes darted towards the door. He'd soon know she'd taken his hoard she realised, raking a hand through her hair. Resentment bottled up for years prevailed and, making an instant decision, Sherry snatched up the money and stuffed it into her pocket, thinking of all the housework she'd done for him and how little he had given her in return. It was only a small part of the wages she had earned but not been paid over the years.

She turned the light off and raced down the hall into the bathroom where her stomach rebelled. A few deep breaths and a glass of water to wash the bitter after taste out of her mouth, Sherry calmed enough to lock the bathroom door. No point in leaving the way clear for Ralph to walk in unannounced as he had done in the past. It was one of his habits to ignore a closed door, as if he had the right to open any door in the house, as if he owned it, and owned his ward as well.

Bathing away tears of reaction, Sherry buttoned her blue plaid western shirt leaving the top buttons undone defiantly. Normally she wore her shirts buttoned high at the throat or concealed herself in oversized T-shirts and baggy track pants. Especially in bed. She had woken one night at a sound and found Ralph standing over her with a strangely intent look on his face.

She'd gasped in fright, her heart pounding like a runaway train when he reached out his hand towards her face. Scooting over in the bed she'd pulled her blankets up to her chin, but when he dropped his hand without touching her she'd looked up into his eyes and realised he must be sleep walking. Unable to speak, she'd nearly wept with relief when he'd turned and left the room without a sound.

She'd leapt out of bed immediately to put the catch on the door. That had been two months ago and every time he looked at her closely after that, her skin crawled even more unpleasantly than usual. Poor Susan. Was this what had happened to her? No wonder she had run away from home.

She looked at her reflection, her large grey eyes defiant. Surely it wasn't a crime to have long silvery blonde hair and clear skin she asked herself. Why, she'd seen in the old photo album that her Mother had looked just like her when she was twenty. Small and slim with large dark lashed grey eyes and dark eyebrows, Rose Delaney had been a beautiful, ethereal woman who seemed as if the wind would blow her away, but she, like Sherry, had been stronger than she looked. She wouldn't have survived life in Archer's Creek mining community otherwise.

Aunt Jo had told Sherry stories about those days, how young men from the Timber Mills had driven over in their cars from Ballarat for the local dances and had tried to take up with the Archer girls, Josephine and Rose, sniffing around like dogs hunting rabbits.

They were wild days in Archer's Creek but once Mike Delaney had shown up no-one else stood a chance with Rose. Back then no-one dared show any disrespect to the Archer family. Being a wealthy land owner, Rose' father had a lot of power in the district. Even the police left Grandpa alone, most of the time.

Sherry was always painfully shy and since Ralph's advent, she'd had no chance to build normal friendships with any males at high school. She'd been told by other more confident girls that there was nothing like hands on experience but had been too afraid to take a chance. In the four years since she'd left school she'd stayed home to clean and cook as well as keep the hens and sometimes help Ralph shovel tailings out of the mine. She'd had no time for anything other than work. Ralph had seen to that.

The only freedom she knew was if she escaped from the house while Ralph was busy elsewhere, usually at night. She would take old boy's clothes she had found in a chest in the upstairs storeroom and put them on, pinning her hair up out of sight and putting an old cap on her head. She would pull on work-boots and a large shapeless jacket then saunter down to the town. She had found if she acted casual and didn't look like she was hiding, she could easily visit the library or window shop without anyone knowing it was Sherry Delaney.

She even deepened her voice successfully when she was asked a question and the whole thing became a game as she tried out her new persona on people she knew and they treated her as a stranger. Her confidence built and she began to think maybe one day she could escape in reality, not just pretend.

She looked at her letter on the table and knew it was finally time to break free, time to abandon the only home she had ever known, a home that wouldn't feel like hers again until she'd earned some money and could afford to pay a lawyer.

Having been an unpaid slave for years she was ready to change things, to take charge of her life. Sherry had waited a long time to find a way out, now that her chance had come she was going to grab it with both hands. And if Ralph didn't like it, that was his tough luck.

Slipping denim clad legs into old leather riding boots outside the back door later that night, then snapping Scrappy's lead on, Sherry felt her throat tighten and her skin crawl with nervous tension. What if Ralph came back early? She'd have to explain what she was doing.

He wouldn't believe her, whatever she said. It was all the same to him. Sherry never told him anything, no matter what he said or did to her in retaliation for her silence. Her defiance drove him crazy and that fact alone gave her a strange dark pleasure.

Even if the bruises he inflicted were visible, there was no-one she could ask for help who wouldn't be vulnerable to Ralph's vengeance. He was a man with two faces. The people of Archer's Creek seemed to think he was perfect. She knew he was not. Her fierce determination not to bow down to him was all she had left of her pride. To give in was to lose a part of herself. Beside which, what difference would it make. She was leaving and, short of locking her up or killing her, there was nothing he could do to stop her.

He'd try of course. Probably he'd begin with his usual emotional blackmail by reminding her of her obligations to him after he'd spent the last twelve years of his life looking after her, not making his own fortune but taking care of her affairs for no reward.

Then, with tears in his eyes, he'd tell her how much her parents had meant to him and how he'd promised her father on his death bed to make sure his little daughter was taken care of. He would remind her of the Administration Order on her inheritance that was valid until she was twenty five.

Since she was ten he'd been manipulating her and shaping her into his puppet, alternating cruelty and kindness, making her dependent upon him, making her believe he was the only person in the world who could keep her safe.

But safety was an illusion she had discovered. He would pick up a squirming Scrappy, holding him aloft with tight hurting hands until he whimpered and Sherry knew a terrible fear that the silent threat to her pet's life would be carried out, without mercy.

Ralph would say he was acting in place of her father when he refused to allow her to leave but she knew in her heart there would come a time, a moment, when he'd stop watching her.

One day his friends who spied on her when she was away from the house would be looking the other way and she and Scrappy would be gone, without a trace. She smiled secretly as she trudged down the road a few minutes later, moonlight forcing her to keep under the cover of trees, Scrappy sniffing and watering every bush, marking his territory. Anticipation was heady.

Eaten away with boredom, Quin lay in bed waiting for the doctor to come and discharge him. The question 'have you ever wanted to disappear?' was haunting him but, trying to put it out of his mind, he was attempting to read the newspaper from cover to cover. After going over the business and employment section while he waited, fidgeting and fuming inwardly that the medical staff took so long to get around to him, he went back to the ad., with a strange compulsion to read it over and over again.

Even the nurses who had hovered over him devotedly when he was first admitted seemed to find his brooding looks and short fuse intimidating. Not that he blamed them. It was almost impossible for him to refrain from dragging his clothes on and heading out the door.

He'd tried to be pleasant but his lack of civility towards the young nurse who was supposed to accompany him to the shower that morning wasn't something he was particularly proud of.

She had fled in tears and been replaced with a dragon who had warned him she was tougher and meaner than he was and would he like to try one on with her. She also suggested that if he had anything different from any other male in the place she'd like to see it.

Resigning himself to her company was hard and he hadn't liked it at all. He'd felt like an exhibit at a peep show and didn't see why they couldn't just leave him alone. He'd been showering himself for the last twenty six years and hadn't done himself an injury yet.

Quin's business was going downhill at speed so unless he got himself out of his hospital bed quick smart and generated more sign writing contracts he'd be closing the doors. He'd even had to let his assistants in the shop go, as well as the men who worked on the outside jobs. If he was forced to close down, rather than live on his investments and savings which, fortunately, were considerable, he'd have to find something else to provide an income.

Since his reputation as a businessman had come under fire, he had wondered if he could become a painter and decorator. He scowled at the thought. He didn't feel he could make a living from landscape painting. Maybe he'd do better heading back to America. No-one would know him there and he could start a new business, and a new life.

He'd worked hard in his business and certainly had the capital and the expertise to start again. He could even find time to look up his family. His mother's parents and various aunts and uncles lived in Cherokee, North Carolina.

His grandmother had once written to his father saying they owned a family run hotel which catered to the crowds of people who flocked into the town to play bingo. She'd asked if he would bring Quin to see them and said they would be welcome to stay in the hotel. He had no idea if his father had replied to the letter or not and at the time Quin was too young to do anything about it anyway.

He didn't know if they had written again but he had found the letter with an address amongst his father's papers. Maybe he would write to them himself some day and reopen the lines of communication. After all, they were his family, his only connection to his mother.

Anything was better than sitting around waiting for the financial axe to fall he decided, forgetting for a moment the danger he was in. Then, as he read William Jones' offer, he remembered. Not only was he threatened with his business closing, his life was in danger. Eventually, the thugs who were out to get him would be successful.

What have I got to lose he asked himself as he read through the ad again? I've little in life to look forward to. My parents are dead. Someone has me on their hit list. I've lost most of my friends over this business and the police are out to prove I'm a criminal or a psycho.

For once his optimism failed him. It was like looking down a long dark tunnel then turning back and seeing the same tunnel behind him.

Quin picked up the paper and read again 'How would you like to disappear, start a new life, get rid of your problems?' What an offer! Who is this Mr. Jones? Is this on the level? Can I really just disappear without a trace? He was intrigued and decided to find out more. After all, it might be the answer to a prayer.

When he was finally released from hospital Quin tried to keep busy in his business, reorganising equipment and completing orders accumulated while he had been out of action. Spare time was spent in his studio painting, slapping oil paint around with indiscriminate vigour, attempting to find a target for his restless anger.

In the end, nothing did any good. All he created was a violently colourful surrealistic landscape with no basis in reality and he thought later it was probably one of his more creative works although not in his usual down to earth style.

Finally, he put the poor abused canvas away and spent the next few evenings at the gym teaching a punching bag who was boss. At least there he could work off some of his angry frustration and develop and extra layer of muscle. He had a feeling he was going to need all the strength he could find in his next job, as a builder's labourer.

Nervous excitement raced through Sherry as she pushed her letter into the post box, hoping no-one was around at this late hour to notice her. It'd be worth a lot to see the look on Ralph's face when he found she had escaped. Yes, she thought, it would be definitely be worth it. Sherry grinned to herself and gave scrappy a pat. 'Come on little guy,' she whispered. 'Let's go back to the house. We don't want to arrive home after Ralph. He'll be really ticked off if he thinks I've been out enjoying myself.'

Archer's Creek was a quiet town of around five thousand regular inhabitants but most of the houses were away from the main street. Street lights were minimal and the double storey red brick and timber shops were silent witnesses as she left the post office and began the walk back through the town, past the hotel and small business district, past the public swimming pool with it's gardens and tall trees, over the Archer's creek bridge and up the long hill to home. It was her town and yet not hers because of Ralph. He'd poisoned it for her by just being there.

Getting back into the house without attracting attention was difficult when Ralph was home but Sherry felt quite confident tonight. She had Scrappy with her so the only dog who might make a fuss would be Jasper, the large brown and white mongrel Ralph kept as a guard dog. Since Ralph was out she felt almost safe. The dogs seemed to sleep through anyone leaving but when people arrived they usually set up a commotion, unless it was someone they knew really well.

As she approached the house through the back gate, all was quiet. Dark upstairs windows seemed to watch broodingly as she tried to open the back door. She found it locked, remembering then that it, as well as the front door, had been locked by Ralph when he went out. She'd left by the window in the study and left it open to save bothering with keys when she returned.

Her boots echoed like gunshots on the wooden verandah floor so she pulled them off and set them down by the back step before padding softly around to the window. Jasper didn't make much noise even then, a muted whine, a stifled grunt, then silence. Sherry was so preoccupied by her letter and thinking about the job as well as the consequences of leaving the only home she had ever known, her radar for keeping out of danger was off the air.

With one leg over the window ledge and both hands occupied pulling herself through the opening, Sherry had no time to duck as large hands grabbed her by the arm and hair dragging her through, making her scream in fright and pain when she hit the hard wooden floor with her hip. This was much worse than she had imagined would happen if Ralph caught her sneaking out.

'Slut,' he snarled. 'I'll teach you not to sneak out at night. When I'm finished with you you'll beg for mercy. Then none of them fancy boys in town will ever look at you again.'

Through her pain and fear, Sherry sensed Ralph's fury with her was out of control and he was liable to take the beating he looked set to dish out a few steps further than he had ever gone before. She had to diffuse his rage but it was clear he was in no mood to be placated, even if she felt capable of it. His eyes glittered with what most folk would see as anger but which Sherry had discovered recently was excitement. The more she fought him the better he liked it. Scrappy began to bark furiously outside the window and Jasper howled from his spot near the door.

'I'm going to make you sorry you were ever born girl,' Ralph threatened softly as he slowly withdrew his thin black leather belt from his thick waist. Sherry knew that belt from old. Wielded by powerful arms, it would cut like a knife. Keeping her waiting was also one of his pleasures and he revelled in it now as he circled her prone body lying on the floor.

She hated what he did, no matter how many times he harangued her and said it was for her own good, how he raved periodically with sanctimonious hypocrisy, even preaching in church about the sin of a child's disobedience to his parents, forcing her to listen to this public rebuke when he wasn't even her parent. She knew never to say what she thought out loud though, in case he hit harder or chose another punishment altogether, something infinitely more creative.

She knew he thought about her, how she looked and how she moved. Something told her it wouldn't be long before that other hidden evil she had glimpsed behind his repellent eyes would emerge and be acted upon. Her skin crawled with fear and revulsion. Some time soon he'd come to her room and there would be nothing she could do about it. No one would be there to hear her scream. No-one could protect her. No-one would care if he destroyed her.

She lay on the floor like a sacrifice, waiting silently, heart pounding, muscles clenched painfully, her throat locked against sound. Then, as if awakening from a paralysing dream, Sherry knew it was time. Freedom called to her from the depths of her anguished soul. She answered that call by gathering her fragile strength and rising to give her tormentor a hard shove as his hands were occupied with his belt. As he lost his balance and fell clumsily with a howl of pain against corner of the desk and down onto the polished wooden floor, she fled through the open window, grabbing her tiny dog in her arms as she hit the wooden verandah outside. Hearing sounds of chairs being violently thrown aside and ornaments smashing as the old mahogany desk was shoved towards the wall, Ralph's filthy curses ringing in her ears and Jasper barking wildly, she snatched up her boots from the step and ran through the yard to the back gate.

Firewalking

It was all she could do not to stop and throw up but fear drove her on. She paused momentarily behind the old hay shed to shove her boots on then ran as fast as she could, carrying her dog, through the rough stubbly paddock at the back of the house.

Weaving her way around bushes and trees, she moved quickly over the hill which contained the old gold mine called Archer's Luck which Ralph had worked with her father, past the cemetery where Sherry's parents, Grandpa and Aunt Jo were buried and down the back way into the town of Archer's Creek.

She dared not go by the main road in case he followed in the truck. She wouldn't put it past him to run her down in his rage. Behind her she heard him shout her name and curse over and over like a chant of retribution. It was enough to make her run even faster, as if the devil was on her heels.

Sherry had a friend, the only one who understood her situation, the only one who was ready, when she said the word, to stand up to Ralph. Most people in the town were either scared witless of losing their jobs at various businesses he ran in the town or in hock to him at the General Store which he owned and ran with the aid of a Manager and a sales clerk.

As Mayor and owner of the only real estate office in the district, Ralph had his hand firmly on the purse strings of the town and most of the public buildings, including the offices of the Town Council, the Police Station and the house in which Sergeant Burns, the Officer in Charge of the Police Station, lived, were leased through him. The Archer's Creek Hotel was also leased through him by one of his cronies, a convenient arrangement since he was a frequent customer and wanted his drinks free of charge.

Sherry wasn't aware of who owned the properties but she suspected it was someone Ralph had firmly under his control.

Full of gold rush history, the town relied upon income from the Archer's Creek Mining Museum and tourist money to keep the town's coffers afloat and pay the salaries of the Mayor and Council staff.

A Tourist Development company also leased property from him and used colonial and mining heritage to attract tourists to the area. They had also built a large modern motel on the outskirts of town.

Ralph had moved into her house when he became her guardian even though he had at his disposal the cabin her father had given him to live in when he originally came to Archer's Creek. Often she'd seen his truck parked at the cabin and heard music and laughter drifting across the paddocks while she was trying to sleep.

One night she had even crept across the paddocks to look through the window. She had crept back home half an hour later with an entirely different view of Ralph and the wife of the bank manager who was usually so refined and ladylike.

She knew he'd been named her guardian and administrator of her estate until she was twenty five in her father's will but the true extent of the property involved was a mystery to her. Even Mr. Slade the lawyer gave her so much double talk she resorted to asking Ralph what he was saying. Ralph told her to leave it to him he'd sort everything out.

As a child she accepted his right to order her life, unquestioning his methods in her need for safety, and had signed papers on the day she turned eighteen giving him the power to continue to run her affairs. He'd kept on doing the job he'd taken on when she was ten and she supposed she should be grateful to him for looking out for her all these years. Somehow though, gratitude had no part in their relationship. Once her name was signed, and witnessed, it was more like a cold psychological war with undertones of fear and a subliminal threat of violence if she broke away from his domination.

Sherry didn't count the times he'd hit her, usually in places that couldn't be seen. She'd recovered after all and the physical scars hadn't been permanent, except for a torn ligament in her left knee which ached in the winter months or when a storm was brewing. She'd run from him late one afternoon and fallen down one of the shallow mine shafts on the hill. She was thirteen years old at the time.

It had grown dark and she became terrified, thinking he would leave her there to die. He came along a couple of hours later and hauled her out with a rope around her waist. He'd mocked her fears of the dark and told her the mine shaft was where he would put her if she ever disobeyed him again. It was the mental scars that refused to be erased. She felt they would be with her forever.

CHAPTER THREE

On a back road just out of town was an old cream and brown weatherboard house, run down with weeds and junk littering the yard. Peter Madigan lived there, a prospector and a friend of Sherry's late Grandpa. Old Pete would hide her from Ralph, Sherry hoped, and collect any mail that came for her at the post office, namely a letter from Mr. William Jones addressed to S. Hunter. She prayed it would come soon before she was forced to find some other way of leaving town.

Unfortunately, there was no other way that she could see. Where could she go? Except for Pete, she knew no-one who would help, had no money, and had only the clothes she stood up in. Not that she had anything worth taking with her except Scrappy, although what she was going to feed him on she had no idea. Perhaps Old Pete would have something? Luckily the little guy was a small eater and used to Sherry sharing her food with him.

The fire Pete had lit in his small front room warmed Sherry right through as she told him how she'd escaped the house. She hesitated to call it 'home' because it wasn't any more. It had become a prison.

It was not only the wind that was cold that night. Her heart was chilled with loneliness. Why did things like this happen she wondered as Pete heated up some soup on the wood stove?

'I'm real sorry this happened, Sherry,' he said after she'd explained her late night presence at his house, 'That guardian of yours is a low life bastard. I'll have a word with him if you like?' His worn but kindly face was troubled.

'Thanks Pete. I appreciate what you're trying to do but we both know he won't listen. He makes his own rules.'

'I suppose you're right. I've known him since he turned up twelve years back and I've never heard a friendly word from him except when other folk are around and he wants to put on a show. He's got some kind of burr under his saddle but I'm damned if I know what it is. Most likely he's jealous.'

'What of, Pete? He's not jealous of you for goodness sake?'

'No, not me, of your whole family. Think about it, Sherry. Your father had everything.

A beautiful wife, a lovely daughter, a place where he belonged, a home with love in it, friends. People loved him you know. They took him into their hearts when he married your mother and he loved them too. He made this town what it is today. I reckon Ralph Marley wanted what Mike had, and when he died, Ralph got it all, except the love. He managed to get everything but the one thing he really needed. Funny really, it's the one thing he doesn't think is worth having. I suppose if you've never had a thing you don't miss it. Poor sod.'

Sherry had never thought of Ralph as poor anything before and it made her think. Was there something she could have done that would have made him treat her differently. Was it her fault he was a monster? Then she remembered her mother saying once that we all make choices and if you're old enough to make them you have to live with the results. She realised then that Ralph was like he was because he wanted it that way and nothing could alter that. She wasn't responsible for his way of life or the choices he had made.

As she sat on the sofa drinking the hot tea Pete had made for her, she felt something in the back pocket of her jeans. Knowing she had brought nothing with her from home in her hurry to get away, she put her hand in and found money. She gasped with surprise and elation. Ralph's hundred dollars. She'd put it in her pocket before going to post her letter and forgotten about it. She spun around and said, 'Pete. Look what I've got.' She held up the bundle of notes.

'Whose is it?' he asked.

'Ralph's.'

'What are you going to do with it?'

Defiantly she said, 'I'm going to keep it. I've earned it.' A slight tinge of guilt began to creep into her subconscious making her feel she had to justify what she had done. 'He hasn't paid me a cent in years Pete. Let him pay now.'

'You can't do things that way, Sherry. It isn't right. Even if Marley does deserve it. Maybe you should send it back. By mail.'

She knew Pete was an honest man and even though he had contempt for Ralph, he wouldn't condone stealing money.

'Maybe I would if I didn't need it so badly.'

'Okay. I'll send him some money to make it up. He won't have anything to complain about to the police then will he. How much have you got there?'

'I suppose you're right,' Sherry conceded reluctantly. 'Dad would have made me pay it back. There's $100. It's just a loan though. I'll give it back to you as soon as I've got a job.'

'Fine. I'll take care of it. Forget about Ralph for now. He's not going to find you here. Not if I can help it.'

As she settled down for the rest of the night on the sofa in front of the fire, Pete noticed her tenseness and said, 'Relax sweetie. No-one's likely to come looking for you until morning and by then I'll have figured something out.' He patted her on the head in gentle affection as he passed and took himself off to bed.

Sherry lay by the fire warmly wrapped in blankets with Scrappy curled up next to her. She looked into the softly waving flames and reflected that she hadn't been entirely open with Pete. She'd only told him she had run away because she got in late and that Ralph was furious with her. The job wasn't mentioned. That was her secret, in case it didn't happen, she reasoned. No point in winding Pete up about it. It was a very strange offer made by Mr. Jones and when she learned more about it she might change her mind about wanting to be involved. It could turn out to be a con trick of some kind, possibly even dangerous.

Ralph and Sergeant Burns came looking for her a couple of days later but she and Scrappy had hidden in a cellar Pete had dug out under the new kitchen he had built on the back of the old farmhouse a few years back. He liked to keep bits of ore and gemstones down there plus a cache of money as well as potatoes, carrots, pumpkins and his home brewed beer.

He didn't trust banks or computers to keep a check on what he earned. He said they had no business knowing what he had and since he lived a simple existence with no apparent comfort no-one else really knew what Pete had either.

Sherry listened for their departure from behind the half closed door of a large cupboard, keeping a firm hand on Scrappy who showed signs of wanting to dive up the stairs and attack. She had to hold his muzzle in case he barked.

She heard them shouting threats and interrogating the suddenly morose and uncooperative Pete, then listened with relief as they stomped out the front door vowing to return soon and turn the place upside down if they didn't find her.

As they roared away in Sergeant Burns' Police car, Pete came to Sherry and brought her upstairs to tell her what had happened. 'They'll never let it rest,' he said, shaking his head worriedly. 'That Marley sure is determined to find you. Make me wonder why seeing as how he treated you so shabbily.'

'I don't know Pete. I have nothing he wants. He ought to be glad I've gone.'

'Well he isn't. He's furious enough to do anything. You better keep well out of sight and if we're real lucky he'll think you've left town.'

'No Pete. If we were lucky he'd leave town, and never come back.'

Ten days later a letter came for S. Hunter care of Pete's Post Office Box. Pete picked it up amongst his own mail. When he came in the back door Sherry was making coffee. 'Mrs. Poole from the Post Office sure gave me some funny looks today,' said Pete as she poured a cup for him.

'I reckon getting a letter addressed to a stranger care of my mail box must have had her tongue burning with questions. Too bad I didn't have any answers. She must be mighty frustrated by now. Probably spreading it around town that I've got a woman holed up here with me.' He took a sip of the coffee and sighed appreciatively. 'This is great coffee, girl. I might just have to keep you here to cook for me. Then Archer's Creek really would have something to talk about.' He grinned with anticipation.

They took their drinks into the sitting room and sat down. Pete said, 'I've heard some of the stories Mrs. Poole has put out about people in the past so I know she has a great imagination. Makes you wonder what kind of books she reads.'

Sherry laughed. 'Probably romances. Some of those juicy ones I've seen in the bookshop look good. Wish I had the money to buy one myself.'

Pete chuckled, obviously amused by the images they'd conjured up involving a frustrated Mrs. Poole. He winked mischievously at Sherry. 'Sounds like the sort of thing I'd like to read too.'

He sorted through the pile of mail and handed her the letter. She held it against her breast for a moment, her eyes closed, too overcome to open it right away. Then she grinned and looked at him cheekily as she sat down.

'She's probably hoping for a bit of excitement. It must be pretty boring sitting around all day in a post office waiting for mail to arrive and be collected. She probably fancies you yourself, crusty old bachelor that you are. Maybe she wants to reform you and make you into a model citizen or something.'

Pete began to shake with laughter. 'Got an uphill job in front of her if that's the case. I reckon I scared her off though. When she looked like she was set to ask questions like 'who have you got stashed up at your place?' and 'who is S Hunter? Is it a woman?', I gave her the look that I used to reserve for brawling miners back in the old days. She sure seemed to back off mighty quick. It was a treat to see I still had the old evil eye.'

'Pete, you should be ashamed of yourself. Mrs. Poole is a bit of a gossip that's all. She doesn't mean anything by it. I think she's lonely, especially since her mother died last year.'

Pete brushed his hand over his face and sobered. 'Yeah,' he said softly, 'I know what it's like to be alone. You keep thinking of the past, wishing you could change things. It's great to have someone to talk to, someone who understands what life was like back when the town was fully alive and mines were working full bore.'

Pete stood and found a silver letter opener on the old sideboard which held glassware and trophies, beer coasters and other things accumulated over the years. 'It's a pity she's sticking' her nose into this business though,' he continued as he sat down again to open his mail. 'It won't be long before Marley and Burns get wind of the gossip and come here looking for you. Then it'll hit the fan for sure.' He began to slice open the junk mail and throw his bills into a pile on the floor.

Sherry tore open her envelope and withdrew a piece of white paper. She scanned the page, gasping with excitement then jumping out of her seat. 'You won't be in trouble from Sergeant Burns if I'm not here to find,' she told Pete excitedly. 'I applied for a job. This is a reply from Mr. Jones.'

Surely it's too good to be true she thought, a chance for a new life, free of Ralph Marley. 'Pete, I'm scared. He wants to see me. I've got an interview for a job. In Melbourne. Will you drive me there?'

'Hold on, Sherry. Talk slow. Who wants to see you? What job?'

'Well, you won't believe this but I answered a job ad in a Melbourne paper, the Herald. It was a couple of weeks old but I thought I'd try anyway.' She began to pace restlessly around the small room.

'What kind of job is it?' Pete asked suspiciously, never having seen Sherry so excited before, except when he presented her with Scrappy ten months ago.

'It's...it's...well, I don't really know exactly. I suppose it's sort of domestic work or something. Oh, I don't know and I don't really care, so long as I get the job and get out of here. That's all I want, just to leave Archer's Creek and make a new life for myself. Is that too much to ask Pete? Is it?'

She raised beautiful haunted eyes to her old friend's face and trembled with emotion. 'You know what my life is like here. Please, help me get away. You won't regret it, I swear. Grandpa would be so grateful to you if he was here. I will be too!'

Pete was unable to deny such a fervent plea, especially knowing her circumstances. He said gruffly, 'Alright young Sherry, I'll drive you. But I'm staying close by while you're in Melbourne in case you need me. When's the interview?'

'Tuesday the 24th. That's a few weeks away isn't
it?' 'Yeah, nearly three weeks.'

'I'll have to keep on hiding out here for a while. I hope you can put up with us Pete, me and

Scrap? I'll cook you some really good dinners to make up for it.'

'I reckon I can suffer through it,' he teased. 'Where's the interview?'

'Somewhere just outside of Melbourne, near Yarra Glen. If you get a street directory we can plan how to get there. The place he says to stay at has a stretch of water called Palm Lake. Must be palm trees planted there.' She handed him the letter and said, 'The address is in there. I have to phone and leave a message for Mr. Jones and he'll book me a room at the hotel.'

'That shouldn't be a problem.' he replied as he read. 'We can ring up and leave the message right now if you like.'

'Thanks, Pete. I'm really grateful to you. You're a loyal friend.'

Pete's weather-beaten skin flushed a dull copper. 'Go on with you, get some rest. No sleeping in come morning. We've got work to do.'

Sherry grinned and hugged him. 'Good on you, Pete. I'll make sure I'll be up before you and give you breakfast in bed for the first time in your life.' All she got in reply was a swat on the rear.

The next three weeks were an agony of anticipation for Sherry. She helped Pete with his animals and cooked his meals, but tension was always present. A constant lookout had to be kept in case her presence was seen and reported to Ralph.

Up early on the day they were due to leave, Sherry packed sandwiches and coffee for the journey. They'd worked out it would take an hour and a half into the city then maybe another hour to find the hotel on the eastern side of Melbourne. She climbed into Pete's dusty ancient utility and they set off for Melbourne, Scrappy checking out the scenery. He could barely see out of the window but it didn't seem to matter to him. It was extremely uncomfortable for Sherry in the first part of the trip as she had to hide under a sheet of canvas in the back in case she was seen.

She emerged half an hour after they'd started smelling of potato dust and mouldy vegetables, a silly grin on her face. Independence was heady. Smiling hadn't come easy in her life, but she promised herself from now on it would be a good start to every day. She'd remind herself of how great it was to be free.

It was a nuisance she didn't have a driver's licence. She could have helped with the driving. She vowed it was something she would learn the first chance she got.

The truck stop on the outskirts of Ballarat was thankfully deserted. Pete encouraged Scrappy to put out his contribution to tree preservation while Sherry visited the amenities. She was tired, hungry and dirty but the feeling of freedom was overwhelmingly heady as she washed her face and brushed her hair. Her only regret was in leaving the house where she was born. Her parents, Grandpa and Aunt Jo were carried with her in her heart.

Sitting in silence inside the cab of the truck, Sherry knew that she'd come a long way from being a scared young teenager. At ten she had been left in the guardianship of a man her parents had trusted. He had betrayed that trust and now she was running away. He had taken her home and possessions and made them his own. He had made her afraid in the town where been born and raised.

She had learned not to trust. Now she was mistress of her own destiny and it was wonderful, a whole new life. The only thing she was taking with her was Scrappy and he showed his appreciation by snuggling up to her and licking her stroking hand. He seemed to know something good was going to happen at last.

It was pleasant at the Palm Lake Hotel/Motel, middle class accommodation, cabins spread around the large lake like cabanas. A small dock with canoes for hire gave guests a choice of fishing or lazing their holiday away on the water.

The large modern three story main building stood alone surrounded by green lawns, palm trees and red flowering gum trees, old fashioned flower gardens edged by fine gravel paths, it's balconies facing low hills in a vivid green landscape.

Tennis courts and a swimming pool were placed close to the main building. The surrounding countryside had a few farms dotted here and there but the closest shops were either in Yarra Glen or towards the city.

Sherry registered at reception and was shown to a cabin which, she had been assured by the receptionist had been organised by Mr. Jones, the bill to be sent to him for the time she would spend at the hotel. She was relieved not have to pay because Pete was the only one with any cash and, after all, Mr. Jones had promised in his letter to pay for her room. He said he'd pay for her meals as well but Sherry felt it would be better to eat some meals with Pete while he was still in town. Her appetite was small and it wouldn't cost much to share with him. Pete had reached into his generous pocket and produced enough cash for Sherry to buy some clothes, sneakers, toiletries and a backpack big enough to hold clothes, her little dog and his food as well.

They had taken time on their way to Palm Lake to shop and Sherry was overwhelmed with the choices and excitement of it all, never being able to buy what she wanted or to choose freely since she was a young girl. She eyed the dresses displayed in the window of a small exclusive store with a sense of deprivation.

She hadn't ever been permitted to wear such beautiful things, had never touched such delicate fabrics. She'd wanted to though, but knew her work roughened hands would be a desecration.

Other girls in Archer's Creek had worn them and had seemed to revel in flaunting themselves in front of her small figure clad in worn jeans and boys shirts. Their nylon covered feet clad in high heeled sandals, those tall confident girls had trampled all over her emerging femininity with total unconcern, secure in their ability to attract any male they chose and some they didn't want, purely to say they could if they wanted to.

As she looked around at girls in the stores with their male companions laughing, listening to music, sipping cokes and having fun she felt a bitter sense of loss. Such freedom and enjoyment had never been hers and it was doubtful she would fit in with their world now even if she had the chance.

As Sherry watched the young people, most of them not much younger than her, she remembered, there had been a boy at school, a tall handsome son of one of the women from church. He was a couple of years older than her and full of the confidence of youth as he played football and flirted with the other girls.

She had watched from the sidelines as he dated first one girl, then another, until he finally started going with one girl who was as smart and outgoing as he was. They were a magical couple, both super achievers, both beautiful and both with families to back them up as they planned for college.

Johnny Piedmont was his name and he was as unaware of Sherry as he would be of an ant beneath his feet. Several times they had been face to face and he had looked right through her as if she didn't even take up air space. His girlfriend was called Karen and she was the daughter of the licensee of the Archer's Creek Hotel.

Firewalking

Of course Sherry knew how unattractive she was, a mousy boring girl with nothing to attract a boy like Johnny, not even a good figure. Ralph had made sure she knew how bad she looked when he caught her looking at Johnny one day. He had been at school to pick her up for some reason and they had gone to the supermarket before going home. Johnny had been there with his girlfriend and Sherry had watched him, not realising she had given her yearning away to Ralph.

Ralph pointed out to her how much she lacked in looks as well as personality. He said Johnny was from a well off family. The Piedmonts owned the most expensive restaurant in the town and couldn't afford to associate with someone as unpolished and clumsy as she was. Johnny himself was planning to go to College and become a master chef and would need a wife who could match him in every way by being a refined and well dressed hostess able to help run the restaurant.

He told her to forget getting a boyfriend or finding a husband. She was going to have her work cut out keeping house for him for a long time, after all, she owed him for years of selfless protection and care.

Sherry turned away from her grim recollection as Pete turned to her with a grin. He pointed out some of the more outrageous fashions and hairstyles. He tucked an arm around her shoulders in reassurance at her wistful gaze and uncertainty.

'Come on sweetie. You're free to buy whatever you want. Provided I can afford it. Only please don't ask to have rings put in your eyebrows or nose. I don't think I could stand it.'

Sherry laughed then and said, 'Why not, Pete? A ring through the nose and I'll do whatever I'm told without question.'

'Not you, Sherry. For sure, now you're out of the cage you're never going back.'

With Pete's help and a large slice of luck, she managed to smuggle Scrappy into the small cabin. He was so excited to be free, he leapt and whirled on and off the double bed like a demented moggy. It was all she could do to keep him quiet but he wasn't a dog who barked a lot normally and she was grateful.

Pete booked into a motel a few miles away towards the city. It was cheap and run down but it suited Pete. 'No fancy trimmings for me,' he told Sherry drily. 'All I need is a place to sleep, a well cooked steak and a beer for dinner.'

She had to agree with him even if she wished he was with her at Palm Lake. He said he'd wait until she knew what was happening and then head back to Archer's Creek, with, or reluctantly, without her.

Sherry panicked for a moment at the thought of being left alone then she reasserted her vow to be independent.

It was one thing to be kept virtually a prisoner in a small country town by your guardian when you were a young girl but once you were old enough and knew how to take care of yourself it was important to take control of your own destiny. It was important not to back down when confronted by your own deeply ingrained but probably irrational fears.

When she was shown into Mr. Jones' hotel suite the next afternoon, Sherry was as nervous as a pedigree cat. Scrappy was being pooch-sat by Pete in his motel room and, last seen by Sherry, they were curled up munching potato snacks and watching cartoons on TV. Now she was on her own and determined to make the most of her opportunity.

Jones was a small middle aged man, slightly plump with thinning fair hair, he had a secretive air but a pleasant smile for Sherry as he opened the door. 'Come in Miss Hunter,' he said quietly. 'Please, sit down and tell me all about yourself.' He indicated the plush velvet upholstered sofa.

She started slightly in reaction and looked around apprehensively, wondering for a moment who he was talking to. Then she remembered. She hadn't grown used to her new name or learned to control her habit of looking over her shoulder. Curling her fingers together nervously she sat down and looked around, trying to make herself comfortable.

Her throat was dry and she cleared it before saying, 'Nothing much to tell Mr. Jones. I said in my letter I felt it would be a good thing if I changed my life. My reasons still stand. I've no money and no qualifications to speak of.'

'And your family? Won't they wonder where you are?'

'I have no family.'

'So you have no-one who would wonder where you disappeared to, who would try to find you? No friends, no enemies looking for you?' He smiled slightly showing small inward sloping teeth. 'No young man?'

'No. I'm all alone.' Briefly Ralph flashed into her mind but she forced him out and concentrated on the interview. Fortunately she'd had plenty of years to practice keeping the truth from being seen on her face. She didn't have to lie exactly, just clear her expression to bland innocence look her tormentor in the eye and wait quietly.

'Forgive me for mentioning this my dear but you are a very beautiful girl. Such lovely colouring and fair skin. Surely there is someone who cares for you.'

'No. There's no-one who cares for me,' she repeated her stand, trying to appear cool and confident. Forgive me Pete, she thought. You care very much. It's just a small but necessary lie. I'll make it up to you one day.

'I find that very hard to believe,' he said, his eyes lingering on her beautiful face for long seconds. 'You are a most unusual looking girl Miss Hunter. Quite delightful, in fact your photograph does not do you justice. You must be about 5 feet 5 but I assumed from your picture you were shorter. And a little younger. Obviously this school photo was taken some years ago.'

'Yes. It was taken at school when I was sixteen. I'm a few years older now and much more able to cope with a job.'

'I can see that,' he murmured looking at her with assessing but vaguely troubled eyes. 'I think you should think this over carefully though. It might not be quite what you envisage and I don't want you backing out later when I've gone to the trouble to make arrangements.'

'Are you trying to put me off Mr. Jones?' asked Sherry with a worried frown. 'I know I must seem to be a little confused but you have to understand. I need to get away. I have no money. My family are all gone and I have some very sad memories. I want to change all that and make a new life with new friends.'

'I assume you're offering a job somewhere, maybe domestic work or typing perhaps. Is it some private organisation who screen their employees very thoroughly for high security positions?' she asked ingenuously.

He smiled slightly as if she had made a tasteless joke. 'Something like that.'

'It wouldn't bother me. I'd be safe then wouldn't I?' Sherry's hands trembled and she swallowed nervously while shifting in her seat. 'No-one would be able to find me.'

'Perhaps there's something you aren't telling me Miss Hunter? Do you have some serious and pressing problem I need to evaluate before I make a decision?' He looked stern for a moment, less the benevolent uncle and more the discern er of lies.

Sherry hesitated, sensing he was about to refuse her if she didn't open up to him. 'There is one thing,' she said slowly, her eyes wide and beseeching as she looked into his. 'A man is trying to find me and I don't want him to.'

'A man. Do you mean a lover?' He raised his eyebrows as if her having a lover was beyond his comprehension.

Not a lover,' she replied, blushing fiercely an confirming her innocence.

'A relative?' he spoke kindly but had a strangely excited gleam in his eye.

'No. He's no relation.'

'What is he then?' he asked. 'I'll admit to being slightly confused my dear. There aren't many other categories for a man to fall into. Perhaps he's a debt collector or an taxation officer? It couldn't be that you're wanted by the police?'

'Oh no, not the police. He's...' she thought rapidly, seeking a description of Ralph which was unlikely to tell Jones of any authority he might claim in looking for her. 'A stranger. He's been watching me. I can't go anywhere without him following me.'

That much was true she reasoned. Ralph was always following her, watching her every move like a reptile watches it's victim before the strike. In fact, Sherry reflected with black humour, his appearance was rather reptilian as well, pale hooded eyes, cold flesh and a vicious tongue.

'Have you been to the police?' asked Jones, breaking into her thoughts.

'They can't do anything unless he attacks me or breaks into my hou...my flat.' She forbore to explain that he already lived in her house and that he had attacked her quite a few times without provocation and would continue to do so if she stayed.

'I'm frightened and all I want is to disappear. I've given up my flat and I'll need to find somewhere else to live if you can't help me. Can you find a job for me Mr. Jones? I'm quite strong and I'm not afraid of hard work. I'm a good cook and I can clean. I can even type quite well and do simple bookkeeping. Whatever it is you want me to do, I know I'll do it well.'

Her eyes filled with unconscious tears as she pleaded with him. 'Please consider my application. If you don't I'm not sure what I'll do.' A shade of desperation was apparent in her voice and her clenched hands which were held so tightly they etched half moons into her palms.

'Alright Miss Hunter,' he agreed in a reluctant tone, his eyes watching her carefully. 'I'll consider you. You do seem suitable for the work I have in mind.'

'What sort of work is it?' Eager now, Sherry couldn't keep an excited sparkle out of her eyes. She grinned at him, unconsciously allowing him a glimpse of the vivacious care-free young girl she could have been if allowed to grow up with loving parents and a normal childhood.

The man paused for a moment and looked her over from head to toe with that same excited gleam in his eye before saying smoothly, 'It's simple work mostly, domestic, cooking, things like that. There will be another woman to work with you and kitchen staff to clean up and serve as well. You'll be able to do it easily. Now I have a few other people to see today so I'll be in touch later this afternoon. If I decide to employ you, I'll expect you back here tomorrow night for further discussion. Wear something pretty. There might be a few other guests.'

'Thank you Mr. Jones. You won't regret this, I'll make sure of it.' She'd worry later about what she could find to wear and how to introduce Scrappy. Whatever happened he was going to be a part of it too.

CHAPTER FOUR

That night, after Sherry and Pete had eaten take-away hamburgers from a fast food place, he dropped her back at the hotel. She sat on the back step of her cabin with Scrappy in her arms breathing in the fragrant country air and feeling the cool breeze from the lake stroking her heated skin. It was a lovely clear night, still warm from the heat of the day. A sleeveless white cotton button-through blouse and a short floral skirt made of silky jersey caressed her bare legs and made her feel reassuringly feminine. Normally her jeans and man-size work shirts covered her from head to toe but she wasn't bound by her compulsion to hide her body any more. She was able to put on whatever she felt like wearing and enjoy it.

Sherry was just thinking about turning in around ten o'clock when a sound came from the front door. Someone was putting a key in her lock. Cold dread woke Sherry out of her dreams of freedom. It was too late to be the manager wanting something, anyway, he'd knock first wouldn't he? She held Scrappy firmly to prevent him growling and crept in through the back door. The light hadn't been switched on so she could only make out the furniture in the room by tracks of moonlight coming through chinks in the curtains. She had no idea who this was but knew that if Ralph had found her she would give him a run for his money. No way was she ever going to submit to his domination ever again.

A deep male voice outside cursed and the man thumped the door with what sounded like a very large fist, as if it was refusing him admittance on a whim. 'Bloody key,' growled the voice. 'It's the wrong damn one.'

Sherry crept to the window and pulled the curtain aside to watch as the large darkened figure of a man strode away down the barely lit gravel path to the main building. She breathed a shaky sigh of relief. A least it wasn't Ralph. But who was it? He'd sounded determined to get in. Probably the wrong cabin she reasoned, remembering his words and wondering if he'd be back. She hoped not. All she needed right now was some man who wouldn't listen to reason. She'd had enough of those to last a lifetime.

She put Scrappy down on the bed and, sitting on a chair in the dark, listened carefully for sounds of movement outside. After a while she heard determined male footsteps approaching her door. Not again she thought, preparing to get rid of the intruder once and for all. Once more a key was shoved into the recalcitrant lock and jiggled, accompanied by more cursing. She was sure she heard the manager's name mentioned in a catalogue of his sins against society and his family tree. Wishing she should introduce her visitor to her guardian so he could evaluate what sin really was, Sherry stood up in fury at the aggravation and abruptly pulled open the door as the man was pushing at it. Momentum carried him across the threshold, causing him to knock her flat in the process, only saving her from being crushed by thrusting his muscled arms out as he fell and keeping his upper body away from her, the rest of him directly aligned with her much smaller frame.

He was a tall, well built man with collar length thick dark hair and an angry glint in his eyes. He looked about thirty but with a lifetime of experience stamped upon his face that removed the surface impression of good looks and replaced it with an aura of danger. His immediate expression said to her, give me any trouble and you'll regret it. Then it changed dramatically to consternation when he realised it was a young and beautiful woman he was crushing with his body.

Winded and unable to make a sound, Sherry felt his hard body touching hers and thought she might be a mass of bruises by the morning. Not that he was moving at all. He was quite still as if stunned by the position he found himself in. His short sleeved black cotton shirt was partly unbuttoned and she caught glimpses of tanned flesh through the opening. Her hand was caught against a hard smooth chest but she was unable to move it away. Her fingers moved involuntarily, stroking the heated skin with fatal fascination. It was like touching a radiator

She began to worry that he was injured in some way but then he moved slightly and she allowed herself to relax, confident he was about to pull himself to his feet. Unfortunately her confidence was misplaced. He made no further attempt to get up. He simply gazed into her eyes as if he had never seen a woman before.

Moonlight shimmered across the floor through the open doorway and shone on her face giving an unearthly glow to her luminous grey eyes and her long straight silvery hair which spilled like warm silk across his hand and arm.

Cave man, she thought, coming back to herself abruptly, squirming her hips in reaction to his touch. This is probably his version of a polite come on line and he expects me to say thank you and yes please to whatever.

Her insides began to vibrate with what she thought was loathing but which quickly pooled into moist heat in areas that had previously known no such phenomenon.

What's happening she wondered, squirming even more, her small hand pushing ineffectively at his rock solid chest. She was beginning to feel really good, flushed and excited, her blood pumping faster and faster, her heart almost leaping out of her chest. I could stay here and do this forever she realised and felt something stirring as he began to move. In her naivety fear was the furthest thing from her mind.

Involuntarily Sherry grasped the buttoned front of his shirt and held him there. 'Don't move,' she said huskily, breathing deeply, unconsciously pleading, moistening her lips.

'Not in this lifetime,' his deep voice rumbled as he shifted slightly, confirming her opinion of his muscles. They certainly were impressive.

She blushed. 'I mean, be careful. You're such a big man and I'm... .'

'You're what? A little girl? A delicious little girl?' He amended, smiling gently, his beautifully curved mouth beckoning her to undiscovered delights, his dark eyes gleaming behind lowered lids. 'Don't worry, I won't hurt you. My name's Quin.'

'I'm Sherry and I think if you move I'll be in big trouble.' She moved her hips and legs tentatively and felt heat rush to her face. Excitement was staking it's claim on her senses and she was offering no resistance at all. Was this what Ralph had not wanted her to know about when he told her boys were trouble and posted no trespassing signs all around the property when she was twelve?

Maybe this what the local girls had termed hands on experience as they laughed about their intimate exploits? Or it could be called whole body experience since the lightning zipping through her blood was shattering her entire body. It was certainly a long way from the tepid emotions the males she'd met so far made her feel. Even John, the boy she had idolised at school, hadn't aroused this kind of feeling and the few foolish ones that had braved Ralph Marley's wrath and chanced a kiss behind the shelter sheds in her final year at high school were now blurred memory. She wished those girls could see her now. Instead of mocking her and calling her Snow White they would call her Rose Red and hate her even more.

'If I don't move you'll be in even more trouble,' he said, his intense gaze wandering wherever he pleased. 'I can personally guarantee it.'

Sherry caught her breath on a sigh. 'Oh,' she whispered, 'Perhaps you better get up then.' She stroked his chest without thinking, slipping her fingertips through the spaces between buttonholes and touching his hot bare chest.

'I wouldn't do that if I were you Sherry,' he said hoarsely, feeling her touch right down to his toes like a firebrand. 'I might like it too much and decide to stay.'

She pulled her wayward hands away as if burned. 'Sorry. I wasn't thinking.'

A small wet tongue insinuated itself into Sherry's ear and began to slurp enthusiastically. Just as she began to protest, 'Scrappy, cut it out.' Quin found his chin being similarly treated to a thorough washing. As the tongue reached his mouth he moved his head away abruptly and looked down into a pair of small black eyes surrounded by long strands of brown and black hair. 'Who are you little guy?' he asked with a grin. As Scrappy began to climb onto Sherry's chest and lick at Quin's face once more Quin protested, laughingly saying, 'Hey, I'm clean. Okay? No need to give me the once over.' The little dog slipped down off Sherry's shoulder and began to bark in a half playful, half serious manner. His tiny stump of a tail was twisting vigorously side to side and he was turning in circles as Sherry said, 'Now Scrappy. Don't get yourself in a knot. This is Quin. He's just visiting for a minute. I think.' She looked at him uncertainly.

Quin looked down a the woman beneath him and, as if suddenly sensing her inexperience and the impropriety of his position, he carefully levered his body away from hers and climbed to his feet. He put down his hand to help Sherry up and said, 'I'd like to say I'm sorry for what happened but it would be a lie and I prefer to tell the truth wherever possible.'

'Can I help you with anything?' she asked, backing away from his tall figure reluctantly and picking up her dog. She had to look up a long way to see his face and he bent his head to look down at her, smiling gently, his expression softening as he listened to the uncertainty in her voice.

'You could,' he said softly, watching her beautiful eyes glisten in the moonlight. 'I doubt if you're ready for that though.'

'Ready for what?' Then she realised what he'd said and colour flowed over her honey toned skin. She replaced Scrappy on the floor at her feet and straightened her white cotton blouse which had become twisted during her sojourn on the floor. She ran her fingers through her long fair hair and wished she had a brush. It was as if she had to have something to do with her hands to stop herself reaching out to him once more.

He sighed and willed himself to be strong and his blood to cool down. He had never known himself to react in such a mindless way to a woman before. Maybe it was his practice of abstinence of late that was increasing his hormone level to that of a randy teenager. No doubt about it, he would have to find a woman to break the drought. But not this one. She was too innocent, too vulnerable. If he followed through on his fevered imaginings, he would only cause her pain. 'It doesn't matter. I've obviously got the wrong cabin. I arrived here yesterday but I've been busy today and haven't had a chance to look around. This place is confusing at night. In the dark the cabins all look the same.' He laughed. 'I suppose I should be grateful I didn't fall in the lake. It's sure to be cold this time of night.' Maybe I should jump in now he thought, knowing it would be a long time before he slept after tangling with Sherry and feeling her soft fingers caressing him, even if she didn't realise she was doing it.

'Well I hope you find the right one. This is number six.' She wanted him to go so she could think over all that had happened yet at the same time she wanted him to stay, to remember cabin six and come to see her again. Scrappy settled the matter by putting his leg up on the man's ankle and drenching his blue jeans and sneakers with ammonia. 'Oh dear, I'm so sorry. Bad doggy Scrap. You naughty thing.' She picked up the tiny hound and put him in the bathroom. When she returned to the door the man was out the door and backing down the path.

'Good night,' she called through the open door. She received a wave of his hand as he turned and strode hurriedly away. 'Goodbye Quin,' she whispered as he hesitated outside another cabin then disappeared inside. 'It was nice while it lasted.'

Quin was furious with himself. What an idiot. Fancy not reading the number on the cabin correctly. That girl must think him a total fool. Thank goodness she couldn't read his mind. She would have run screaming for help and had him ejected from the Hotel. Not that he regretted what had happened, except for the dog that is. The ammonia smell wafted up to his nostrils on the breeze from the open window and he sat down on the bed to remove his squishy sneakers. Quin grinned as he thought about what had happened. That was one smart little mutt. He knew how to repel boarders. He took off his soggy jeans and socks and rinsed them in the bathroom. The sneakers had a tiny pool in the bottom and were beyond being washed, they would need to be replaced.

Sherry. An intoxicating name. The tiny blonde with those gorgeous grey eyes was a treat he hadn't expected to encounter. Pity he wouldn't see her again. Tomorrow was his second interview with Mr. Jones and after that, who knew what would happen.

He'd had enough trouble with the first interview when he'd tried to make up some plausible explanation as to why he answered the ad. He wasn't a good liar but he'd done his best, saying he had gambling and other debts he couldn't pay and creditors who were hounding him to death. Jones had seemed convinced but Quin wasn't so sure. He didn't trust Jones at all and that was the problem.

Still, regardless of his efforts to remove her from his mind, Quin dreamed long and hard about invitingly soft lips, a voice that poured over exposed nerve endings like melted honey and hair like slippery satin flowing down over small breasts to a tiny waist he could almost put his hands right around. No other woman had ever made him forget what his main goal was before and he wished it hadn't happened now. He needed all his concentration to discern what Jones had in mind. The man might not be completely what he seemed but was he a con-man or just holding his cards close to his chest?

One thing for sure, Quin was desperate to get away. A few days before, another attempt had been made on his life and this time they had almost succeeded. Early in the day, he'd climbed into his van which was parked in a side street and driven around past the front of the building containing his upstairs apartment, intending to go to his store in the city.

Looking in the rear-view mirror, he'd seen his cat prowling around on the footpath. He'd braked and got out to take the animal back inside to the building manager who took care of the cat while he was at work or away on weekends.

The two men had been walking back out the front door when Quin's van had exploded into a wall of flames, shattering the front windows of the building and making debris spin through the air to litter the deserted street. Both of them had been thrown back through the building's front door and were showered by flying glass. A second explosion had ripped through the air exploding the painting supplies contained in the van and the petrol tank.

Mr. Scallini, the building manager, had cuts and flash burns on his face as well as hearing loss and concussion. His arm was broken as he had fallen against the door frame and he was in a state of shock. Quin had been protected from the worst of the blast because he'd been behind Mr. Scallini's substantial figure just inside the door but nevertheless he had bruises where the man had landed on him and superficial lacerations to his hands and face. His back where he had fallen was extremely painful and he had difficulty in thinking and hearing clearly.

It was a few minutes before the fire department sent a truck and when the flames had been doused the fire-chief examined the burned out shell. 'Remote control device,' he'd said to Quin, looking at him curiously as an ambulance officer checked him for injury and cleaned up the blood flowing from a few fine glass cuts on his hands and arms. 'Someone wants you dead my friend. And that's a fact. They must have watched you get into the van and set the timer going as you drove away. They weren't to know you'd stop and get out just around the corner. Just as well you did though. You would've been char grilled for sure.'

'Thanks,' said Quin drily, wincing as a particularly nasty cut was swabbed with antiseptic. 'You'd be a riot at your end of year barbecue.'

The Fireman slapped him on the back and said, 'You're alive mate. That's always a bonus. If I were you I'd think about getting a different set of friends. The ones you've got play a little too rough for my liking. Disappear for a while and give them time to cool down.'

'Good advice,' Quin said thoughtfully. 'I'll think about it.'

'Don't think too long,' advised the fireman as he scanned the area at the crowd of people who were gathering like ghouls at a feast. 'The bastards who did this little job are probably watching us this very moment. Someone in that crowd might have their finger on another button in another few days and then you'll be history.'

The police arrived in screaming police cars flashing their lights and swarmed all over the area. Even more people seemed to arrive from nowhere. They stood and gaped, getting in the way until a couple of uniformed officers began to close off the area to traffic and put up barriers. Both Quin and Mr. Scallini were taken to hospital in the ambulance for observation and treatment.

A couple of police detectives turned up soon after the two men reached the hospital and began questioning Quin about his lifestyle and gambling habits, ferreting for information on anyone who might feel he'd cheated them. They treated him as if he was a major offender with a string of unpunished crimes to his name.

One officer said, 'We know all about you Jameson. You're a trouble maker and you bring problems on yourself. You'd better keep your nose clean or we'll be taking you in for a closer look at your affairs. Keep that in mind when you decide to point the finger at anybody.' They left then, leaving Quin fuming with frustrated anger and trying to come to terms with the police's attitude. It seemed he was in a no win situation. Mr. Scallini they passed over as an innocent victim and hardly questioned him at all, merely asked him what he had seen. He could tell them nothing.

A television crew had been at the scene soon after the van exploded and their report came on TV after the police had left the hospital. Quin watched in anger as they announced that, after questioning the parties involved, the police could find no evidence to show who had planted the bomb or why.

It was mentioned that the van contained chemical substances and hinted that they were the cause of the explosion, thereby blaming him for the whole mess. Police indicated that enquiries were still proceeding.

Quin wondered if they would be more thorough if it was someone other than himself involved and the thought created a fierce desire to make them beg him for help. He wanted them to publicly apologise to him and plead his forgiveness. Then reality kicked in and his anger died, leaving only the empty realisation that he was on his own, that for all the good his father had been to him during his growing years, he had always been alone.

The authorities would never apologise, never admit they made an error in judgement. Once they labelled you a trouble maker, that's the way you stayed, forever marked and fed into their soulless computer. And once the police computer has you on its debit list, he thought cynically, you're finished as far as your business or personal reputation is concerned. You might as well fold your tent and go home, wherever home would be once you'd lost everything that meant anything to you. It was a bit like being fed into a waste disposal unit. Everything you had liquefied and funnelled down the drain like garbage.

Quin discharged himself after a couple of hours. He had things to do that couldn't wait. Anyway, Mrs. Scallini was fussing around her husband and making him comfortable in the hospital ward so Quin felt he was leaving his friend in the best hands. He felt responsible for what had happened but knew it wasn't really his fault. It was just another thing he had to live with.

Taking the advice of the fire-chief to heart, Quin made arrangements to lease out his business. Mr. and Mrs. Scallini had assured him they would keep the cat who spent more time with them anyway and the apartment could be sub-let until the lease ran out.

It was one thing to stay and fight openly but what good would it do him if he was dead or someone else was injured or killed because of him. He couldn't live with that. Some day he would regain what he had lost he promised himself silently, anger beating inside his head like a live wire as he put his personal equipment and paintings in storage. It would take time but some day he would rebuild his business bigger and better than ever but he'd never want to live or work in the inner city again. He'd choose a place where he was unknown and make a new life for himself, a fresh start. It was something to look forward to.

Until the explosion destroyed his van, Quin had been uncertain whether to follow through on the letter he had sent to William Jones. It all seemed a bit fanciful and beyond reality, wishful thinking on Quin's part and maybe a possible scam by Jones. Who could tell? But after the van disintegrated in front of his eyes, he realised the people who wanted him dead couldn't care less if they killed innocent people as well. He knew then it was time to disappear, one way or another.

The day after his encounter with Sherry in the cabin, Quin was asked to come to Jones' suite around five o'clock. He knocked on the door and, when Jones opened it, walked in and found several other people there having drinks in the kind of restrained atmosphere present when strangers meet and have no basis for friendship or communication. He hoped this was when he would discover where the job was situated.

Initial questions had informed him that the people Jones worked for were recruiting staff for a secret project. He was to be part of a team working on restoring a large old building. That was all he had managed to find out so far but if all was as it seemed, he'd be quite happy to go along. It was, after all, a job and he would be well paid. Then he noticed Sherry.

She was standing near a couple of young women at the side of the room, looking jumpy as a rabbit and sipping a glass of what looked like orange juice. She was dressed in a simple A-line high necked dress of royal blue jersey with short sleeves and looked entirely out of place but still the most delicately beautiful woman in the whole room.

What are you doing here he wanted to ask. This is no place for an innocent like you. Go home where you'll be safe. Forced by circumstances beyond his control, he said nothing, deliberately making his expression cold and hard in the hope she would take fright and leave.

Sherry noticed Quin right away. He was dressed in navy pants and a white shirt with a camel coloured sports jacket. Tall and dark haired, gorgeous dark brown eyes, he looked the embodiment of fierce male beauty without the rough edges of their previous encounter.

It's not fair she thought sadly, I was beginning to think he was a lovely dream. Now he's here and I want to talk to him and find out about him but he looks as if he hates me. Maybe if I smile at him a little...she tried but nerves made her tentative approach look like a grimace.

She gave up then and looked away but even that effort at distancing herself was doomed to failure. It seemed her eyes had a will of their own. Who are you really Quin, what are you doing here, was her silent plea?

After speaking to their host, Quin glanced across at Sherry, a frown gathering on his dark brow. Their eyes met and clashed, his saying fiercely, 'Go away, I don't want you here'; hers pleading, 'What's going on? What have I done to make you look at me like that?'

I wish you weren't here so I didn't have to worry about you he thought with a flash of self-disgust at the pain in her eyes, pain he had caused.

She shivered and turned away, suddenly aware of being separated from all she knew.
Last night he had seemed warm, a man she could trust even though he was a stranger. Now he was cold and, even from across the room, intimidating.

At that moment William Jones called to all the people in the room, 'Everyone, thank you for coming. I thought it would be pleasant for some of you to meet since you'll be working together on our little project. I know this is confusing for you but I will speak to each of you later to explain the situation. In a few days when the details are complete, you will be taken to a secret location where you will be informed of your duties. Your hotel bills here will be paid for you, not the extras though. You can pay for your champagne and massages yourselves.'

Several people laughed slightly and Jones looked like a jovial master of ceremonies intent on holding a captive audience in his hand. He stopped smiling and went on, 'You are to discuss this job with no-one outside this room. Anyone who talks about our business to another person will be excluded from the project and their employment terminated immediately. They will also have to pay their own hotel bill. Is that clear ladies and gentlemen?' When all nodded assent Jones smiled again and said, 'Fine. Relax now and have some wine and savouries, get to know each other. As I said in the advertisement, there's no need to give your right name. It's up to you. I'll talk to each of you later. Thank you and good luck.'

No-one stayed for long. Quin talked to men of varying nationalities, digging a little but not coming up with any answers. No-one wanted to talk about who they were or where they came from but that was okay, he didn't either.

He didn't talk to Sherry or the other women who seemed uncommunicative and nervous. Like you, they want to disappear, he reminded himself, wondering what could make a sweet girl like Sherry need to leave her home and family. It must be something pretty catastrophic he thought, fighting against the urge to barrel up to her and ask. He said his name was Con to any who asked and left it at that.

By the time Quin left, Sherry and the women had gone. Just as well he thought morosely. I wish she wasn't involved in this, that I'd met her somewhere else, some other time. I've a feeling there's something strange about this whole project so we'd both better be on guard. The problem is, how do I explain my instincts to her? Would she even listen to me if I did?

After a couple of hours pacing his room restlessly, Quin decided to go to Sherry's room and talk some sense into her. He had been going over and over in his mind all the things he'd been told about the job, which was almost nothing of any use. The whole thing was beginning to feel like a big mistake. He put on his jacket and walked out into the night, heading over to Cabin number six, hoping she would listen to reason. A little voice in his head whispered, wake up and see the light man, that's not all you want is it? You want to see that beautiful hair swinging around the smooth bare skin of her shoulders and those eyes that look at you with such incredible heat that you're warmed right through to the core. You want to go back to the night before when she was beneath you on the floor, squirming with banked down energy like a volcano, when she looked at you with an innocent kind of hunger, the kind of hunger that makes women crave to be fed and men kill to satisfy that craving.

CHAPTER FIVE

Quin knocked on the door of Cabin six, a loud assertive knock betraying the impatience of the warrior. Sherry looked through the curtain covering the window next to the door and saw it was Quin waiting outside. She almost melted at the sight of his strong handsome face silhouetted against the light from the moon. He looked fierce, as if he had something on his mind other than a pleasant conversation with a fellow employee. She hesitated for a moment then opened the door. As soon as he entered the room he pushed the door shut and said harshly, 'You shouldn't open the door to strangers Sherry. It could be anyone out there. I could be a rapist or a murderer for all you know. Don't do that
again unless you know who is out there.'

'Don't be so bossy Quin. I knew it was you. I looked through the curtain.' Her feelings of joy at seeing him were being eroded by his scowling face and his obvious upset that she had let him in. 'But don't worry, next time you come calling I'll set Scrappy onto you. He'll make you sorry you tried to get into my room and take advantage of me. He might even attack if I tell him to.'

'This isn't funny. You don't know me yet. I could be anyone at all and you'd never know what hit you if I decided to take what you so generously offered to me last night.'

An indignant tide of red flowed up Sherry's face. 'Dream on Mr. Ego,' she said fiercely. 'I offered nothing to you last night. You'd be lucky if I gave you the time of day much less anything else.'

'You offered alright. I don't think you meant to but I can read body language, especially when the body in question is pressed up against mine like sticky tape. If I'd been so inclined you would have been putting out right there on the floor. I wouldn't have even needed to ask.'

'That's not true Quin Jameson,' Sherry yelled. Losing control of her temper, she began to pace the room. 'I'm my own person and nobody can tell me what to do, not any more.
You're imagining things if you think I would have let things go any further than they did.'
She stopped in front of him and glared, wanting to hit him for his stubborn opinion of her morality, wanting to kiss him at the same time, her desire for him almost overwhelming any

shred of self protection she had left.

Then she committed the ultimate error. She lied. 'I don't even like you that way. I don't want you.'

Quin didn't even hesitate. In a second she was in his arms and being convinced beyond a shadow of a doubt she did like him in that way. In fact she desired him that way with such ferocity that she would have done anything he asked without further thought, would have given him her soul if he had asked it of her. His lips plundered hers thoroughly, taking and giving with such delicious savagery, his tongue curling inside her mouth, urging her to give back as much again in sweet surrender.

His large strong hands moulded her body to his, stroking and learning every hollow and curve with the finesse of a master potter moulding his clay into the perfect form. Her breasts swelled with desperate need as he stroked them, the nipples burning, needing to be freed to the cool night air. She couldn't get close enough to him, wanted to climb inside him and make him as hot as he made her.

His voice was hoarse, his breath ragged as he said, 'So you don't want me huh? I like the way you don't want me Sherry. Don't want me some more.'

His words were like a blast of cold air. She pushed him away from her and fled to stand on the other side of the room, the sofa and coffee table between them. She picked up Scrappy as if she needed him as a shield making him squirm in her arms. She held on tight as she confirmed shakily, 'I don't want you Quin. All that was just the heat of the moment. When I can think clearly, I don't want you.'

Sherry's face was flushed and her hair all over the place as she put Scrappy on the floor and re-buttoned her blouse which had become undone with the wild flame that had taken her apart and scorched her to the core. Quin looked just as wild, his flushed skin feverish, the darkness of his pupils burning with desire, his long dark hair tangled from her hands running through it.

'It was a hot moment alright. Very hot. Almost spontaneous combustion.'

'Okay, Okay. It was hot. That's why I'm not coming near you again. It's too dangerous. I need to keep my cool, and my job.'

Quin ran his hands through his hair and looked away, unbearably tempted to vault across the sofa and take her in his arms once more. Instead he said, 'Yeah. The job. That's what I came here tonight to talk to you about.'

'You could have fooled me. Hey, you did fool me.'

'Yeah. Well, I really did come about the job. I don't want you to take it. It's not a good idea for you to go to work for Jones. He's not what he seems Sherry. I don't trust him one bit.'

'He seems alright to me,' Sherry said, a puzzled frown on her face. 'Why don't you trust him? Do you know something I don't.'

'No, but I don't trust this whole setup. How do we know what's on the other end of the line. What's the story on the secrecy angle? If he was on the up and up there wouldn't be any need to hire people who want to disappear. It stinks to high heaven and I don't want you to be caught up in something you can't control.'

'I need this job Quin. It's the only thing between me and ...' she hesitated, 'going home. I can't go home. I've burnt my bridges and I'm not going back.'

'Let me help you then. I can find another way out for you.'

'No. I need to do this on my own. Call it independence if you like, it's the first time in my life I've felt truly able to manage my life on my own. I'm free to do what I want, when I want.

And I like it that way.'

'It's dangerous Sherry,' said Quin as he edged his way across the room toward her. All he intended to do was hold her in his arms and convince her to let him take her some place neither of them would be found but she backed away and kept the furniture between them.

'Go away Quin. Go back to your room and leave me alone. I can't think when you get too close. My brain turns to hot toffee and I do things I regret.'

'Hot toffee tastes wonderful,' he crooned as he came within touching distance, reaching out a finger to stroke her cheek. 'It's sweet and delicious and melts on your tongue. Forget about Jones and his job offer. It's too dangerous to fly off into the unknown. Who knows what kind of world is waiting for you out there.'

Sherry slapped his hand away at the same time as she caught her breath. He was too close for comfort. How did he get so close without her knowing? 'Forget it Quin. I'm going. Now go back to your room. I've got to get some sleep. We keep early hours in the country and I'm tired. It's been a long day.'

Quin looked down on grey eyes that were drooping with weariness. 'Alright Sherry. I'll go. But give it some thought will you? Don't commit yourself to a situation that could be much worse than the one you left.'

As he stepped out the door of the cabin he thought he heard her whisper fiercely, 'Nothing could be worse than that. It was hell and I'm never going back. Not ever.'

Quin turned back, momentarily tempted to quiz her on her words but all he said was, 'Don't open the door to anyone else Sherry. It's not a good habit to get into. This is the city and all kinds of things happen here.'

'It's a bit late for that advice,' she countered, her sense of humour coming to the fore. 'The fox has already been in the hen house.'

'Ah, but he hasn't eaten his fill yet,' Quin laughed, his voice husky with unfulfilled need and a promise. 'He'll be back.' Then he turned and continued on to cabin number nine, where he should have gone in the first place. A believer in destiny, Quin couldn't find it in himself to regret his mistake at all.

*　　　*　　　*　　　*

ON the afternoon of the next day, William Jones rang and asked Sherry to come to his suite. All morning she kept a look out for Quin but he remained elusive. Reluctantly she drew the conclusion he had no intention of being seen or had left the hotel so she tried to put him out of her mind.

It was only while she had lunch with Pete at his motel that she was able to forget him because they talked about home and the situation there. The sad and bitter memories which came flooding in clouded her mind of anything else.

She was worried and once again unhappy. What was she going to do with Scrappy? She thought of asking Pete to take him back home but the thought of parting with him brought desolation. Ralph would be sure to find out and Pete would probably be accused of doing away with her or something.

He would take Scrappy from Pete and who knew what he would do to him. He was all she had left. She loved her little mutt and he loved and trusted her completely. She needed to ask if she could bring her dog with her to the job, knowing full well she would be unable to bring him undetected.

Jones opened the door to her knock. 'Miss Hunter. Come in and sit down. You seem a little tense today. Is something wrong?'

'I've got a dog,' she said abruptly as she walked in the door. 'He's very small, a Yorkshire terrier. I promise, he wouldn't be a nuisance.' She sat on the sofa opposite the door with her knees pressed tightly together, her hands twisting themselves into knots.

'You want to bring your pet with you, is that it Miss Hunter?' Jones seemed bemused. 'Yes please Mr. Jones. If I could?' Her eyes pleaded unknowingly for his compassion. 'This is the first time I've been asked to bring an animal along. I suppose you could, so long as he's kept on a leash and doesn't bother anyone.'

'Oh thank you. You're a kind man. Scrappy and I are very grateful.'

'It's nothing my dear. Anything to keep our employees happy. Now I need to explain what your duties will be. Mostly cooking I'm afraid. You did say you could cook didn't you?'

Sherry was so happy she would have agreed to anything, almost. 'Yes, I like cooking. How many people to cook for?'

'Possibly eighteen or twenty on a regular basis. Sometimes more or less. I'm not sure of exact numbers. There will be another woman as well who is experienced in catering and another two to help with preparation and washing up. Is that alright? Not too much for you?' He looked over her slim build, obviously doubting her ability to cope.

'I'll be fine thank you. I'm stronger than I look.' She thought momentarily of the work she had done for Ralph, hard slogging work shovelling tailings in the mine, washing and ironing for him too. Cooking his meals. Cleaning the house. Pity she hadn't had the guts to put a little something extra in his food. Like Epsom Salts.

Mix the Epsom salts with sugar in the sugar bowl and he'd would have put it in his tea without a clue what he was doing. Three teaspoons per cup of tea or coffee, eight or nine cups per day.

That would have settled his account very nicely she thought with a burst of malicious pleasure. He wouldn't have had time to give her any trouble. Slightly ashamed of her thoughts but unrepentant, she gave herself a mental shake and asked, 'Where is it we're going exactly?'

'I can't say at the moment,' said William Jones looking at her curiously. 'That was a very strange look you had on your face just then Miss Hunter. Are you concerned about something?'

'No, not really. I just remembered something I should have done but forgot. It's nothing.'

'If you say so. You must realise I need someone who can carry out orders and not cause problems. If you've got something on your mind put it aside or tell me now so we can deal with it. The man in charge of the project, not me by the way, doesn't like employing girls who cause problems with the other staff. He says it makes the men restless and unreliable if you know what I mean.'

'No, I'm not sure. Why would they be restless and unreliable?'

'Women are a distraction. Men see them as available or unavailable and act accordingly. If women set themselves up to be noticed the men are going to be thinking of them instead of the job.'

'I think I understand? But there's nothing to worry about Mr. Jones. Everything will be fine. I promise not to distract anyone from their job.' She smiled sweetly, reassuring him of her gentle pliability.'Will the other people I met here be coming too?'

'Oh yes, plus one or two extras you haven't met yet. You'll be one big happy family.' He beamed at her as if he was a travel agent delighted with the arrangements he had made. 'I'm sure you're going to enjoy working for us as much as we'll enjoy having you.'

Later that night Sherry thought of Quin and was glad he was included. She longed to see him and talk to him and even if he rejected her again, it would be worth it to know he was nearby. Somehow she felt she could depend on him in a crisis. And there was always the chance of some more of those mind blowing kisses. They were the sort of thing she could easily become addicted to. It was a pity he dished them out just to prove to her how much she wanted him. Blow hot, then cold. It seemed he couldn't make up his mind. All she knew was that he didn't want her along on the job with Mr. Jones, didn't trust Jones at all.

For the life of her she couldn't see anything dangerous about the little man. He was just offering a security conscious job for people who wanted to change their lives for a while. It was all very simple if you looked at it that way. Maybe Quin would decide not to come along in the end. She wouldn't be surprised. She'd miss him though, even if he was hard to understand and difficult to get along with. She hoped he would decide to come. He was one person she would like to distract. Why it had come into her mind that there might be a time when she needed help was beyond her. Unless it was Quin going on about how dangerous it was to accept a job in such a way with people who seemed so secretive about the destination or anything else about the position.

After all, with Ralph Marley only a bitter memory, she was in no danger and ready to begin her new life. She had Scrappy for companionship and her life was finally heading in a positive direction. What more could she want?

During the night when the subconscious takes control, she remembered, reliving over and over again how it had felt to be held close by Quin when they had first met, even taking their second encounter in her cabin a step or two further in her mind. A little voice taunted her with possibilities, tingling her fingertips and forming sensual images in her mind. A man, tall, strong, dark haired, impossibly handsome, name of Quin Jameson. A man who knew what he wanted and made sure he got it, who would fight for what he believed in, a pirate and a renegade but oh so exciting, a man with kisses so hot he was like a volcano on the verge of eruption.

Sherry squirmed in her lonely bed, strangely feverish and desperate for the touch of Quin's hands, needing to hear his deep voice curling around her nerve endings, to feel him penetrating the fragile shield of her innocence. She woke then, breathless with unsatisfied longing, ruthlessly stifling the voice singing Quin's praises in her head and trying to sleep. It was going to be a long hot night.

Quin spent the evening after the cocktail party and all the following day thinking. He still wasn't sure whether he should give the whole business away and find some other way out of the mess he was in.

Unfortunately whenever he decided to quit a vision of an innocent, defenceless Sherry in serious trouble would slip past his common sense. He'd then decide to find out more before he finally made up his mind, knowing his conscience wouldn't allow him to leave her to face the unknown unaccompanied even if it meant going into a bad situation unprepared. He tried not to let the fact that he wanted her influence his thinking in any way. Unfortunately his body seemed to have no direct connection to his brain.

This type of vacillatory behaviour was alien to Quin's normally forceful outlook but since he'd met Sherry, he seemed more inclined to have his mind on things of an introspective nature as well as on the young woman who seemed to have taken over his emotions and his mind, not to forget his body. It has to stop he decided ruthlessly, as that afternoon he ploughed up and down the length of the hotel swimming pool, forcing his muscles to burn and stretch with exertion; who can tell where such thinking might lead. I might find myself needing her and then falling in love and then married with a few children, a little girl with long fair hair and a boy with grey eyes and dark hair who would be everything a man could want in a son. A loving family to take care of and protect....

At that point he stopped thinking altogether and ordered himself a meal from room service, the most expensive item on the menu because, fortunately, Jones was footing the bill and he had to be good for something.

Late the next evening, Quin approached the door of Jones' hotel suite. William Jones opened the door when Quin knocked and said, 'Come in Mr. Jameson, take a seat. Drink?'

'Whisky and soda thanks,' Quin replied, sitting on the plush sofa and making a mental note to only sip his drink. He needed to keep his mind clear.

'I suppose you want to know what the job entails?' Jones sat on a matching chair and crossed his legs, his black knife pleat trousers pulling up to show cartoon characters on his socks. It was an aspect of Jones Quin hadn't realised existed. The man had to have a sense of humour hidden somewhere amongst his tight smile and sophisticated manner. It was somewhat reassuring in the overall scheme of things.

'Yeah. It would help me to get my bearings. I like to know what's what.'

'Well I don't mind giving you a few details. With your background in sign writing you'll be amply qualified for painting and finishing off detailed scroll work. Some repairs will need to be carried out before you paint but I'm sure you'll be able to manage that. It's important to do the job properly because the building is of historic value and very likely will be opened to the public at some time in the future. Some woodwork and plaster work must be repaired and that will also be your job. Sound okay so far?' Jones smile was confident, his eyes sharp.

'Nothing I can't handle. Where is it? The house I mean?'

'In the north of Australia. I'm unable to divulge the exact location I'm sorry to say.' He didn't look sorry but Quin listened closely, hoping for a clue.

Jones took another long sip of his drink then continued. 'The house is in an isolated area and contains many things of value, antiques mostly, with a few significant paintings as well. The greatest secrecy needs to be kept in case word of it's acquirement by a certain high profile gentleman leaks out. I'm sure you understand.'

Having been in business himself, Quin understood such precautions. He had also had close encounters with the press and knew of several fortunes that had been lost through premature disclosure of a project.

'Yes, I understand very well Mr. Jones.' Quin nodded in agreement. 'Naturally, I'm still curious but I accept your need for secrecy. Although I hope you'll let me know what's going on as soon as you can.'

'As soon as I can tell you anything I will?' Jones smiled and spoke gently but his eyes turned as hard as granite. 'You don't need to know anything else Mr. Jameson. And I suggest you don't ask any more questions of a sensitive nature, especially when speaking to the other prospective employees. Just accept that you'll go where you're needed and that we will pay you well to go there. Is that understood?'

Quin nodded his head, holding back his contradictory words. He knew he wasn't going to find out anything of importance by aggravating his host. 'Yes,' he said, knowing he was being warned but feeling, more than ever, that he must see this thing through. Especially if Sherry was involved.

There was no way he could leave her alone now, feeling as he did about her. He'd see this thing through to the end even if it meant his freedom, or his life.

Quin was forming a question in his mind about the other employees when the other man stood up and strolled over to look out the window. Jones took a box out of a drawer and opened it, sniffing delicately at the cigar he had chosen then clipping it before turning back to Quin. He leant against the desk casually, crossing his ankles and watching Quin carefully.

'Are you partial to women?' Jones asked softly, with a bland smile which could have meant anything. He put the unlit cigar between his teeth and continued to look at Quin assessingly as he lit up and drew the bitter smoke into his lungs. The doubts in the back of Quin's mind were put on hold as he contemplated the question Jones had asked.

'Sure I like women,' Quin's voice was wary, wondering what the man was getting at. Was he in the procurement business or just being helpful? Maybe he thought Quin was gay? Maybe Jones was gay? Who could tell these days.

'I mean,' Jones said with exaggerated patience, 'Do you fancy any of the women you met here yesterday?'

A tiny blonde with a dimple in her cheek Quin thought longingly. She had been in his dreams again last night. The vividness of it was still with him in the morning necessitating a very cold shower. Frustration could be hell, especially when the cause of it was only a few doors away.

'They were very interesting Mr. Jones,' Quin replied as he remembered where he was, 'But I haven't had a chance to get to know them yet.'

'Don't worry Mr. Jameson. I'm sure that can be remedied. We like our people to be happy in their work and well looked after in their leisure time. If you let me know of your preference, I'll see she's accommodated close to you when we reach our destination.'

'That's very generous of you Mr. Jones. I like a few creature comforts when I'm away from home. If there's anything I can do for you in return I hope you'll let me know.' Quin, deciding to keep on Jones' good side just in case he needed someone in his arena later on, wondered whether all the male employees were to be given such special treatment. It seemed suspiciously like the women were being brought there for the exclusive pleasure of the men, staked out for their inspection like a slave market.

He was positive Sherry didn't know the women were being set up. He knew she would back out immediately if she did. Still, he was only surmising. Probably Jones was only doing him a flavor, man to man, and it had nothing to do with the policy decreed by the head of the company, whoever he was.

He put aside his misgivings, trying instead to discover from Jones any more details about the job. There would be time later to change course if he found it was not what he wanted, time also to persuade Sherry it wasn't what she wanted either.

Breathing space away from his problems was what he needed now and a chance to recoup some of the money he'd lost when his business went downhill so fast, before a bunch of thieves and murderers had decided he was expendable.

Firewalking

After a final meal at a McDonalds restaurant and a tearful farewell, Pete got reluctantly into his utility truck to drive back to Archer's Creek. Sherry took Scrappy for a short walk around the lake, keeping to the shadows in case any employees of the hotel or any inquisitive guests decided to interfere in her business and inform the management she had a dog. It wouldn't do to get thrown out just as she had secured a job and a place to go.

A little after midnight that night they were due to take off for parts unknown. Jones had told everyone they had to be ready outside the hotel at eleven thirty PM. Sherry wasn't looking forward to that because of the coldness of the air at that hour, conversely she was excited about it as well. It was the beginning of a new life for her.

She was coming round the far side of the lake when she saw a person hovering around the cabins, specifically around cabin number six. She froze and pulled Scrappy further into the bushes where the darkness would hide them. She watched for a few minutes then, going from bush to bush, she slowly crept closer. She had to see who it was.

When she was close enough to see it was a man she began to shake with fear, her skin becoming clammy, her breathing laboured. As the man peered into her window then turned to walk around to the back of the cabin before disappearing from view she almost fainted with recognition. It was Ralph Marley.

Even in the darkness he was familiar, like a putrid cold sore that had been probed with the tongue over and over again until it was recognised for the pain it could produce, a cold sore that wept toxins into the mouth even while it was being soothed with that same gentle tongue.

Medium height stocky build, he was wearing a neat navy blue suit and a black felt hat. He was even wearing a red patterned tie in proper church going fashion. The proper mode of dress was something he insisted on. It was part of his disguise, the donning of a mask, the deceit of overlaying evil with the sterility of polished manners, good clothes and gleaming shoes. He had an expression of benign goodwill down perfectly, except when he was with Sherry, then he could be himself.

After standing in the suddenly cold air for a full five minutes, Sherry broke out of her fear induced trance, picked up Scrappy in trembling arms and ran back the way she had come. She blended into the trees on the far side of the lake before finding a spot to crouch down and think. What was she going to do? How could she come so close to getting away then Ralph turns up like the black spot in Robert Louis Stevenson's Treasure Island. As far as she could remember, the black spot meant death. She knew now it was true. If Ralph caught her she would die.

As she hid under that tree and shook with reaction she wondered, was she destined to be always imprisoned by her fear. Rationally she knew he couldn't do anything to her. She knew she was twenty years old and capable of going wherever she chose but something in her caused the fear to well up, her skin to grow cold and her breathing to hyperventilate the moment she saw Ralph or heard his name. It was like she was programmed to be like that, which of course she had been. He had begun the indoctrination of his victim from the moment he had taken control of her when she was ten and had continued with it every day of her life until she had escaped from the farmhouse just a few weeks ago.

After sitting amongst the trees for about an hour, Sherry knew she must find Quin. He was the only one who could help her, who would be likely to understand. She realised she didn't know him very well but he was at least big enough and strong enough to get in Ralph's way.

She crept close to the cabins, once again keeping to the bushes where it was dark. There were some garden lights strung out along the various gravel paths among the cabins but she avoided the paths and kept to the close to the walls of the buildings. Gravel was noisy to walk on and she didn't want to be heard, by anyone. She only hoped no-one noticed her creeping about and called the management, or the police.

It would be the worst thing to be held up for questioning, especially now when Ralph had come to look for her. He would be sure to hear what was going on and come out from wherever he was lurking and claim her. He'd probably spin some tale of how she was mentally incompetent and, because of his standing in the church as a deacon, he would be convincing.

After making sure Ralph wasn't in the vicinity of cabin nine, Sherry knocked on the back door. The pine cabins were set out as if they were a small house on their own with garden beds and trees close by. With a tiny back and front porch, one or two bedrooms, a sitting room, bathroom and tiny kitchenette, they were ideal for family holidays.

The door was pulled abruptly open. Quin loomed in the doorway taking in his visitor, a surprised look then a wary smile on his face. 'What's going on Sherry,' he asked. He looked around outside briefly then stood aside for her to enter. She walked in quickly, pulling Scrappy with her. In her haste she almost tripped on a floor rug but Quin caught her by the arm and steadied her.

'Thanks. I'm a bit clumsy tonight.'

'You look frazzled. Is something wrong?'

'I just needed somewhere to sit for a while.'

'So sit.' He indicated a comfortable armchair in the sitting room. 'Why do you need somewhere?'

Sherry shrugged, trying to appear calm, as if nothing was going on. She tried also to stem the tears of reaction that trickled down her cheeks but was unable to stop Quin's hand from wiping away those tears. 'It's nothing. Just someone I want to avoid.'

'Who?'

'Just someone. A man. He's looking for me.'

'I take it the man is here. You've seen him?'

'Yes. I saw him about an hour ago outside my cabin. Looking in the windows. I can't go back there tonight in case he's still hanging around.'

'He must know you've got that cabin Sherry. Probably asked at reception. He wouldn't be looking in the windows otherwise. He might be arrested for being a peeping Tom.'

'Yes. I'm sure he knows it's my cabin.'

'Did you tell him where you'd be going?'

'What! As if I'd tell him anything. I'm not that stupid.'

'How did he find out then? And why is he looking for you?' Quin, looking puzzled, dragged a hand through his long hair and rubbed his eyes. Sherry thought he looked tired. 'Who is this guy?'

She looked hunted, her eyes not quite meeting Quin's as she explained, 'He's just someone I want to get away from and I don't know how he found out. Maybe I left Jones' letter behind somewhere, probably at a friend's house. Maybe he followed me.'

'Reception wouldn't give out your cabin number to just anyone.'

Sherry looked hunted. 'He must have said he was a relative.'

'Is he?' Quin looked into her eyes, his determined gaze probing through a minefield of memories and fe ar.

She was unable to hide the truth. 'In a way. He's related to me by marriage. My dad's cousin was his wife. I used to call him uncle but he isn't really.' She took a deep breath.

'Look Quin. Forget about this.' She made to get up but he stopped her with a hand on her arm. She looked up at him with pleading eyes. 'You don't need my troubles on top of your own. You're tired and it's time I sorted this out for myself. I'll go back to my cabin and get my things then I'm out of here. It's the best way.'

'Then what would you do? You don't know your way around here and that friend of yours who dropped you off has gone back home by now, wherever that is. There's nothing to stop this bloke finding you again. Is that what you want?'

'Of course not. But I can't stay here.'

'Look, we're off tonight. Remember. Eleven thirty start out the front. It's not that long and we'll be flying away and he won't be able to find you no matter where you go.'

'What then? What shall I do about my things?'

'You stay here with that little dog of yours. Give me your key and I'll get your gear. You have packed haven't you?'

'Yes. I've packed. All except for my toothbrush. It's in the bathroom.'

'Right. I'll sneak over to your cabin and be in and out with no-one any the wiser. I'll return here as soon as possible. Put the jug on will you and I'll be back.' He grinned. 'If you feel the need to do something useful, I could use a coffee. There's biscuits in a tin in the kitchen. Help yourself to whatever you need.'

She handed him the key, the skin of her fingertips tingling as she touched his hand. Her hand seemed to want to linger, to touch and learn all the secrets of his palm but she drew back, determined not to be held to ransom by this unwanted sensation of desire she seemed to feel for this one man.

As he was opening the door she called softly, 'Quin. Be careful will you. He's not above putting you in to the police if he thinks you're helping me. He'd make up some story or other about us and we'd both be kept for questioning. The plane would be gone long before they let us out, if they let us out.'

'He won't even see me.' Quin turned back and grinned reassuringly. 'By the way, what does he look like? This ogre of yours. What's his name?'

She grinned back. 'Oh, not tall, not thin and not very nice. His name is Ralph Marley.'

'That's a lot of negatives. Is there anything positive you can tell me?' 'Well, there is one thing.'

'Go on?'

'He dresses like a minister. Very clean, very neat. He even wears a small gold cross on his lapel and his shoes shine so much you can see your face. If you talked to him he would sound like a very nice fellow, very law abiding and trustworthy.' 'I take it he's not a nice fellow? This Ralph of yours.'

Her eyes went curiously dark, a haunted expression on her face. 'He's not mine. I don't want him. Not at any price. He's not nice at all. The way he is, well, it's the sort of thing you only find out about a person if you live with them.'

Quin felt a sense of shock. 'You actually lived in the same house with him?'

Sherry didn't notice his expression. She was caught in a deep well of sadness as she remembered all she had lost to Ralph Marley. 'Yes. I lived with him for twelve years.' At his sharply in-drawn breath she looked up into his face, abruptly turning away and saying, 'I don't want to talk about it anymore Quin. It's a bad memory and all I want to do is forget it. You better go if you're sure you want to do this. Just watch out for any medium height, middle aged men lurking around outside. He has very large strong looking hands with a lot of scars.'

At Quin's inquisitive look she went on, 'He used to be a fisherman down in Portland. Trawlers, deep sea stuff. If anyone like that is hanging about don't go inside my cabin. He'll know you're connected to me and he'll follow you.'

'And what do you think he can do to me?' Quin stood with all the confidence of a tall, super fit man in the prime of life, primitive in his abilities to defeat anyone who tried a physical attack of any kind.

'Oh, he couldn't beat you in a fight on his own but he could have friends or people working for him. He'll never fight fair Quin, in any way. You can't trust him to play by the rules. He makes his own.'

'I'm not above making a few rules of my own Sherry,' Quin said, a grin of anticipation on his face. He hadn't grown up on the back streets of Sydney without learning a few dirty tricks. 'I'll see you in a little while. Meantime you fix those drinks and settle in to the spare room. I'll take care of your visitor if I see him, make no mistake about that.' He turned and went out the door shutting it gently behind him.

CHAPTER SIX

Outside the cabin the air was cool. Quin stepped carefully onto the path, looking around in case Ralph was nearby watching number six. He wasn't anywhere to be seen so Quin walked up to number six and unlocked the door. He went inside and turned on a small lamp so he wouldn't trip over anything and was about to check out the small
sitting room when he heard a sound. Instinctively he turned and the man in the process of tackling him from behind went down with him onto the floor, upsetting the small coffee table and knocking the television askew. A coffee cup broke as it hit the wall and shards of pottery lay in wait for Ralph's bulky form as he rolled, his momentum bringing him onto the sharp points which dug into his right buttock, ripping the blue linen of his suit and leaving a trail of blood on the carpet.

Ralph howled with pain and pressed his hand to his backside bringing it up to his eyes to see if he was bleeding. He was. Profusely. 'Bastard,' he roared, conveniently forgetting who had started this confrontation. Red veins stood out in his face and neck and his breathing was harsh. 'I'll teach you some manners. You and that little bitch. Where is she? Where's Sherry. She belongs to me.'

Heaving himself to his feet he lurched himself at Quin who was now on his feet and nursing a badly bruised hand which he had caught on the edge of the television. Quin stepped to the side as Ralph reached him, head down and bellowing like an enraged bull, hands bunched ready to pound his victim senseless.

The bulky man's velocity carried him past Quin and into the wall head first. When he hit the plaster, flakes of white broke away and showered his suddenly unconscious body, the air conditioner rocking on its support as if ready to fall and crown him. The sudden cessation of noise was like the eye of the hurricane and Quin knew, in moments, the man would wake up and begin again. Such fury could not be limited to one engagement. It was the kind of overwhelming rage that made wars of domestic violence and made people kill. If this was the man Sherry was escaping from Quin was not about to step aside and let him take her back. He would do all he could to protect her.

Carefully stepping over the prone body of his assailant, Quin went into the bedroom, turned the light on and collected Sherry's bag. He put back in it all the things that Ralph had strewn all over the room, Sherry's meagre personal clothing, a small toilet bag, her purse and a brush and comb. He went into the bathroom for her toothbrush then stepped over Ralph who was lying on the floor groaning and coming back to consciousness.

Ralph's gaze pierced Quin as he reached the door. He tried to get to his feet, his face once more a red mask of murderous rage.

'Come on. Fight like a man you filthy coward,' he snarled, putting his hands to the floor and pushing his knees forward before putting one foot flat on the floor. He levered himself upright by holding on to an armchair, swaying as he stood.

He tried to take a step toward Quin but stumbled, grabbing hold of the shelf holding the air-conditioning unit which promptly fell and smashed on the floor, large pieces of which landed on Ralph's foot. His rage by now was uncontrollable as he hopped on one foot and called Quin all the foul names he could think of.

'Sorry to disappoint you mate,' said Quin blandly, highly amused by the performance of Sherry's tormentor. His language certainly wasn't original, Quin had heard it all before. 'I've got better things to do than touch vermin. And just for the record, Sherry doesn't belong to you. She's a free woman, free to go wherever she likes and to see whoever she likes. If I were you I'd think twice before I kept following her. She doesn't want to live with you any more, if she ever did.'

Quin decided to add a little comment because having read between the lines, he sensed that Sherry's relationship with Ralph had many question marks upon it. 'If I were to point the police in your direction I wonder what they would find.'

At the sudden paling of Ralph's ruddy features Quin knew he had hit a nerve. He grinned. 'Ah, I see you have something to hide. It might be a good idea if you took yourself back to wherever you came from and left Sherry alone. I'll leave you now. You look like you could do with some medical attention. I think the nearest public hospital is in Box Hill.'

Ralph glanced down and touched his hand to his left buttock. His linen trousers were ripped and a pair of gaudy satin Marilyn Monroe boxer shorts, also ripped, showed through the tear. An expanse of fat pink backside lay exposed as well. His hand came away covered in blood.

Flakes of plaster rained down from his thinning hair onto the shoulder of his once pristine suit and he winced with pain as he touched his bloody hand to a huge bump on his forehead which was already turning purple. 'I won't forget this,' Ralph's voice was a low feral growl. 'I'll find out who you are and then there will be nowhere you can go I won't find you. You and that bitch will pay, I promise you.'

'Tell me, just as a matter of interest, what's that gold cross on your jacket for? What does it mean to you Ralph?' Quin smiled slightly, knowing he was in much better shape than his opponent, especially now. He was ready to leave the man with something to think about.

Ralph's face twisted with rage, spittle appearing at the corner of his mouth. 'It means I have the power to make or break you boy. I have the right to take Sherry back home and to call the law in to dispose of you. It also means people respect and obey me. You're on your own if you want to take me down and you won't do it because I have the power of God on my side. That's what it means.'

Quin's laugh was pure cynicism which enraged Ralph even further. Ralph's breathing was harsh, his fists clenched into weapons ready to inflict serious damage and his glaring eyes glittered as if, in the absence of physical ability, his will alone would propel him across the room to lay his enemy flat out on the floor.

'I wouldn't hold my breath for God to help you Ralph. I reckon you might have done your dash where He's concerned. I don't reckon He takes kindly to a man taking advantage of a young girl like you've done.'

'You know nothing about it at all. I've looked after her for more years than she deserves. She owes me and I aim to collect.' Ralph collapsed onto the sofa as if his legs would no longer support him, his face white, blood seeping sluggishly from the wound on his forehead.

'Yeah, she owes you alright. And one day she's gonna pay you back for all you've done. In the meantime, forget it. You're finished. You've lost the power to hurt her any more. Go back home and be thankful she's not a vindictive person. Remember though, if you keep on with this, I won't forget and I can be a unforgiving bastard when I choose. I'll pay you back, with interest.'

'I'll call the police.'

'Go ahead,' agreed Quin. 'Before they arrive you'd better think of a reason why you're in Sherry's cabin. It looks like you've smashed the place up a little. Not a good thing to put on your resume I wouldn't think. See you.'

Quin turned and walked out the door with Sherry's pack. He wanted very badly to slam it but knew the value of a quiet but victorious exit.

After taking a roundabout route back to his cabin, Quin found Sherry curled up on her bed asleep. Scrappy lay next to her also fast asleep. She had twisted her blankets until they had knotted and half fallen to the floor, the track of tears on her cheeks clear evidence of her distress.

Now that he had met Ralph he understood her need to get away and was determined to help her in any way he could. It was the least he could do for this small defenceless girl who had taken hold of his heart and given him a reason to believe in himself again.

It was half past midnight when the group of passengers arrived in a bus at the small airstrip outside Lilydale. About fourteen people were milling around sorting their belongings, a fact which allowed Sherry to avoid looking at Quin. After the previous few hours she had spent in his cabin she had no idea what he was thinking or what he wanted of her.

He had woken her up with a gentle shake on her shoulder and since she had slept fully dressed, there was nothing to do but make a quick cup of coffee and haul her things out to the front of the hotel. Scrappy was easy to manage and Quin was as uncommunicative as usual.

He'd helped her by picking up her things at her cabin earlier in the evening but beyond saying he'd seen Ralph and taken care of the problem, he'd said nothing. She wished he would tell her something, anything, about what had happened but he was a close mouthed as ever. Did he talk to Ralph personally? Did Ralph promise to leave her alone.

She desperately wanted information but in this she was denied. She hadn't seen anything more of Ralph and it was as if he hadn't even been there. She began to think she had imagined it all, if it wasn't for the strange hollow feeling in the pit of her stomach and the fierce headache hanging around.

Everyone was allowed one main piece of luggage which was stored in the plane storage area and one hand held carryall which was to be kept with them. Scrappy was tucked up under Sherry's left arm while she held her backpack in front of her with the other, giving her attention to Mr. Jones who was welcoming them.

At first glance there was nothing unusual about these travellers, except for their appearance. They were all good looking, handsome, well built men and women with healthy trim figures, beautiful faces and lovely hair. There were equal numbers of men and women. All wore sneakers and casual gear of jeans, sweaters and jackets in varying degrees of quality.

Most seemed to be filled with suppressed emotions at the great risk they were taking, flying into the future, destination unknown. Even Jones seemed excited they were on their way. Maybe, Sherry reflected broodingly, the whole thing will be like a fun vacation...then again, maybe not.

She stroked her little dog for comfort, feeling as if she was spinning out of control. His warmth was her only security. Then Quin sat next to her on the plane and all Sherry's nerves began to jangle as she felt the long length of his hard thigh next to hers and the heat of his body as he shifted to get comfortable.

It was all she could do not to leap out of the plane and find a nice safe place to hide, a refuge where her emotions weren't tossed about by a man who had no feelings for her at all. For the last twelve years she had been either ignored, ridiculed or beaten and to find herself attracted to a man who seemed to be able to forget she existed even when they were in the same room was too much for her.

She wanted to talk to the other women but they seemed to be unapproachable, as if they had shut themselves off in case someone got too close and discovered who they really were and where they had come from. Even though they were lovely to look at in their own distinctive ways, the women were clearly not looking to be friends with someone like Sherry.

She was the youngest of the group and all she received in return to her friendly overtures was a forced smile from one young woman and advice from another to mind her own business or she could run into a pile of trouble. She gave up then and kept to herself.

It would have been nice to make a friend thought Sherry, another woman who could explain what it was about men that made them act as they did, who would understand her feelings about Quin.

On second thoughts maybe that wasn't such a hot idea. Another woman would be sure to want him for herself. Good grief, she thought, any woman would want him, all he'd have to do was look their way with those brooding dark eyes that could see into a person's soul and they'd melt like chocolate in the hot sun. He wouldn't even have to smile that rare and beautiful smile for them to form a queue.

'Are you okay now?' asked Quin politely, obviously trying not to touch her. He seemed offhand and she tried to understand his hot-cold treatment, even return it. Even a slight smile from him would have stilled her growing fears and made her more able to deal with what was ahead. She nodded her thanks and looked away.

Scrappy was behaving well, looking around and sniffing the air. She'd said a tearful goodbye to Pete the day before and he'd left reluctantly, warning her to be very careful and to send a telegram or phone him if she needed help.

Assuring him she would be fine was hard because she wasn't sure herself if that was so. It was a massive bluff on her part because she was determined to take the job and get on with her new, independent life and she didn't want him to worry. He would have been beside himself if he knew that Ralph had turned up at the hotel the night before. Of all the people in the world, Pete Madigan was the one who knew what lengths Ralph would go to get what he wanted. He'd been on the receiving end of one of Ralph's mining swindles and had lost a lot of money in the process.

They'd been flying for a couple of hours when they stopped at a small deserted airfield for fuel. It was cold and windy as the passengers huddled into a small Spartan building and consumed hot drinks before climbing back onto the plane once more. The one bright spot for Sherry was when she went outside with Scrappy and bumped into Quin.

He grasped her gently by the upper arms and said, his deep voice a rumbling echo in the night, 'Is everything alright?' Just the fact that he was near generated a wave of heat inside her. His touch was something else again. Something much more compelling. The hard strength of his hands was almost too much for her to bear. She wanted him to keep touching her and never let her go.

Determinedly she pulled her arms free. Now was not the time or the place for letting go of her emotions. 'Yes, thanks, of course I am. But it's all a bit weird isn't it? Flying off in the dead of night like this to who knows where. It gives me the creeps.'

He gently brushed her cheek with his finger and looked down into her eyes, a grim smile on his lips. 'It is a bit strange. You should have listened to me Sherry. I warned you things would not be quite what you imagined they'd be. Now all we can do is wait and see. I'll catch up with you later on,' he said, 'Take care.' She shivered, wanting desperately to respond to his touch but chained by her inexperience to a wall of silence.

After giving Scrappy a scratch under the chin Quin walked around the corner and into the dimly lit building, leaving her to her thoughts. They were turbulent and she was prey to unimagined longings as she pictured in her mind what could happen if he wanted her too.

But, she reminded herself harshly, he doesn't want you. A couple of kisses mean nothing to a man like that. He probably kisses women all the time and makes love to them too. You can't compete with experience like that.

He can see you're a novice at relationships. Why would he want to get involved with a girl who doesn't know anything about love or how to please a man in bed. There's plenty of women out there as well as here on the plane who would be only too pleased to keep him happy in and out of bed. Sherry's thoughts were tumbling through her mind like clowns at a circus, tormenting her and making her look inside herself for the answers.

She remembered all the negative things Ralph had taught her to feel about herself as she drank a cup of tea in the corner of the small lounge of the airport. Then she reminded herself of the way Quin acted towards her when anyone was near. He treats you almost like a stranger, one whom he hasn't the slightest interest in getting to know any better. Just because he helped you out of a difficult situation and spoke a few friendly words he might use to anyone doesn't mean he's interested in you at all. Even those two kisses she remembered so vividly were simply the result of proximity. She was there and so he kissed her, nothing more.

Still the memory of his touch was burned into her brain. How could she manage to live and work near him and still get over the effect he had on her? How could she ever forget him if he went out of her life and she never saw him again?

The long hours of worry took their toll and for most of the remainder of the flight Sherry slept. There were another couple of stops during the night for fuel but they were uneventful and passengers stood around in the cold while the refuelling took place.

When she woke after a final fitful sleep it was a cold and inhospitable dawn and they had landed at yet another small deserted airstrip which looked more like a rough and overgrown track through flat sparsely treed paddocks.

Large white parrots and pink galahs noisily announced their presence in the trees as the weary passengers exited the plane and collected their luggage. This time there was no building and no sleepy attendant to bring them drinks.

Instead, marshalled together like school children by Jones and two drivers, they were herded carrying all their belongings a hundred meters or so towards two medium size busses.

Sherry took Scrappy for a much needed investigation of a tree and was told sharply by one driver, Jones called him Walker, to get back to the bus on the double and stop messing around with the dog or he'd leave the mangy mutt behind. She scooped Scrappy into protective arms and hurried back into line, wondering what on earth she had done. Quin had been right. There was something wrong about this business if a man like Walker was employed to shove people around. For a moment she almost wished she was back in Archer's Creek but that thought didn't last long. Anything, even being bullied by Walker, was better than being back under Ralph's domination.

The driver was rough and abusive as he swore crudely and pushed some of the passengers along, hardly giving them time to move before shoving them forward once again.

Even though some of the passengers complained of the way they were treated, the other driver and Mr. Jones seemed content to step back and allow Walker to practice his own efficient but ruthless method of packing them into the busses. It was only when the were finally on their way and headed through a gateway and down a narrow gravel road lined by lemon scented gums and wattle trees that Sherry could breathe the sigh of relief which came when Walker had climbed into the other vehicle with Jones.

Squeezed together like sardines in a can, they were a silent and strangely uneasy group who looked out the side windows and watched as native birds and kangaroos set about their morning search for food. Some people fidgeted, embarrassed and not looking at each other as stomachs growled in hunger and other more personal needs became paramount.

Quin was in one bus and Sherry in another so she couldn't take comfort in his presence. She could only remember his words of reassurance and trust that they would end up in the same place at the same time.

As they drove a long distance along deserted roads, some hard packed sand and some paved with bitumen, the sun began to rise and slowly heat the air, bringing with it the refreshing tang of eucalyptus and pine as well as every now and then the distinctive aroma of cattle.

After crossing a couple of wooden bridges over sluggishly flowing creeks, the vehicles turned down another dirt road on what seemed like a vast property with no buildings in sight.

After a while, they reached a gateway and cattle grid over which they rattled and rolled, forcing everyone into an alertness that they neared the end of their journey.

The morning sun was just creeping over the top of the tall trees when they reached a heavy iron gate in a cyclone wire fence topped with barbed wire. Vast grounds were cultivated with a few thirsty flower beds and swathes of long grass while jacaranda trees plus many other native flowering trees were spread out around what appeared to be a large three storey homestead. White iron lace-work decorated wide verandahs and twin towers graced each end.

The cream painted weatherboard and brown stone house stood majestically on a slight rise looking out over pastures stretching to the west with endless tracts of native forest. Sounds and smells of the sea filtered through the air punctuated by the warbling of seagulls. It was clear to Quin they were somewhere on the north coast of Australia but there was no way to tell where. The wide tropical sea could be seen from where the busses stopped outside the gates.

The gates were opened by a man who, after checking the vehicles and occupants carefully, allowed the busses to drive through. Sherry caught a glimpse of another man inside a small stone gatehouse. To her dismay, both men were armed. Gasping, she looked toward her fellow passengers but none gave any sign they had noticed anything amiss. It was enough to make her hunch down in her seat and clutch Scrappy's warmth to her breast.

Suddenly all her doubts and worries, half formed when she emerged from the plane, came to stinging vivid life. It was doubly clear to her that she shouldn't have come, especially when she saw Walker climb off the first bus and saw he also had a gun tucked into his waist band. She hadn't noticed it before because he wore jeans and a plaid shirt with the tails hanging out, as did most of the men. Now, as Walker began to speak with the other men at the gate he unbuttoned his shirt and took it off revealing a white singlet and muscular tanned arms. His face was clean shaven, his dark hair cut very short but that was as far as civilisation had reached him. Sherry listened at the open window of the bus and heard his voice as he questioned the guards, not the words but the tone. It was savage and not happy.

What on earth is going on here she wondered?, twisting slightly in her seat and peering around as Walker climbed back on board and the busses proceeded through the gates and up to the house.

Up close she could see that the house was extremely large. Built on a stone foundation which stood a man's height up off the ground, it was a huge barn of a place supporting a timber frame with wooden weatherboards painted cream and a dark red colour on window frames and doors. Additional rooms had been attached seemingly at random and the third floor was shown by extended attic windows whose frames were also painted dark red.

Wide wooden verandahs with wide stairs leading down to overgrown gardens were attached to every part of the ground floor visible from the front and sides of the building and the roof of that verandah formed balconies for the next floor up.

Windows were topped with carved wooden mouldings painted dark red and creepers wandered over walls like threads of green embroidery on a cream background

Strangely frightened of the house and its yet unknown occupants and wondering what they might mean to her life, Sherry gathered her courage around her like a shield, thinking nothing could be worse than what she had already endured. At least Quin would be nearby. He was a big strong man and, even if he didn't want to be involved with her personally, she was sure he would still be willing to give her a hand in a crisis.

As the word crisis played through her mind she berated herself. 'You're imagining things Sherry,' she whispered. 'There's nothing to be afraid of. It's just a big old house dumped out in the bush.' She closed her eyes for a moment against the glare of the sun and thought, you're here to work and make a new life for yourself. Forget about horror stories and pull yourself together. Forget about Ralph Marley and Quin Jameson too. He doesn't want you and you'd better get used to it. Find yourself another man, one who'll love you and never leave you, one who looks at you as if you're the only woman in the world.

Sherry climbed out of the bus and looked around as she put Scrappy on the ground for a short walk.There were two small wooden bungalows toward the back of the house. They were grouped together surrounding a large yard containing a few pieces of rusty machinery, a windmill and several huge water tanks.

A few large and small sheds were spread around as if they had been erected as needed on the spot, some dilapidated and some quite new. A few more run down bungalows were hidden among trees like a small town. Much of the area around the sheds was overgrown with grass and shrubs. Large trees, mostly Australian native eucalyptus gums, grew close to the buildings giving much needed shade. Sherry could smell the tang of freshly cut grass, wattle flowers and salt in the air.

Her mind was jack-rabbiting all over the place trying to make sense of what she had seen when a grey haired man of about forty in a dark business suit came out of the front door, down the steps and strode across the gravel forecourt.

He shouted, 'Alright people. Listen up. My name is Merton. I'm in charge here. Let's get you settled in, then you can look around the house. Try not to get lost. I don't want to send out search parties. It's expensive.' He grinned jovially but his eyes were cold dark pools. 'I'll see you all in the dining room for breakfast in an hour. Later on you'll be told what your duties are. Mr. Jones has maps of the house and name tags so I'll know who each of you are.'

Without waiting for comment, the man turned and marched back into the house, leaving them to William Jones who handed out simple layout maps of the house and told each of them their room number. He said, 'Mr. Merton isn't a man with a great deal of patience so I suggest you move along now. I'll leave you to find your rooms yourselves. If there's anything else you need we'll discuss it at breakfast. Remember, you only have one hour. Don't be late.'

'What is this place?' someone in the group asked.

Jones smiled slightly. 'I believe it was originally a homestead build by a pioneer family in the 1800's. They wanted to bring a piece of the old country with them but they couldn't so they built this to compensate. I rather think they overdid it though.'

'Where are we Mr. Jones?' asked someone else.

'I suppose it can't hurt to tell you now. We're in Queensland. On the coast.'

A sound rippled through the group. 'What part?' asked someone. 'It's not near Brisbane that's for sure. This place is nothing like that, it's too isolated. How are we going to get away for vacations and weekends off?'

'You're not going to get away...yet, are you? You wanted to disappear if I remember rightly and you signed on for a year, no vacations and no whole weekends off, only Sundays.'

'Doesn't seem fair,' a woman muttered loud enough to be heard by everyone.

A hard note entered Jones' voice. 'You're being paid very well for this job. I suggest you don't blow it by complaining. Remember, there are always other people who want work, people who will do anything for money. Any more questions will be answered at breakfast.'

Muttering among themselves the group collected their belongings and went toward the building. Sherry shivered with a strange dread when she looked out over the grasslands beyond the built up area and almost turned to walk back to the bus before she remembered, she had signed on for a year in this lonely place. There was nowhere else to go and the gate was now closed.

The man named Walker had gone back to speak to the men at the gate in a low voice and left them carefully watching the new arrivals before returning to chivy his passengers along.

Sherry looked at her map which showed the first floor at ground level, second floor then the attic or third floor. Her room was on the attic floor. She looked over at Quin but he was looking away from her, his gaze following the line of the barbed wire fence as it disappeared into trees in a far off pasture. The only thing stopping the line was a second wide gate complete with cattle grid on a dusty track coming from the trees at the back of the bungalows.

His mouth was compressed and his eyes narrowed as he stood waiting for Jones to hand him a map, his bearing tense, radiating a readiness to move into action. Sherry knew she should talk to him as soon as possible. Whatever was disturbing him was enough to make her worried too. She was determined not to be left in ignorance. As she had found out to her cost in the past, ignorance was definitely not bliss.

Quin had seen something that disturbed him greatly. A truck was being unloaded behind the sheds. He could see the tray from where he stood near the bus he had arrived on. Not a huge truck, it had what looked like large olive green metal boxes on the tray which he assumed were extremely heavy from the way the men were lifting them. One of the boxes slipped out of their hands and was caught before it hit the ground. Panic seemed to hit the men and a heated argument broke out as it was carried away from the truck and Quin saw stencilled writing on the side. It read M26 GRENADE. That was all he saw before the box was lifted once more and taken through a door in a nearby shed. No wonder they panicked. If that lot had hit the ground the guys would have been crow bait.

He turned back to where the people were gathered in front of the house before anyone noticed where he was looking, knowing it was something he had to keep to himself. If anyone knew what he had seen he might suddenly, conveniently, disappear, not voluntarily like last time but a forced evacuation in a pine box.

When Sherry reached the third floor she found it contained two long attics divided into totally enclosed bedrooms like timber partitioned dormitories with a central corridor. Both a male and female communal bathroom were situated at each end of the corridor close to the entrance to the tower rooms.

The view from the central balcony was spectacular, showing the sea curving into two small bays. Huge granite rocks seemed to guard the outlet channel to the sea. Crescents of sand and scattered driftwood were being washed by sea foam but most of the shore was rocky and interlaced with scrubby bushes and trees.

Sherry had last seen the sea when she was a small child and was overwhelmed by its power. She watched it ebb and flow for a while, mesmerised by its seeming life-like aura, its rhythmic motion as it stroked the sand, the rich green of the depths and the translucent aqua blue of the shallows. It was a miracle to Sherry, a child of the inland, whose home place in parts had been mined continually for gold for over a century, leaving huge piles of tailings and some hills dry and barren, the goodness sucked out of them by predatory man and now topped with the occasional scraggly bush or tree and holes in the ground to trip the unwary.

The lush green of the grounds and the trees made a heady impact on her and she wished she had someone to share it with. Quin sprang into her mind but she rejected his image immediately, feeling it would be better to distance herself from him before she became too dependent on his support.

She hadn't seen him come upstairs, had no idea which floor his room was on and couldn't, wouldn't, ask. Everyone else had disappeared into rooms or gone back downstairs for breakfast or to look around.

Scrappy squirmed against her as she looked up and down the corridor. He seemed eager to investigate but she wasn't about to put him down until she had explored the place herself. There might be all kind of passages or stairs he might fall down. It was such a huge place that, once missing, he could be lost to her for a long time, or forever if Walker got hold of him. She almost wished she'd left him with Pete. At least then he might have been safe, here she wasn't so sure.

Afraid in a deeply instinctive way she'd never known before, even with Ralph, she'd noticed the way Walker watched her with her tiny dog, assessing everyone, scowling and making remarks to the other men and women of a nature which suggested he despised women and used them, threatening to get rid of her dog if she refused to co-operate with him. Not knowing what he really wanted from her, she wished he would leave her alone because she didn't trust him, not at all.

The white painted room she had been given wasn't large but adequate for one person. Bare floorboards creaked slightly as she walked across the room towards the window. On the left, the single bed was covered by a plain dark brown cotton spread. An old oak wardrobe with built-in drawers, wooden handles and a musty smell took up much of the space on the right hand side, except for another door.

There were no mirrors so Sherry brushed her hair and straightened her jeans and blue cotton shirt tidily. 'You'll do,' she told herself, hoping Walker would think she was suitably boring and unattractive. 'After all, you're here to work, not fool around.' She opened the window and the smell of the sea wafted in like the cleansing breath of spring.

Scrappy demanded a hug when he bounced up onto the bed, then stuck his head under the pillow. 'Hunting for a bone are you Scrap?' she asked. 'Too bad little guy. It's a good thing you aren't a big dog. I reckon we'll hunt out a little something for you to eat downstairs in the kitchen. It'll probably be people food though. I haven't seen any other dogs about.'

She continued to talk to Scrappy as she put her few thing in drawers. 'If this is typical of the size and condition of the rooms I can see why the owners want to remodel.' She looked to Scrappy for agreement. He'd rolled over onto his back, legs in the air. He was asleep and snoring gently, his tiny brown chest moving with his sighs, feet quivering with each outgoing breath. How she loved him, her tiny companion. He was sweet and loyal, the one thing in her life she trusted.

Sherry tried the door in the wall opposite the bed and found it was locked. She wasn't overly concerned. 'It's probably just another room like this one,' she said aloud to herself. She was curious about the unusual carved cornices in the room which were trimmed with dark red, dark green and charcoal grey to make them look like intertwined roses. The high ceiling prevented her from examining the work too closely but she decided to acquire a chair for her room from somewhere later and stand on it to see. Sherry had grown up in a harsh environment with few luxuries to soften the hard edges of life. Decorative surroundings were a novelty but, she decided, things were changing.

She was beginning a new job, admittedly a tough job, cooking for a lot of people, none of whom she'd met before. It was time to create a new image for herself and do away with the old Sherry. She was sick of being a victim. It was time to live the life she had always wanted, free and earning her own money. Then a tiny voice whispered doubt in her ear, slithering into her insecure subconscious. If only she could be certain that this was the place she was meant to be?

Quin was a side track she had no intention of going down. He hadn't shown any interest in her as a woman, apart from that first night and the time he came to talk her out of taking the job, so from now on she was going to take things in her stride. She'd try to look and act differently, not scared any more, confident and assertive. She'd tell Walker to shove off. Also, Jones had promised a change of appearance in the ad. I'll ask for some new clothes, she thought. After all, what could it hurt to ask. He'd either agree or not. Maybe it was even part of the deal.

CHAPTER SEVEN

Sherry left Scrappy asleep in her room and went back downstairs, deciding to bring him something to eat later. Right now it was time to join the others in the dining room, have breakfast and find out about the work she had to do. She hoped Quin would be there because she wanted to ignore him. It was time to stop acting the besotted idiot and lay down her own set of ground rules. Number one of which was, I will not fall in love with the first man I meet. I intend to show everyone that I'm a woman to be reckoned with.

Unfortunately Quin wasn't there. Mr. Jones beckoned her over to where he sat at a long table with several others and, standing up, introduced her. 'Everyone, for those who don't know her already, this lovely lady is Sherry. She's one of the ladies who will prepare wonderful dishes for us and who must be kept sweet or our stomachs will suffer.' He smiled jovially and pulled out a chair for her.

Quiet greetings came from the ten or so people as they smiled at her, a few telling her their favourite dishes and making jokes, others silent and obviously nervous at being among strangers.

She smiled back, went quickly to select cereal and fruit from the buffet. Sitting down to make conversation, all she could think of was the man who had turned her life upside down. So much for making a life of excitement and romance with some unknown man waiting in the wings. All she could think about was Quin and the turmoil of how he made her feel.

Then he came in the door, tall and lithe, windswept dark hair, hard muscles in his legs flexing as he strode across the room. He wore faded blue jeans, brown leather boots and a royal blue T-shirt but the civilised clothing barely disguised the untamed look of primitive male which he wore so un-selfconsciously. He looked like he had discovered a secret, the like of which he could not, would not share with anyone. He gave her a sardonic glance and turned to say, 'Mr. Jones, those paintings in the gallery on the first floor are unusual. They look like originals. Are they?'

'This is Mr. Jameson my friends. He's here to work on restoration. Yes, we have a wonderful collection of art,' Jones agreed. He smiled smugly at Quin, his enthusiasm when talking about the paintings highlighted by an upper crust British accent. 'And yes, they're all originals. Our employer is a collector. Just one of his many little sidelines. The paintings will soon be put in storage so you won't have to worry about them too much longer.' Jones' suspicious gaze focused on Quin's profile as he said sharply, 'I hope your love for fine art extends to your packing them carefully Jameson. We wouldn't want to damage anything would we?'

'You can be sure I'll be careful.' Quin turned away and walked toward the other side of the room where a separate buffet table was set up for hot breakfasts. Some people had gone over to fill plates or find a place to sit. Others had finished and were just sitting with their coffee talking and getting to know each other. Pairs were being formed and relationships developing already.

Sherry was left on her own for a moment, focusing inwardly and drifting into another reality as she contemplated Quin's words. So he knew about paintings did he? What else did he know about?

Did he know how her heart picked up its beat when he entered a room? Was he aware of the way her eyes followed him, devouring and drinking him into her mind so she would be able to recall every single detail of his face and body, asleep or awake, even when he had gone away from her forever. Did he know how she yearned to walk on the beach with him, talk long into the night and then explore all the ways they could please each other.

Did he realise how unlearned she was and how she longed for him to be the one to teach her, to share with her the mysteries of love. Suddenly she knew a terrible hunger. Not for food. For love and physical communication with the man she loved. All she could think of was him and how he made her feel, how much she wanted his arms around her, holding her tight, crushing her body against his until he could not contemplate life without her.

Sherry made herself collect a plate and fill it with toast and a poached egg. Unfortunately, her food when she got it seemed tasteless but she knew it wasn't entirely the present cook's problem. It was her own faulty taste-buds that dried up at the thought of Quin. She couldn't have said what she ate later on. It was eating but not tasting, drinking with no awareness except of the fact that she must not look at him, must not make him aware of her feelings. She must endeavour to ignore him and put him from her mind. Sadly, it was easier said than done. He sat at the table talking with Mr. Jones and she knew it was much too late. She was already in love and a vast hunger for him was clamouring at the walls of her heart.

Quin was in his room hastily putting his belongings into the wardrobe. He'd left the dining room after breakfast, intending to explore the house. As far as he could tell, the job was going to be a breeze. Hard work sure, but no more than he was used to in his own business.

Early this morning he had been overwhelmed by the display of paintings adorning many of the walls but since then, he'd had time to think, and wonder. What place was this? Were the jobs they'd been given all there was to these people being brought here in the way they had? None of it seemed to make sense to him.

He couldn't forget what he'd seen in the few minutes he'd grabbed to take a look around outside. Were the array of weapons he'd glimpsed inside one of those innocuous sheds for the use of the men manning the gatehouse? Something stank about the whole set-up and it was getting worse with every minute.

Quin's knee-jerk reaction was to grab Sherry and find some way to get out of there immediately. To add to his disquiet, he noticed men patrolling the grounds, all of them looking tough and efficient. Seemingly under the control of the man named Walker, they were strolling about casually but he had the feeling they carried concealed weapons and knew how to use them.

Were they there to protect the obviously expensive works of art or were they patrolling for another, darker purpose? He needed answers but knew he wouldn't get them from Jones who had proved capable of sidestepping any question with a plausible explanation and a bland smile. He would have to do a little investigating, but carefully. If he was caught snooping who knew what these people would do.

Quin couldn't stop thinking of Sherry. Who would protect her if something happened to him? She was such a fragile woman, innocent, a gentle lamb in the company of wolves. He wished she hadn't come to this place. It could turn out to be a very dangerous job for her, and for him. At least she would be safe enough in the kitchen for the moment.

He remembered the look she had given him at breakfast. Hope had appeared in her eyes when he looked at her but when he didn't smile that hope was soon followed with confusion and, to his shame, hurt. He felt like a heel as her eyes became a beacon for her soul and moistened with unshed tears.

Nevertheless, he continued his policy of coldness towards her knowing if he appeared partial to her Jones or Merton would notice and possibly use it to their advantage. They seemed to have enough weapons at their disposal already.

For the rest of the meal she had kept her expression carefully neutral. She must be a good poker player he surmised as he left his room and headed down the stairs. Sometimes you can't tell what she's thinking. Just as well. If he couldn't tell what she has on her mind then no-one else will either.

'Good morning Mr. Jameson,' said the smooth voiced Jones as Quin reached the first floor landing. 'I hope your quarters are to your liking?'

'Spartan but adequate, thanks,' replied Quin, unable to relax with the older man and feeling a simmering distrust of someone who could persuade others to fall in with his wishes so easily. His pride was in tatters as he silently acknowledged that his eagerness to escape his problems may have provided another set equally as bad if not worse. At least in Melbourne he could have simply got on a plane and gone to another part of the country but now he didn't even know exactly where he was much less how to get away. But if he hadn't answered the damn ad he wouldn't have met Sherry and found out what love was all about.

Jones smiled as if he had done something special for someone and was waiting for them to notice. 'Have you met your neighbour yet?' He licked his lips and the sweet stench emanating from his cologne drenched skin as he perspired made Quin feel slightly nauseous.

'Which one?' asked Quin. 'Have you forgotten, there's at least ten rooms on the attic floor as well as another ten on the next floor down and most of them are occupied.'

'I refer to the lady in the room next to yours. A very nubile young woman.'

Quin began to get annoyed but tried to remain cool. He didn't want to react and give Jones ammunition. 'Is this what you were referring to back at the hotel in Melbourne, a woman to help keep me happy after working hours?'

Jones' plump face fell slightly, a frown of confusion settling on his brow. 'I realise you would prefer to choose your own woman Jameson but this particular girl is a beauty. She's young and healthy and I think comparatively inexperienced. She'd be wasted on most of the men.'

'You sound like you have a personal interest. Do you?'

'I admit. I like her. She seems a nice little thing. I only want the best for her.'

'What's this paragon's name?' As if he didn't know. Quin ground his teeth as he waited for Jones to answer. Then he'd knock Jones' teeth down his throat.

'Marina.'

'Marina! Who the hell is Marina?' Quin was beginning to wonder if Sherry had opted for a name change when Jones continued in an oily persuasive manner.

'Surely you've noticed her Mr. Jameson. She has certainly noticed you. She told me so. Wanted me to introduce you to her. I told her I would but then I remembered I'd already put her in the room next to you. I decided you could do your own introducing.'

'Get to the point Jones,' growled Quin. 'Who is Marina?'

'No need to take that tone,' Jones whined. 'I'm only trying to do you a flavor.' When Quin took a step toward him he stiffened and backed away, Quin's superior height and muscular build menacing in the shadowed light of the hall.

Jones continued quickly. 'She's the young woman with long dark hair and brown eyes. You know the one, very attractive. Looks foreign, exotic in a Mediterranean kind of way. She's had a difficult life I believe but I'm confident she'll do well here. You just have to talk to her, get to know her.'

'I thought you were talking about the little blonde?' Quin said, deciding to probe a little but expecting to hear that Sherry would be too busy in the kitchen to be anyone's plaything. His relief was short lived.

'Oh no.' Jones appeared startled before lowering his voice and confiding, 'Sherry is a delightful young woman but we have other plans for her.'

'Like what?' He decided he'd be better off knowing what she was doing than worrying all the time he was working.

'Well, for a start she's doing the cooking,' intoned Jones as if reciting a menu. 'Then, when our employer arrives next week, she's going to be entertaining him during the evenings. He might decide to let her off cooking if she proves amenable and creative. We'll have to see how it works out.'

He didn't see the darkness in Quin's eyes or the murderous clenching of his fists as he fought against his inclinations to throw Jones over the railing to the floor below. Jones continued talking softly as if he was the procurer quietly providing the best meat for his most affluent customer. 'I think he's going to be very pleased with that little morsel. I knew right away she was going to be the one. A virgin too. Not many of those left these days. A real prize.'

At that moment Quin looked down, hearing the sound of footsteps on the stairs below just before Sherry came into sight, her lovely grey eyes startled, the straight fall of silver blonde hair flowing over slim shoulders encased in a soft violet blouse open over a white tank top. She took Quin's breath away but he was too angry to think about how she affected him at that moment. She paused to say hello to the two men, appearing startled at the violent expression on Quin's face. She smiled nervously and touched her lips with her tongue, unconsciously echoing what Quin was longing to do.

Jones smiled unctuously and said, 'Miss Hunter. I hope you're settling in alright.'

'I'm fine. Thank you. This is a lovely place to work Mr. Jones. I think it's going to work out just fine.' Sherry had no intention of telling Jones she wished she'd never seen the advertisement in the paper about the job just in case he decided to send her back to Melbourne alone.

She glanced at Quin who was watching her intently and said nothing as she hurriedly continued upward, gently rounded hips swaying in slim fitting blue jeans, disappearing out of sight around the angle of the staircase. Quin was taken aback at the sight of her. She'd obviously taken the time to shower and change her clothes since their arrival and he wished he'd managed to do the same. Of course, he'd seen her at breakfast behind a table but not close enough that he could smell the fresh lemony scent of her hair and see the softly glistening lips which were parted to show white even teeth.

Everything about her was a pleasure to him, even the trembling hesitation in her left leg as she lifted her right foot to step up the stairs. He especially enjoyed it when she watched him thinking he was not aware of her. He could have told her he always knew when she was near. It was a kind of physical telepathy.

Quin watched until she was out of sight before turning back to Jones who was smiling in that secretive way and nodding his head as if he had all the answers. Smug bastard, thought Quin! How I'd love to rearrange your face.

He knew no good would come of smashing Jones in the face even though he would have taken much pleasure in making him suffer. The way he had spoken about Sherry was degrading. She was his woman, Quin reasoned savagely, the woman he....cared for... loved.

Did he love her? Or was it the feelings of a strong man for a helpless girl, one who needed him. More importantly, did she love him?

Quin had never been in love. He'd never needed anyone to hold his hand or see into his soul. He'd never wanted the responsibility of a wife or children, never known the joy of holding his own baby in his arms, the deep satisfaction in coming home to the one person in the world who loved him more than life itself.

His mother had died when he was a child of six and, since then, he had never known what it was like to be loved unconditionally by anyone. Except maybe his Australian Grandmother who had died when he was ten. She had lived in Adelaide and he hadn't seen her often enough to know if she loved him that way or not.

Upon losing his job when Quin was eleven, his geologist father had proved to be an unstable alcoholic, a poor influence in his life at best, at worst a danger to his emotional stability as well as his physical well-being. Police had come to his school to tell him his father was dead when he was fifteen but he hadn't been able to mourn for a man who had never seemed to care enough to stay sober for more than a week at a time.

This was not the time to be thinking about his muddled feelings for Sherry, he decided ruthlessly as they paused on the ground floor, pushing the image of her walking away from him up the stairs from his mind. It was time to give Jones something to think about. 'Your Marina sounds like she's just what a lonely man needs Jones. I appreciate your thinking of me.' He smiled, hoping the other man wouldn't see the falseness of it or the danger in his tightly clenched fists.

'Think nothing of it Jameson,' said Jones. 'I know what it's like to be in need.'

I bet you do thought Quin. 'I wish you luck sending the little blonde to your boss. She's probably not as biddable as she appears though.'

'I know,' Jones chuckled. 'But he prefers a girl with spirit. She'll be perfect.' 'Yes,' agreed Quin. 'She's perfect.' Perfect for Quin, no-one else.

'Well, I must get going,' said Jones jovially, rubbing his hands together. 'I have some darkroom work that needs doing.'

Thinking he'd better take the chance to see as much as possible Quin walked down the stairs with Jones and, as they reached the ground floor, said, 'I've some experience with developing and printing. Perhaps I could help?'

'Not at the moment thanks. These pictures are a little over exposed for anyone to help but I'll keep you in mind.' He chuckled as he turned away, walking quickly and disappearing through a door down the other end of the corridor.

That break into his blind emotional response had given Quin the ability to reign in his instincts. He looked around for a moment, his eyes hard as he assessed his surroundings, then walked outside. He was wondering what that strange look on Jones' face had been for. Had he said something to make Jones laugh or was he just a weird kind of guy who like to take strange pictures? What did he mean by saying the pictures were over exposed?

Later in the morning Quin came across Sherry sitting on a deck chair just off the rear verandah overlooking the sea. Someone had mowed the lawn earlier that day and the freshly cut grass gave off a wonderful spring perfume. She had an iced fruit drink and a sun umbrella provided a small amount of shade.

Scrappy lay nearby on the grass soaking up the sun. Quin wanted to tell her everything he'd seen but decided to wait until he had more evidence of what was going on. 'Better watch that sun,' he said abruptly, unknowingly curt and preventing Sherry from asking the questions that were on the tip of her tongue. 'It can cause skin cancer even at this time of year.'

'You're not my baby-sitter,' she fired back, determined to show him he wasn't wanted. She remembered his words that had floated up the stairs after her earlier encounter with him and Mr. Jones. Something about a woman called Marina. The rest of his words had vanished in the echoing hallway but the damage had been done.

'Why don't you go annoy someone else? That dark haired girl for instance. She's been eyeing you like a famished crow ever since you came out here.' Scrappy got to his feet and sniffed at Quin's shoes making him step back.

'Oh no you don't you little monster,' he said, grinning. 'Not again.' Scrappy wagged his tiny stump of a tail and went to lie back down. Quin sat down on a deck chair and said, 'It's not very nice calling Marina a crow Sherry. She's more like a glossy bird of paradise.'

Sherry scowled but said nothing as she turned to look out at the ocean view, the salty breeze catching the ends of her hair. She had taken off her blouse and her shoulders were becoming slightly red from the sun's rays.

'Believe me Sherry, I'm not interested in anyone else.' Quin's dark eyes smouldered with frustration.

She turned back to him and said, 'Why should I believe anything you say? You should make up your mind. One minute you're kind and thoughtful and treat me like you would a child, then you're coming on to me as if I've suddenly become the only female left on earth. The next minute you'd think I'd killed your granny and you loathed the sight of me.

This hot and cold stuff is a pain. I never know where I am with you and I hate that kind of treatment Quin, so say what you want to say and then leave me alone.'

'I am interested in you Sherry. Your welfare is very important to me.'

'Well hooray for the cavalry. Just what I need, someone to rescue me from the white slavers. Get real Quin. I'm a big girl and I don't need a man to save me, okay?'

'Cut it out Sherry. You're in real trouble here. I only want to help you.' He stood up and said, 'Come for a walk with me. I've got some things to show you about this place.'

'I told you Quin, I'm not interested. Go find yourself another girl.' Sherry was determined not to give in to him, otherwise he'd just go on treating her hot and cold and she'd never know what to expect.

'I wish you'd stop playing matchmaker. I told you before, I'm not interested in another girl.'

'You better be. She's coming over right now and she looks like she's got plans, for you. If she was the only girl left on earth you'd have no trouble at all. A re-population program would be first on her list of things to take care of.'

He turned to see Marina swaying in their direction and smiling, her tall lush body ripe with promise, her melted chocolate eyes and long black hair gleaming in the sun. When she arrived at his side she put her hand on his arm and looked up into his face with an invitation on her richly painted red lips.

'I hear we've got rooms next to each other Quin,' she purred. 'I like that. It'll be nice to tap on the wall at night and talk to each other won't it? I'll know when you get up and we can have breakfast together.'

Sherry coughed and stood up, pushing her deck chair out of the way and slipping her sandals back on. She wished she had high heels so she didn't feel like a child at an adult picnic. 'It's nearly time for lunch and I have things to do.'

'No need to run away Sherry,' Quin said, looking back at her. 'Have another drink. After all, we work tomorrow. This is our last day of freedom.'

'No thanks.' She plastered a saccharin smile on her face. 'I have to take my dog for a walk and you need to work on your own program for tomorrow. See you.' She picked up Scrappy's lead and walked rapidly around the corner of the verandah and away into the gardens.

'What's with her?' Marina tried to look upset Sherry had gone but failed.

Quin said casually, 'Beats me. Come on Marina, let's have a drink and get to know each other better.' He hid his lack of interest in a show of manners but inside he was marking time until he could go after Sherry. He wanted to talk to her but had no idea what he was going to say. He was tempted to shake her but knew he wouldn't. As soon as he put his hands on her he would want to kiss her and touch her, and go on kissing her. She was a thorn in his flesh but not one he wanted removed. He wanted her embedded there forever. One thing was sure, any re-population program would begin and end with her, no one else.

Sitting facing Mr. Jones who had his back to the room, Sherry spent lunch trying to avoid watching over Jones' shoulder as Quin made time with Marina. Time after time her eyes were drawn back to them as she picked at her own meal of fish and salad. Quin appeared to be enjoying himself enormously, collecting a drink for Marina, laughing with her, feeding her pasta with his fork and tasting her offerings of potato salad with enthusiasm. She was far too close to him in Sherry's opinion, practically sitting on his lap. It was indecent, the way they were carrying on and she wished she had a jug of ice water to toss over them and cool them off.

'It's remarkable what one man can do for the economy,' said Mr. Jones as he sat opposite Sherry and laboriously chewed his way through a rare steak, waving his fork around for emphasis as he spoke. 'Mr. Wilson is such a wonderful employer. He makes things happen and that's why you're here today. He organises people to work for him and gives them experience in the workforce. You'd never know it my dear, but I was out of a job a few years ago and without qualifications of any useful sort. I met Mr. Wilson in a bar in London when I was contemplating ...well, forget I said that, I don't want to depress you.

Anyway, Mr. Wilson said, 'I'll give you a chance. Come to Australia and work for me in my Melbourne office. If you're still working for me in six months, you'll be with me for life'. I still work for him and I'm a happy man Miss Hunter, a happy man.'

'It sounds just like a dream Mr. Jones. I'm sure you deserve to have a good job.' Sherry sighed, wishing she could get up and leave the room. She'd waded half way through her meal and was beginning to feel trapped. Surely she could make some excuse...

'What about you? Are you really happy to be here Miss Hunter? No regrets.'

'Oh, yes. I'm happy. Who wouldn't be. Beautiful views, a room of my own, a good job. All I need is some decent clothes. I hope you'll arrange for me to be taken to town one day Mr. Jones. I really need some things and you did say we could change our appearance.'

'I'm glad you're happy my dear. I like to see our employees in good spirits. Unfortunately a trip to town is out for the moment. Perhaps in a few weeks when you're more settled. However, we do have anything you might need of a personal nature in the store. It's fully stocked and is situated in one of the bungalows. There's a sign up so you can't miss it. Just go and choose what you want, write it in the book and we will deduct your pay at the end of the month.'

He hesitated for a moment then said, 'Would it be presumptuous of me to ask you to go for a walk in the garden. It's a lovely day and we could sit in the shade of that huge old flowering gum tree near the orchard. What do you say? Will you walk with me?'

Sherry swallowed her disappointment about the trip to town. After all, she was used to being denied, it was nothing new. The trapped feeling intensified at Jones' invitation but Sherry could find no reasonable excuse. 'Alright Mr. Jones. Just for a little while. Then I must sort through my things for tomorrow.'

'Excellent. I'll look forward to it. Would you like some coffee to finish off this delightful meal?' Without waiting for her reply he turned and looked around the room for the woman who was serving. He held up his hand when she noticed him and she came to take their order. When she had left he turned back to Sherry and waved his arm vaguely toward the corner of the large room saying, 'Those two hit it off rather well don't they?'

'Which two Mr. Jones?' asked Sherry, not about to admit she'd been watching that corner surreptitiously for some time.

'The two in the corner. Quin Jameson and Marina Angelli. They look like they were made for each other. Both tall, dark and handsome. A perfect match.'

'I don't know. She looks like she's got a temper waiting to erupt and he's got arrogance written all over him. I wouldn't be surprised if they can't tolerate each other after a while. Both probably want their own way a little too much.' Sherry was appalled at the jealous way she had spoken but relieved when Jones didn't appear to notice.

Smiling at her in a way that had her biting her lip nervously, Jones said, 'I'm glad to see you're a reasonable girl Miss Hunter. You realise you can't have your own way all the time. Have to give the other chap a chance sometimes. May I call you Sherry? My name is William if you care to use it.'

'Thank you...William. I'm not sure reasonable is a correct description of me you know. I do get angry sometimes, especially when people push me around. Then I get most unreasonable.' 'I see. Well, I shall be careful not to push you.' William Jones smiled then, making Sherry wish she had left the dining room straight after lunch. She certainly didn't want to go strolling in the grounds with him. Something about him suggested a hidden purpose, a secret person hidden inside the outwardly helpful and friendly man who was in the business of providing escape routes for people wanting to disappear.

Sherry shivered and stood up from the table saying, 'Look, can I take a rain check on that walk Mr. Jones...I'm sorry...William. I'm feeling a little tired. All that travelling, you know how it is. I think I'll go upstairs and rest a while if that's okay with you.'

'Certainly my dear. I'll see you later on. Maybe you'll feel more like it then.'

Jones stood also and pushed in her chair for her accidentally touching her arm. It took a lot of willpower not to flinch but Sherry had years of practise remaining outwardly unmoved by a man touching her. Ralph had loved to get her to react to him by brushing against her just as Jones had done but she had beaten him by refusing to acknowledge him. Picking Scrappy up, she began to turn away.

'Of course, you brought your little dog with you. I'd forgotten.' William Jones smiled slightly at her and she tried to smile back. He put his hand out to touch Scrappy's head and the little dog bared his teeth ferociously and growled low in his throat. Jones jumped back and scowled as he said sharply, 'Do try to keep it under control won't you Miss Hunter. The dog better not take a bite out of anyone or I'll have to get rid of it. Keep it clear of furniture and off carpets as well? Some of these things are worth a lot of money, especially the Persian floor rugs in the main salons. They're Mr. Wilson's pride and joy.'

'I'm sorry he growled Mr. Jones. That isn't like him. He's probably nervous in a new place.' Sherry felt an embarrassed flush on her face as she tried to explain her pet's belligerent behaviour. 'Scrappy's usually a good boy. He won't damage anything,' she asserted, hoping Jones would leave it at that.

All she wanted now was some fresh air. Somehow he made her lungs constrict and breathing difficult as he loomed over her. Quin had done the same thing and her reaction had been entirely different.

'We'll see Miss Hunter,' he said as he walked towards the door. 'I'm not making any promises concerning the dog. If it makes a mess or destroys anything there will be a price to pay. Mr. Merton will see to that I assure you.'

At Sherry's fear filled silence Jones frowned back at her and continued sternly, 'So I'll say it again. If you want to keep the dog make sure it's out of the way at all times. Especially don't let Walker near it. He hates dogs even more than Mr. Merton, or me. It seems to give him great pleasure to destroy things.'

He turned and left the room, leaving Sherry shattered by what she had been told. How could anyone hate such an innocent little pup as Scrappy. These people were monsters. Then she ground her teeth in sudden anger as she also left the room, allowing the door to slam on her way out, wishing several heads could be disposed of with such ease. No way was she going to let anyone hurt her pet, even if she had to run away in the night to keep him safe.

CHAPTER EIGHT

Seething with frustration, Sherry thought of Quin. Added to the threat to Scrappy she had to cope with the sight of the man she wanted with Marina. It was eating away at her like an acid burn. She had seen him leave with the dark haired beauty while she

herself had stood talking to Jones, before he had spoken about Scrappy. Marina had slipped her hand through Quin's bent arm and walked closely with him as they left the room, brushing her body against him like a cat desperate to have it's fur stroked.

Sherry felt an irrational urge to follow them and rip out some of that black fur by the roots. Jones had called her reasonable but she knew if she had the chance, she would tell Quin what she thought of his womanising ways. She longed to physically tear him out of Marina Angelli's arms and give the woman a black eye for her trouble as well. That would sink her fancy little boat before it sailed alright.

Not that Sherry had any claim on him. She was completely on her own in how she felt. He had shown no interest in her at all as a woman after those first two times they'd been in contact and she had better get used to it. But it was hard, almost impossible, to get him out of her mind.

It was especially hard when she ran into him in the corridor at the foot of the narrow back stairs which led up to the second floor in the west wing. She'd decided to use the back stairs thinking he would take the main staircase which was a more direct route to the third floor where their rooms were.

Striding towards her in his tight fitting blue jeans, black leather boots and a partly opened soft white button through shirt with the sleeves rolled up to his elbows, Quin looked like a buccaneer, a tall dark man with the fierce beauty of a warrior. 'Where's your room?' he asked abruptly, his lean jaw clenching with tension as he waited for her reply, his hot dark gaze boring through her flimsy covering to the fragile body beneath.

'None of your business.' Trembling inside, she had no idea why she answered him like that. Some evil genie had taken over her tongue and was saying the opposite of what she wanted to say.

'I haven't got time to play games Sherry. Where's your room?'

'Why do you want to know?' She wished he'd stop looking like he wanted to devour her. She picked up Scrappy as if for protection but the tiny mutt looked at Quin as if he was the only person in the whole world he trusted. He set to, wagging his stumpy tail and grinning like a besotted fool. little traitor.

'You'll find out,' he replied grimly, absently patting the pooch gently on the head with one hand, his free hand reaching out to firmly grasp her arm. 'Where is it? I haven't got all day.'

'I don't like to be touched Quin,' said Sherry defiantly, pulling away from him, her evil genie continuing to speak without consulting her. 'You can say what you want right here.'

'No. I can't.' He began to take a few short impatient steps up and down beside her.

She could see a muscle in his jaw twitching slightly and knew she was getting to him. Even his shoulders were tense. Any moment now she thought, fascinated, he's going to do something explosive.

Prompted by her evil genie, she decided to fire-walk a little. 'Don't try to throw your weight around with me. I'm not interested. Why don't you go back to your little friend Marina. She obviously admires your Neanderthal charm. Just flex a muscle or two. I'm sure she'd never be so boring as to say no to you.' Probably had never found a use for the word in her life thought Sherry nastily, feeling thoroughly ashamed of herself.

Quin stopped suddenly and grinned. 'There's no need to be jealous Sherry. Marina's just a diversion.'

Misunderstanding his words she reacted with scorn. 'I bet she'd appreciate hearing you say that. Women like to be treated with respect.'

'Damn it Sherry,' he growled, the grin replaced by a glare. 'I don't want to discuss my non-existent relationship with a woman I've only just met. I need to talk to you. It's important.'

'Well I don't want to talk to you. And where my room happens to be is no concern of yours. Now leave me alone Quin Jameson or I'll scream so loud everyone will think you're trying to molest me. Come on Scrap, let's go.' Sherry turned on her heel and hurried off around the corner of the passageway. She was intending to hide downstairs in a small store-room off the kitchen. Scrappy would have to wait a few minutes for his walk until Quin had left. It was time that man learnt he couldn't have what he wanted whenever he wanted it. Sherry would see to that even if it killed her.

Maddening little wretch thought Quin admiringly as he watched her taut rear end disappear with poetic rhythm. She sure has a nice exit line. And fantastic muscle control. He appreciated her tenacity in rejecting him and knew it was one of her most appealing features, that stubborn refusal to give in.

She appeared fragile and sweet, a girl who might blow away in the wind but underneath she was strong both emotionally and physically, a perfect fit for a man, a perfect mate for himself, if only they could survive their current situation.

Marina, an exuberant kind of girl, had been a fount of information. Quin now knew they were on the east coast of Queensland, not far from Fraser Island. He had no idea how far from civilisation they were but knew something strange was going on. Marina had been chatting to one of the guards who had boasted to her that his boss made art movies, some of which the guard himself had appeared in. Marina had asked the guard what kind of part he'd had but he refused to say anything else.

From her account, he'd leered at her, suggesting she come to his room in one of the bungalows that night and he would tell her more. She'd said she would. He'd told her they'd have a good time because the boss liked his employees to be well taken care of. 'Of course I told him I wasn't that kind of girl,' she'd said to Quin unconvincingly. 'He told me I could come if I liked, it was no skin off his nose either way. So I went. I was curious and he was kind of attractive. Besides, I was bored and lonely and I had to have someone to talk to since you were unavailable.'

*   *   *   *

As he hung around the dining room waiting for Sherry to reappear, Quin reflected on the differences between the two girls. Marina was bouncy and garrulous and she'd made it clear she was not averse to a little after hours activity. She'd left a husband who had lost a lot of money gambling and who was now hiding from his creditors somewhere in America.

After a no contest divorce she should have been free to keep the money she earned as a cosmetic consultant, that was if the men looking for her ex-husband didn't find her first. She'd seen the same ad as Quin, and, after one or two strangely sinister accidents in her car and numerous threatening phone calls, had taken it as the perfect escape route.

Sherry was somewhat different from Marina. She was quiet and at times hardly spoke, except when she was arguing with Quin. She seemed content in her own company, not frenetically trying to fill up the spaces in her life with activity and noise. He knew she'd had a hard life and was running away from Ralph Marley but still she had a quiet serenity about her, a deep reserve of peace that was an intrinsic part of her. He envied that peace even while he knew it was not something he could achieve on his own. He needed to tap into hers and become a part of her life.

Marina had said what she missed most of all was her TV, movies and dating but Sherry seemed to be able to read a book or sit peacefully looking out at the sea. Sherry's face often had a withdrawn and sad expression as she sat, isolating herself not only physically but within her own mind as well. Quin wished he could see into her head and unlock the secrets that were so carefully hidden. He felt there was so much she could share with him if only she would trust him.

That thought was swept away then as he looked out a window and saw her walking toward the house. She went through the kitchen garden, in through a back door and, from his vantage point near the door to the kitchen, he saw her step up the back stairs with Scrappy trailing behind on a lead.

He allowed her to go on ahead, then, after a few minutes, climbed the main stairs to the third floor and settled down near the head of the main stairwell just inside the doorway of a small linen store-room.

It was mid afternoon and, feeling sure she wouldn't keep Scrappy cooped up in her room for the rest of the day, he intended to wait until she came back and then persuade her to sit down and listen.

Sherry spent ten minutes in the bathroom then poked her head back out into the corridor. She sensed Quin would be somewhere around wanting to continue their earlier confrontation. Unable to see him, she hurried along to her room carrying her dog and, expecting to be relieved he'd taken her at her word and left her alone, she was horrified to find herself on the verge of tears. He'd given up on her she thought miserably, left her so he could chase after that overblown tart, Marina Angelli. Anyone could see the woman was anybody's, for the right price.

What a nerve he had, approaching her after being with that woman then leaving just because she told him to go. Surely he had more going for him than to do what he was told without question. He hadn't seemed like the sort of man who'd obey a woman or anyone else. Still, you never could tell, some people were all wind.

She sniffed and wiped her eyes with the back of her wrist. 'He's probably just a wimp, a paper maché dragon with his wings clipped,' she said to Scrappy as she put him down on the ground to walk.

'I reckon a man like that's no good to me anyway. I want someone who'll stand up for me and protect me, someone who won't take no for an answer, a real man, not a pretend one who'll lie down and let other people walk all over him, even me.'

Scrappy was content to stay in the bedroom while Sherry took herself down to the bathroom again. She needed to wash a few things out so she'd be ready for work in the morning. On her way back from the bathroom for the second time she was humming to herself and planning what she would do the next day when she sensed something wrong.

That psychic vibration of danger had helped her in the past when Ralph had been in one of his rages and she slowed her pace to assess her surroundings. Most of the doors were closed but she still maintained caution. She shrieked sharply as a long tanned arm snaked around her waist from behind and snatched her off her feet.

Struggling to free herself she kicked her captor with her heels, swearing vividly as she elbowed, punched and pushed against a wide solid chest and strongly muscled forearms. Finally, after she had resorted to biting the wrist of his free arm and pulling his hair Quin hauled her through the open doorway of a bedroom. Swearing vividly, he tossed her down on the bed and stood back to view his captive, rubbing his wrist. She brushed aside her tangled hair and glared at him silently before sitting up to straighten her blouse. The room was a mirror image of hers, in fact hers was the next door along but she wasn't about to tell him that.

Sherry stood up quickly and backed away from him to stand by the window overlooking the sea. 'What do you think you're playing at?' she asked in a shaky but defiant voice.

Quin closed the door and leaned against it, broodingly watching her retreat. 'I told you I needed to speak to you Sherry. Didn't you hear me before?'

'I heard you Oh Master, I just refused to obey.'

'Cheeky wretch.'

His strong face gentled as he looked at her and she was compelled to soften her own words. 'Why are you so horrible to me Quin? I don't understand the way you are.' Her eyes pleaded with him to explain.

'It's complicated Sherry. I'm trying to take care of you.' He rubbed his hands over his lean jaw in frustration before taking a deep breath. 'To protect you.'

'Protect me from what?'

'From things that are happening here. You know I'm concerned for your safety?'

'Yes. I understand that but how can staying away from me help. If you wanted to look out for me you'd talk to me and hang around. Instead you act as if I've got some social disease and you don't want to know me.'

'I do want to know you,' he asserted, taking hold of her hand. 'I just don't want to hurt you. I'm not a very good person to be around. I've nothing much to offer a girl in the way of security. My life is a shambles and I have major problems to work out if I ever go back to Melbourne. If we became involved, you could be in trouble too.'

'What's that got to do with the situation here?'

'If the people here see us together it might put you in danger. They might try to use our involvement to their advantage.'

'I don't understand Quin. What possible advantage could they gain by using either of us.'

'They're in the business of making movies here so if you're not careful you might find yourself the star feature in an X rated movie theatre.'

'What are you talking about?'

'You might have a starring roll in a movie.'

'What kind of movie?' Surely her ears had been deceiving her when he said X rated. 'In consideration of your delicate ears I'll call it an art movie.' 'You mean one of those movies where they take their clothes off.'

'Something like that.' Lord, she was innocent Quin thought, watching the colour come and go in her face.

'Are you telling me they make pornographic movies here Quin?' It was hard for Sherry to verbalise such things but she felt she must. It was time she reacted like the adult she was instead of a silly embarrassed child. Instead of firm and adult though, the words came out as aggressive and loud.

'I believe so. Marina told me about it.'

'Maybe she stars in them?'

'Not nice Sherry. Put away your claws. Marina found out by talking to one of the men guarding the place. I'm not sure she wants anything to do with that sort of thing either.'

'No, well I'm sorry if I misjudged her,' Sherry replied, shrugging her shoulders, not believing for a minute she had misjudged the other girl. If ever a person was ready to do whatever it took to get ahead, it was Marina Angelli. Sherry had heard her talking with some of the kitchen staff one day and knew what her goals in life were. It wouldn't surprise Sherry at all if Marina decided to take advantage of the money to be made in X-rated movies.

'She's had a tough life Sherry. We mustn't think badly of her because she enjoys herself now and then.'

'Well I wish she wouldn't enjoy herself with you,' she burst out, instantly putting her hand over her mouth as if to hold back the words. 'I mean....here, with anyone here.'

Unable to stay away from her, he reached out and pulled her into his arms. 'I know what you mean.' He kissed her then, his mouth gently preparing her lips for the hungry assault he knew was not far below the surface. It was all he could do to hold back, her innocence a temptation and a delight, but he knew to rush her was not the way to keep her. She was inexperienced and he must give her time to accept him. He needed her to trust him, knew also he could not allow anyone to see them as anything other than casual acquaintances.

Sherry knew she had come home. All her life she had waited for this moment, a point in time when she could say 'this is the man I will love forever'. She slipped her arms around his waist and held him, opening her mouth to him, instinctively taunting him with sweetness too delicious to resist. He deepened the kiss for a long moment and then pulled back, his breathing ragged. 'Sherry, sweetheart, I want you to be very careful. You mustn't say anything to anyone about what I've told you. You don't know who you can trust.'

'I don't care about that,' she said recklessly. 'I trust you Quin. Kiss me again. I need you.' Unable to resist such pleading he gave in, lowering his mouth back to hers and tightening his hold on her, their passion spiralling rapidly out of control. He was lowering her to the bed when an alien noise intruded, a whimper of distress, coming from behind the closed connecting door to the next room.

Quin lifted his head like a deer scenting a predator, then, letting her drop the rest of the way onto the bed, straightened up and strode to the door. Sherry was still locked into a sensual haze and found it difficult to make the instant transition from willing participant in love making to a seemingly discarded and uninteresting nuisance.

When he asked abruptly, 'Sherry, is that your dog howling in the next room?' she too became alert and, except for a tingling of her lips and the rapid beat of her heart, she put aside her feelings of desire for him.

Nothing meant as much to her as Scrappy and if he was unhappy or hurt, so was she. The fact that Quin too was thinking of her pet helped her forgive him for abandoning her.

The key was in the lock so, not waiting for an answer to his question, Quin turned it, Sherry clinging to his side. He opened the door and walked through to find a tiny pathetic bundle of black and brown fur sitting whimpering in the middle of the bed, black eyes moist and reproachful, a wet patch darkening the bedspread near the pillow.

'My poor baby, ' cried Sherry, tears threatening as she hugged him to her breast. 'You've wet the bed. Oh dear, I'd better take you outside. Mummy won't leave you again my precious. Next time you can come with me wherever I go. Okay?' For answer he licked her chin over and over, wagging his whole body to and fro, tiny stump of a tail moving to a faster beat.

Quin looked at the two of them and knew the bite of jealousy as he realised she had completely forgotten him. Second place to a mutt, he thought disgustedly, or maybe he didn't rate at all. Still, Scrappy sure was a cute little guy, even if he did have trouble figuring out where to put his liquid deposits. 'What are you going to do with him in the kitchen Sherry? I shouldn't think pets will be allowed where food is being prepared.'

'He can bed down in the pantry store-room on my jacket. No-one will be able to see him there.'

'That Merton character doesn't seem the type to allow pets. How did you manage to persuade Jones to let you bring him with you?'

'I just asked and he said okay. I'm not sure if Mr. Merton knows about him.'

'Well, keep him away from people if you can.'

'I'll try,' she said and then, her eyes worried, she asked, 'Quin, how do you know the guard was telling the truth about the movies being made here. Maybe he was just spinning a yarn for Marina's benefit.'

'I don't know. But if it's true, you could be in danger.'

'Why? I'll be doing the cooking, nothing else.'

'If these people are making movies legitimately, why go to the trouble of finding workers to restore this building in such a clandestine manner? Why not advertise locally and in trade magazines for qualified workers. Why look for people who want to disappear? Something very suspicious is going on and I aim to find out what.'

'How?' Sherry grabbed his arm as he made to return to his room. 'What are you going to do Quin? Go up to Jones and say 'what's going on mate? Do you make porn movies here or what?'. He'd either laugh and say you're crazy or he'd offer you a part in one of the movies.'

Quin gently took her hand off his arm and strode to the connecting door to his room. Over his shoulder he said, 'No need to get in a knot sweetheart. I'm just going to take a look around. See you later on.'

He disappeared, then, moments later, stuck his head back through the doorway, 'Oh, and by the way Sherry, I'd say no, just in case you were wondering.' His grin was pure cheek.

'Say no to what?'

'The part in a porn movie.'

She chuckled. 'Why? Don't you think you've got what it takes?'

'Oh I've got what it takes all right. Never doubt it. No, it just wouldn't be fair.'

'Oh?' A blush stained her cheeks as her imagination took over.

'Yeah. It wouldn't be fair to get some young lady's hopes up then have to back out of the deal.'

'Back out,' she breathed tautly, wondering when he was going to get to the point.

'Yeah, back out. You see, I have this thing about privacy.' Quin's voice deepened to a honeyed flow as he strolled back into the room and casually leaned wide shoulders against the door frame, hands flexing inside his pockets as if he couldn't trust them near her.

He watched her steadily with slumberous eyes as he said, 'When I make love to a woman. I like it to be just the two of us. No directors, no cameramen, no angles. Just me and my lady doing whatever comes naturally.

I'd whisper sweet words in her ear and discover all the hidden places, all the softness of her. I'd stroke and explore and ask the same from her. She'd call my name and I'd give her everything I had and then find more to give. I'd want everything she could give me and more. And do you know what else?'

'No, what else?' Sherry's voice was a husky croak and she was unable to look away. 'I'd make it last all night and through the day until it was time to start all over again.' Sherry's throat closed completely. Not a sound was heard as he stood straight and tall, his own breathing ragged. 'I'll be back later,' he rasped. 'Take care.' And then he was gone, leaving Sherry clutching Scrappy like a lifeline, her heart pounding like a drum.

After a visit to the bathroom to cool her heated skin, Sherry went back to her room. The door was still open to Quin's room so she lifted Scrappy into her arms and looked around. It was the same as her room, small window overlooking the sea, fancy moulding on ceilings and cornices, brown cotton bedspread on a single bed. All his things had been put away leaving the room sterile and plain except for a trace of sensually scented aftershave hovering in the air. Unwilling to remain in case Quin returned and found her there, dreaming about him, she turned to go and spied the key in the connecting door.

Now she had calmed down and could see her involvement with Quin objectively, Sherry decided she was being a bit hasty allowing such liberties as he had taken already. Perhaps it was time to dampen his enthusiasm a little. After all, she was very inexperienced in these matters. If she encouraged him it could be a big mistake. Added to that, she couldn't forget he'd been all over Marina like a rash.

Still, one thought comforted her as she slipped the key out of the lock and re-inserted it on her side, locking the door firmly against intruders. That single bed was hard as a rock and too narrow for Marina to fit with such a large man as Quin. One or both of them would fall to the floor the instant either of them rolled over. Sherry clipped Scrappy's lead in place and headed downstairs for a walk, satisfied that Marina would not be satisfied.

Quin's thoughts were running in parallel with Sherry's that afternoon. He too had envisaged the single bed provided and mentally occupied it with two people. Whereas Sherry viewed the space inadequate, Quin saw it as promising. Instead of seeing Marina curled up invitingly with her head on his pillow, he had an entirely different woman in mind. Sherry.

She would fit perfectly he decided, tucked up against him in the narrow bed, her beautiful moon-glow hair trailing silkily down his chest, his arms cradling her slender body firmly against his to prevent her sliding to the floor, giving in often to the urge to double up, going to sleep with her draped across him like a sheet.

It was a stimulating thought but that's all it could be for the moment. He had to remain on guard and ready to intercept any problems that might arise. He had no idea yet when they could make their escape but knew it had to be before things got out of hand. No way was he going to let Merton get his greasy hands on Quin's woman.

Casually but carefully, he went over every inch of the house looking for emergency exit points, especially the windows, and talked to the other men without arousing suspicions about what he was doing.

He had no idea who was who and which of them could be trusted. The people who had accompanied them on the flight from Melbourne were doing as he was, inspecting the building or taking a look around the grounds. Some sat on the verandah and drank beer or lemonade, some sat talking or reading.

It was like an unfinished holiday resort with patrons waiting for tennis to start or the evening entertainment to begin. Only there wasn't going to be any entertainment, at least, Quin reflected cynically, there won't be unless it's us.

He tried to find some excuse for Jones luring them there to work and all the time planning to use them in X-rated movies without their consent as the guard had intimated to a very accommodating and interested Marina.

He hadn't figured out how they meant to do it but sensed it had something to do with hidden cameras in bedrooms. Some of the men had told Quin they'd been paired off with women and were having a great time getting to know each other.

They made it seem as if the good life had suddenly arrived through the connecting door and was to be lived to the fullest.

He wondered what would happen to them once their usefulness had worn off. Probably give them their marching orders and shovel them back to where they started from. That was what he hoped would happen but the worst case scenario was a lot colder and a lot more painful. It was not to be taken lightly.

Sherry lay in bed that night wide awake, thinking. She heard Quin enter his room and waited for him to try the door and find it locked. When he didn't she was at first relieved, then furious.

Who did he think he was, kissing her one minute and the next ignoring her. The least he could do was try to use the door and show her he cared enough to make the effort. A few minutes later she heard him leave again and wondered where he was going. It was past midnight and everyone else in the house was asleep or trying to sleep. At least, she thought they would be trying to sleep.

Maybe some are posing for the cameras she wondered curiously, speculating on which of the people who had come at the same time as she and Quin, would be offered work in a film. Now that she thought about it, the group were all good looking people, some exotic and all reasonably slim and athletic. All were under thirty five. Even the guards around the place looked good. Some didn't fit the movie star criteria.

Merton, his secretary Ms. Macklin, and Jones were older. And of course, there was Sherry. She had no illusions about her own attractions. As Ralph had repeatedly told her, her looks were nothing to write home about.

Jones had never given any inkling that he was part of such an organisation. He'd always appeared to her as a middle aged gentleman, a serious minded, aloof but kind man who let her bring Scrappy with her even though he knew it could mean trouble with Merton who seemed to now be in charge of everything.

Of course there was the sometimes curious way Merton looked at her? What did it mean? Was he playing games with her, waiting for a moment when he would propose an illicit liaison or even physically threaten her. Did his almost military-like exterior hide a devious and cunning mind planning a future for his victim disagreed upon and unwished for by her.

It was enough to stop sleep coming for a long time and, when at last she lapsed into dreams, her troubled imagination wove nightmare images until she woke again, sweating under hot blankets and desperate for a walk in the cool night air.

Sherry opened the window and climbed back into her bed, the cool breeze drifting past filmy curtains over her hot flesh. She thought back to that afternoon. She'd gone back downstairs after Quin had left, restless and anxious to start doing something, even if it was work.

Scrappy was happy enough lying on the grass and tied up to one of the verandah railings, a bowl of water and food next to him, his beloved mistress within sight as she sat on a lounger.

Every now and then he would get up and come over for a reassuring pat and then return to his spot on the grass.

Jones had gone to work in his darkroom soon after they had arrived and Merton had then asserted his authority at breakfast that day by demanding to see each person separately during the day to discuss their work. Walker had stood by the doorway, his surly demeanour and large build intimidating to say the least. Needless to say, the interviews took up the whole day.

When Merton had sent his assistant out to get her, a Ms. Macklin with dark brown hair scraped back in a bun, glasses, thin legs and a severe frown, Sherry had been relieved to have something to do. She'd followed the sharply efficient woman inside the house and tried in vain to keep calm as Merton raked his hard blue eyes over her face and body.

He'd made no overt movements toward her but she'd seen that look before in another man's eyes. Thoughts of Ralph had filtered through from her subconscious making her shiver with loathing. It would be a long time before the memory of his callused miner's hands faded from her mind.

Merton had asked about her experience in cooking and cleaning but she could see he wasn't really interested. It was more like a formality which had to be got through before he came to the real reason for their interview. He'd asked, 'What about your life before you came to us Miss Hunter? Where did you say you lived?'

'I lived with my parents in a small town in Central Victoria. They died.' Sherry refused to say when they died in case he asked who she had lived with until recently.

'So now you're all alone. Poor little girl. That's tragic.' He smiled consolingly but his assessing eyes told a different story. 'I hope we can become family for you my dear. May I call you Sherry?' As he spoke his hand came to rest casually on her tense shoulder.

'Sure, if that's what you'd like, Mr. Merton.' Wanting desperately to move away from his clammy hand, she was confused by his words. He'd sounded as if he wanted to be friends and help her, not as if he wanted her for a movie. She decided to listen to him carefully before she believed Marina's story. There could be some perfectly reasonable explanation for everything.

'How old did you say you were Sherry?' Merton had looked into her guileless eyes, mesmerising her, his own eyes dark and piercing, thick brushed back grey hair scraping his collar, face thin and grooved. Not a tall man, he nevertheless had presence and authority, and an aura of ruthless determination.

'Twenty. I'll be twenty-one soon,' she had replied, almost paralysed, a lump forming in her throat making it difficult to speak. His hand was still on her shoulder, the thumb rubbing softly backwards and forwards making her nerves twitch.

'So young,' he mused, sounding sympathetic. 'No boyfriends, no-one else to support you?'

'No boy-friends. No-one at all.' She relaxed a little then, thinking, this isn't so bad. So far he'd asked nothing she couldn't answer with a polite negative or a vague response. He hadn't even asked about the man who was supposed to be stalking her back home. Sherry could only think that, for his own reasons, Jones hadn't passed that little bit of information on. She was very grateful for that even if she didn't understand it. It seemed the left hand was working independently of the right, a fact that could work in her favour.

'Well my dear, we're very lucky to have you. I have in mind a little project you could help me with. For the moment it's in the planning stages so I'll discuss it with you another time. Perhaps I'd better warn you though.' He patted her on the arm in a manner designed to reassure. All it did was make her uneasy.

' Some of the men here are rather starved for female companionship,' he continued. 'I'd be careful and not have too much to do with them. They may make nuisances of themselves. Do you understand what I mean?'

'Yes, I see. I'll be careful. Thank you for thinking of me Mr. Merton.'

'If you do have a problem, please let me know, or Mr. Jones or Walker. We will deal with it. Go now and tell Ms. Macklin I'm ready for the next one.'

He'd smiled at her as she left the room on the ground floor where he had set up an office. It wasn't a pleasant smile, more one of a 'job well done' and a 'trap's set, wait for pigeon' kind of grimace. All in all, she remembered how grateful she had been to get out of his presence and into the fresh air. He had seemed to have a mind numbing effect on her.

CHAPTER NINE

The next day was the first day of work for everybody and Sherry was up at five to prepare breakfast. The other woman who was going to cook was to do the main meal at night and help with lunches. The two women and one man who had been working
in the kitchen for the first few days were grateful she had come to take over some of the cooking. They were happier with their roles of serving and cleaning up. The man was really the groundsman who mowed lawns and dug flower beds. He was grateful to be allowed back outside and having been so grouchy about being kept in the kitchen, everyone was grateful to let him go.

It was the first of a couple of weeks of long hard days working to the point of exhaustion and going to sleep in the early evening so she could get up at five to work again. Sherry saw almost nothing of Quin since she herself and the other kitchen staff ate after the other workers. He made no attempt to contact her and she felt as if he was something wonderful she had dreamed up to bring a little excitement into her life. He hadn't knocked on the connecting door at all and she was so tired she slept soundly through any noise he might have made in his room.

Scrappy was the least of her worries. He stuck to her side like glue and slept in the large pantry store-room most of the time. The spring weather was calm and warm but not overly humid so Sherry left the window open for him.

Sherry saw nothing to indicate movies were being made there and no-one asked her to audition for anything. Disappointed, Sherry decided she wanted to be asked and to be allowed the pleasure of turning it down. So few times in her life had she ever been given a choice in anything. Marina occasionally came into the kitchen to find something and most times she looked at Sherry with contempt and occasionally something akin to amused pity though she never said anything personal directly to her. The other kitchen staff were of the non-talkative variety which made for efficiency if nothing else.

Merton turned up now and then to assert his authority but said nothing beyond polite queries about stores and food to Sherry. She remained wary of him, especially after the interview on the first day when he almost had her believing he was harmless. A little while away from him had cleared her mind and brought back all her fears and instincts where he was concerned. She sensed he was waiting for something to happen before he talked with her about her future and that little project he'd mentioned.

Whatever it was that held him back, she was grateful for it. Surprisingly, he had seen Scrappy in the kitchen and said nothing, merely raised his eyebrows at Sherry and left.

Maybe, she thought charitably, like Ralph there were still some human qualities waiting to be found. All that was needed to change the situation was a catalyst but she had no intention of being around long enough to be one.

The only threat to disturb those first weeks was Walker. He'd stroll through the kitchen before each meal and check on whatever they were doing. He seemed particularly interested in Sherry and insisted on testing everything she made. He watched her as she sliced vegetables and mixed cakes, stood close behind her as she rolled dough out on large floured boards to make pies. He was becoming quite a nuisance but Sherry felt she could handle the situation until one day towards the end of two weeks he did something she could never forgive him for. He kicked Scrappy a glancing blow with his boot when the tiny pooch inadvertently got under his feet.

Walker lost his temper and snarled at Sherry, saying, 'Get that bloody dog out from under my feet. He's a damned nuisance. I'm always tripping over him.'

Sherry had come out fighting mad in defence of her pet and replied, 'It's you that's the nuisance. I'm trying to cook here and you're always hanging around, distracting me when I'm working. I wish you'd go away Mr. Walker. Just get out of here and plague someone else.'

'It would be to your advantage to be nice to me,' Walker took hold of Sherry's hand and squeezed, just enough to hurt but not break the fragile bones.

She pulled away from him with as much strength as she had and wiped her hand on her apron, glaring fiercely. 'Don't touch me ever again or I'll find another use for those sharp knives I use all day.'

'That's it,' he said, 'I've had enough of you and your fussy cranky looks every time I come into the kitchen. It's my job to check up on you. You'll find I'm not a nice person to get on the wrong side of Miss Hunter. I can make you very uncomfortable around here.'

'You already do,' she returned unwisely, keeping her white face under control while keeping an eye on Scrappy who was quivering under a nearby chair.

'I'd keep my mouth shut if I were you. You're only making trouble for yourself?' he gritted, his hands flexing and his eyes like chips of ice.

She could smell the alcohol on his breath as he leaned close to her. 'Why don't you shut up and leave me alone. I've got work to do.' Defiant, even as he intimidated her with his size, she forced herself not to back down. Every nerve in her body remembered the kind of pain that happened to girls who answered back.

'Maybe this will teach you a lesson in obedience?' Walker stooped and grabbed Scrappy by the scruff of his neck from the floor and strode to the back door with his tiny body held in one huge hand. The dog yelped and squirmed then tried to bite Walker's hand, receiving a cuff on the ear as payment. 'Shut up you mangy hound,' he growled. 'You and I are going outside for a little walk.'

Sherry screamed, 'Walker. Bring him back. He's only a baby. Don't hurt him.' She ran after the man and tried to get her dog out of his hand but he gave her a vicious shove which made her fall in a heap on the floor. Bruised and shaken, she climbed to her feet and ran to the door but Walker had disappeared with his pathetically yelping burden. Tears pouring down her cheeks, she decided it was time to call for help but first she had to find out where her saviour was working.

Quin was spending the week working on the restoration of a large reception room on the second floor. It was a beautiful room with carved ceilings, ornate panelled walls and a huge marble fireplace with a mahogany mantelpiece.

Merton seemed to haunt the place, turning up unexpectedly to stand behind him, watching silently and, it seemed to Quin, with hostility.

Did Merton sense a threat or was it something else that drew him? Maybe he had seen him talking to Sherry and wanted to make sure it didn't happen again. After all, his plans for Sherry would be hard to carry out with another man in the picture. Unable to ask outright, Quin decided to say nothing, just to wait and observe.

He was a patient man except when it came to Sherry but he knew people were watching him so he stayed away from her. She was safe for now even if she was working so hard she was ready to drop. That angered Quin but comforted him too. At least she hadn't yet been handed over to the boss for him to use as a plaything.

Quin's comfort was shattered when he heard his name called. Sherry was racing towards him as he stood on a high step ladder painting the ceiling. He was alone. She grabbed his leg and pleaded urgently with him to climb down.

'That man, Walker, has taken Scrappy away. I think he's going to do something to him. Scrappy didn't do anything except get in his way. He sounded as if he wanted to kill him or something. Please Quin, help me. I have to get my baby back. I love him. He's all I've got. ' Tears of terror and helpless rage flowed down her pale cheeks as she clung to his arm.

'Calm down honey,' said Quin as he wiped his hands on a rag. 'We'll get Scrappy back. We just need to find out where Walker has taken him.'

'I think they've gone to Walker's bungalow. At least that was where Mr. Wallace the gardener saw them headed.'

'We can't just go up and confront him. It would link us together and that's not a good thing. They've got enough leverage over us as it is.' Quin hugged Sherry to him in comfort. 'It's almost dusk now. You sneak around to the back door of his place and I'll try to distract him in front long enough for you to get inside and spirit Scrappy away. When you've got him try to keep him hidden. There's no telling what a low life like Walker is capable of.'

'Okay Quin. That's what we'll do.' Sherry's tears had dried at Quin's practical approach to the problem. She knew she could rely on him to help and trusted in his calm judgement. She just hoped Walker wasn't as violent towards Quin as he had shown himself capable of being.

Darkness was falling as Sherry approached the back of the bungalow. Quin knocked on the front door which was opened by Walker. 'Yeah, what the hell do you want Jameson? This better be important.' Quin could hear a television blaring in the background.

'I thought you might have some beer and smokes over here,' asked Quin, trying to appear frustrated and bored. He hunched his shoulders and sniffed like he'd seen some junkies do on city streets at night. 'The night life in this joint is a bit on the slow side and I sure could use a drink.'

'What do you think this is?' Walker snarled. 'A damn holiday resort.' Swearing viciously, he came out onto the step to confront the whining Quin who looked suitably scared of the savage creature he had unleashed. 'I ought to report you to Merton. He'd give you something to think about besides beer. Something much more painful.' The sadist laughed, clearly enticed by the thought of Quin in pain.

'Please don't tell Mr. Merton.' Keeping his eyes down, Quin backed away from the creature masquerading as a human being that was Walker. 'I'll just get back to the main house and forget about it. It's not that important.' He turned and headed rapidly back toward the house having seen the shadowy form of Sherry slipping around the side of Walker's bungalow and into the dense trees, carrying a small bundle.

The last thing he heard as he stepped up onto the verandah was Walker's threatening shout, 'Don't come back here again you pathetic scum. I wouldn't share good beer with someone like you. You gutless pretty boys make me sick.' The words were accompanied by crude laughter and the slam of a door.

Back at the main house Sherry was distraught. She held the soft body of her little dog in her arms and cried. Quin came in through the back door and put his arms around her, muffling her sobs in his shirt. 'I'm sorry Sweetheart. I wish this hadn't happened. Poor little guy.'

He looked down at the tiny black and tan dog and thought, that bastard will pay for this. Then one of Scrappy's ears twitched and he realised the dog was alive. He had been obviously been smacked around and thrown away like so much garbage before Sherry had collected him.

'Quin, he moved.' Sherry's voice was a thin thread of escaping tension. 'I thought he was dead. I found him on the floor just inside the back door of the bungalow. He was just lying there not moving.'

She began to cry again, this time in relief. 'I wanted to go in there and kill Walker. I've never felt like that before. Not so violent and uncontrolled. I just wanted to do something, anything to punish him for what he did to my baby.'

Scrappy lifted his tiny head and licked Quin's hand, then sighed. He snuggled further into Sherry's arms and whimpered. He seemed to be okay, just shaken.

They smiled over his head like fond parents and Quin walked with her upstairs. 'Keep him out of sight from now on,' he said gently, vowing such a thing would not happen again no matter what they had to do to prevent it. Walker was a dangerous man and must be avoided at all costs.

From then on Quin kept his eyes open and his ears keen. Several of the other men often discussed things they had seen and heard, one of which was the crates of equipment which had arrived the previous day. Only selected people had been allowed to unpack whatever it was and those people had said nothing, only smiled smugly and kept working at various jobs of restoration.

Those same people seemed to disappear after the evening meal and turn up late each morning, bleary eyed and snap tempered. It was obvious they had been active during the night but at what none would say. Quin had his suspicions but had no way of finding out.

He had tried to follow some of them one night but had come across a man, obviously a guard, who had informed him that certain areas in the east wing had been closed off for a reason and were off limits. He was told to be grateful he had a bed to sleep in with good food as a bonus and not to anger the boss with nocturnal wanderings. He could gather himself a pile of trouble going where he wasn't wanted.

Quin took the hint and kept to the main rooms, not because he was scared but because he didn't want to draw attention to himself. There would be time enough for that when he and Sherry made their escape. That they would be kept there against their will if they tried to leave was no longer a supposition on his part. It was a certainty. Another man who tried to leave was brought back by Walker and two brawny men then taken to a room in one of the bungalows. It was called the sick bay.

After a few hours he was returned to his room by the men and had refused to talk about what had happened. He seemed haunted and jumpy, eating little and talking even less. Then one day he disappeared and his friends were told he had decided to have a break, a nervous breakdown was given as the reason.

His clothes were packed and he was gone, leaving a tinge of fear in his fellow workers and questions on their minds if not on their lips. Why had he wanted to leave? Where had he gone? How had he gone? No-one had any answers but Quin was determined to find out. His gut feeling was that the man would never be coming back.

The next night a tapping noise from the connecting door woke Sherry from a deep sleep. She was dreaming restlessly of Quin in full war paint wearing nothing but a pair of leggings, bronzed muscles gleaming, feathers and a headband in his long hair and riding on a black horse.

With bow and arrow poised he was chasing Ralph who was running barefoot across a desert plateau, his fancy suit in tatters and cries of terror on his lips. It was a most satisfactory dream and she was cross at being brought back to a dark forbidding room with nothing warmer than scratchy blankets to keep the night chill out. The tapping was now accompanied by a whispered, 'Sherry, wake up. It's me, Quin. Open up.'

She rolled over and put a pillow on her head but the sound of short yaps forced her to move and open the door. Scrappy was determined she would let Quin into her room and she knew he would keep up the pressure until she gave in.

Her tiny pooch seemed to have taken a great liking to the large dark man who haunted her dreams night and day, especially since the rescue. Quin was as gentle as could be when he petted Scrappy or when he picked him up. He even tolerated his face being licked at a furious pace while the stump of a tail circulated like a fan.

Sometimes Sherry felt excluded and little flames of jealousy flicked her. Unfortunately she couldn't make up her mind whom she was jealous of, the dog or the man.

When he entered the room Quin urged her, much against his will, to get dressed. 'I want to show you something Sherry. Leave Scrappy in your room and come to the head of the stairs. There's no-one about right now. The guards are in that small sitting room off the dining room watching television until the next round which is in 45 minutes time. We can be back in our rooms by then if we hurry.'

'You must be off your head Quin,' croaked Sherry, before yawning hugely and shaking her long hair out of her eyes. 'What's this about guards? It's four o'clock in the morning. Go back to bed and lock the door on your way out.' She turned back to the bed, forgetting the key to the connecting door was on her side.

'Come on,' he whispered urgently, 'there's no time to waste. Wear your sneakers. We need to be as quiet as possible.' He picked up her jeans and shirt hanging over the back of a chair and tossed them onto the bed.

'Hold on,' she asserted, questioning suspiciously as she began to wake up properly. 'Just what is it you want to show me?'

'There's no time to explain. Just get a move on. I'll wait near the stairs.'

Sherry knew when to give in so she said ungraciously, 'Oh, alright Quin. Get out of here so I can dress will you. I think you're crazy and so am I for going along with you.'

She pulled her hair into a pony tail and dragged her sneakers out of the cupboard. 'This better be damn good or I'm going to feed you snakes and cockroaches even if I have to go out and hunt for them myself! Witchetty grubs too if you're not careful.'

'Delicious. At least I'll be getting plenty of protein,' taunted Quin softly as he left the room, hearing the rush of a pillow as it followed him. She sure was grouchy first thing he thought fondly. What a great start to the day to soothe her first and then get the adrenaline going.

Yes sir, that's what I want, a kick start to the day with a fire walking woman. We're gonna make one fantastic team alright. Right now he wished he could stay and help her dress but knew they wouldn't get far. All seemed to think of was undressing her and he knew she wasn't ready for that yet. He was ready though, more than ready. Had been since the moment they'd met in the cabin at the hotel.

The darkness of the stairs and the empty corridor daunted Sherry until her night eyes kicked in and she could make out a short hallway on the right which led to one of the tower rooms. The dim glow from the moon filtered in through a window at the far end. Further down were the closed doors of bedrooms and bathrooms. As she approached the staircase to her right, Quin said quietly from a doorway, 'Good, you're here. What I want to show you is on the next floor down. Be careful on the stairs, the carpet is threadbare and loose in places.'

He took her small hand in his and moments later they were moving downstairs and then treading softly along a corridor to enter a large bare room with huge uncurtained windows. It was in the process of renovation. Quin switched on a torch. The ladders and scaffolding loomed in the moonlight, throwing tall dark shadows on the walls and across the floor. The place gave Sherry the creeps and she shivered nervously.

'This is where I've been working today,' he said quietly, looking around.

'What am I supposed to see Quin?' Sherry's voice was a whisper.

'This!' He touched a small button on the body of one of the angelic figures carved into the mantelpiece. A panel slid open in the wall close by, big enough for a small person to get through, not quite big enough for Quin unless he bent low then crawled on his hands and knees.

'I've taken a look with the torch and it seems quite safe,' he said as he peered into the darkness. 'There's a tiny room behind the wall and a ladder down to the ground floor below. It might lead further on to the outside somewhere or possibly down to the cellars. I won't know until I explore further.'

'Why would anyone build something like that here, in Australia? Out in the bush. It's weird. How did you know it was here?'

'I found papers, plans and records of who owned the house. They were down the back of an old Victorian oak sideboard. I moved the thing, damned heavy it was too, and there they were. Must have fallen down there at some stage and gotten lost.

I'm sure Merton hasn't a clue about it. Anyway, it tells of how the people who built the place wanted a replica of their family seat in England. He was a younger son who came out here to make a new life for himself.' Quin laughed. 'Just like us. Anyway, there's a letter with the plans. Says he added verandahs because he wanted it to have an Australian flavor as well. Must have found out how hot it gets out here compared to England.'

'What did he want it for?'

'I guess he was just a kid at heart.' Quin grinned. 'Maybe he wanted to get away from his wife in the evenings. He could have kept a mistress down the road a bit and gone out that way to avoid trouble.'

Sherry punched his arm. 'Maybe she knew about it and wanted him to leave so she could get something going with the butler. Did they have butlers back then?'

'No idea. Probably. You know, this could be our escape route. I don't think anyone knows about it so we could use it instead of sneaking out using the stairs and trying to dodge the guards.'

'I'm not sure about this Quin.' The black hole beckoned to her and she shrank away both mentally and physically, her skin clammy, heart pounding.

Quin's eyebrows drew together in a puzzled frown at her reaction but he shrugged and went on, 'Anyway, I thought you might like to come with me now and have a look. I've got the torch so it'll be as bright as day in there.'

'No! I'm not going in there! I hate small spaces. And spiders.' She trembled with the force of her reaction, her voice echoing her fear. She backed away from the hole and said anxiously, 'And what happens if the torch fails? I'm not going in there Quin, no way.'

'Hey, I'm sorry Sweetheart.' He put his arms around her and held her close to his chest, stroking her shoulder. 'I had no idea you would feel like that.'

'Yes, well, you weren't to know about my phobias.'

'Did you get a fright as a child Sherry?'

'Oh Quin,' she sighed in his strong arms as she listened to his heart thud beneath her cheek. 'I feel as if I've been scared all my life. First my parents died and left me in the guardianship of my Aunt Sylvia's husband Ralph. He's the one that turned up at the cabins in Melbourne, the one I was running away from.

Well, Aunt Sylvia, she wasn't really my aunt, just Dad's first cousin, she died about twelve years ago and he came to work for my dad just after. We have an old gold mine on our property and sometimes I have to work inside the tunnel. When the electricity fails and the light goes out, I have to will myself not to panic. Ralph says I act like a snivelling baby but I can't help it, I get so scared of the dark. I can hear those spiders and insects tramping their feet and rubbing their feelers together inside my head every time I close my eyes to sleep.'

Quin knew he hated the absent Ralph, had hated him since he'd first heard of his treatment of Sherry and more so since he'd met him at the cabin. The man was a reptile. If he ever had a chance to even up the score with him, he would take it with both hands. The thought of Sherry shivering in terror inside a black tunnel made him want to put his fist through the wall or preferably her guardian. If he had anything to do with it, she would never have to go back to that kind of life. She would be free to be and do whatever she wanted. He hoped she would want to be with him as much as he wanted to be with her.

Taking her hand in his, he led her across to the corridor where he paused for a moment to touch her palm. He asked gently, 'What have you done to your hands Sherry?'

He turned one over then the other, stroking the calluses gently with his fingers, holding the torch slightly away with his other hand so he could see. He probed a thin scar on her thumb. 'Is this the result of working in the mine tunnel?'

Sherry's face went blank at the reminder of pain. She had perfected the ability to hide her emotions from Ralph to save herself from a beating and any mention of what she had gone through with him brought out the same reaction. Quin was having none of it.

He said, 'Don't hide yourself from me Sherry. Tell me about it, about your guardian. What did he do to you to make you like this.' Her face was unwittingly giving away secrets she would rather no-one knew, especially Quin.

'Shovelling stones and gravel wrecks your hands. I can fix it though, with lemon juice and sugar. After a while they'll be as good as new, especially if I don't have to work in the mine.' She looked at him, silently begging him to stop asking unanswerable questions. His face was grim as he looked back at her. What he was going to say remained unsaid. It was not the time or the place to bring back distressing memories.

'Forget about the mine,' he said gruffly. 'Don't think about that hole in the wall either. The plans could be wrong. It's probably just a trick cupboard that goes nowhere.'

'You could go down there if you like Quin. Just because I can't manage it doesn't mean you shouldn't.'

'It's okay. I'll leave it for now. I just thought it could be a useful place for us to hide in or escape through. Just in case.'

'In case of what?'

'Look, just forget it Sherry. It was a bad idea.'

'No. Tell me,' she insisted.

Quin looked uncomfortable. He ran his hand through his hair exasperatedly and said, 'You might want to hide somewhere if they try and force you to do something you're not ready for. It's not like you've got lots of experience of this kind of thing.'

'What kind of thing?'

'You know. Porn movies. Skin flicks.' He hesitated. 'Sex.'

'How do you know what experience I have Quin.' Sherry blushed fiercely but she was woman enough to want him to take a longer look at her and see her as an adult and not a wilful child.

He laughed shortly. 'Believe me Sweetheart. I know. You might as well have Virgin tattooed on your forehead. It's as clear as anything you have no familiarity with people like we're encountering here. And, I'd like to keep it that way. At least until you can make your own choice in the matter. Okay?'

'Okay,' agreed Sherry in a small grumpy voice. 'You win. I'll hide in your ridiculous hole-in-the-wall if necessary. It won't be easy but I'll do it. Just make sure you stay out of trouble too. Otherwise I'll be left on my own and I wouldn't like that at all.'

She didn't tell him her fears for his safety were greater than her fears for her own. She didn't have to. He knew.

'I wouldn't like it either. Don't worry. I'll find some way to get us out of here. In the meantime, we'd better get back to our rooms before the guards start patrolling the upper floors. They get really bent out of shape if anyone strays out of bounds.'

'Look, are you really sure we need to leave here Quin? I haven't seen anyone making movies and I don't know what I'd do if I had to go home again. I think I'd rather take my chances here. At least I'm free.'

'No, you're not free Sherry. You just think you are.'

She looked up into his sombre dark eyes and he was lost. All that she couldn't say was in her beautiful grey eyes and he fought desperately against the urge to hold her tightly in his arms and make her forget all the pain she had suffered in her short life. Instead he kissed her gently on the lips then turned away, clenching his hands tightly around the torch to prevent them reaching out. He began to move towards the door knowing they had to get back upstairs before they were caught.

'Things have been happening Sherry. I can't explain right now but we definitely have to get out of here. Trust me on this will you?' He stopped for a moment and looked down at her, willing her to understand and to agree. Without her consent things would be much harder to arrange. He had to make her see the danger she was in.

'What about Marina?' Sherry hated to bring up the woman's name but felt compelled to know what was going through his mind about her.

'She knows what's going on here but I'm not sure she cares any more. Certainly she doesn't intend to leave with us.'

'Did you ask her?'

'I had to. We couldn't go without asking her to come too.'

'I could. I don't want her along with us.'

'That's not like you Sherry,' he said, frowning. 'You're a sweet generous girl and if Marina needs help you'd give it to her, if you could.'

'Maybe. I still don't like her. She looks at you like she wants you for dinner.'

He laughed softly, amused at an image flashing into his mind of him on a plate and Marina poised with knife and fork, saliva dripping from her chin. 'Maybe she does but I'm only on your menu Sherry. Anyway she won't come with us. She said she plans to make a lot of money as a movie star.'

'Do you think she'll be able to do it?'

'Unlikely. I don't think the setup is quite what she's expecting. Time will prove whether I'm right or wrong however. I hope it isn't too late for her then. We'd better get back. It's five o'clock already. Almost time to wake up.'

He walked with her quickly and silently up the stairs and back to their rooms without encountering any guards then said good night before shutting her door after her.

He didn't kiss her or touch her because he knew it wouldn't end at a kiss and that any minute two men would come along the corridor on their rounds. If he was going to have a confrontation with anyone, he preferred it to be on his terms and in a place and time he chose.

The next afternoon Quin saw Jones going into a room on the ground floor and decided to ask him a few probing questions. He knocked and went into a room which served as an office with a lot of fancy computer equipment and a telephone. Making a note of that fact, Quin decided to return later that night to see if he could make an outside call. Then he noticed the lock on the phone and realised it would do no good unless he could find the key.

Meanwhile, he looked around for Jones who had certainly gone into the room but was nowhere to be seen. Then he saw another door with a red light above it. A darkroom. This must be where Jones disappeared to all the time. Quin remembered him talking about developing photos.

The light was off so Quin took a chance and turned the handle. What he saw when he entered the room confirmed his belief about why unskilled workers had been brought here. There were hundreds of photographs lining the walls. Some of the people in the photos he recognised as fellow workers, some he had never seen before.

All were in various stages of undress, men and women together, some just men, some just women, some alone, a few group shots. Most seemed to be engaged in sexual activities which should never have been seen by a camera lens or any other person.

William Jones turned from a sink to look at Quin. He said abruptly, 'What are you doing here Jameson. This place is out of bounds.' A strong chemical odour hung in the air.

Quin forced a jovial grin to his face hoping to disarm Jones who looked like he was going to have a seizure any minute. 'I just wanted a word with you about something. Guess I got more than I bargained for hey?'

He looked around for familiar faces, especially his own and Sherry's. What he found was Marina with one of the guards and another of her with a man who worked with Quin on the renovations.

He had no idea she was so athletic. His eyes narrowed slightly as he wondered if she knew she had been photographed.

Jones' anger seemed to evaporate when he saw Quin's amused reaction to his work. 'You really shouldn't be here you know. Mr. Merton would have a fit if he knew. Still, I suppose now you're here you might as well take a look.' He went across to the board and drew down a couple of large glossy 10 x 8 prints and handed them to Quin. 'What do you think of these beauties. Fantastic angle don't you think?'

It was all Quin could do not to laugh at his boyish quest for approval. He wasn't quite sure how the three people managed to get themselves into that position in the first place and had serious doubts as to their survival intact but it was indeed a fantastic angle.

Having seen quite a few adult magazines plus photographed, sketched and modelled in clay more than his share of nudes during his thirty years, Quin was accustomed and mostly immune to the display of naked flesh before him but he felt nauseated at the knowledge that these photographs were probably taken without the subject's knowledge or consent.

On further study he saw that some shots seemed to be taken from a high angle, as if from a ceiling or high on a wall. How had they been obtained he wondered, resolving to investigate those intriguing cornices and ceiling mouldings he had thought so interesting in the bedrooms. Maybe the light fittings would have some answers. But first he had to talk his way out of this darkroom with its strangely twisted tenant, William Jones.

Then he noticed they key ring dangling from Jones' belt and knew it wasn't much use coming back for the telephone. And he shrugged mentally, who would he call? Who would be interested? No-one.

CHAPTER TEN

'THESE are very interesting photos Mr. Jones,' Quin enthused. 'Did you take all of them yourself?'

'Well, I develop and print all the still shots, most of which I've either taken myself or arranged to have them done. They're from a video camera with a motion detector. The same sort of thing they use for security surveillance. Some are photos I took from a different group of people, willing people.' Jones was warming to his subject as he put the glossies back on the wall. 'These ones I took last year. I think they even enjoyed it. I paid them so they couldn't complain.'

He indicated a series of shots of several women on their own. Beautiful women in very candid shots. Then he pointed to another group. 'These girls didn't know there was a video camera being activated. Wonderfully natural aren't they?' Jones was obviously very proud of them and saw nothing wrong in filming them unaware. 'A bit like the sixties isn't it. Let it all hang out.' He laughed as if he'd been the first person to use the phrase.

'It's amazing what you can do with an ordinary camera though. Take a look at this one. I used subdued lighting and a soft focus filter.'

Jones produced from a drawer a photograph of a thin older woman in a dark blue nightgown, fine gauzy material with spaghetti straps, her long light brown hair flowing over her shoulder. She was lying on a bed presumably asleep. Quin thought it looked strangely like Ms. Macklin but he couldn't be sure, she looked so different from her normally scowling appearance. 'Some people enjoy the ritual of being photographed for a portrait. They turn it into quite a ceremony.'

'I'm sure they do,' agreed Quin. 'Is there some reason for taking them?' 'I guess you could say we're talent spotting.' 'Oh? Why is that?'

'We need to see if our employees measure up.' Jones began to chuckle at his own humour. 'Measure up, get it? You know, sometimes I surprise myself. I never found much enjoyment in life before I met my present employer. I knew a lot of things about technical stuff but didn't know how to use it to the best advantage. Making money if you like. Now I do. And I find humour in many things these days where before I wouldn't have noticed the joke. I even find myself telling off colour stories without getting embarrassed. It's very liberating.'

'What are your employees measuring up for?' Playing along and laughing too, Quin had to ask even though he had a strong suspicion he already knew.

'Mr. Wilson, our employer, enjoys making movies Mr. Jameson. He has to make sure the people he employs are suitable for the roles he has in mind for them. Hence the talent spotting parade. It's only fair to give everyone a fair hearing.'

Jones sighed and took down a photo of a young blonde woman who was a stranger to Quin, saying, 'Take this one for instance. She's blonde, beautiful, has a lovely body. But there's something missing. It's something our Miss Hunter has in abundance. I think it's that quality of innocence that appeals to me. It's just a pity she's so young. I would have liked...but no, I probably wouldn't have had a chance with her. She's not interested in an old man like me. Anyway, it's out of my hands. Merton has her marked for the boss and one thing is certain, she won't be innocent for long. That will be such a pity but it's inevitable.'

'Do any of the people here know they're being photographed?' Quin ground his teeth to avoid the words that were bursting to be said in condemnation of both Merton and Jones and the whole setup.

'We like to get a video and hard copy before we select. It saves time and disappointments in the long run. So no, they don't know. And if they don't know they can't be unhappy when they aren't selected can they. It's only fair. Next week we'll be installing extra audio equipment in all the bedrooms as well as video cameras. At the moment they're just in the bathrooms and a few of the bedrooms. We'll get the whole show on the road, voices, action, the lot. Fantastic.'

'I really get a kick out of watching them you know.' His eyes gleamed. 'It's like looking into their minds and seeing all their naughty little secrets spread like a smorgasbord. You have no idea what people do when they think they're alone. Unbelievable.'

Jones shook his head as if he couldn't believe the nature of humanity. His voice became hushed, as if he thought he might be overheard. 'It's even better if you're in a city. Apartment buildings are perfect for watching. Everyone doing their own thing and thinking they're alone. They don't realise they're never alone. Always someone is watching and maybe planning an intrusion. Someone is always listening. Sometimes someone is watching the watchers as well and that makes it doubly interesting, especially in huge cities like Hong Kong or New York where people are living on top of each other like packed zoological specimens.'

'It sounds very interesting,' said Quin, thinking, what a creep you are Jones.

'Remind me some time to show you the new long range photographic equipment we have. It's state of the art. Very sophisticated. You can even see skin and hair in fine detail.'

'Thanks Mr. Jones. I'd love to see what you've got.'

Quin had never been into voyeurism but Jones brought a new enthusiasm to the habit. It seemed his hobby was not confined to this place but had been practised all over the world. He decided to milk Jones for as much information as he could because who knew when or if he'd get another chance and it might be useful. 'Why get amateurs for a job like this one? Why trick people into coming here who haven't a clue about acting or anything else connected with movies?'

'Let's be realistic Mr. Jameson. My employer is a man of infinitely creative taste. He has many diverse interests and hates to waste money. He refuses to pay when he can get something.

for nothing, or almost nothing.'

He laughed cynically. 'You can hardly blame him for that can you?' Jones looked smug, as if he'd drawn the most logical conclusion possible.

He went on, 'Good looking people cost a lot of money, especially when the work is unusual, and if he can get away with paying much less for a bunch of amateurs he's entitled to do it. Most actors wouldn't be caught dead in a dump like this. They like to be seen, get their pictures in the paper, their name in the credits of a movie shown at cinemas and all that. Perfect paparazzi fodder.

'He's also got a hold on you people in another way. It's isolated out here in the country. You can't get away even if you want to. All of you have lives you're running away from, especially you Jameson. You're such a big spender you ought to be grateful someone is willing to pay you.'

'I suppose you're right,' Quin wondered how Jones had acquired his particular variety of malformed logic. He knew he'd better get out of there before he said or did something to totally wreck his chances of escaping unscathed from this mess he had got himself into. 'I'd better get back to work now. Merton can be a slave driver when he wants something done. I can see you're busy so I'll talk to you later on.' Quin started to walk out of the room.

Jones said, 'What did you want to talk about Jameson? I might not be here later. I have to leave for a few days tomorrow and when I return Mr. Wilson will be with me and I'll be too busy.'

Quin thought quickly and said, 'I just wanted to know if I could borrow a bike from that storage shed near the garages. I'd like to get some exercise.'

Fear and anger warred on Jones' normally placid brow giving him the appearance of a man torn between opposing forces. 'How did you know there were bikes in there? Those buildings are off limits to everyone except appointed personnel. Stay away from them Jameson or I won't be responsible for what happens, alright.'

'Okay, okay.' Quin put his hands up placatingly. 'I just thought I'd ask. Someone was riding one of them the other day and parked it outside the shed. I thought it would be okay.'

'Just stay away from those buildings. Keep to the house or nearby. Remember, I'm not always here and Mr. Merton has a very bad temper. I wouldn't want to cross him in any way Jameson. Do I make myself clear?'

'Sure do,' said Quin, backing away and opening the door to the hall. 'I'll be sure and keep to the house Mr. Jones. Catch you later.'

He quickly slipped out the door in case Jones came to the belated conclusion that Quin had indeed seen into the sheds and that he knew what was in there. He'd broken into the sheds to take a closer look at the metal boxes a few days ago and found there were not just bicycles, there was the box of guns he had seen when he first arrived. The stencilled label read M60 - CAL 7.62MM GPMG. On further inspection Quin found they were military issue machine guns.

They were serious weapons intended for serious purposes although most still had a thick coating of black grease on them being still unused and probably having been stolen while on their way to the ARMY base at Townsville.

It was a very strange accompaniment to the restoration of an old homestead or even an X-rated film shoot. Something was not right in this place and he intended to be long gone before it erupted. And Sherry would be going with him whether she liked it or not.

Firewalking

The next day, during the break for lunch, Quin brought out his sketch pad and pencils. He took some sandwiches and went outside to sit under a large shady tree. Intending to sketch the house and grounds so he could study them later and form a plan for escape, he was so engrossed in his work that he didn't notice Walker standing behind him like a giant shadow until the shadow moved and growled, 'What the hell do you think you're doing Jameson?'

Luckily Quin had only just started and not made any written notations on the page as yet. He slipped into his persona of a spineless ineffectual artistic type and said, 'Oh, Mr. Walker. I'm just sketching the house. It's a great piece of historical architecture. I just love the way those towers have been built on the ends of the place. It's so romantic.'

Walker leant down and ripped the sketch book out of Quin's hand. 'If you know what's good for you, that's the last time you'll try drawing anything around here. Photo's and pictures are banned. Got it pretty boy?' Savagely ripping the sketch book in several pieces, he threw it down contemptuously then turned and walked away, leaving Quin feeling lucky he'd only ripped the book and not his head from his body.

That afternoon Quin watched as Jones climbed into a car and was driven away by Walker and another man. He was relieved Walker had gone because Sherry would be able to bring Scrappy out without the danger of Walker seeing him.

Walker had brutally told her the dog had crawled off into the bush and was probably dead by now when she asked him where he was. She'd been forced to ask so the guard wouldn't know the dog had been taken back by his owner.

Showing an acting ability to be admired Sherry had cried as though her heart would break. Walker had left the kitchen where he had given her the news, grinning with satisfaction that she had been suitably punished for her insolence towards him.

As soon as he'd gone she slipped away from the kitchen and told Quin what had happened. She knew Scrappy was bored and unhappy cooped up in the bedroom but that was better than having him disposed of like unwanted garbage.

Quin knew they should make their escape attempt within the next few days, before Wilson arrived. He decided to tell Sherry about the photographs lining the wall in Jones' darkroom.

He knew she would be shocked but felt he had no choice. If she refused to come away with him he would have to kidnap her and that would be awkward, especially with Scrappy to advertise what was going on.

How he was going to transport them was another worry. Could he steal a vehicle or should they take a couple of bikes and sneak away quietly? He was in flavor of the bikes since they would be forced to go at night and the sound of a car or jeep would broadcast their presence to everyone. An added bonus was the full moon that should shine their way.

Sherry was in the store room gathering ingredients when Quin found her. He checked that no-one was about before sliding in through the door and closing it firmly. They would at least have a modicum of privacy to talk. Scrappy was curled up asleep in a box on the floor. All he did when his favourite appeared was wag his tiny tale and shut his eyes once more in total trust. Quin began to talk about the things he had seen and heard.

'A wall full of photo's,' Sherry exclaimed. 'How exciting. What are they pictures of?' Having just explained that Jones' photos proved there was filming going on he felt he could leave out the content of the photos. Saying a little as possible was his own way of staying out of trouble but this tiny blonde with insatiable curiosity was having none of it.

'People.'

'What people Quin? Come on. Tell me. You've made me curious and I want to know. Who is in the photos? What are they doing?'

'It's just some of the staff who work here. No-one important. They're not doing anything special, just lying around.' Quin nearly choked on the lie as his inner eye recalled just how inventive those people were just lying around.

'That sounds fascinating. I'd like to take a look if I can.'

'No Sherry. I think it would be better if you stayed in your room. Just believe me when I say it's proof that something funny is going on around here and we should leave.'

'Look. I'm sick and tired of people making decisions for me. I'm all grown up Quin and even you can't tell me what to do. Now you can show me the photos or I'll sneak out tonight and have a look by myself. I know where Mr. Jones has his office and I'm real good at sneaking out. I've been doing it on and off for years.'

'It's too dangerous. You're crazy to do this. What if Walker or one of the other guards found you. They could do anything they liked to you and you wouldn't be able to stop them.'

Sherry shivered at the thought of Walker or his cronies catching her but, thinking of all the times in her life she'd backed down from a challenge, she decided to go ahead with her plans. After all, she'd got away from Ralph and a small thing like sneaking downstairs to look at pictures in an office could hardly be more paralysing than that. 'Sorry Quin. I'm going to do it. Come if you like but if not I'm going alone.'

She looked up into his gorgeous dark brown eyes and almost melted. It was like looking into an infinity of heated pleasure filled nights. Momentarily distracted, she blinked then smiled slowly. 'Come on. Give up. You might as well come too Quin. It'll eat away at you if you stay here. Besides, I need you.'

Quin was lost. She needed him. He'd seen himself reflected in her luminous grey eyes and seen the soft yearning she had been unable to hide.

He'd also seen the stubborn glint that had preceded the softness and having found out in previous encounters that she meant what she said, that she would do whatever she decided was right for her, he decided to give in, just for now.

'Alright. We'll do it your way, just this once. But you'll do as I say. No going off on your own. I can't protect you if we're separated can I?' He turned and picked up the huge box of potatoes she had been trying to lift when he came in and lugged them to the door. We'll talk later on tonight.'

As he left the kitchen and went carefully back to his work repainting the decorative centrepiece of a ceiling, Quin reflected that, however much he might prefer her not to see the photos, the content of them might shock her into realising that these people were into some very strange and dangerous activities and that she should bow to his superior knowledge and leave with him as soon as possible.

They sneaked out that night and, with the aid of Quin's torch, reached the darkroom and office on the ground floor. Quin produced a credit card and slid it up through the lock.

No sign of any guards led him to think the staff had relaxed slightly now that Jones was gone. Merton hadn't been seen much since they had begun working and was obviously busy on errands of his own.

Firewalking

Sherry swallowed nervously when she saw the darkroom for the first time, astonished at the variety of the photographs. She had never seen anything like it and her education in anatomy was completed in one swift glance around. Never had she thought to see such a blatant display of male and female flesh in one small area. Her innocence had taken a dramatic nose-dive and she blushed fiercely, stammering to Quin, 'I think I've seen enough Quin. I believe you now about the movies being shot here. Perhaps we'd better get away while we still can. I don't want to end up as someone's x-rated entertainment.'

Relieved she had taken heed of his warnings, Quin said, 'I'm sorry you had to see this Sherry but I think it's best to get out while we can. Don't worry though, you won't be forced to return to your Ralph Marley. He can't make you do anything you don't want to do.'

Sherry had been hoping he'd say they would stay together but when he didn't she replied sadly, 'You don't know Ralph. If he wants you to do something, you do it. He has a strange power over me, like he owns me or something. I fight against it but I always seem to go back and be a victim again.'

'Not this time Sherry,' asserted Quin, not knowing how he was going to help her and not in a position to promise help but determined to do so.

'You left him once. You can do whatever you want. Tell yourself he has no power over you, that you have the strength of break free of him and live your own life. I'll help you as much as I can, okay?'

'Okay.' She glanced again at the photographs as they left the room and saw the one of Marina. 'Look at that Quin. I think Marina wants to stay. She seems to like it here.' Then she saw tucked partly behind another photo something he clearly hadn't noticed. A photograph of herself, standing in her room dressed in tiny lace bikini panties and nothing else. She was looking out the window brushing her hair. It was a very revealing photograph in more ways than one.

'I wonder when he took that shot?' asked Quin, looking appreciatively over her shoulder. Sherry whipped it down from the wall and said, 'I don't know and I don't care. The nerve of that man, taking photos of me without asking. I'm going to have a few things to say to him, I can tell you!' Without another word she turned, spine stiff, and marched out of the room.

Quin grinned and followed her out, shutting the door carefully and turning out the light. He wished he could snaffle that picture for himself but she had such a tight grip on it, he feared he's never get hold of it before she ripped it up and threw it in the garbage.

In the outer office Quin noticed some filing cabinets. 'Hang on a minute Sherry, I reckon while we're on the job we ought to take a look at what's in there.'

'Could be some clue as to who these people are. Maybe even some paper evidence to indicate why we've been brought here.'

'I thought it was to take pictures of us and get us to make disgusting movies. Isn't that enough Quin?'

'Maybe that's not all there is to it. Anyway, I'm taking a look. You stand near the door and keep a look out. The guards aren't due for another half hour but you never know.' He turned to the cabinets and began to pick to lock with a thin spike attached to his pocket knife. Sherry turned to the door.

Well, thought Quin, what do you know? Photos of the people who came on the plane with us. He picked up a folder full of postcard size prints and negatives and found himself looking at his own image. The row of showers in the male bathroom had curtains for privacy but he was alone and the curtain was not pulled across the opening. Fury clouded his mind as he took in his state of undress.

He was standing under the spray of the shower with his face held up, his hands raised to push his long hair back from his forehead, eyes closed. The video camera must have been rigged at an angle to take in the whole of the shower but he couldn't think of where it could have been hidden. Maybe it was in the air vent on the wall over the hand basins. Of course, at the time he hadn't been looking but he would from now on. He'd check everything very carefully and then pull every camera apart piece by piece. And he'd enjoy every minute of the destruction.

He took the photo out and laid it on top of the filing cabinet then turned to look once again into the folder. Many of the shots were the same as his, singles, either in showers, bathrooms or bedrooms. Many of them showed how enjoyable many of the people found their life in the homestead as they paired off with other people, especially at night. Those intricately carved ceilings could harbour secrets thought Quin, and the light fittings. Maybe even the air vents in the bedrooms.

Then he found the photograph that nearly blew his mind. She was standing side on to the camera in front of a full length bathroom mirror. Her filmy nightgown was drifting over her body as a breeze caught it as well as the white nylon curtains on the window.

With the sunlight from the window filtering through it her small perfect body had a translucent glow which matched the dreamy expression on her beautiful face. Obviously unaware her privacy was being invaded, Sherry's eyes were half closed and unfocused, not seeing her own image in the mirror but looking inward, thinking about someone or something so pleasurable that it was unearthly.

She held a fine silver neck chain up to her mouth as if she was tasting it, a faint smile hovering on her lips. He recognised it as his own chain which he had accidentally left in the same bathroom.

Pulsating with frustrated desire, Quin quickly shoved all the photographs back inside the folder and picked it up plus another one he hadn't time to look into. Holding them in front of him, he hurried over to the door where Sherry was peering outside and waiting for him.

'Let's get out of here,' he said, not quite steadily, 'Those two guards will be around any minute now and we don't want to be caught here with the goods. They'd make mincemeat of us.'

Together, without another word, they sneaked back upstairs to their rooms. Quin left her at her door with a swift hard kiss and disappeared into his room, leaving her wondering what she had done to make him so angry. She cuddled up with Scrappy and surprisingly enough she slept.

Quin, next door, wasn't so fortunate. He lay wide awake with the folder of photographs under his pillow and every now and then took one particular one out. It burned all thoughts of sleep out of his brain leaving him hollow-eyed and wild-cat mean all the next day.

Trying to distract himself from his ill humour as he cleaned plaster and painted skirting boards, Quin took some time during a sandwich lunch in the privacy of his room to take a look at the other folder he had picked up. It contained some very interesting and enlightening photos.

Quin wondered how and why these pictures had been taken. Walker was portrayed as a man with delicately perverted tastes, quite alien to his normal aggressive persona. The man with him looked like Merton but Quin couldn't be sure because of the long wig the man wore. They were engaged in what could only be described as an impossible feat, for normal men that is.

Laughing to himself, Quin realised this must be Jones' version of insurance, if he ever dared to use it of course. Not a very safe road to travel at all. He could just imagine what Merton would do if he knew Jones had the photo. One thing for sure, Jones wouldn't have very long to make his confession. He would be exterminated like the strange little bug he was imitating, the dung beetle.

In the early hours of the following morning Quin made an inspection of the bathrooms. He took his pocket knife and carefully pried suspicious looking mouldings apart, carefully feeling for rough edges and gaps with his fingers. He looked behind light fittings on the ceiling and took the covers off air vents

What he found were spaces where video cameras could have been placed and in one instance a movement sensitive camera itself, still and waiting for the morning rush of showers. He left the equipment as it was, knowing that he would soon be gone and not ready to advertise that someone was aware of their game.

Early the following afternoon a helicopter circled overhead landing in the open area at the side of the house. At the propeller blades slowed some of the guards came out and unloaded some boxes. They seemed to be keeping the area secure.

Several business clad men and women climbed out of it and followed a tall immaculately suited fair-haired man of about age forty onto the back verandah and into the house. Jones and Walker had arrived back in a car a while before and came out to meet the guests.

The helicopter rested silently as the pilot finished checking his equipment and then also went inside. Quin sensed the tall fair man was Wilson, aka the boss, and wondered why they had returned earlier than Jones had said. He waited for something to happen and was perversely disappointed when it didn't.

Quin spent that afternoon and the next couple of days painting the walls of the room which contained the secret compartment and Sherry worked hard cooking meals for her usual crowd plus extra fancy food for Mr. Wilson and his guests. Crates of gourmet delicacies, vegetables and fresh meat had been brought in by helicopter and stored in huge refrigerators.

Sherry had spent nearly two hours unpacking the goods as well as preparing the meals and was exhausted. Scrappy was once again confined to barracks as Walker prowled the house and grounds like a feral cat.

Quin spoke to her quietly in the corridor outside the dining room after lunch on the third day, asking if she'd heard anything about the guests and why they were there. She looked around nervously saying, 'Quin, Mr. Jones asked me to serve dinner to Mr. Wilson and some of his guests in the small dining room tonight. Me, not Julie who usually does it.'

'You can't go. Tell him you're sick or something.... anything! You can't go!'

'I don't have a choice. If I don't turn up he'll come and get me.'

'Send Marina. She'll jump at the chance to make time with Wilson.' 'I can't do that either. Jones asked for me.'

'I don't like it Sherry. Why would he ask for you specifically? What's his game?'

'I've no idea but I have to go.' Seeing the worried look on his face, she said, 'Don't worry about me Quin. I'm a big girl. I can take care of myself?'

'You're not that big. Those people are sharks. And I'd rather take care of you myself.' The glow in his eyes told her how he felt without words.

'Quin, you say the most incredible things, especially when I can't do anything about it.'

'Be careful Sherry. I'll wait here until you come back but it had better be within thirty minutes or I'm coming to get you whether you like it or not.' Quin's dark blue eyes flashed with a fierce desire to protect her, his mouth a hard line of determination.

'You mustn't do that. They'll realise you suspect them and it could provoke them into something dangerous. Better to wait and see what they're going to do.' She stood on tiptoes and gave him a hurried kiss before disappearing into the kitchen. It all he could do to stop himself following her and dragging her upstairs where they would explore all the possibilities of what she could do for him.

Reluctantly, Quin stayed out of the way that evening when Sherry took a tray into the small dining room. Watching from under the stairs as she knocked on the door, his large hands bunched into tension filled fists. He wanted to be ready in case something happened, in case she called out or needed him in a hurry.

Feeling felt beads of sweat break out on his dark brow as he waited in the humid alcove, he impatiently wiped them away. It was going to be hell for him to wait the half hour but he forced himself to think of other things, such as how they were going to escape from this place.

As far as he could tell, the guards who patrolled the outside carried weapons. They strolled about casually as if they were workers just like the rest of the men. He hadn't seen them paint or do any of the other repair work being done.

He'd seen them watching him and knew they were wary of him. He supposed it was because of his size and, for the first time, he thanked God he'd chosen to take work as a labourer to earn extra income to pay for university fees instead of a cushy job loading shelves in a supermarket as most of his friends had done. He'd kept his insurance investment intact plus the back-breaking work in a road gang when he was eighteen had built up his muscles and stamina. He'd never lost that strength having kept up hard physical exercise in a gym or jogging even when he began his sign writing and art supply business.

Even his landscape painting had helped him to stay fit because the scenery he wanted to paint was inaccessible by road and he had to climb for it. The mountains were his playground and he loved the sheer ruggedness of it and the incredible unearthly colours which radiated from rock walls in the sunlight at different times of day. Thinking about what he would do when he was able to take Sherry away took up the half hour he waited. Then he looked at his watch and counted the minutes, deciding to give her a little more time.

After cooling his jets for an hour, Quin was ready to charge into the room and take on anyone who would try to stop him. He took deep breaths and tried to calm himself down, realising how stupid it would be to attack the people who held all the cards.

They had strength of numbers and probably weapons in the room. He decided to wait five more minutes and then knock on the door and ask for Sherry politely, saying she was wanted in the kitchen for something. It was the hardest and most frustrating decision of his life and he would have rather chewed nails.

Five minutes passed. He walked up to the door and knocked gently but firmly, held back from smashing the door in by an indomitable strength of will. He was very controlled even when door opened and Merton gave him a suspicious look before asking what he wanted.

Asking if he could speak to Sherry, he looked past Merton's immaculately dinner suited figure into the room and saw a large table laid with a white cloth and silver cutlery. Plates with left over food sat neglected while red candles blazed amid used wine glasses and bottles. Over-flowing ash trays polluted the atmosphere with acrid smoke. Taped music played softly in the background. Two other men in black dinner suits and three young women in colourful evening dress lounged on chairs but there was no sign of Sherry or any guards. Merton tried to shove the door shut in Quin's face saying, 'She's not here Jameson, so take off.'

Quin's warlike side erupted then with all the passion of his untamed and savage ancestors. The man had no time to react as the door slammed open again. He bounced away from it and sprawled on his back on the floor, a howl of pain bursting forth as he banged his head on the leg of a chair.

'Where is she?' Quin demanded, hauling him up from the floor by the shirt front and shaking him fiercely. The others in the room stood up suddenly, backing off, their faces mirroring their fear and incomprehension as Merton struggled unsuccessfully to free himself from Quin's hold. One woman started shrieking like a demented galah.

Gasping as his collar was twisted, Merton croaked, 'She's gone.'

'Where?' Quin's dark eyes glared into Merton's face, daring him to lie.

'Upstairs.' This short answer earned him another shake. 'With the boss,' he continued.

'Where upstairs?'

'How the bloody hell should I know,' the man snarled as Quin eased up his grip. The hard hands twisted again. Quin said gently, 'I never did have a lot of patience.'

The answer came in a rush, 'The tower. They've gone to the north tower.' He landed on the floor again as he was dropped, the breath forced from his body.

Gasping for air as he climbed to his feet, Merton's bloodshot eyes drilled into Quin's back with hate as Quin left the room and took the stairs two at a time. The other people in the room stood back, shaking their heads, obviously grateful he hadn't turned on them.

Merton climbed to his feet and rasped, 'Why didn't you morons help me? That bastard nearly choked me to death. Shut up Cynthia. Stop that bloody stupid noise. Anyone would think it was you he strangled.' The woman gasped and fell silent, nervously pouring herself a drink. Merton didn't wait for a reply but keyed in a code on a hand held receiver. 'Walker! Get in here! Immediately. We have a situation!' He straightened his tie, smoothed back his hair and lit a cigarette with a shaking hand. The other people in the room stood in stunned silence.

CHAPTER ELEVEN

As Quin pounded up the stairs, scrunching the threadbare carpet with his boots, all he could think about was Sherry, that sweet innocent girl who had come into his empty existence like a shower of pure life-giving rain. She had tempted him with her unconscious sensuality and in her innocence had made him want her past her own understanding. She needed him, and his warrior spirit, which had been slowly drained by the problems besetting his life, had been lifted up. In needing her as well, he had been given the precious gift of hope.

How could I have let this happen, he berated himself mercilessly as he climbed two steps at a time to the top floor? She was counting on me to protect her and I let her be taken away by a pervert who makes porno flicks, a man whose whole operation stinks of corruption.

I can't believe I let this happen. The man has hand grenades in his shed for goodness sake. I saw the damn things, I should have done something sooner. I'd better get her out of here. Any way I can, as fast as I can. He stopped thinking then as he approached the top of the stairs and, soft footed, sliced his way along to the doorway of the east tower.

The door leading to the tower was unlocked. He stopped and listened for a moment and when he heard nothing, he entered the doorway and went silently up the narrow stairs, halting just before the entrance to the tower room. Peering around the door frame Quin saw that the hexagonal room was furnished with two long couches, coffee tables, a bar and liquor cabinet, plus a giant television screen. Maroon velvet curtains were drawn closed on the windows facing the sea. One candle flickered in a corner of the room. There were no other lights.

Two people sat on one of the couches. Quin could not see who they were in the darkness but knew it had to be Sherry and Mr. Wilson the mysterious 'Boss' Merton and Jones always referred to in hushed tones as if he was some kind of deity. Quin would have bet anything at all that Wilson wasn't his real name. He had to be the tall fair haired man who alighted from the helicopter like a prince overseeing his hunting lodge, his minions scurrying to do his bidding.

The screen was alight with movement and sound, a couple making love in an exotic bedroom cavorted and writhed across the screen, crying out their pleasure with animalistic groans and soft screams.

Quin was transfixed for a moment, then turned his attention to the couple on the couch whose shadowed figures were silhouetted by faint candle-light. The man leant over the woman and peeled her blouse off over her head. He started to kiss her and the woman linked her arms around his neck, kissing him back and making the same guttural sounds as the woman on the screen.

She was obviously enjoying what he was doing to her thought Quin savagely. How could she do that he wondered, bile rising in his throat, his Sherry, a young inexperienced girl playing up to a man she'd only just met. But maybe Quin was the fool and she was a gifted actress who got her jollies from duping people. Maybe she knew exactly what she was doing and had done all along.

Pain shattered his heart, preventing him from breaking into what was obviously a mutually satisfying arrangement. As Quin walked softly back down the stairs, he was confused and heartsick at what he had seen. He was in love with her and she was in the process of giving herself to another man, one who was going to use her for his own ends. Or maybe she was the one doing the using. Who could tell? Was he so blind he hadn't seen the truth of her deception?

When Quin reached the second floor he opened the door and stepped out into the corridor. He was so overwhelmed by what he had seen that his usual instincts for danger were absent.

Instantly he was surrounded by armed guards and escorted downstairs. Walker seemed to take great pleasure in shoving him so hard he fell against the stair-rail several times and had to pick himself up off the floor at the bottom of the stairs.

He silently wished for the opportunity to make Walker pay for what he had done to Sherry and Scrappy as well as himself. Just because she had betrayed him didn't mean he wished her harm. All he really wanted to do was love her.

Merton was alone in the dining room and smiling grimly as Quin was escorted roughly into his presence. 'So, Mr. Jameson. How nice of you to visit us again. We have some things to discuss wouldn't you say?' Merton had straightened his dinner suit and dispensed with his elegantly dressed companions but still retained a flush of anger on his lined face. His voice was hoarse and his thin mouth twitched. A purplish lump had formed on his forehead.

'Get on with it Merton,' snarled Quin, wondering what was coming next. For sure it wouldn't be pleasant if all he'd heard about Merton from some of the workers were true. Mr. boss man Merton had a whole bunch of bad habits.

'Certainly. You realise I cannot have people attacking me like you did. That was very foolish of you. It sets a bad example to the rest of the staff. I can see you're rather an impulsive man and that you rather fancy that delectable Miss Hunter. Otherwise why would you come after her like you did?'

Quin made no reply and Merton went on, 'Nothing to add to that Mr. Jameson? Fine. I rather fancy her myself so I understand what you're going through. I, of course, am able to have her whereas you are not. A fact which I find vastly amusing. What's to be done with you is another matter. I'm afraid I can't allow you to leave here. You've caused us a great deal of inconvenience by interfering in matters that are not your concern. The girl is here to do a job and nothing you do or say will alter that fact.'

'You people are vultures, preying on young innocent girls.' Quin wanted to take his tormentor apart piece by piece. 'Why don't you find experienced women to work for you. At least they'd know what they're getting into.'

'So you know about our little film making project do you? I'm sorry about that. It gives me a double reason to keep you here. Don't worry, we're not usually violent people, at least,' he smiled reminiscently, 'not all the time and not outside our films. We prefer more subtle methods of persuasion.'

'What are you going to do then? Keep me here forever?'

'If you behave yourself, you will be freed when we're finished with this particular project. We only stay in one place for a year or so then move on. The building renovations will be completed and the place sold, possibly as a hotel. The paintings and sculptures also. This once so respectable house will be returned to whence it came and none shall be the wiser. It will be as pure as a new born lamb. The employees contracts will be terminated and they will be free to go. However, there are quite a few months to go before that will happen.'

'What am I supposed to do all that time. Stay in my room like a good little boy?'

'No need to be sarcastic Mr. Jameson. There is an alternative to staying in your room.'

'What's that?'

'Making movies. Willingly of course. We could use someone of your height and dark looks. One of our scripts calls for an Indian warrior who steals a beautiful white girl from her parents and takes her back to his village. You can imagine what happens then can't you? Great script!'

'No way. You're just a sleaze Merton.'

'Not a sleaze Mr. Jameson. Just eminently practical. My employer pays me very handsomely for what I do. Just think, I might even pair you up with the little blonde in another movie I have in mind. How would you like that eh? She'd look fantastic in a bit of black leather and chained to a wall.'

'So what about this great Boss you keep prattling on about. Is it that guy upstairs? Who is he really?' Quin ignored the taunting reference to Sherry with great difficulty. He knew he had to keep calm and cool to regain control over the situation he'd found himself in.

'His name is Mr. Wilson as I think you know already. At least that's the name he uses in this country. He can be a merciless opponent so I urge you to co-operate with him.'

' What will happen if I don't?'

'That's another story. While I abhor unnecessary violence I'm afraid Mr. Wilson has no conscience at all. He has his own methods of obtaining the co-operation of his employees. Mr. Walker will attest to that and he does so enjoy his work. You've seen Mr. Walker in action haven't you. He likes to make an impression.'

'What does that mean Merton? What kind of methods does Wilson use?'

'Well might you ask. Mr. Wilson doesn't know about your little effort tonight as yet. He's too busy with your pretty little blonde girlfriend to pay us any attention. If you participate fully in our film,' Merton bared his teeth in a cruel smile, 'by that I mean give the job everything you've got without making trouble for us...If you participate enthusiastically, I'll make sure he doesn't hear about your little rebellion. Miss Hunter will be saved a lot of anguish and pain too if he doesn't find out. Otherwise, he might believe you and she are in league with each other and he's a man who finds it very hard to trust, or forgive. When he finds a person doesn't measure up to his requirements, well...' Merton shrugged his thin shoulders, 'I wouldn't want to be that person. I hope you understand?'

Fear for Sherry, even though she'd betrayed him, raged fiercely in Quin's heart and mind.

He couldn't deny he was furious as well as tormented by what she had done but if he refused to make the film they would both be at the mercy of this bunch of sadists.

Quin had no illusions as to the true nature of a man like that. He would be ruthless in the extreme and likely both he and Sherry would be disposed of in a very short time and as unpleasant a manner that could be envisaged.

'Alright,' he found himself saying. 'I'll do what you want. Leave Sherry alone and I'll make your damn movie.'

'Very good Mr. Jameson. But just as a safeguard, I'll have to keep you locked in your room when you aren't working.'

'Look I'll give you my word, I won't make trouble.'

'I'm afraid that won't make any difference. You see, I don't trust anybody, ever. Not even myself. I, more than most people, know how easy emotions take over a person. I've seen people persuaded to do things they would never have done if their emotions weren't raging out of control.'

'By emotions I suppose you mean sex?'

'It's the same thing in my opinion.'

'Most people have something in them to make them human but you seem to have missed out,' Quin taunted his opponent. 'It's obvious you've never been in love.'

'No. And I don't intend to be. It only leads to financial ruin as far as I can see.'

'I suppose there's no use appealing to your better nature Merton?' Quin tried one last time to find a way out of such a distasteful career change.

'I don't have a better nature. This is as good as it gets. You should be thankful Jameson. For a while I contemplated a far different fate for you, especially after you attacked me tonight.' Merton pointedly rubbed the bump on his head. 'Pain makes me do things I usually regret.'

'You're a low life Merton. You deserve everything that's coming to you.'

'Very likely. Unfortunately for you though, I'm in charge and what I say goes. Now head off back to your room before I change my mind about having Mr. Walker teach you some manners. Tomorrow morning I'll expect you to be ready to begin your new occupation. With enthusiasm.'

'Are you going to tell me what I have to do in this skin flick?'

'You'll find out. Don't bother to dress up though. It won't be necessary.' Merton was still laughing hoarsely as Quin left and was roughly escorted up to his room by a granite faced guard. Fortunately for Quin, Walker stayed behind with Merton. He didn't fancy getting the stuffing kicked out of him again. Once a night was enough. His door was locked after the guard had checked the connecting door to Sherry's room. It was already locked and the key was nowhere to be seen. Quin just sat on his bed and stared at that closed door, his immediate senses numb, his rage too fierce to contemplate, his pain too deep to fully comprehend.

It was 2 am. Quin checked the time on his luminous watch face then turned the light on, wondering what had disturbed him. He'd finally dragged his clothes off and fallen into bed after the traumatic events of the evening and, against all odds, had lapsed into sleep immediately. Then he realised what had woken him. He heard a whine from next door. Scrappy he thought, confused by his whirling emotions. That must mean Sherry was back in her room.

Did he want to see Sherry or not? He didn't know. She'd been with that bastard for four hours at least. What had they been doing all this time? As if he didn't know. His heart burned anew as he remembered seeing her in that man's arms, being undressed and uttering cries of passion.

How could she? he asked himself again. Why didn't she wait for him to help her escape? He'd told her he would. And if she had wanted something more physical she only had to ask. She must have known he wanted her. He would have willingly given her everything he had and more.

Then he heard it. The faint sound of a tortured groan then silence. Scrappy whined again and suddenly it was too much for Quin. No matter what she'd done he had to go to her. Then he remembered, the key wasn't in the lock and he was locked in. What could he do?

Climbing out of bed, he dragged on his jeans and knocked gently on the door between the two rooms. Half a minute later he heard the key grate in the lock. The door opened to reveal a dishevelled Sherry, yawning tiredly as she tried unsuccessfully to hold the front of her thin robe together.

'Quin, what is it? What are you doing?'

'You sounded upset Sherry. No matter what you've done I had to see if I could help.' He looked into her sleepy face and smiled gently. She was like a child now, clinging to the door frame and rubbing her bare feet together, her long blonde hair tangled over her brow. How could she be expected to know what people like Wilson got up to? He must have been mistaken about her willing cries in the tower room. Maybe she had gone to him unwillingly and they were really cries for help. That thought made him scowl furiously. That bastard he thought with primitive determination, I'll feed him to the sharks one piece at a time.

'I was asleep and you woke me up,' said Sherry. 'What are you so savage about Quin? You look as if you'd like to kill someone, not me I hope.'

Sherry's attempt at a smile was pathetic. Quin grated, 'What happened tonight Sherry? Why did you go upstairs with Wilson. Didn't you know what he would do?'

'How did you know I met Mr. Wilson? Did you see me go upstairs Quin? Were you watching me?'

'Of course I was bloody well watching you. At least, I was watching out for you. I told you I would. I didn't see you leave though did I? Must have been easy for him to spirit you out through the other door, snake bellied mongrel that he is.'

'Calm down Quin. We left by the other door because it's more convenient to the kitchens.'

'That's rich. The man takes you up to his private viewing room to seduce you but stops by the kitchens on the way in case you'll need a snack afterwards.' Quin was rapidly developing a headache and his temper was close to boiling point.

'What are you talking about? What private viewing room?' She looked confused for a moment then said, 'Oh, you mean the tower room. Yes, I remember, there was a giant TV.'

Quin hardly heard what she said, his fury was so great. 'You mean you didn't pay much attention to the TV? It was showing the movie of the week. One of his own no doubt. Did you go with him willingly? Did you say yes to everything he asked of you Sherry? Did you?' He forced himself not to grab her and shake the answers out of her.

'Of course I went willingly. I wanted to get....'

She was cut off in mid sentence as Quin snarled, 'What the hell did you do it for? I'd made plans to get us out of here. You knew what the situation was. All you had to do was wait for me.'

'All I was going to say was I wanted to get...'

'What? Wanted to get what Sherry? Some experience with a man? I was ready to do that for you. All you had to do was ask.' He glared at her with pain in his eyes. 'Maybe you wanted some wine to drink to your future as an X-rated movie queen, or maybe you think he wants to marry you or something. Come out of the clouds girl. The man wanted to use you and you allowed him to do it. I can't believe you let him make love to you like that. I wanted to kill the both of you, on the spot.' He began to stride around the small space, breathing harshly with fury. Scrappy whimpered on the bed, unused to this strangely furious man inhabiting his favourite's body. 'If you wanted a man that badly I was here. I was right next door.'

'I didn't...'

'Didn't what? Want a man? Enjoy it? I'm surprised,' he jeered, looking down into her white face, 'The man's a professional. He's had a lot of practice making sex enjoyable, on the screen that is. How he does in real life could be another matter entirely.'

'I didn't do it Quin.'

Sherry had spoken quietly but Quin heard every word. 'Don't bother to lie to me Sherry. I know you did. I saw you.' His anger was fading as he came to the conclusion that no matter what she did he would still want her. He wanted her now, even when she'd just been with another man.

'Listen to me Quin Jameson. And listen good! I did not do anything with Mr. Wilson. Did you hear me? I did not have sex. I didn't even kiss the man let alone let him put his hands on me.'

'You didn't? Then who was it I saw in the tower room?'

'It was probably Marina? You know, the prospective movie queen.'

'Maybe you'd better tell me what really happened?' Quin, rapidly cooling down, was beginning to realise his behaviour had been way out of line and the only excuse he could give was blind jealousy. That ugly green monster had completely taken over his reasoning abilities to the detriment of the only woman he'd ever loved. He sat down on her bed and, cradling Scrappy in his arms, said gruffly, 'Start talking. It's three in the morning and I've got to start a new job tomorrow.'

'Well, as you know, I served the dinner party their meal. When I'd finished Merton introduced me to Mr. Wilson. They insisted I sit down and eat with them. I think Merton hoped his boss would like me enough to use me in a movie. He kept saying things like 'she's very photogenic', 'good skin' and 'that hair would show up well on camera'.'

'I can see that you'd look absolutely beautiful Sherry. I'm not surprised they want you.'

'I am. I'm not an actor Quin. I haven't any ambition to be one either.'

'They don't want actors. They want bodies and faces that look good. They can be the puppet masters and all you have to do is lie back, stand on your head or whatever. You just do exactly what you're told.'

'I'm not standing on my head for anybody. I'd get vertigo and throw up. Then they'd be sorry.' Sherry turned determined eyes upon Quin.

'It's just a figure of speech,' he said. 'I mean you'd co-operate with them.'

'Yeah. Well the only way I'd cooperate with them would be if I was unconscious. Anyway, they talked about movies for a while and I had a drink of wine. That woman, Cynthia, is such a snob. She thinks she owns the world and that every man in it should worship at her feet.'

'Forget about her. She has no control over anything here. She's just another puppet for Wilson to use and discard when he's done. You know you shouldn't have taken a drink from them Sherry. They could have drugged it.'

'Well they didn't. You're so suspicious Quin. You don't trust anybody.'

'No, I don't. Especially ruthless men like Merton and Wilson. Jones can be manipulated but I still wouldn't trust him. Walker I'd classify as plain mean and dangerous. I wouldn't deal with him at all.'

Sherry yawned and rubbed her eyes. 'I'm tired Quin. Let me finish the story and then you can go back to your own bed.'

He didn't like the sound of that, he'd rather stay in hers. He said abruptly, 'Yeah, sure. Just get on with it.'

Sherry looked at him suspiciously but continued, 'Mr. Wilson asked if I would take some food upstairs to the tower room. He told me he'd help me by carrying the tray of food if I would take the wine and some glasses.'

'I'll bet he did.'

'Quin. Stop it. The man was a gentleman. He'd done nothing to suggest I was his intended playmate for the night.'

'Alright. Go on.' Quin gritted his teeth against the reply that hovered on his tongue.

'I went through to the kitchen via the other door because he held it open for me. I filled a tray with snacks, you know the sort of thing, crackers and caviar, and then I went upstairs with him. All he did on the way up was ask me more questions about myself. I didn't tell him much because there's nothing much to say without going into boring details about mining and living in the country. I didn't want to mention Ralph.'

'What happened then?' Quin's lips tightened. He felt sure Sherry was leaving something out, something she had felt or that Wilson had done.

'When we reached the tower room he put the tray down and turned the light on.' Sherry looked uncertain for a moment and Quin thought, here it comes, the crunch. What had really happened in that room? He waited and then she said in a rush, 'I don't really know what would have happened next if Marina hadn't arrived on the scene. She sort of flowed into the room in a low cut sleeveless silk top and a pair of transparent harem pants. I didn't know where to look Quin. I haven't seen anyone wear clothes like that before. Wilson was looking at her and I could swear his mouth was watering.'

Quin knew how Wilson had felt only he was thinking of how Sherry looked with her filmy night dress peeping out from behind her robe. He put those lustful thoughts aside with great difficulty and said hoarsely, 'What did you do then?'

'I took myself out of there while I had the chance. Marina gave me a look that said I'd missed out, tough luck for me, but Wilson hardly noticed me leave. They didn't say a word after that, just kept looking at each other like ravenous dogs.'

'Thank God for Marina,' exclaimed Quin. 'That girl has beautiful timing.'

'Beautiful everything if you ask me,' said Sherry glumly. 'I'd like to have her looks. I'll bet she makes a fabulous movie star and makes stacks of money doing it too.'

'She will indeed. But you won't.' Quin looked sternly at Sherry.

'Why not?' Sherry bristled with her newfound independence. 'I reckon I could look almost as good as her, with a bit of that fancy eye make-up.'

'You'd look better no matter what you did to yourself. And you don't need loads of make-up. I like you just the way you were born. Natural and beautiful.'

Sherry blushed at his praise, not really believing in her own attraction but hoping he would go on saying such wonderful things to her. She said breathlessly, 'That won't help us get out of here though Quin. I think Wilson will play games with Marina and use her but he'd still like to put me in a movie as well. He as good as said so while we were talking.'

'Then we're getting out of here tonight. No more dragging our feet. It's time to move.'

'It's almost morning. How can we do this without getting caught?'

'We'll have to be extra careful. Anyway, if we don't take off now while we can, yours truly will be starring alongside you in a film and it won't be the kind of movie your grandmother would go to see.'

'What do you mean Quin? Why will you be in it?'

'When you didn't come back to the kitchen through the hall, I confronted Merton in the dining room. I wasn't very patient with him and he didn't appreciate the methods I used to get information. After I tracked you down, as I thought, upstairs with Wilson, Merton sent his thugs to bring me to him.'

'What happened Quin? What did he do to you?'

'He threatened me, and you as well. Said if I didn't co-operate and participate in his skin flick willingly, with enthusiasm, he'd give us both over to Wilson. I'd no intention of dragging you into this but Merton said Wilson was ruthless and had no conscience. He'd do anything, including dispose of people, to get his own way. Naturally I agreed to do the movie, hoping I'd be able to get us away before filming began.'

Sherry looked at his smooth bare chest and hard muscles dreamily, 'I think you'd make a wonderful movie star.' Watching his beautiful mouth curve as his deep voice curled around her nerve endings, she licked her lips, unconsciously provocative, needing his touch.

Quin groaned low in his throat as he looked back at her. 'Thanks for the compliment honey but I think I remember telling you I prefer to do my lovemaking in private.'

'So do I. Or, at least I would, will....oh, you know what I mean.' Sherry turned slightly so he couldn't see the scarlet colour on her face but the shade was also in her voice.

He grinned. 'I know what you mean. And I can say you will for sure. But only with me.' 'Yes Quin. Only with you.' Scrappy began to whine as he was crushed between them. Their mouths meeting for a moment in mutual promise. Sherry looked ruefully downward at the small terrier and smiled. 'It's okay Scrap. You too.'

'Hang on,' laughed Quin, 'I'm not into threesomes. I think we'll leave that to Marina and the rest of them. For now we'd better grab whatever we can carry and hit the road. If we're lucky and the guards aren't about, we can steal a couple of bikes and be out of here before dawn.'

Quin and Sherry were within five steps of the second floor when the stairs creaked. He cursed silently as the sound echoed through the deserted hallway. It was dark except for a small globe at the head of the stairs which shed minimal light in the upstairs corridor and no illumination at all at the foot of the stairs. Both of them stopped still and waited for a response to the noise they had created.

After a few moments when nothing happened they moved on through the long hallway towards the back of the building where the back stairs were situated. Quin grasped Sherry's hand to guide her and she followed him blindly, trustingly, through the darkness, their footsteps muffled by the carpet.

Scrappy was firmly enclosed in Quin's pack, right next to the slim folder of photographs and other evidence, including videos, he'd filched from Jones' private office and darkroom. He'd tried to use the telephone but found it needed a key so he gave up on phoning for help. When it came down to it though, who could he call? There was no-one.

A rumble of voices began, drifting closer, becoming more distinct. One was heard to say, 'I think I heard something on the stairs Mack. I'll have a look around then I'll come back for another round. Poker's my game you know and this time I'm gonna rub your nose in it.'

Another voice said, 'Sure Jack. Every day. Go on then, check on the mice. Place is probably over-run with the little rodents. Don't forget to take your big gun.' Laughter sounded from the direction of the kitchens as booted feet could be heard walking through the tiled walkway from the kitchen wing to the main entrance hall.

'I think it's too chancy to try to get out through the kitchens Sherry,' whispered Quin as they stood in a dark alcove at the end of the second floor.

'I'm scared. What if they catch us Quin? They've got guns. Do you think they'd use them on us?'

'I hate to say it but yes, I think they would. Especially Walker. Between the two of us we've really ticked him off. I don't like to ask it of you honey, but will you try the secret escape route I showed you the other day?' She swallowed nervously, her eyes wide with dread.

'I promise I'll be there with you. I really believe it's our only chance. If they don't see us go we might have some hope of getting a fair distance before they realise we aren't in our rooms and start looking for us.'

Trust was important thought Sherry, dazed at how much she believed in this man. He had showed himself a man of honour as well as a man who could take charge and get the job done. She knew it was time to return just a little of the caring support he had shown to her during their stay in this fancy prison.

Not counted was his reaction to what he thought was her betrayal with Wilson. Anybody would have believed the same. She smiled at him with all the confidence she could dredge up and asked, 'You promise you won't leave me?'

He kissed her gently. His words came from deep within, an unequivocal pledge to protect her no matter what. 'I won't leave you my love. I'll never leave you again, I promise.'

Sherry's eyes shone with complete trust. 'Then let's go Quin. It'll be daylight soon and we haven't a moment to waste.' He smiled and took her hand, her small fingers curling around his large ones, the heat from the connection sealing their bond of love and commitment to each other.

CHAPTER TWELVE

Quin and Sherry sped on silent feet past empty rooms, moonlight splashing through uncurtained windows. The room with the secret door waited like a beast of prey ready to devour the frightened girl whose senses were heightened by fear.

Her skin took on a clammy sheen and her breathing quickened as she battled to contain her revulsion of small, dark spaces. Knowing it was just a set of walls with floor and ceiling made no difference. Some inner primordial directive claimed her and moulded her into a being controlled by fear.

Quin put his pack with Scrappy inside on his back and took her in his strong arms. He held her tight, whispering sweet words of reassurance in her ear as he helped her adjust her back-pack, comforting her until she calmed and allowed him to lead her inside the dark chamber. He stooped down onto his hands and knees and crawled ahead slowly, urging Sherry along behind him with gentle words. Even Scrappy seemed to sense the need for quiet.

From the moment of entering the darkness she blanked out her churning emotions and mind locked-with Quin, moving as one, crawling behind him, standing up and stepping where he stepped, crouching where he crouched, until they reached the ladder going down.

Fortunately, after they managed to stand up, the small torch he carried lit the way, dispelling most of her demons, and they were able to climb down the steps with confidence. 'I've been in here before Sherry,' Quin told her before they climbed down to the floor below. 'There's an entrance to the cellar down here. It's quite safe.'

The trap door opening into the cellar was closed. He said, 'I'm going to turn the torch off just in case someone's down there. I hope you don't mind. It's safer this way.'

Still in thrall to Quin's magnetism and the way his touch helped her control her fear, she nodded her head and whispered, 'I don't mind. I trust you Quin.'

'That's my girl.' He smiled to himself as he extinguished the light. Her trust was more precious than anything he'd ever had in his life. He only hoped he could prove worthy of it as he pulled the trap door open slightly to make sure no-one was waiting on the other side.

All was dark and silent so Quin hauled on the heavy wooden flap, pulling it open all the way. Unfortunately, the scraping sound of rusty hinges flowed into the silence like a freight train on disused tracks.

They sat still and waited for a few minutes more before moving on, breathless with fear and excitement, adrenaline charging along their veins in case they had been heard Then, with Quin leading the way, they slipped silently through the hole in the floor and down the ladder.

As they reached solid ground, they sank out of sight behind some wooden packing crates having heard one of the guards ambling along the corridor upstairs. The ground floor cellar door on the other side of the room had been left open and vivid torch light swished through the opening, across the steps and down to the floor like a searchlight moving from side to side.

The two fugitives crouched still for a moment, listening, hearts throbbing to a strangely slow hypnotic beat, Quin keeping Scrappy quiet with a gentle hand over his nose. It took quite a few moments before their eyes adjusted to the darkness.

They were very careful where they put their feet in case they tripped over the stacks of junk furniture and boxes of household goods. One of the boxes contained potatoes and another cooking apples. They each scooped up half a dozen of the green fruit and put them in their packs, both knowing it was going to be a long time before they would be able to get a meal.

'Where are we going?' whispered Sherry nervously.

'I've been doing a little private investigation. There's a passageway to the outside down in this cellar. It opens onto the beach. Amazing. These English settlers really went for it when putting down roots. This is most likely a copy of the cellar in their house back home. Should be good in the cyclone season.'

'It's dark Quin. I don't think I can handle being down here.' Sherry was shaking and nauseous, her voice was a thin thread of sound.

Quin took her damp hand gently. 'It'll be okay honey. I'll be with you just like before. You can trust me.' He turned on his small torch and shadowed it with his hand.

'I know that.' She looked up into his eyes in the dim light. 'Scrappy trusts you too. I've never seen him take so well to anyone before. It's wonderful. Anyone would think he was your dog and not mine. Traitorous hound.'

'Yes, well I'm kind of attached to the little guy too.' He stroked Scrappy's head and received a lick in return. 'He introduced himself to me when we met and I've never forgotten it. Even had to buy myself a new pair of sneakers.'

'Oh, I remember. He certainly made sure you knew who was boss didn't he?'

'He sure did. We'll have to have a little talk one of these days. I'd like to explain to him about size. I'm bigger than he is and therefore I'm the boss.'

'Hey, size doesn't make you the boss. We're partners in this Quin and don't you forget it. I don't think Scrappy would listen anyway. He's his own dog.'

Sherry smiled as she remembered her tiny dog's lack of fear. He'd faced up to Ralph many times for her, been beaten for her, always coming back for another go even when the chances of winning were zero to none.

'He thinks size is irrelevant,' she said. 'The bark is the thing that keeps him going and he's got more heart than many dogs twenty times his size.'

Quin had to agree. 'He's the best Sherry. I couldn't wish for a braver companion.'

She stifled a sigh and said, 'Well, I suppose we should go before I chicken out altogether.'

'Yes. Let's go, now, while we can. I don't think we'll get another chance.'

The dank mouldy smell wafted around them as they stood for a moment assessing their surroundings. Quin shifted his pack to his chest so Scrappy would be more secure then enfolded Sherry's small hand in his large one. He switched on his torch and turned to take the first step.

She felt then that even though she and Quin faced a frightening journey and were preparing to once again push on into unknown territory, regardless of what might happen, they were linked to each other by more than hands or even friendship.

They were sensitive to each other without the intrusion of light as they had never been before, each breath taken, each sigh, every time one moved even a little, formed another thread that bound them together.

The perfume of her hair, the faint masculine aftershave, the contrasting textures of their skin as they held hands, the almost electrically charged physical awareness, all helped to form an impenetrable magnetic field.

It was cold in the cellar and becoming more so as they went on but the heat generated inside their bodies and minds by their close proximity and shared experiences and emotions warmed their spirits and made them move as one.

Quin felt a tiny wet tongue on his smooth bare chest inside the opening of his shirt and he smiled. It was like a canine seal of approval.

Quin played the torch light over the low ceiling of the timber walled passageway which was lined with small rooms. Some were filled with boxes of tinned food and equipment for film making, some filled with wooden crates and olive green metal containers stencilled with numbers and the letters SLR ASSAULT RIFLE 7.62 Cal MM. Another box had Fragmentation Grenade M36, yet another had BROWNING CAL 50MK2 HB. More boxes were stacked with the letters unreadable. They stood for a moment looking at the cache of weapons in the torchlight, silent with dread. A cold draught of sea air seemed to hover around them then drift away before they moved on, saying nothing but holding hands to keep out the chill of fear in their hearts.

After making their way down the passageway by the thin light of the torch, eventually they reached a rusty hinged wooden door. An old ornate key was hooked on a nail beside it. Quin put the key into the lock and turned it with difficulty before opening the door cautiously, Sherry standing close behind him. The hinges creaked noisily so they took it very slow.

On the other side of the door a long tunnel carved into stone led directly down a slight slope, spaced intermittently with shallow steps. A damp cave with a sandy floor and black porous rocks opened out onto a small sandy beach peppered with tiny rock pools and sharp broken shells. Waves crashed on rocks close to the beach as the tide washed the shore and seagulls could be heard faintly over the sound of the surf . Dawn was approaching.

Quin and Sherry came out into the open air and pale moonlight with a feeling of liberation. They had traversed the first obstacle and escaped the house unseen. After looking around their tiny inlet, they discovered they could take off along the beach if they chose. It stretched to the next bay then appeared again before disappearing into the distance. It was too dark to see just how far it went or whether there were cliffs or sand dunes to climb along the way.

Not having any idea where the beach would end up and knowing they could be followed easily with footsteps in the untouched sand, they elected to return to the grounds surrounding the house via a narrow sandy path which snaked its way through large rocks and straggly trees back to the top of the cliff.

They sat for a moment on the sand to rest before climbing the path giving Scrappy a chance to stretch his legs and check out whether it was safe to proceed. He took his duties as guard dog very seriously.

Having only the moonlight to guide them and, using the cover of the trees to their advantage, they made their way upwards heading for the shed where Quin had last seen the bicycles. They didn't dare use the torch in case they were seen.

As they climbed Sherry asked, 'What do you suppose is in those packing cases and metal containers? The green ones. Is it guns?'

'Stolen military hardware. Weapons. Ammunition. I'm not familiar with what the army issues to troops but I know a little about rifles and grenades. Who doesn't if you watch television or videos.'

'I don't. I've never seen videos except at school and they're not movies. They're educational stuff, mostly environmental or science videos.'

'Sorry Love. I had no idea Ralph was so mean he wouldn't let you watch TV. Bet you didn't even have a VCR in the house? Did you get to go to the movies?'

'No, never. I think it was just an excuse to keep me ignorant. Don't worry. I'm learning fast. So they're guns in the boxes are they. Sounds dangerous, and illegal.'

'Yes it is. We should be glad to get away from there. It's a powder-keg down in that place. You know, I wouldn't be surprised at what little sidelines Merton and Wilson have going. They're pretty dangerous characters no matter what kind of front they use. X rated films seem pretty tame after stealing from the military.'

'Would they use violence on us though Quin? We haven't done anything to them. All we want to do is leave.'

'A cardinal sin I believe. In their minds, if we leave we're traitors and informants. We need to be removed from circulation. They don't care about anything else except profit and to make the kind of money they want they have to be free to do whatever their minds can conceive. If we talk to anyone about what they're doing here the police will start asking questions for sure.'

Sherry was shaken to the core. She'd seen plenty of violence in her own life but never from outside sources. The world had seemed a place to run towards rather than from and now everything was changed.

The only stability in her life at the moment was Quin and even he would soon disappear back to his other life, a life she had no knowledge of. Nothing of what she was feeling showed in her voice though as she said, 'Well I'm all for getting out of here. Let's find those bikes and just go, now!'

Sherry took Scrappy, put his lead on and let him walk for the last part of the climb up to the cliff-top. The little dog was being very good about being bounced around and she was grateful he was so quiet. She didn't know what she would do if she lost him. Having been without any close friends for a long time, he'd filled a huge gap in her life when all she could see ahead was emptiness and pain.

The man patrolling the grounds walked silently past them without turning his head and holding Scrappy closely to prevent him giving them away, both sighed with relief. Fortunately they'd seen him coming and had crouched down behind some thick bushes just in time. All Sherry had to do was gently tap Scrappy's nose and he was quiet.

Quin put his mouth close to Sherry's ear and whispered, causing shivers to run up and down her spine. 'The guard walks round past the front of the building now then he goes round the back past the old tennis courts where he has a smoke for a few minutes. It takes him about forty five minutes to do the circuit so we have to move quickly. I'll go first and if anyone comes duck back behind the shed and keep out of sight.'

'What if we're caught?'

'We go back to where we were before. Don't worry, I don't think they want to hurt you Sherry. You're too valuable to them.'

'What about you Quin? What will they do to you?'

'Nothing. I'll make their blasted film for them and after a few months they'll let us go.' Quin was fairly certain it wouldn't end there but he wasn't going to say anything to Sherry. Why worry her with something that might not come to pass.

'But you don't want to get involved in that sort of thing,' she stated, secretly fascinated but ashamed of herself for it. 'It's so degrading.'

Quin grinned, his teeth shining white in the starlight. 'I'll have to do what you ladies are supposed to do, lie back, close my eyes and think of England.'

She tried not to laugh and her voice came out sounding like a croak. 'It's not funny Quin. I don't like to think of you making movies like that.'

'It'll be okay honey. We won't get caught.' He reached across and slipped his hand behind her head into her hair, pulling her close and kissing her, a short but passionate kiss that tempted but denied satisfaction. When he let her go he said, 'Give Scrappy back to me and I'll tuck him into my pack again. We'd better wait for the guard to come past again and then we'll make a run for it. He should be back here in about five minutes.'

Sherry was shaken to the core by the caress of his hand and those wonderful firm lips that could reduce her legs to jelly and set her heart thumping so hard it could leap out of her chest. She wasn't used to being kissed or touched in a loving way and it took long moments for her to regain her breath.

'Yes, you take him,' she whispered, passing the tiny bundle of fur over to Quin who stroked him gently. 'He'll be safe with you. He trusts you.' As she said the words she knew it was also true for her. She trusted Quin completely.

He tucked the warm little body firmly into his usual place in the pack and said, 'Okay Scrap my boy. It'll be sun-up in a couple of hours so it's almost time to hit the road. Try not to make a sound or we're finished.' He could have sworn he heard the pooch give a tiny grunt of agreement.

Once the guard had passed by a second time, the bikes weren't hard to find. Old but still usable, they'd been recently oiled and were propped up outside the shed as if waiting for someone to ride them. Someone was.

Quin was busy tightening a loose nut on one bike with his pocket knife so Sherry started off ahead of him, impatient to be gone. She rode off around the corner of the shed and a minute later Quin jumped on board and followed.

She was gone! He rode along the rough dirt track past tall gum trees and thick bushes looking to see where she was ahead of him. It was still dark and the moon was almost gone so the starlight was the only illumination. He couldn't hear her bicycle creaking or anything except a soft breeze blowing through leaves and the sound of insects clicking. He knew it would be total disaster to call out to her but the urge to do so was almost overwhelming. Where was she? How had she gotten ahead of him so quickly?

After riding for five minutes Quin could see the track straighten out ahead of him and knew something must have happened to Sherry. She had completely disappeared. He stopped the bicycle and looked back along the track, desperately hoping she was playing some sort of practical joke. He wished she would suddenly jump out of the bushes and scare the living tripe out of him. At least then he could tell her off and they could be on their way, no harm done except to his nerves. Ten years off his life wasn't much to give for her safe return.

He turned back along the track and rode as fast as he could towards the shed where she had disappeared. Either she was hurt somewhere or had gone in the wrong direction.

There were several side tracks she could have gone down in her haste to get away from the homestead. One of them led to the bungalows where some of the original homestead staff had lived and now the guards were housed. Quin took that track and as he rode he realised there was a dim light in one of the buildings.

He stopped riding well before he reached it and, tying Scrappy to a tree with the lead, put his pack on the ground nearby. He went quietly along on foot, scanning the area as he did so. He took along his pocket knife just in case.

There was no-one about but he heard a faint sound coming from an open window. Creeping closer, he listened, peering over the window sill. Sherry was sitting on a ladder back chair in the kitchen with her hands tied behind her back then tied to the chair. Her jeans and shirt looked as though she'd been rolling in dust and her hair was tangled. Her face looked bruised along the cheek bone.

Walker was leaning against the sink drinking from a bottle of beer. He was dressed only in a pair of baggy blue shorts, his large body full of aggression. As he turned towards the window to thump his empty bottle down on the counter Quin ducked down out of sight, listening carefully.

'You can't keep me here Walker,' said Sherry shakily, her voice rising as she pulled uselessly at the thin nylon rope he'd used to tie her hands. 'The Police are going to hear about this. It's kidnapping. Australia is a free country and I can go anywhere I like. I can leave this place if I want. Anytime. You can't stop me.'

'I have stopped you in case you haven't noticed. Anyway, I really can't see why you want to leave.' He ran his eyes over her body, a salacious grin on his swarthy face. 'A girl like you could be a lot of compensation in a place like this. No-one would have to know. I'd look out for you. Mr. Wilson, he listens to me. I'm his security. He needs protection, I'm it. He doesn't make a move without me there. I've got all the muscle he needs.' He flexed his arms and shrugged. 'After all, it's probably a better deal than what you were getting down south.'

'What do you know about that?'

'Jones told me about the stalker. He said someone was after you and you needed to get away. At least with me you know what to expect.'

'No, I don't. Things change from day to day. You're nuts if you think your job is secure Walker. I've seen the way it is. They'll use you then throw you away. Anyway, I'm not like Marina. I can't handle things easily like she does.'

He gave a feral grin, looking distracted as if remembering the way Marina handled things. 'No, you're not like Marina. She knows when to come across.' His tone changed and he snarled, 'Not like you, you stuck up little bitch. You think you're too good for a working man, a real man, like me.'

Her voice became urgent, persuasive. 'Why don't you let me go and we'll say no more about it. I won't tell anyone anything. I'll just get back on the bike and find my way back to Victoria where I belong. No big deal. I'll just disappear out of your life the same way I came in. Blink and I'll be gone. What do you say?'

Walker laughed. 'You're good. There's no doubt about it you'd make a great actress.' Sherry gasped and he said. 'Yeah, I figured you'd found out about Merton's little project. He's got a fantastic setup here. Everything laid on to make great skin flicks. And best of all, the skins are free. They come here to escape from their crummy lives and we give them something to live for, something exciting with pleasure as a bonus. I don't see anyone else complaining except maybe that idiot Jameson. He's a pain in the butt.' His eyes sharpened. 'Where is the hero anyway? Trying to find the courage to come out in the dark?'

'He's not an idiot. I think you're jealous of him because he's the only real man I can see around here.

He's not a bully who torments anything smaller than he is just for fun. A real man wouldn't hurt a defenceless little dog like you did. You're a sadist. I'd like to tie you down on an ant heap and torment you. Then we'd see who enjoys pain. You'd soon be crying like a baby.'

'Shut up you stupid bitch. What do you know about pain? I'll tell you. You know nothing! You ought to join the army. Then pain would find you and you'd probably die of shock. A thirty mile hike with a full pack, half a cup of water and starvation rations would have you screaming for your daddy to come get you.'

As tears welled in her eyes at his mention of her father he snarled, 'Cut out that damn snivelling. All I've done is tie you up. Anything else was because you wouldn't co-operate.'

She stiffened her spine and asked cuttingly, 'What did you think? That I was going to let you do whatever you liked without protecting myself? Call Quin an idiot, you must be a prize idiot yourself. No wonder Merton makes you live in this grotty bungalow. It's a hovel and it suits you right down to the ground. He probably doesn't trust you up at the house with all those fancy furnishings. You'd drop cigarette ash and burn holes in his expensive carpets.'

At the sound of Walker cursing and a door slamming violently Quin looked through the window once more. Sherry was alone at the table. She was twisting frantically, trying again to free herself. She was jumping up and down with her bottom on the chair attempting to move it over to the kitchen drawer. He guessed she was going to try to locate a knife to cut the rope and realised that now Walker had left the room he could do something about her situation. Trying anything before Walker was out of the way would have put the woman Quin loved in even more danger.

Swiftly he pulled the insect screen out and climbed in the window. Before she realised he was there, he was beside her cutting the knots around her wrists with his pocket knife. She sagged with relief and said, 'Thank God you're here. Hurry Quin. He'll be back in a moment. I think I ticked him right off. He's so angry he slammed out of here in a rush muttering something about finding some handcuffs over at the house.'

'Then it's just as well I got here first. What were you thinking of, taunting him like that? It's no wonder he's in a rage.' He began on the ropes around her feet.

'You think that's a rage? You should see Ralph. He cornered the market on anger a long time ago. Sometimes he'd get so red in the face I thought he was going to have a heart attack. God help me, but sometimes I even wished he would, then I'd be free. I hated myself for that but it was true. I wanted him to die.' She took a deep breath and smiled shakily as he pulled the ropes away and helped her to stand, holding her arm as she steadied herself. 'I learned to live with his anger and sometimes even use it to my advantage. If you can make a person mad enough you can get them to do stupid things. They stop thinking with their brains and use their emotions instead. Then you've got them.' She began to shake her feet and bent to rub them vigorously. 'Ah no, I've got pins and needles Quin. That beast tied those ropes so tight it cut of my circulation.'

She sat down suddenly and he bent to rub her feet also, saying, 'Sherry, that's a dangerous way to live. What did you hope to achieve with Walker?

He could have totally lost it and really slammed you around, not just tapped you for fun.' He stroked her bruised cheek with his finger and she flinched.

Shrugging defensively, she rubbed her wrists and stood up. 'He left didn't he?' 'Yeah. He left. But only to get handcuffs. He's coming right back.' 'Well I'm free aren't I?' She moved toward the window and looked out.

'Only because I came along. You're going to have to learn self defence if you insist on baiting the tiger. I'll show you some moves. Might keep you alive.'

'Oh, for heaven's sake Quin. Let's discuss this later. You can teach me how to fix Walker but we'd best get out of here before he returns with the cuffs. '

He heard the sound of bare feet slapping on the verandah steps and said, 'It's already too late. He's back. Quick. Get down beside the fridge. I'm going to see if I can buy us a little insurance.' He stepped behind the door and waited.

'What are you going to do?' she whispered.

'Just get yourself hidden,' he replied quietly. 'And stay out of sight.' Moving a plastic bucket out of the way, she slipped inside the tall thin broom cupboard between the fridge and the window wall and held her breath.

The door opened at that point and just as Walker strode through it he cursed fluently. 'The bitch,' he snarled. 'She's gone out the bloody window.'

He turned to the wall where there was an intercom. He pressed a button and spoke into it. 'Katz, get out here. That girl, Sherry Hunter, she's loose on the property and trying to get away. She knows everything...I don't care if you're asleep or what's going on.

'Tell Marina to give it a rest and get your backside out here. And don't tell Merton or Wilson. Not yet. I want a bit of time alone with her. She needs to be taught a lesson. I'll meet you out by the jeep.'

Walker went over to the window, thumped the window sill as he looked outside, then scooped up the rope from the table. He threw it down, swore viciously, then turned to walk toward the door.

As he reached it Quin, who was hidden behind it, put all his considerable strength into slamming the heavy old door into Walker's face. He fell, smashing his head on the corner of the fridge as he fell and lay groaning on the floor semi-conscious. Quin was relieved it was so quick because Walker was a big man with a lot of weight and could have easily overcome any assailant if he had been upright.

'That was great Quin?' Grinning with delight, Sherry swung a pair of handcuffs in her hand. 'What are we going to do with him now'

'Tell me Sherry,' Quin asked, a gleam in his eye. 'Would you really like to tie him up on an ant's nest?'

'You bet,' she agreed enthusiastically. 'Meat ants. It's just the place for him. The ants would be well fed for at least year.'

'You could turn into quite a monster yourself,' he laughed ruefully. 'You'll have to curb those sadistic tendencies for now. Turn the lights off so they think he's gone. No point in showing them we're here. The window has no blind.'

'Okay.' Black enveloped the room, then a torchlight pierced the blackness before being shaded by Quin. His hand glowed pink and red between the fingers.

'So what are we going to do with him,' asked Sherry worriedly. 'We can't just let him go. He'll wake up in a minute. The other guards will be swarming here soon anyway and they'll be armed.'

'We can't do much to him no matter how tempting it is. We don't want to lower ourselves to his level. We'll tie his ankles, gag him with his own belt, put those handcuffs on him, and shackle him to the leg of the old cabinet in that store room out the back. It's heavy enough to slow him down a bit and he'll be hidden from the other guys, at least for a while.' He pushed Walker onto his front with difficulty, Walker was a heavy man, and pulled his hands back behind him.

Quin grinned as he used the nylon rope he'd found in a drawer and tied his ankles tightly together. 'Then we're going to leave him here with his headache and head for the hills. We need to get going quick smart if we're going to escape this mess. As soon as people start looking for us they'll also see Walker isn't around. They'll have people out searching straight away so we need to go, now.'

'What if they follow us?' she asked as she put the handcuffs around Walker's brawny wrists behind his back.

'Maybe we need to leave a little distraction. You remember over behind the bike shed there's a hay storage shed. No walls, just posts, a roof and hay.'

'Yes. I know the one.'

'I'm going to set a fire in it.' At her horrified gasp he grinned. 'Don't worry Sweetie. No animals are going to burn. There's plenty of water in the tank close by and hoses for just such an emergency. They'll have it out in no time but in the meantime we'll be gone.'

'You're a firebug aren't you Quin.' She grinned at his unrepentant expression.

'Yeah. But I keep it under control.' He grinned like a small boy and she loved it, loved him, so much she could hardly speak for the emotion welling up inside her.

Before dawn broke they were away, pedalling along a tree lined, overgrown, dirt track bypassing the primary access route and the main gate. The dirt road led in turn to a paved main road. An orange glow could be seen behind the house with shouting men trying to contain the sudden fire which had sprung up in the hay shed.

As the sun rose two hours later they were coming close to a wooden slatted bridge when they heard vehicles coming along the road behind them. Quickly they turned down another overgrown dirt track and hid under the bridge. Sherry held her breath nervously and prayed, her heart beating like a drum as the cars rattled over the wooden slats, the sunlight flashing through the holes as the wood moved. Quin simply held Scrappy in his arms and asked for a miracle.

Three vehicles passed overhead and sped away. Quin said, 'I think if they don't find us on this road soon they'll come back and this is the most logical place to look. We'd better head back along the road to that other track we passed. There's a farmhouse in some trees down there so maybe we could call the police.'

'It's a bit close to the homestead Quin. Maybe the people in the farmhouse are part of the setup and we'll be in just as deep as we are now.'

'We'll just have to chance it. Come on Honey. Other than giving up it's our only choice.' He added softly, 'I haven't seen you giving up lately. It's not your style. You'd rather go down guns blazing than play dead.'

Thanks Quin.' She laughed. 'I'll remember you said that when you're trying to get me do something I don't want to do, like climb down into a tunnel. You'd better buy yourself a bullet proof vest. You're gonna need it.'

Sherry and Quin rode up to the weathered timber frame house and hid their bikes under some bushes behind a tree. They looked around. It seemed to be deserted but so many old houses had that same neglected air so they knocked on the door anyway.

They heard sounds from within after a few minutes and footsteps coming towards the door. Seconds later an elderly bearded man stood there in pyjamas and a robe carrying a shotgun, his rheumy eyes half closed against the early morning light. 'What's going on? Who're you?'

Quin stood in front of Sherry and said, 'Sorry to disturb you sir, but I wonder if you could help us?' He hesitated to lie and say their car had broken down. Something about the old man had made him rethink this doubtful strategy. He decided to be as honest as possible in the circumstances. 'The truth is sir, some people are looking for us and we have nowhere to go. We have to get help.'

'You from the big homestead on the other side of the peninsula?'

'Yes Sir. We're trying to get away. Can you help us?'

The man stood blocking the doorway, the darkness of the hall making him seem momentarily menacing with his gun and a scowl on his weathered face. Then he moved closer and his face seemed gentler in the early morning light. 'Can't see as how I can do anything for you.' He'd started to close the door when an elderly woman shuffled up beside him in loose slippers and a voluminous apron over a long nightgown and pink chenille robe.

She peered at her visitors through blue framed glasses and asked, 'What's going on Sam. You keeping these young people out on the step all day. They could probably use a cuppa and some breakfast.'

'Go back to bed Margie,' he said firmly. 'There ain't nuthin' for you to worry about here. These folk are just about to go on their way.' The old man glared at them, daring them to dispute his ruling. The woman hovered in the background, clucking anxiously about denying hospitality to people in need. Quin and Sherry turned to leave and the man began to close the door once more.

The bark seemed to come from inside Quin's chest. Scrappy set up a commotion which could not be ignored by anyone. 'Hush Scrap, we'll soon be able to give you a run.' Quin tried to soothe the little beast and Sherry murmured to him as she would a small child but he would not be quiet. The old man came out onto the porch and said, 'What in blazes have you got in there? Sounds like a Great Dane.'

Sherry laughed. 'He certainly thinks he's a Great Dane.' Scrappy pushed his head out into the open and looked around, his little black button eyes blinking.

Margie came out onto the porch and smiled. 'He's gorgeous. Bring the little one in here then. He's probably hungry and thirsty poor little scrap.'

'That's why I called him Scrappy,' said Sherry, smiling. 'When I got him he was the smallest of the litter and he looked half starved. He was only able to eat tiny scraps of food. He fitted into the palm of my hand.'

Quin and Sherry looked at the old man and he nodded. 'Looks like that little fella makes his own arrangements. It's cold this early in the day. Come on in and we'll talk. I'm Sam Bryce and this is my wife Margie.'

'I'm Quin and this is Sherry.' They shook hands with Mr. and Mrs. Bryce. 'We really appreciate this. It's been a difficult night for us. We took some bikes from their shed and took off but they know we've gone and are out searching.'

'Maybe there's something I can do to help.' Sam stepped back to allow them to enter his home. 'Never did think much of those folks takin' over the homestead. It's downright disturbing what goes on there.'

'What have you seen Mr. Bryce?' asked Quin as they went inside the farmhouse and sat down on carved wooden chairs at the huge old pine kitchen table. The kitchen smelt of herbs and flowers and the welcome aroma of freshly ground coffee bubbling on the wood stove which also gave welcome warmth.

'I've noticed lots of strange things, boats coming and going at night, sometimes noises like guns going off, people up and down the road at all hours. Jeeps and men in camouflage gear. It's like the army round here sometimes. Then there's the weird ones.'

He looked embarrassed for a moment and then said, 'You know what I mean. Men who dress like women. I saw a car load of them driving past here one evening. I was down in the paddock checking on some sheep. I'd swear the idiots were drunk, car swerving all over the road, hooting and laughing fit to kill. Margie and I stayed well out of sight that night. Probably on drugs or something. You never know what people get up to these days.'

'No,' agreed Quin, his eyes locked with Sherry's. 'You never can tell.'

Sam rubbed his whiskery chin and said, 'Margie, you get these folks some breakfast, I'll go and get myself dressed and then we'll have that talk. If you need help to get away, well, maybe I've got an idea.' He got up from the table and left the room.

Margie smiled at her unexpected visitors with delight and said, 'Now, what can I get you. Eggs and bacon, toast? Some cereal. Maybe a cup of tea or coffee?'

Scrappy was munching happily down on the floor and being observed by a large tortoiseshell cat whom he ignored. 'That sounds lovely Mrs. Bryce. I could eat a horse,' said Quin as he sat down at the table and held Sherry's hand.

She eyed him with the perception of a mother and said, 'Horses we don't serve but what I give you will taste just as good. You look like you could used a little TLC Quin. You too Sherry. How about resting here for a bit. My two sons have married and moved away. Their rooms are empty and you'd be welcome.'

'Thank you Mrs. Bryce,' said Quin gently, shaking his head. 'You've been very kind to us already but we couldn't put you in danger too. Those people will probably come looking for us and if they track us to you who knows what they'll do. It could be extremely dangerous.'

'Nonsense young man. I wouldn't hear of you leaving. Anyway, there's always the storm cellar to hide in. You eat your breakfast and while you do, I'll nip down into our little dugout and make it comfortable for you. We built it in case of cyclones you see. No-one will ever find you there.

'It's the perfect hideout,' Margie continued coaxingly. 'The sort of cellar you wouldn't notice unless you fell into it. You never would though because the door to it is hidden inside one of the sheds. My husband built it like a bunker in wartime. He was in the army you know. World War 2.'

'Now Margie, what are you going on about?' The old man came back into the kitchen.

'Sam. These young people want to leave because they think those people down the road will come here looking for them. I say we hide them in the cellar. It's safe there and they won't be found.'

'Sounds good to me. Better listen to Margie. She's usually right.'

'Well, if you say so Mr. Bryce,' said Quin. 'I won't argue. We're very grateful to you.' He smiled at the two people who had been so kind and they smiled in return. Sherry felt it was like being part of a family once again.

CHAPTER THIRTEEN

Quin and Sherry spent the morning resting at the Bryce farmhouse while keeping eyes and ears alert for approaching cars. Scrappy feasted on pieces of mutton then slept on the grass in the shade of a red flowering gum while the Bryce's old female Labrador kept an eye on him. He didn't even seem to mind when she began to wash him with her long wet tongue.

They discussed how they were going to get away without running into Wilson's men and finally decided on a rowing boat which Sam kept moored in a nearby inlet. The bay was not open sea so they could, in calm weather, row across the water and reach the small fishing community of Cobbs Point. They decided this was much safer than travelling by road to a closer town and being spotted.

Looking out when they heard a helicopter overhead, they saw it was the one Wilson and his cronies had arrived in and when it had gone over and returned several times, Quin said it seemed like it was following a grid pattern search. Obviously it was looking for something, probably them. They decided to stay well out of sight.

Quin wrote an account of their stay at the old homestead and Sam said he would take a trip to town the next day and mail it to the police. Quin hoped that would put an end to Wilson's activities in the area permanently. He included an account of how he'd seen the boxes of weapons and the number of guards he'd seen as well as describing the large crates in the cellars. He also described the man who had gone missing in the hope he could be found safe and well.

When Sam heard about the guns he said, 'I remember one newspaper in Brisbane reporting the theft of weapons from the Army Base in Townsville. Police found some of the stolen weapons in the back of a sports store in Sydney.' He laughed. 'Stupid idiots thought they could sell the stuff under the counter. Now they're searching for the rest of the haul in a joint operation between Army Police and Commonwealth Police . They reckon the thing's a threat to national security.'

'They're gonna find plenty of goodies tucked away in the cellar of the homestead,' said

Quin. 'Probably the same mob. We were lucky to get away when we did, and in one piece. It could turn out to be a war zone out there.'

Sam agreed. 'Yeah, it'll go bad for them I reckon. I've lived here all my life but I've never seen such strange goings on at that place before. It used to be owned by God fearing people who had owned it for generations. Unfortunately the bank foreclosed and they lost it. A real shame.' He turned his head towards the kitchen where his wife beckoned. 'Let's forget it for now. Time to eat.'

Margie fed them huge quantities of chicken stew and apple pie with custard for lunch then they talked and lazed the afternoon away in the shade of trees on the beach. The spacious cellar in which they were to hide was nearby so they could reach it quickly in case anyone came or the helicopter returned. It was cool and ventilated by a door opening out onto the beach. A cluster of rocks and tall tea-tree bushes hid the door from view. Another hidden entrance was in a shed.

In the late afternoon of that first day there came the sound of two vehicles pulling up to the house. For a moment it was panic stations, then the four looked at each other and Quin and Sherry quickly headed into the shed which contained the door to the storm shelter. They had just shut the shed door opened the inner door to the shelter when they heard the sound of harsh male voices. One of them belonged to Walker. They could hear every word as though he was next to them.

'Mr. Bryce, we're looking for a couple, a man and a woman. They left the homestead early this morning.'

'Why are you looking for them?' asked Sam. His voice was inhospitable.

'They stole something from us. We're going to hand them over to the police.'

'Well, I'm afraid they're not here. Haven't seen them,' lied Margie.

'You don't mind if I look for myself,' demanded Walker implacably.

'I'm not real happy about it,' said Sam. 'It's an invasion of privacy. Why don't you check out buses at Cobbs Point. Those two are probably long gone.'

'Look, if you don't let us look around old man we could come back later tonight.' Another man spoke in a tone designed to intimidate. 'And if we have to come back tonight we won't be happy and neither will you. Understand?'

At the implied threat Sam said, 'No need to do that gentlemen. Feel free to check out the house. Don't damage anything will you. I wouldn't like that.'

Quin and Sherry could hear doors opening and shutting and then a short time later Walker said, 'Come on you blokes. They're not here. We're wasting time.' Engines started up and two vehicles roared off down the track.

Within the next five minutes the Bryces were opening up the beach door. 'Come on you two,' said Margie. 'They've gone, thank goodness. I really thought we were done for.'

Sam put his arm around his wife and said, 'Margie, you were wonderful. I'm hungry after all that negotiating. How about some tea. Come on Quin, let's find a drink. I think we've earned it. I've some home brew that's about ready.'

'Thanks Sam, Margie,' said Quin. 'Look, I'm sorry about all that. I had no intention of putting you in danger. That man was Mr. Walker. He's not a nice character at all. Really vicious and cruel. We'll leave first thing in the morning.'

'Nonsense,' said Sam. 'Nothing much happens around here. This is the first bit of excitement we've had in months. It's better than worrying about my arthritis anyway. You two relax and rest for a few days. Those blokes won't bother coming back. And if they do it's into the cellar again. Okay?'

'Yeah. Thanks. It's a great cellar Sam. Just right for two.' Quin smiled and put his arm around Sherry. 'We're really grateful for all you've done.'

'We've done nothing yet. Wait 'til you see the boat. Then you can thank us.' Sam began to laugh. 'If you have time that is. You'll probably be busy bailing water out of it.' Margie began to laugh too, then Sherry and Quin. There was a wonderful feeling of relief for everyone that Walker and his men had gone.

The two fugitives spent the next couple of days in the same relaxed fashion, Sam having reported no sign of the men looking for them when he drove around the coast into Cobbs Point to post the letter. At night though, they curled up in sleeping bags in the cellar each battling their own demons.

Quin wanted desperately to reach out and bring Sherry's shivering form into his own sleeping bag and protect her from the nightmares which she seemed to be plagued with. She kept calling out in her sleep and pleading with Ralph to stop. Quin wanted to find Ralph and dispose of him, as inhumanely as possible.

If he did as his body craved and curled up beside her he knew what could happen and knew also that it wouldn't be fair to make love to a girl in Sherry's confused state. He loved and needed her too much to start something which might only be temporary. What good was that to an innocent girl when he might have to leave her soon and let her make her own way once again. It just wouldn't be fair.

Sherry knew Quin was uncomfortable sleeping in the same room as herself but she tried to ignore his restlessness. If he wanted to sleep somewhere else all he had to do was say and Margie would find him a place in the house. She wished he would come to her and hold her but was afraid to ask in case he thought she was easy like some of the girls at school or the women Ralph seemed to find attractive.

She'd seen one or two of them on occasions when she crept up to his old cabin at night while Ralph was entertaining. Blonde hair seemed to be his preference as well as substance. He seemed to enjoy women with plenty to say which was why she couldn't understand why he seemed to be obsessed with herself. She was quiet and withdrawn and completely inexperienced, a total opposite to his usual woman.

Never before in her life had she come across emotions that drained your strength and destroyed your ability to remain in control. She was alternately wanting Quin and rejecting him in her mind even as she tried to find excuses to be near him. He confused her utterly, saying he loved her, looking at her with scorching glances, taking her hand and laughing with her but making no overtures of a close personal kind. Did he think of her as a child? Was he really in love with her or was it just words. The not knowing was the worst cut of all to her fragile self esteem and she had no idea how to ask for what she wanted.

Late in the afternoon two days after arriving at the Bryce farmhouse, Quin rowed the small boat across the sea and waved goodbye to the wonderful old couple that had proved to be such a God-send.

Scrappy was nestled comfortably in his mistress' arms while she reclined in the bottom of the boat with nothing to do but think of Quin and how she felt about him. The only acid to corrode her thoughts was the future. What was she going to do when she and Quin parted company as she knew they would eventually. He had said he would always be there for her but what did that mean? Would he be available on the end of a phone line or would he be with her in person?

Would she be forced to go back to Ralph and her former life? Or, would she strike out on her own once more, only to find herself alone and friendless in a strange city, unable to find work, living in the slums on welfare.

It was almost better to go back home. There at least she would have a roof and food to eat. Anyway, what did it matter what she did or where she did it, without Quin her life would be empty. All she would have would be her tiny Yorkshire terrier and even he, because of his devotion to Quin, would remind her of all that she had lost.

Before Sherry could sink further into despair, they reached the beach below the town of Cobbs Point. A few people were strolling along the sand, enjoying the last of the sun's rays. Quin pulled the boat past the high tide mark and they walked up a rocky pathway to the road.

Shops lined the wide street and cars passed by as Quin looked for the bus depot Sam had said was there. Lights were appearing on the foreshore and a brisk breeze sprang up to cool the day. Sherry grabbed him by the arm and dragged him into a clothing shop.

He was taken by surprise but went willingly enough saying, 'What's this for Sherry? We don't need clothes.'

'Idiot!' she exclaimed, looking back over her shoulder. 'I just saw Walker and a couple of his men coming down the street. He looked so mad he could spit ground glass. They were looking into every shop as they came. What are we going to do Quin, they'll see us.'

He thought quickly and said, 'We'll have to try some clothes on, pretend we're customers. Grab something off a rack to try on and go into the cubicle at the back. I'll do the same. After a while we should be safe to leave but we'll have to get out of this town a.s.a.p.'

After about half an hour when the saleswoman had supplied about ten items to try on Sherry said, 'I don't think any of these will suit. Thanks anyway.' She left the woman muttering about what a waste of time it was serving tourists. Quin met Sherry at the front of the shop and they looked out carefully but could see no sign of their pursuers. It was now dark outside and a crisp breeze had sprung up.

'Looks like it's clear,' said Quin and he stepped before her out of the shop, lights along the street showing the way. They hadn't taken more than ten steps when a large hand grasped Sherry by the arm and a rough male voice said, 'Hang on a minute.' Crowds of people walking along the street flowed around them.

She whirled round to see a large crew-cut man in camouflage pants, black T shirt and loose khaki jacket holding a plastic shopping bag. 'You forgot this,' he said in a slight American accent and she breathed in relief at not recognising him.

'No,' she smiled shakily, her voice trembling. 'It's not mine. I didn't buy anything.'

'I think you'll find it is,' he insisted. His hand remained like a steel manacle on her arm and she began to feel trapped. 'Allow me to introduce myself. I'm Jerry Katz. You can call me Katz.'

'Quin, tell him, this isn't my shopping bag.' She looked to him for confirmation and found another man in faded blue jeans, a white singlet and a loose jeans jacket standing on his other side. 'What's going on?' Sherry's voice was a thin thread of sound. 'Quin. Do you know these men?'

'No. But I don't think that matters to them honey.' Quin turned to the man holding Sherry and said, 'What is it you want?' Rage was building in him as he saw the man touching Sherry. 'Take your hands off her. Now.'

'Sure pal,' said the man. He took his hand from Sherry's arm and put it under his jacket where Quin noticed a small handgun. 'Whatever you say. Mr. Merton just wants a little chat with you and the girl.'

'So you work for him do you? You must be one of the new guys who came last week. Where is Merton?' Quin looked up and down the busy street.

'Back at the house. He leaves retrieval and disposal to us. You, we retrieve.'

'You're nuts if you think we're going back to there.' Quin took Sherry's hand in a firm grip and pulled her to his side.

'You two don't want to make us get rough do you?' asked Katz, his heavy-jawed face hard and humourless, his large frame tense. 'We'd like to do this civilised if possible. You caused the boss some grief so we've come to pick you up and take you home. Simple.'

'You don't have to do it at all,' said Quin. 'Just tell Merton you didn't see us and that'll be that. I'll pay you.'

'Oh yeah, what with? You got money we don't know about?'

'Hey Katz! The guy's got money?' broke in his thin wiry companion whose dark eyes took on a predatory gleam as he looked Quin over and grinned, 'He won't need it where he's goin'.'

'Shut up Dooley. I'll decide what goes down around here.' The large man glared at his voluble companion who had attracted unwanted attention from passersby with his outburst. 'How much you got Jameson? And don't even think of lying. We're gonna search both you and the girl.'

Dooley began to laugh softly and look Sherry up and down like she was on sale. 'I'll do the girl,' he said licking his lips, a feral odour emanating from his stained white singlet.

'I've got a few thousand in cash. A watch, a gold ring. Things you could hock,' Quin said, trying to contain his rage at the thought of them searching Sherry. He ground his teeth wishing for the chance to poke Dooley's lights out. He was also trying to keep them talking long enough to think of an escape plan.

'We better keep this quiet Katz?' said Dooley. 'Making a bit on the side works for me but we better make sure Merton never finds out about it. He's not a forgiving man.'

'For once you're showing some brains Dooley. This will just be our little secret, providing you can keep that big mouth zipped up.' Katz glared at his companion threateningly then turned to Quin. 'Okay, where's the cash Jameson and no funny stuff? I'm watching everything you do.'

'I can't give it to you here,' said Quin. 'We're attracting too much attention as it is. People might think we're selling drugs then the police will get involved. You don't want that do you? Let's go down to the beach.' True enough, several shoppers were looking their way with interest. Quin was sorely tempted to ask them for help but knowing Katz had a gun couldn't take a chance on their safety.

'But Quin...' began Sherry, casting a worried glance at the two men, their minds clearly on a cash reward, their hard faces unimpressed with her soft blonde hair and her beautiful dark lashed grey eyes. 'The Police...'

'Relax honey. Bringing the police in now would be too dangerous. There's too many people around. Everything will be fine. These two gentlemen seem quite reasonable. We'll make them a little deal and then we'll leave.'

'Are you sure. I don't trust them,' Sherry whispered, shaking with nerves. He realised he would have to calm her fears so he could carry out the rest of his plan of escape. No way were they going back to the homestead. Not if he had anything to say about it.

'I'm sure,' Quin gave her cold hand a squeeze. 'Come on honey. Let's get this over with.'

The four walked down the street and round the corner heading towards the beach, Quin taking the lead with firm steps, Sherry following behind him less confidently. The area was becoming quite crowded with tourists and locals heading towards the carnival which had taken over the beach and the nearby park.

The noise was gathering volume as children gathered to buy tickets for rides, stall holders shouted invitations to buy, music played from loud speakers, buskers with guitars sang country and western songs and shouts were heard from high on a ferris wheel as its cars began to move around. Coloured lights flashed as delicious smells of hamburgers cooking wafted over the scene and hot dog sellers vied with ice-cream vendors who played calliope music to attract customers.

It was a scene of excitement and fun which seemed incongruous to Quin as he wended his way through the crowds to a spot on the beach which was relatively unpopulated and unlit by the huge lights shining over the park.

'This is far enough.' Quin stopped and, turning to the two men, said, 'What guarantee do I have you won't go back on your word?'

'What do you take us for Jameson?' demanded Katz.

Quin said drily, 'A couple of honest blokes who can be trusted to shut their eyes?' Not bloody likely.

'Yeah, well, hand over the cash and the other things and we'll see won't we?'

'Quin,' said Sherry, tugging on his arm. 'Don't trust them.'

'I have to Sherry. We're down to our last choice and they're it.' Holding her hand tightly, he tried to infuse her with trust in his abilities to get them out of trouble but realised her fear was draining her confidence in him.

'He's right sweet cheeks,' drawled Katz, an incongruous ear-ring glinting in his earlobe in the moonlight. 'If you don't trust us it's back to Merton. You two really rattled his cage didn't you? He's not a very friendly guy at the best of times and right now he's about to explode. He's even got Jonesey spinning like a top looking for you two, not to mention our friend Walker. Now there's a man to be scared of. He just loves hurting people and has been looking for you guys for a long time, especially you little girl. I believe he has something really special planned for you. He said something about ants but I couldn't be sure.' He laughed as if he enjoyed the idea. Dooley laughed too, then they turned to Quin. Katz said, 'Okay, let's get to it. Show me what you've got.'

Quin gritted his teeth and began to take off his gold watch and a signet ring which had a ruby embedded in the gold. 'This should cover some of my account.'

'The money,' said Katz, taking the watch and ring and inspecting them closely. 'Hand it over Jameson. If you've got it?' he glared at Quin as if he knew he was a liar.

'Keep your shirt on Godzilla. I've got it.' Quin took out his wallet. 'This is it. A couple of thousand was all I brought with me.' He tossed it down onto the sand and said as they bent to retrieve it, 'Enjoy it for what it's worth.'

Then, holding Scrappy in his pack firmly against his hard chest with one hand and grabbing Sherry's hand with the other, he ran with her through the darkness and into the park where they melted into the crowd.

Dooley started to run after them but his partner grabbed his arm and, as he picked up the wallet, said, 'Relax. They're still here in town. There's nowhere they can hide for long. Walker's around somewhere and we've got men on each end of the street and at the bus depot as well as several guys walking through the town. Let's have a look at what Jameson left us before we go hunting.'

'What then. Do we take them back to Merton?'

'Sure we do. With this little haul we get double the pay. You didn't really think I was gonna let 'em go did ya?' Katz was laughing as he looked into the wallet but the grin faded rapidly as he erupted in fury and swung around towards Dooley. He threw the wallet down furiously. 'Five dollars,' he shouted to the breeze. 'Five lousy stinking dollars. I'm gonna get those cheatin' bastards if it's the last thing I do.' He turned and marched furiously up the beach and into the crowd with Dooley trailing behind like a forgotten appendage.

When the two men had gone, Sherry stood with Quin under the cover of the trees for a moment more and said, 'That was a good idea you had, doubling back to hear what their plans were. So, what do we do now? They seem to have us trapped.'

'Now, we find a way out of here. You heard what they said. They won't rest until they find us. Neither will Walker. He's looking for blood. Our blood.'

'I'm scared Quin. They're dangerous men. I don't want to be forced back to the homestead. Especially now we've managed to get free.'

'There's always the boat,' he said, his mind working furiously.

'But where would we go?'

'That's a point. I don't know this area well enough to take a chance. We can't go back to the Bryce place. I don't want to place them in danger too.'

'Maybe we could go to the police.'

'I'm sure our friends will be watching in case we do. In any case, what could we say? They didn't actually imprison us or hurt us and we became involved of our own free will. We can't prove anything without hard evidence and I've mailed all that I had to them already. Unfortunately it's Saturday and mail isn't delivered until Monday. I'm not even sure it would reach them by then. Sometimes, according to Sam Bryce, things take quite a few days by post to get to where they're going .

'In any case, who is to say they'd believe us anyway? It's been my experience that they only believe what they want to believe.' His voice was hard with cynicism and he looked away from her soft face, unwilling to let her see his disillusionment.

'Quin.' Sherry reached up to stroke his lean jaw and bring his eyes back to her, wondering why he had this thing about the police. 'You have to cultivate a little trust. Not all policemen are prejudiced, or corrupt. That would be impossible. Anyway I have an idea. How about doing a little dressing up?' Sherry said, her voice quivering with mischief.

'What are you talking about?' Quin asked, his dark brows drawn together.

'Disguises. We'll go to the second hand market I saw near the park and buy scarves and some other clothes. Also, I happened to see a wig on one of the counters. It looked a bit grotty but that won't matter. I can brush it well.' She grinned, delighted to be taking the initiative for a change. 'The only problem is money. Hopefully we wouldn't need much. Dare I hope you have some more tucked away?'

'Don't worry about that,' said Quin, handing her Scrappy's lead and putting the little dog on the ground for a walk. He unbuttoned his shirt to reveal a tautly muscled chest and a money belt around his waist which he unsnapped and opened to reveal credit cards and plenty of cash.

'Quin,' breathed Sherry admiringly, 'You're a genius. Where did you get all that money.'

'I used to be a boy scout. Be prepared was a particularly helpful trait they encouraged. I've always had the feeling I'd need some spare cash some day so I always carry this around with me everywhere I go. Looks like now is the time.'

'I'll say. I can't believe it! I've never seen so much in all my life.'

'It's only money Sherry,' warned Quin seriously. 'It buys things but doesn't guarantee safety. Those guys are still out there and we'll need a streak of luck to get away.'

'We'll make plans then. Disguising ourselves will help. You can be a woman and I'll be your son.'

'I'm too tall to be a woman.' He grinned at her, 'Besides, I'm not built for it.'

'You wouldn't be too tall if you were in a wheelchair.' She looked back at him, delight at her plan making her eyes glow.

'You're crazy Sherry. I'd stand out in a minute if I did that. Those guys would notice us for sure. Whatever else, they're not stupid.'

'Don't be so negative Quin. Trust me. I know about disguises.'

'Oh yeah, how's that?'

'Remember I told you I often disguised myself as a boy when I wanted to get away from Ralph. People would tell him they'd seen me all the time, like a spy network. Everywhere I went he'd know about it, everything I did he found out and punished me. I was so fed up one night that I dressed up in my Aunt Jo's short haired brown wig and some of my father's clothes from when he was a boy. Ralph never found out where I went even though I walked around the town and spoke to people who usually reported on me. After that I went often. It was the only way I could be free.'

'Ralph must be blind. You don't look at all like a boy.' He eyed her curves and shapely breasts like a grateful connoisseur. 'You look very female to me.'

'Yes, well, it's amazing what you can do with adhesive tape.' Quin was still laughing silently as they hugged the darkness on the walk back to the shops. She was a girl of many facets and he had only begun to scratch the surface. What a delightful way to pass the time he mused, if only we can get away without running into any more trouble.

Sherry woke feeling stiff and sore having spent the night on the hard bunk of a tiny camper van she and Quin had hired overnight. It had been the last one available at the beach-side park. There were two bunks side by side and a small table with two tiny bench seats at the end plus a mini-sink, stove and fridge.

Quin was too big to fit comfortably in a bunk so he put one of the mattresses down on the floor and spent the night between the bunks. He was very restless and Sherry had been kept awake not only by his thrashing about but by his very proximity.

Sleeping with a man in the same room might seem small change to most people but to Sherry it was like a revelation. She didn't count their time in the Bryce cellar because there had been a lot more space between them then and they weren't virtually doubled up. Not that he seemed to be aware of her she thought with chagrin before dropping off into an uneasy sleep. Most of the time he treated her as if she was a little girl and not a grown woman.

It was the dawn light shining through the open window that woke her. She turned over and rolled out of bed without thinking, falling on top of the man lying below her on the floor and forcing her breath out in a painful rush.

The trailer rocked and he grasped her around the waist and hips with arms like steel, saying in a sleepy morning voice, 'This is very nice. The perfect wake up call.'

Blushing vividly, Sherry tried to lever herself up and away from him. She had worn an extra long T-shirt and bikini panties to bed but the shirt had become twisted around her waist and she worked in vain to pull it down. 'I was climbing out of the bunk.' She attempted to speak with composure but her voice came out slow and husky.

'Keep still Sherry. You're causing me some damage here,' accused Quin softly as he stroked an investigatory path down and up her vertebrae before pulling her head down to his and teasing her lips apart gently.

Sherry tried to say 'don't' but ended up emitting nothing but a sigh of pleasure as their legs tangled together, hair roughened flesh against smooth soft skin creating explosive friction. She was not able to say a word then as he continued to shape her lips to his and to probe the depths with his magic tongue.

His arms gentled as he held her and she was lost in a storm of feeling, wishing it could go on forever. She moved against him and felt his body react and move with hers. He had slept in satin boxer shorts but they weren't able to shield her T-shirted body from the effect of his.

Tension rode hard upon both of them as they communicated their deepest needs without words but, in the midst of the conflagration another element intervened. Quin dragged his lips away and said, 'Damn it Scrappy. Get off!'

Startled, Sherry lifted her head and was licked all over her face for her trouble. Scrappy had jumped down from the bunk and was having a wonderful time teasing his mistress and making her notice him. He wagged his stumpy tail rapidly and tried to climb from Quin's shoulder onto his bare chest. His toenails scored in the smooth muscles as he tried to keep his grip making Quin use several unprintable words about dogs that should be kept in kennels or used in Chinese food.

'He doesn't mean that Baby,' crooned Sherry as she sat up and straddled the large body beneath her, picking up Scrappy and reluctantly climbing to her feet. She pulled her T shirt down over her long slim thighs and stepped back carefully from Quin's prone body, carefully not looking at the evidence of his desire. She stroked her pet, saying, 'He's just a big bear in the morning. Take no notice.'

She was unable to look Quin in the eye so she hugged Scrappy to her breast before putting him on the floor and, turning, she began filling the small electric jug which was supplied with the camper-van. 'Sorry I fell on you Quin. I hope I didn't hurt you.' She kept her face turned away and studied the contents of the fridge as if they were all that was on her mind.

Grinning at the image evoked by her words, he sat up and pulled on his jeans. 'Not likely. You're a featherweight. It seems to me we've been in this situation before though.'

'Not me,' she asserted. 'I don't do this sort of thing, ever.' She hunted for the jar of coffee she'd purchased with a few groceries the night before in the shop attached to the park. She'd hidden her hair under a scarf she borrowed from the park manager's wife and worn a shirt of

Quin's to shop in. It was the best she could do to disguise herself at the time but they needed to eat. As it was, she saw no-one suspicious and was fairly certain she wasn't followed.

'Don't you remember the first time we met?' Lying back on the floor with Scrappy now contentedly crawling up over his body, Quin propped his head up on a pillow and smiled indulgently. When she didn't answer he continued, 'I do Sherry. You were incredible. That was when Scrappy introduced himself to me.'

'In the motel? That cabin? Of course I remember.' How could she forget the most incredible moment of her life? 'I didn't know you then.' She laughed softly, feeling a long way from that naive young girl who had simply wanted to disappear. 'That was different though,' she went on, 'Our positions were reversed.'

He grinned at her and said, 'They certainly were. That time I was on top.'

Sherry was almost speechless. Determined not to show the flare of heat that his words evoked, she glared at him and said, 'That wasn't what I meant.'

Taking pity on her embarrassment, Quin asked, 'What did you mean then?'

'What I meant was, when we met, both of us were trying to get away from all our problems at home and now we're trying to get back there again.' The kettle boiled then and she occupied herself making coffee and toast. Quin stood up and, pulling on a shirt, seated himself on one of the built-in vinyl seats at the tiny formica covered table.

'I'm not sure I want to go back to the city again,' said Quin. 'Maybe it would be a step backwards. I reckon I could go anywhere in the country, maybe overseas. What about you?' He hoped she would say she wanted to go with him, wherever he went, but she didn't.

She turned her face blank and said, 'How many sugars in your coffee?'

Frustrated by her lack of response Quin was unconsciously cruel as he replied, 'Two. I suppose it's no use me saying don't go back to your guardian?'

'No use at all.' She replied quietly, looking down into her coffee, her shoulders tense. Unless you can offer an alternative she asked silently, hopefully. While she waited, slowly dying without an indication of how he felt, he got up off his seat and opened the door. Then he stamped out of the camper van with his coffee and went to sit outside. The sun was beginning to make inroads into the night but all the lush pinks and violets of the sky could not erase the foreboding in his heart. His black scowl prevented her from going after him and talking about the situation. He was an unapproachable as a rogue stallion and looked twice as mean.

After an hour during which he slowly cooled down, he came back to the door of the trailer and said coolly, 'Well Sherry, what do we do now? Time is precious and we've got things to organise.' His set expression said any moments of intimacy and sharing were over. Even anger was put on a back burner because it was time to plan their next move.

'So now we go shopping.' Sherry said, thinking, if you can be cool so can I.

CHAPTER FOURTEEN

Crowds already milled around the beach park where the carnival had been held the previous night. Clearly it was going on for the whole weekend or longer. The camping grounds and stores which were opening all weekend for the carnival also came in for a fair amount of traffic, a fact which Quin was grateful for.

Sherry tied her blonde hair up in the borrowed scarf and picked up some boy's clothes at the market as well as a very large long sleeved cotton frock and underwear for Quin. She even managed to purchase a large pair of brown sandals for him as well as the wig she had seen earlier. Fortunately it was such a mess no-one else had wanted it. A small General Store held all the other things she needed and she was lucky enough to find a pharmacy open to hire a wheelchair.

Quin was waiting impatiently in a shaded area of the camping park as she arrived back from her shopping spree and all but pounced on her as she stepped into the shade of the tree. 'Where the hell have you been Sherry? I've been waiting here for ages. Did you catch sight Walker or the other two, Katz and Dooley? They're like slime, creep in where they're least wanted.'

The tenseness in his voice showed her how worried he'd been and she wanted to kiss him for his concern. No-one had been like that for her since her parents had died and she hugged it to herself as a memory of their time together. 'I didn't see anybody I recognised. They can't be everywhere at once.'

'Don't be too sure about that. Merton and Wilson are both very tricky characters. They've got plenty of money too and can afford to pay a lot of people to search for us.'

'Maybe they've given up.' She looked at him with hope in her eyes which faded as he returned her look with a cynical one of his own.

'No way. As long as we're out here with what we know they're going to be looking for us. I'm sure Walker won't ever give up. He's a man with an axe to grind and we're top of his list.'

'What about in Melbourne? Will they follow us back there.'

'Probably. But I hope they won't find us. I only supplied a box number and cancelled it before I left town. What about you?'

'I gave them a false name so they won't find me either.'

'Did you?' He looked at her impatiently. 'Well, would you like to tell me what you real name is? In case we get separated and I need to look for you.'

'It's Delaney. Sherry Delaney. You don't seem surprised.'

'I'm not. I just wish you'd told me before now. I accepted you would have made some changes just so you could come on this little jaunt to Queensland. I made some fairly radical changes myself. Anyway, before I left Jones' office I looked around and found several files on the people who came with us on that flight. Very interesting reading. Yours and mine I collected up and brought with me. I haven't had a chance to check them out yet.'

'Why did you do that?'

'Just in case they decided to look for us I decided to remove temptation from their path. Without those files they won't know where to look for us. We'll be safe unless Mr. Jones has the memory of an elephant and recalls your box number.'

'I doubt it. He's too involved with his cameras and video recorders and peeping into people's private lives to take much notice of anything else. Horrible little sleaze. Maybe someone is also watching him. I hope they are.'

'Someone is. Wilson. He has files on everyone, including Jones I bet. All their nasty little secrets recorded for posterity. You know, it's a good thing you changed your name or you'd be hiding forever.'

'They'll probably still know I'm from Archer's Creek. It's not a very big town. They could find me there without any trouble. All they'd have to do is describe me. Everyone knows who I am.'

'We'll just have to pray Jones'll forget. They can't refer to missing files and hopefully that will make it okay. If not, we'll deal with it as it gets here.'

'They'll probably still come looking for us.'

'Guys like that never stop looking for you if you're a threat. Take it from me, they never give up.'

The bitterness in his voice shocked her. 'You sound really angry Quin. You haven't told me much about yourself. Is someone looking for you? Is that why you wanted to disappear?'

'Yeah, someone wants to see me curl up my toes. They've tried a couple of times in the city. That's why I took this job with Jones in the first place, to give myself some breathing space and to save my life.'

'I'm glad you did. Otherwise we wouldn't have met. I would have been at the homestead with no-one to protect me. Then I'd have been in it up to my neck.'

'You sure would honey. But I wouldn't have let you go alone. I knew I had to be there for you.'

'Thanks Quin. That means a lot to me. So, why is someone out to get you. What have you done to them that could be so bad?'

'It's a case of seeing too much and saying too much to the wrong people, namely the cops.'

'So the police are after you?'

'No. Guys who were pretending to be cops. They think I can identify them. I can't but that's beside the point. If they catch me I'm history so I packed up my stuff and got out of town via Jones' advert.'

'What a terrible injustice. It seems so unfair.'

'Yeah, well your life hasn't been a picnic either Sherry. But we have to go on and make the best of things. For now we have to get away from here and onto a bus. When we reach Maryborough hopefully we can vanish for a while, maybe hire a car and drive back to Victoria or catch a plane to anywhere else we want to go. And we'll do it together.'

'Anywhere but here would be wonderful.' She gave him a sweet but mischievous smile as she opened a plastic shopping bag. 'So, Quin, look what I've got for you. Isn't it super. Just the right colour.' She handed him a dress which was dark blue with large white flowers in a shirtwaist style with lace on the collar, a petticoat, a large straw sun hat and a pair of flat brown unisex sandals which looked huge but fitted him quite well.

She also brought out a razor and advised him to shave his legs. When he objected she said, 'Look at this in a scientific way Quin. When your legs are smooth it cuts down the wind resistance.' When he looked blank she continued with a grin, 'It's in case we have to make a run for it. Besides, women with lots of dark hair growing on their legs look extremely masculine. It makes people stare and we don't want that do we, hmm?'

When Sherry handed him a large size old fashioned lacy white bra, some beige coloured nylon stockings and a giant box of facial tissues Quin went pale. 'Don't tell me I have to wear this contraption? It's a torture chamber.' He indicated his flat masculine chest which, although well developed, had nothing to offer a bra of such proportions.

'I've got nothing to fill it.' He looked puzzled for a moment and then asked brightly, 'And the tissues? Don't tell me, you're expecting me to catch a cold in this outfit? I'm gonna sneeze, right?'

Sherry laughed drily. 'Very funny Jameson. Stuff your bra with tissues then put the petticoat and dress on. Then the stockings. Make sure your bosom is round and smooth or everyone will know it's fake. Don't let it hang too low. And paint your toenails and fingernails. I've brought a couple of colours for you to choose from with lipstick to match.'

'How do you know all this padding stuff,' he asked, gazing at her T-shirt, the rounded flesh under which clearly needed no padding to make itself noticed.

'I used to do it when I was a girl.'

'You're still a girl.'

'Not any more Quin. I'm growing up fast. These past few weeks have been a real education to me.' She brought out another shopping bag. 'Here's a few extras to doll ourselves up with. Might as well go the whole hog,' she said, grinning. 'I want to be proud of my mum. We'll fix your hair later. I assume you've got underwear.'

'Yeah, some without lace. I won't wear lace on my jocks. It doesn't feel right. Hair later. Just don't cut it, okay? These weeks have been educational for me too you know,' Quin began looking in the bag. 'Tell me, where exactly do you use the sticky tape.' He grinned when she made a slashing motion across her breasts, flattening them slightly. 'I see.' Sherry's face and neck turned a lovely shade of rose pink because she knew he spoke the truth. He really did see.

Quin took his new clothes into the male amenities block and carried out her instructions, knowing it was necessary if he was to pretend to be a woman. As if anyone would be fooled he thought disgustedly, inspecting himself in the mirror.

A man going into the block passed him as he was on his way out and stared. Quin said aggressively, 'Yeah, what are you gawking at mate?'

The man backed away with his hands raised saying, 'Nothing. Not a thing. But if you're going to dress like a woman you'd better use the ladies. It would be more convincing, and safer.

Guys in Queensland can get a little aggro over that kind of thing.' Quin swore, scowling so darkly that the man took off at a run calling to a woman standing near a camper-van in the carpark, 'Get your things back in the van Lucy, we're leaving.... now. This place has gone to the dogs.'

*   *   *   *

Sherry changed in the ladies amenities block. She walked up behind Quin who was holding Scrappy's lead and giving him a drink of water. He started in surprise when she spoke to him, her voice husky with banked down enthusiasm.

'You look great Quin, sorry, I mean Mum. I'm going down to the pharmacy to get the wheel chair,' she said. 'I hired it when I was down at the shops before but they had to get it out of storage for me and I didn't want to hang around. Now that I've dressed like a boy hopefully no-one will recognise me.'

She'd put on baggy blue jeans with a white T-shirt under a man's denim shirt. After adding high top sneakers and a shoulder length brown wig with a basketball cap she looked like a teenage boy. He was amused to see she even walked like one and her breasts also seemed to have disappeared via the magic of sticky tape.

Quin looked like everybody's nightmare of a mother. He'd shaved the dark hair from his calves and put on the brown sandals. To give himself an authentic look he'd given in to Sherry's persuasion and painted his toenails with vivid red to match his fingernails and lips.

His bosom certainly looked impressive. It was large and smooth, slightly higher than Sherry would have wished but she said, 'You look very nice. Very...' she hesitated, 'Very...motherly.' She saw his look of disgust and laughed then went on in a contemplative tone, 'Or perhaps stepmotherly. You know, the wicked stepmother in Snow White.'

Pushing him into a chair, she took a brush and began to work on his hair. 'It's the dark eyebrows I think. They look very...masculine. I think you'd better pluck them and then shave. Your whiskers are showing under the liquid make-up. Wash it off then put more on after. Women with beards attract attention and we don't want them offering you a job in the carnival do we Quin?'

'Anything else,' he grated, looking like an overgrown small boy who'd been into his mother's make-up case. 'You supplied the nail polish so perhaps you'd like me to wear perfume as well.'

'Yes,' she crowed. 'That's what's missing. Some Night Magic. It's a very sexy perfume. I've got some in my pack. Got a sample from the chemist. Hang on while I get it. And don't touch that hair. It's perfect and just the right colour.'

Self-consciously Quin touched his hair. He was used to having his long dark hair tied back in a pony tail or loose. Hair sprinkled with baby powder, teased mercilessly, moulded into a puffy bun on top of his head with hair clips and sprayed with perfumed hair spray made him feel like he was someone else, someone not in control of his life, someone who was vulnerable.

He reasoned it had to be the nakedness at the back of his neck or the grey strands making him look like a granny. Or maybe it was the bra and floral dress that did it? Who knew? 'Don't worry. I'm not going anywhere,' he said gloomily, rubbing his hand over his rough chin. 'Norman Bates eat your heart out. I think I'll check out that razor again.'

'I'll be right back with the perfume and then I'll go get the wheel-chair. I'll bandage your ankle and with grey hair no-one will recognise you, especially if we put on some extra face powder. Maybe plastic ear-rings and a bead necklace. We can get on the bus for Maryborough and everything will be fine. Alright?'

'Right. Just Hurry up Sherry,' Quin growled. 'This mascara is beginning to make me cry. I don't know how you women can wear this stuff. It's disgusting. Maybe you should have got a waterproof one just in case. And a bigger pair of pantyhose. At this rate I'll have a genuine high pitched voice, permanently.'

Two hours later Quin and Sherry approached the bus depot where tourist buses picked up long distance passengers. Quin took Sherry's hand where it rested on the back of the wheelchair. He looked back at her and said softly, 'That bus for Maryborough seems to be filling up. We should buy our tickets now. It might be our last chance to get out of Cobbs Point so we'd better be on it.'

'Whatever you say Mum.' Sherry felt a tingling in her hand as his fingers caressed hers, making her oblivious to her surroundings. Katz and Dooley could have jumped out at any moment and she wouldn't even notice.

'The problem is how are we going to get on board without giving ourselves away.' Quin tugged on her hand and said, 'Are you listening Sherry.'

She gave a start as she was pulled back from her sensual haze. 'What was that?'

He chuckled at her glazed eyes and said, 'We need to get on the bus without attracting attention to ourselves. Got any ideas?'

Plenty, her wayward inner self replied. Most of which are totally incompatible with the mother and son relationship. She replied, 'I guess we just have to play it by ear. If anyone looks suspiciously at us we could create a diversion.'

'Like what?' Quin was intrigued. What more could this ingenious girl think up to confound their pursuers.

'I could steal that little kid's book.' She indicated a small boy in a push-chair looking through a book with goblins on the cover. 'He seems to be ignored by his mother most of the time. She'd never even notice a thing. Too busy flirting with the ticket operator.'

'Yeah. That could work,' he said in a sarcastic tone. 'He'd be screaming fit to kill and everyone would have their eyes on you. The police might even arrest you, and me as well for being an accessory to theft.'

With exaggerated patience she replied, 'I wouldn't really steal the thing. I'd just borrow it temporarily. When the kid screams I'll just say he dropped it and I was handing it back. He's too young to say any different. By the time the fuss dies down you'll be on the bus and I'll be the flavor of the month for picking the book up and handing it back. I'd only try it if we were desperate.'

He looked doubtful but said, 'I suppose it's worth a try. As a last resort.'

She looked at him drily and said, 'Your enthusiasm is overwhelming. It's a good thing I'm in charge of the wheelchair and you're being pushed around. I can just see you pinching a kid's book and his mother whacking you around the head with her handbag. The powder would shake off and we'll all be up that smelly creek without a paddle. Walker would have us parcelled up and shipped out and no-one would do a thing to stop it. The mother of the kid would probably give him a medal for services to humanity.'

'Okay Sherry. I get the point. Anyway, since I am squeezed into this bloody wheelchair and you're walking, there's nothing I can do. By the way, couldn't you have got a wider one? I think it'll take surgery to get me out of here. It's tighter than those rotten pantyhose you insisted I wear.'

'It was the only one they had. Breathe in and squeeze your legs together or cross them. Lots of ladies cross their legs. It shows off their ankles.'

'Mine are too hairy to be shown off. I forgot to shave that far down and I've left a little black stubbly fringe. It looks disgusting.'

'Don't worry Quin. If anyone gets that close hairy legs will be the least of your worries. Just relax and let me buy the tickets and get us on the bus. If you're so worried about a little bit of fluff, when we reach Maryborough you can nick into the ladies and finish shaving your legs. I'll even lend you a new razor. It's pink.'

He raised his eyes to the heavens and sighed. 'Okay, forget I mentioned the legs. Just be careful. These guys aren't playing games. They're going to do everything in their power to take us back with them, even if it means forcing us to go with them at gunpoint.'

'I'll be careful. Don't worry. I've got a lot of experience not being me.'

Quin shifted uneasily in his tight chair, a white elastic bandage on one ankle and Scrappy on his lap inside his backpack, his black button eyes peeping out under the flap. Quin's hair was covered by a wide brimmed straw hat with red and yellow material flowers around the brim. He had a spiky fringe and a few tendrils curling around his ears.'You know, I feel ridiculous,' he whispered in a gravelly voice as they went up to the double doors leading into the depot office and public lounge, Sherry pushing the chair and Quin sitting like an invalid, his knees almost touching his chin, pack with Scrappy on board in his lap, the dress falling down around his ankles, one bandaged. His feet looked huge, and male.

'Don't worry Quin. Your secret's safe with me,' Sherry laughed at his obvious discomfort. It was amazing how relaxed and safe she felt with Quin around, even with all that had happened to them and in spite of their current dangerous situation.

She knew that at a moment's notice he could get up out of the chair and protect her. She also knew that she would fight with all her strength to protect him if necessary so it went both ways.

She pushed the chair into the bus depot and bought their tickets, explaining that her mother could not walk owing to an injured ankle. She requested that, after they'd got on board the bus, someone take care of the wheelchair until it was collected by the pharmacy as arranged.

When she pushed Quin out to the bus it was filling rapidly with tourists, mostly day trippers returning to Maryborough after a day at the Carnival and beach. Quin kept a look out for anyone who looked as if he might be scanning the crowds, particularly anyone he recognised.

He was reassured by the lack of interest shown in them by their fellow travellers. In fact if he didn't know better, he'd think people were deliberately looking away from him. Surely he didn't look that grotesque?

'Sherry,' he whispered in a broken falsetto, grasping her arm and pulling her down towards him. 'Do I look alright or do I look weird.'

'You look fine Mum,' she whispered back. 'Except for the way you keep poking your chest. It looks like you're playing with your breasts.'

'They're itchy,' he muttered, thoroughly uncomfortable and scowling

irritably. 'Stop it then. You're like a little kid, always fiddling with yourself.'

'You're going to have to pay for that remark,' he husked softly, looking at her with intent in his dark eyes, in a way no mother ever should look at her son.

'Okay Mum. I'll do that just as soon as we get back home,' she said aloud and people around them nodded with approval.

One elderly woman nearby said, 'I like to see a boy who looks after his mother. It's a nice change. You're a very lucky woman and he's a fine handsome boy. You should be proud.'

'I am,' said the proud mother. 'He takes care of me very well.' His eyes promised Sherry that he would also take care of her very well. Very soon if he had his wish, very soon indeed.

It was Quin's turn to get into the bus. The driver came to assist his afflicted passenger up the step. Sherry stood behind them as the man helped Quin stand on one foot and balance so he could hop on board holding on to the safety rail.

It was a difficult maneuver, especially when Quin stood towering over the other man, his backpack with Scrappy inside draped around his shoulder. The driver looked at him with astonishment and Quin forgot his role as a woman and said in his normal deep voice tinged with impatience, 'Come on man, don't just stand there, help me up the rest of the way.'

The man stared at him, clearly confused, then started to smile knowingly, rolling his tongue across his thin lips, his freckled homely face alight with interest. He put his beefy bare arm around Quin and squeezed as they moved up, sliding his hand down surreptitiously in a slow sweep towards his rear end. Quin's look could have sliced through steel. He opened his mouth to tell the guy he'd cut his hands off if he went any further but was forestalled by a large woman lugging a screaming red faced toddler and a folded push chair up onto the bottom step below them. It was the same woman Sherry had decided to target earlier by taking the child's book to create a diversion.

Creating a diversion of her own, the woman started yelling at them to hurry up in language guaranteed to get attention. Quin took the opportunity to move further into the bus and away from the attentions of the bus driver.

He said in as high a voice as he could manage, 'Looks like you've got your hands full driver. Better get to it or she'll break the bus in half.'

'I wish I did have my hands full,' leered the driver, looking at Quin's enlarged chest and slowly licking his lips again. 'Maybe we can make a date in Maryborough. My name's Charlie Woods and I'm available. Okay? Call me at the bus line office and I'll come pick you up. We could go to the movies... or something.'

'Or something, sure,' replied Quin, his mind flitting through 'or something' scenarios but not finding anything remotely possible. He was definitely not amused but, wanting to get out of the sticky situation intact, said 'Pick me up Charlie. I'll call you and we'll make a date.' He had a feeling he knew what Charlie's version of 'or something' would turn out to be and wanted to be long gone.

The screaming child was now totally out of control and the bus driver gave a rueful look at Quin as he went to help the mother. Before he went he reached up as close as he could to Quin's ear and whispered, 'Between you and me Chickie, I'm grateful you're past having kids. It's just not my thing if you know what I mean.'

Quin nodded in agreement. 'Not mine either,' he said, forgetting to pitch his voice higher. He grinned with relief as the driver gave him a startled look and left, shaking his head.

Sherry had missed the confrontation with the driver. She had quickly taken the wheel chair back inside the depot and then headed back to the bus where Quin was sitting on a seat half way down the almost full bus. The driver was now standing outside on the pavement talking to a man who was dressed in camouflage pants and a khaki jacket. It was Katz.

Sherry almost turned and ran back inside the depot where he couldn't see her but then she thought of Quin, on the bus already and half way to being free. She steeled herself and walked as casually as she could towards the bus, past Katz and in to where Quin sat, looking out the window, a dark frown on his face. 'Katz is out there ferreting. Let's settle down low in our seats before all hell breaks loose,' he whispered hoarsely as she sat down beside him. 'Maybe we'll be lucky.'

'It's okay Mum,' said Sherry softly, holding his hand and trying not to let her heart leap out of her chest. 'We're nearly there. A few more minutes and we'll be on our way home.'

With Quin against the window, they sat as low in the narrow seats as possible which was hard for someone as tall as Quin. They waited tensely, hoping Scrappy wouldn't give them away. He was tucked down in the backpack well out of sight although the flap was open to give him air. Squeezed together like Siamese twins Sherry and Quin were both trying to ignore the sensation of thigh against thigh, hip to hip, squirming as they shifted trying to get comfortable. Ignoring it would not make it go away however but neither one would have changed places for anything in the world. They were both exactly where they wanted to be. Together.

At last, after Katz had climbed aboard, checked out the passengers himself and found nothing, having given the two fugitives a thorough inspection as he went down the aisle and back again, the bus took off, minus Katz. They breathed a sigh of relief and linked hands in silent gratitude as the bus left the town centre, the driver obviously intent on making up for lost time. The two escapees didn't mind though. In fact they even contemplated giving him a bonus for making a quick getaway.

Sherry whispered in Quin's ear, 'I sure am glad Scrappy isn't a Labrador.'

He grinned, reached into his pack and patted the little dog. 'So am I.'

After they'd been travelling for a while Sherry asked quietly, 'Quin, are you alright? You seem rather restless. I thought once we'd escaped from that place you'd be happy as a duck who survived hunting season.'

'I am happy,' he growled, not sounding it at all.

'Don't fib. Tell me what's wrong. Are you sick or something? Maybe the bus driver has some antacid? I could ask him for you?'

'Don't do that!,' he grated quickly, then seeing she was determined to interrogate him he said, 'It's the bus driver. I'm sure he thinks I'm one of those lonely widows, desperate for a man.'

'What gives you that idea?'

'He groped me on the backside. Pinched me too, the creep. I had no idea women had to put up with stuff like that. I've probably got a bruise. You know I really wanted to punch his lights out, in fact I still might.'

'Seems to me that he likes you. I've heard that a man usually only gropes like that when he thinks a woman is sexy.' Sherry grinned up at him and whispered, 'He wants you Quin. He wants you bad. Are you going to give him what he wants?'

'That's another one I owe you. Pretty soon it'll be time to give me what I want Sherry. I hope you're ready for it.' He eyed her boyish appearance with deliberation. 'I rather like boys clothes on you. Especially when I know what you look like underneath. There were some photos in Jones' collection that looked rather like you. Gorgeous.'

She gasped. 'I didn't know that. The rotten beast. What was I wearing? What did you do with them?'

He patted his pack. 'Relax. You had on that blue nightie.' He didn't mention the one of her in her briefs near the window. Somehow he knew it would worry her to death. 'I've got them safe. You don't need to worry.'

'I want them.'

'I'll give you copies.'

'Originals Quin. That's what I want. And the negatives. I hope you've got them.'

'Yeah, I've got them.' He grinned. 'Jones was up on his filing thank goodness. H and J were almost together. I didn't have to look far.'

'Yes. That's a relief.' A tide of red colour washed over her expressive face but she returned his look with a cheeky one of her own. 'Maybe you better stick to the bus driver. At least he seems keen enough to pursue the matter. He might even have a wedding ring in mind.'

Quin looked up and saw the driver giving him a long hot look in the rear-vision mirror. He had a feeling it was going to a lengthy trip to Maryborough, and only hoped the bus would stay on the road while the driver looked behind. Either way, they were travelling now and would soon be able to hire a car for the long trip back to Victoria.

What would happen then he had no idea, he only knew it would be heaven and hell to travel with Sherry who was both innocence and temptation in the one package. If they survived he would certainly have to make some changes in his life, changes that would include the girl at his side.

Quin decided to spend the extra cash and fly home. He weighed the pros and cons of days and nights on the road and after consulting with Sherry decided the best thing was to get out of Maryborough as quickly as possible.

The amorous bus driver followed their halting progress through the bus terminal and offered to assist Quin to find another wheelchair. In the midst of their refusals, he dashed off and a returned a few minutes later with a small chair he had hired from a local pharmacy. While he was gone Sherry managed to take Scrappy for a little walk outside. He was back in Quin's back-pack before the bus driver returned.

Quin squeezed himself into the wheel chair seat reluctantly, keeping his belongings on his lap, feeling more trapped by the minute as the driver offered to collect his own car and convey them to wherever they wanted to go. Sherry was trying to keep her voice deep but she was hard pressed not to burst into giggles at the expression on Quin's face as he pitched his own voice as high as possible and made numerous excuses, telling stories of plans they had made which would prevent them from accepting his hospitality.

After promising the driver they would return in a minute, Sherry and Quin left him sitting in a lounge area ordering coffee and fled down a corridor towards the public amenities where they were forced to take turns in the wheelchair section. They decided to leave by another outside door to avoid having to make up any more lies to the over zealous bus driver.

The only real problem came when no ramp was provided and Sherry had to push the chair down a step. Several people stopped to watch as Quin was tipped one way and then another, almost falling out of the chair. Unable to get up and walk, he was cursing softly under his breath and Sherry was red faced with exertion and embarrassment before the chair was righted allowing them to go on their way.

They were able to catch a bus to the airport almost immediately, Quin trying not to leap out of the offending chair and take charge of his mobility once again. He was frustrated and irritable at Sherry having to push him along, the forced inaction reminding him of his stay at the hospital in Melbourne and how he had been treated like a fractious child. The fact that he had behaved like one was not something he wanted to think about.

Another helpful bus driver helped him aboard the bus and they left the wheelchair by the ticket office where they hoped someone would notice it and return it to the pharmacy. They didn't dare find Charlie Woods and ask him to do it. He might have insisted on driving them to the airport and Quin wasn't in the mood. He'd had enough of pitching his voice high and fending off hands.

At the airport, Quin hobbled along shouldering his pack and leaning lightly on Sherry as they went slowly through the concourse. His bandaged ankle made him feel very conspicuous and he only agreed to continue the charade of being an invalid when Sherry pointed out to him how determined Merton was to find them. 'He could be anywhere around Quin,' she said quietly, looking around. 'His men are probably all around us and we don't even know who they are.'

'I'd almost welcome a confrontation with them,' he snarled. 'This invalid stuff is driving me nuts and that stupid bandage is itching like hell.'

'Calm down. We're almost home free. Just be patient a little longer.' Sherry patted his arm and slipped her hand around his waist. 'Just lean on me Mummy and I'll take care of everything.'

'That's another one I owe you son. The debts are mounting up by the minute.' He grinned an evil grin that had Sherry wishing she had been more careful of her choice of words but the feel of his warm solid body beneath her hand was worth any amount of retribution.

Quin purchased some magazines and some local and Brisbane newspapers. 'Hey, Sherry. Look at this!' he said, nudging her in the ribs with a hard floral covered elbow. 'Remember that guy at the homestead who took off. You know the one I mean. Young, fair hair. Good looking. Looked really troubled, almost desperate. Jones said he decided to go back home, wherever that was.'

'Was that the one they said was sick or something.' She looked inquiringly at the newspaper he was reading and waited for him to go on.

'Yeah. There's a picture of him. It seems he turned up at some coastal town not far from here. Washed ashore with the incoming tide. People are being asked for information because the man hasn't been identified. It seems he drowned, poor guy. It says here 'Police are treating it as murder because of certain information that has come anonymously into their possession. Inquiries are being made.' Look here.' He pointed to the photo on the front page. It was of the young guy Quin and Sherry had known only as Danny, a withdrawn confused man who was no trouble to anyone, just himself. All he had wanted in the end was to go home.'

'Oh now I remember what happened. That's the man who disappeared one night and then when he came back a day or two later he decided to go back to the city,' said Sherry excitedly. 'That's our proof Quin. They killed him and threw him into the bay.'

'I know Sherry. But we don't need proof any more. I sent a pile of photographs and papers to the police when we were at the Bryce farm. I even found a couple of video cassettes with some interesting stuff on them. Sam posted them for me.'

'Where did you get stuff like that?'

'From Jones' office. I did a little quiet pilfering one night just for insurance.'

'Great. Now they'll really get what they deserve.'

'I sure hope so.' Quin was doubtful whether they would but it was now out of his hands. It was too much to hope none of Merton's men were waiting at the Airport and they were right to worry. In fact they saw Walker speaking to a couple of khaki clad men who looked like very determined rough characters. Sherry vaguely remembered them hanging around the old homestead.

Turning aside, Quin and Sherry entered a souvenir shop and kept out of sight. Since her companion's appearance was eye-catching even under normal circumstances, when he was dressed as a very tall woman he graduated to spectacular, Sherry went to buy their tickets. Quin went quietly out the other door of the shop and sat in the departure lounge. Crossing his legs and pulling his skirt down demurely as he'd seen some older women do, he hid behind his newspaper and stroked Scrappy in the backpack, waiting impatiently for Sherry to get back, worrying all the time in case she was found and taken away by their pursuers.

Finally she returned, breathless and nervously looking over her shoulder. 'What's the matter?' he asked. 'Did anyone see you?'

'Yes, they saw me...'

'Let's get out of here then. Next thing we know they'll be dragging us back to the homestead and we'll never get away again. They'll either lock us up and throw away the key or we'll end up like Danny, floating in the bay.'

Quin made to stand up and took her by the arm. His grip was strong and determined but she pulled against him, holding on to the chair arm and remaining seated. She pulled her arm away and took his hand. He relaxed for a moment giving her a questioning but impatient look. 'What is it? We haven't time to talk about this. If they saw you we're history.'

'Calm down Quin. Yes, they saw me. They didn't recognise me though. They thought I was what I look like, a teenager with a chip on my shoulder. I did a lot of scowling and shrugging at the ticket office while I bought our tickets. I even swore a little. I hate saying that F word. Makes me feel sick but I said it anyway. My voice should have a permanent croak in it.'

'Why didn't they recognise you? They must be blind not to see beyond that hat and hair. Anyone with eyes could see you're too pretty for a spotty teenage boy.' Then he noticed her face. Quite a few small reddish spots were dotted artistically on her cheeks, forehead and nose. 'What the hell have you done to your face?' he growled, putting his finger under her jaw and turning her to the light.

'A little extra insurance. I nipped into the ladies to add a little war paint. Now I really do look like a spotty teenager with zits and attitude. Suits me don't you think?' She preened and grinned up at him and he almost grinned back, but somehow the thought of Merton or Walker being anywhere near her was enough to make his stomach churn with the need to protect her.

'Go on Sherry. What happened next?'

'Somehow I knew someone would be hanging around the ticket counter in case we showed up. I was right. Just as I was about to get our tickets Walker came past and stood there for several minutes looking around. He looked at me and scowled, then he looked away again. It was like being passed over for the guillotine.'

Quin gave a strangled sound, much like a growl and said, 'Hell.'

Sherry grimaced. 'Yeah. Well, I paid for the tickets and took off back here as soon as I could. When I left he was standing outside the men's room checking out every tall man who walked by. Maybe we'll be lucky and he'll be arrested as a pervert. It would serve him right.'

Sighing his relief Quin settled back into his chair, his mind and body unable to relax. He was a tightly coiled spring and nothing would change that until they got far away from there. He watched everyone who walked past like a hawk and kept the paper held in front of both of them as a shield. It wasn't metal but it was the best he could do.

Finally, after waiting a good two hours, they managed to board a plane, Quin shuffling like the invalid he was pretending to be, Sherry the concerned and helpful teenage son. They carefully smuggled Scrappy on board tucked inside Quin's backpack which Sherry had taken charge of. It was while they were standing on the portable steps at the plane's door that a commotion began just inside the terminal.

Police cars screamed onto the tarmac and three men were immediately surrounded. Quin and Sherry looked on in stunned disbelief as Walker hurled abuse and he, accompanied by two companions, were restrained in handcuffs and hustled inside the vehicles. Out of the crowd were led Katz and Dooley. They were also placed in a police van and driven away. It would seem Quin's envelope full of information had arrived at the police station and they had acted immediately on the information received.

Quin figured out they must have raided the homestead the day before and finally caught up with the rest of them at the airport. Not wishing to become involved any more than they had already, Sherry and Quin were grateful they were already on the plane. Fortunately their flight took off moments later and they were at last on their way to freedom.

CHAPTER FIFTEEN

Maryborough Queensland soon became a distant memory as Quin and Sherry flew through the night and after changes at Brisbane and Sydney, landed many hours later at Melbourne's Tullamarine Airport. Outside the building, Sherry put Scrappy down for a walk around and turned to Quin saying, 'I suppose you'll want to go back to wherever you came from now. It wasn't such a good idea to run away was it Quin? We only got into worse trouble than before.'

'I don't know Sherry. If I hadn't answered the ad I wouldn't have met you. I'm glad I did.' He looked down at her aching to take her in his arms, a brooding half smile on his lean intelligent face. He decided to wait until she gave some indication as to what she intended to do. After all, he didn't have much to offer a woman. Sure he had money but what use was that if you lived in terror for your life, always looking over your shoulder in case someone is following you, intending to kill you.

'I'm glad too,' she said, her eyes moist and sad. 'At least now I know there's a whole world out there. I might be able to find some place to fit in. I'll just have to keep looking.'

'What are you going to do now?' he asked.

'Guess I'll go home for now. Nowhere else to go is there?' Her voice was without hope.

'I don't know. Where do you want to go?' Quin wanted to make a couple of suggestions and was about to speak when Sherry touched him on his arm and moved imperceptibly closer. 'I don't know either. It's scary being alone. What will I do about the money I owe you for my plane ticket and bus fare and other stuff,' she asked. 'I can try to get the money from Ralph somehow.'

'You don't owe...' Quin paused, his face thoughtful, then his eyes lit up as he said, 'I reckon I'll have to come with you to Archer's Creek and have a few words with Ralph myself. Can't let an investment slip away now can I?'

'No,' she smiled as if he had given her everything her heart desired in one sweet package. 'Ralph will have to pay you what I owe. If he doesn't I'll go to the solicitor. He might be able to make Ralph pay because some of the money from my dad's estate must belong to me. The

property belonged to my parents after all. So, you'll have to come. To get your money I mean.'
'Yeah. I'll come. So, do you want to spend the night here in Melbourne before heading off? It's getting late in the day and I have a couple of things I need to take care of before I disappear again.'

'What do you mean...spend the night?' Sherry's eyes questioned him intently.

Quin took her hand and led her to a seat. He said, 'I want you Sherry. I need you. I think I have from the first moment I saw you at the cabin. I'd like you to stay the night with me but if you don't want to I'll understand. I'll still come with you to Archer's Creek.' He watched her with an unblinking dark-eyed gaze, taking in her flushed beautiful face, her lovely grey eyes, fine dark eyebrows and silver hair. She was everything he ever wanted but he knew she had to want him as desperately as he wanted her or it wouldn't be any good for either of them.

'Oh Quin. I'm so confused. I want to stay with you but I'm not sure I'm ready for that. Could we just take one day at a time and see what happens when we get there?'

'There's no more to be said my lovely girl. We'll confront Ralph Marley together and then we'll make time for ourselves. Maybe I'll stay a while in Archer's Creek. If you want me to that is?'

She flung her arms around his neck and, tears pouring down her face, cried, 'Oh yes. I want you to come with me Quin. More than anything in the world. I've a friend you can stay with, the one who brought me down to the hotel. Pete Madigan lives on the other side of the town from our place and he'd be glad to put up any friend of mine.'

'It's settled then. We'll go to Archer's Creek and the rest we'll sort out later. I have a couple of small errands I have to do before we leave though. I haven't any place to stay in Melbourne at the moment so I think we'll spend the night in a city hotel.' He grinned at her suspicious look and continued, 'Separate rooms, much as it torments me. I won't push you for anything you don't want to give Sherry. But if you change your mind...?'

'Don't wait up....' Sherry grinned at his look of sensual longing and almost changed her mind. Then she steeled herself and said, 'Stop looking at me as if I were prime rib Quin. It's very disturbing.' She snuggled into his waist like a homing pigeon, almost squashing little Scrappy between them.

'That's good. I like to disturb you. I'd disturb you a whole lot more if you'd let me.' He frowned as he began to think about being back in the city. 'You know, my apartment in Carlton was rented. All my things were put in storage including my wheels. But the reason I left is still here.'

'Will you be able to come back to work here some day?'

'I don't know honey. I don't even know if I want to come back on a permanent basis although a visit would be okay. A whole lot of trouble happened to me here as you know. I'll tell you more about it someday soon. In the meantime we'd better find a taxi. We can drop the little guy off at my old landlord's flat for the night and then we'll book into a city hotel and find a nice restaurant. I think we owe ourselves a treat before we head up country. We've quite a way to go tomorrow and who knows what we'll find when we get there.'

'Ah, Quin, aren't you forgetting something?' Sherry unwound her arms from his waist and stepped back a little, grinning widely as she surveyed him.

'What?'

'You need to have a small sex change operation. You're still a woman.'

A man passing by looked at them and did a double take at Quin's distinct five o'clock shadow. Quin glared at him and he went hurrying on his way, muttering about gays and closets and the Donahue show. Sherry laughed until tears were pouring down her face. 'Go change out of your dress before I have to bail you out of jail for defending your honour with your fists. I'll wait here for you.'

'Are you sure you'll be alright?'

'I'll be fine. Go! Go!' Sherry smiled as he went and sighed. Life was certainly changing for the better. She hadn't laughed so much in ages, if ever. The only problem now was how to deal with Ralph. Thankfully she had Quin to help with that. If only he would stay around permanently, if only he loved her as much as she loved him, life would be paradise.

After securing a taxi and dropping Scrappy with Mr. And Mrs. Scallini, they booked into the Victoria Hotel in Little Collins Street, single rooms as Sherry had decided.

Quin had changed his clothes at his friend's apartment and, much to their bemusement and Sherry's delight, had emerged as a man once again.

They had spent a busy but wonderful hour explaining what was going on, not all the details but in general. Sherry had found a mother in Mrs. Scallini who had taken her in her arms and hugged her with Italian enthusiasm when she heard of the traumas she had undergone. When they had finally left, the two women had been in tears and the two men had shaken hands in secure friendship. Quin knew that if anything happened to him, the Scallini family would welcome Sherry with open arms. Scrappy seemed to be settling in with a ham bone as big as he was in the kitchen and hardly noticed they were gone. He was also busy guarding his bone from the cat.

Dinner that night was wonderful, a superb blend of old world charm and exotic flavors that pleased both Sherry and Quin even though neither could tell afterwards what they had eaten. He walked her back to the hotel with his hand firmly linked with hers, protecting her from the crowds of people milling around outside the cinema complex in Burke Street, pulling her back from the kerb when she would have walked blithely across against the traffic lights. He said, 'Careful honey,' as he put his arm around her shoulders. 'I don't want to lose you.'

Startled, she replied, 'Oh, sorry Quin. Thanks. I must have been dreaming. I always seem to need rescuing lately. It's getting to be quite a habit.'

'It's a habit I like. So long as I can do the rescuing.' Quin bent and kissed her gently on the lips and asked, 'What were you dreaming of?'

'Oh, this and that.' They were walking past the huge Myer Department Store windows watching the displays, especially the one with real people walking around in the window like it was their apartment or office. The four men even had a bathroom behind a curtain much to her surprise. 'Isn't that fascinating. Those people in the window don't seem to care people are watching them. One of them just made a rude sign with his hand. I think they can lip read.'

'I'd be rude too if people stared at me. See what it says on the sign. They're in there for a week, spending the whole time in a living display. Must be hard to go to the bathroom with everyone watching.'

'Crazy. You can't help looking though. I've never seen anything like it.'

They walked on after a while then turned back up the Bourke Street Mall to Swanston Street. Quin said, 'So, you were going to tell me about your dream.'

'Was I?' She looked down to prevent him reading the truth of her dream in her eyes. That all she really wanted was to change her mind and take what he had offered her previously, a night of love in his arms. A night that would have to last her forever because tomorrow she would return to Archer's Creek and Ralph's domination.

Even though Quin would be with her and had promised to help her sort out her problems with Ralph, she had a deep fear that her guardian would manipulate and twist things until he found a way to destroy her and anyone who became involved with her. It was one of his talents, one which he enjoyed practising on everyone who came in contact with him.

Sherry had the feeling that, if Quin knew how tempted she was to change her mind about sharing his bed that night, he would be unable to stop himself trying to persuade her. Although it would probably be the most wonderful night of her life, it would also be against all her deepest moral convictions absorbed during the first years of life with her loving family. Unfortunately, the flesh and the conscience didn't always see eye to eye and she was determined to see that her conscience won.

He might have read her mind because he said in a voice husky with emotion, 'Let's go back to the hotel.' Then he began to walk quickly, forging through the supper crowds with a fierce determination, firmly but gently shouldering past anyone who got in his way.

Breathless from the speed they walked, Sherry wished they could stroll slowly, enjoying the fresh spring air and unusual aromas emanating from exotic sidewalk cafés and restaurants. The streets were filled with lights and the sounds of laughter spiced with such interesting faces and wonderfully dressed people it was hard for her not to stop and stare.

Most people seemed so tall and confident and sophisticated. Sherry wanted to be just like them, striding along as if she belonged, as if this was her city. It was an exciting new world and she wanted to savour it like a child sucking a hard boiled candy, licking the tingling flavor of sherbet from her lips and crunching the texture until it dissolved in her mouth with unbelievable sweetness.

'Why are we hurrying Quin? You're going too fast for me to see anything.' He hurried her past a busy pancake café with patrons sitting at tables set out on the sidewalk, crossed Swanston Street against the lights and turned into the narrow street where their hotel entrance was situated. 'Hey, did we just jaywalk back there?' she laughed, tugging at his arm.

'I thought you were a law and order kind of guy. You know, I could get to like living on the edge. It sure beats staying at home washing clothes or ironing.'

'You've been living on the edge Sherry. In fact you've taken it to the limit by answering that damned advertisement. Somehow though, I don't think the edge is what you really want.' He smiled down at her. 'You'd rather be safe.'

'Yeah,' she acknowledged with a wry grin. 'You could be right about that.' She knew what she really wanted. A life with the man she loved, free of fear.

Quin paused in the shadows outside the hotel and put his arms around her, drawing her close to his body, making her tremble with unfulfilled needs. She clenched her hands against his chest and tried to keep from sliding her fingers up to the naked skin of his firm tanned throat and running them through the thick soft hair touching his shoulders.

She could feel the tension in his body as he moved deeper into the darkness of a doorway and as he swept his hands down her spine to stroke her hips and thighs, the urge to say yes to anything he asked was overwhelming.

His voice was a husky purr as he said, 'What I really want is to take you back to your room and show you what it's like to need something so badly it will kill you not to get it. But I'm not going to. I am going to kiss you though. For as long as I can stand it without dissolving in a puddle on the floor. Then I'll leave you alone to sleep... if you can. I certainly won't be able to.'

His lips descended to hers and made a mockery of all her protestations. She was on fire and the only way to put out the flame was to allow him access to the very heart of her.

Sherry was sinking into a deep well of sensation where the slide down to oblivion was filled with total breathless pleasure. She was moving so fast without a hope of stopping the ride when a harsh voice intruded into her consciousness.

A man was chivying a woman about her drinking too much as they walked past Quin and Sherry and entered the hotel. It was a cold and abrupt end to a flight which had begun with the simple touch of skin to skin.

She shivered in the cool night air and drew away from Quin who tightened his arms momentarily then let her go. 'What's wrong darling? Are you cold?'

'I'm sorry Quin. I wish I could be casual about things.' She looked away, not wanting to see rejection of her ideals in his eyes. 'I can't be what you want. My life is so complicated at the moment. It's just that...well, you know how it is.'

'Hush my darling. I do know how it is. Someday I hope you will too. I won't put any more pressure on you. I just want you to know how I feel right now. I love you so much, it hurts to let you go. But we have all the time in the world to become more than friends. When the time is right we'll become lovers too.'

Sherry sighed, knowing that there was no other man for her, knowing that he was putting aside his own needs and desires in order to keep her safe and respect her wishes. She loved him for his passion, his strength and for his honour. It made him a remarkable man, one she wanted to keep with her forever.

The next morning Sherry woke up to a loud knock on her door. For a moment she tensed in fear but as the veil of sleep slipped from her eyes she realised it couldn't be Ralph or anyone who meant her harm. It could only be the man she loved, the man who'd come to mean more to her than her own safety, her own life.

Hopping out of bed, she put on a hotel robe and let Quin into the room. He was remarkably cheerful as he said, 'Come on my little zombie. It's after nine. I want to do a little shopping and talk to the guy who took over the lease on my shop. Plus I need to pick up my car from the long term garage. We can grab a quick breakfast in the café downstairs and catch a tram to Carlton.' Determinedly he looked away from her dishevelled silver blonde hair and sleepy grey eyes.

It was too much to hope his intense desire for her had gone away during the night. His promise to her was to keep her safe and he wasn't going to let himself betray her trust just because he was alone in a bedroom with her and tempted almost beyond endurance.

'I'd like to say get lost but I know you won't.' She yawned through her words and hurriedly covered her mouth with her hand. 'It would be too much to expect.'

'Ah, you're not a morning person.' He grinned at her scowl. 'Don't worry my darling, you don't have to say a thing until lunch time except yes or no. I'll do all the talking.'

'I can speak for myself thanks very much.' She was beginning to come alive.

'I'm sure you can,' he replied soothingly as he dragged jeans, underwear and a T shirt out of her pack. 'You're just a little grouchy right now.'

'I'm not as grouchy as I'm going to be Quin Jameson,' she snarled as she snatched her plain white cotton briefs from his hand and buried them in the pocket of the robe. He grinned as he handed her the rest of her clothes and gently pushed her into the en-suite bathroom and shut the door.

He packed her things for her and when she emerged showered and fully dressed he handed her a hairbrush. After she'd tugged her sneakers on and made a soft silver cloud of her long wet hair by using the drier supplied by the hotel, he picked up their two packs and opened the door.

In the lift he pressed the button for the ground floor and she looked at him sternly, saying, 'Offending people is an art. That's your department and may I say, you do it very well. I'm impressed.'

'A caffeine fix and you'll feel more human,' he said as if she hadn't spoken.

'For the last time I am not grouchy in the mornings. I'm perfectly nice to be around. I'm never rude or offensive.' That was the last word she said in the lift because he kissed her until she was shaking with pleasure and then they were on the ground floor.

Quin paid their hotel bill and they went into the café to order breakfast. He was glad they'd left Scrappy with Mrs. Scallini because he didn't think the café or the hotel would appreciate a visit from the mutt, cute as he was. It was while they drank their coffee that he asked, 'What are you going to do about Ralph?'

Sherry's appetite died on hearing that name. 'I have no idea. I can't even think about him without feeling sick. He's like an open wound that won't heal.'

'Well, we can discuss it on the way to Archer's Creek if you like.' Quin smiled at her reassuringly and took her hand in his, stroking it gently. 'We need to talk about it some time before we get there but perhaps it's better not to spoil the time we have together in Melbourne. After all, it's not very often I get to tour the city with such a beautiful companion, especially one with such a fresh and interesting viewpoint.'

'Keep talking Quin. I like the way you distract me. All I want to think about right now is shopping. I've never seen so much stuff for sale. It's paradise.'

'Yes, it's paradise,' he returned drily, not wanting to spoil her fun but knowing she had to be aware of the dangers. 'It has a large variety of serpents though. Many of them just take your money but some might take your life if you aren't careful.'

'I'm not worried,' she said without really taking in the warning message behind his cryptic comment. 'I have you to protect me. Anyway, what's wrong with shopping. I haven't any money but looking is more fun than spending anyway...at least, I think it is. I've never had any money to spend anyway.'

Quin smiled but inside he was troubled with her naive outlook. He wouldn't always be with her and even if he was, who could tell if his presence would be enough to keep her safe. He didn't even know if he could protect himself.

With trepidation Sherry climbed on board the tram that carried them to Carlton. It was green with polished wooden seats and colourful advertising posters on each side. She'd never been on a tram and found the whole process to be rather frightening until she found her tram legs.

Then she enjoyed the sway and the sudden stops and starts along with the clattering noise, uneven tracks and the fascinating variety of people who seemed to find the whole thing rather boring. She even enjoyed the clanging bells when the tram stopped and started and the cars that cut in and out of traffic around the tram.

Quin smiled at her almost child-like enthusiasm but kept his eyes alert and hands ready in case she put a foot wrong as she seemed to frequently do. It was distressingly easy for the novice tram traveller to trip and fall getting off.'I want to give you a first-time experience you'll associate only with me,' he whispered in her ear as the tram clattered up Swanston Street. He hoped deep inside it would be only one of many first-times she would enjoy with him.

They visited Quin's old business and Sherry learned that the present lessee of the store had changed the name. Because of the write up about Quin's involvement with the police in the papers and the association of his name with the business, the man told them he'd decided not to try to keep the goodwill, which had dissipated anyway in the tangle of lies printed by the press.

John Allen ran the same type of business that Quin had, sign writing and art supplies, but with a revised client base and fewer men working for him. 'Sherry, would you like to sit in the café next door to the shop and have a coffee while I go to see John Allen. I think you'll be better off not being seen with me for a while.'

'What's wrong Quin?' Sherry looked around nervously. 'Is it dangerous?'

'Could be. I'd rather keep you to myself for a bit. I'm rather well known around here and you never know when a reporter might be looking out for me. They've haunted me in the past and I don't want them doing the same to you.'

'Okay. I'll have a drink while I wait. Don't be long will you?' She kissed him then went into the café where she sat at a window seat and looked out at him.

He entered the building where he had worked and run a successful business for nearly five years. It brought back a wave of nostalgia but not regret. His life had moved on and he had met Sherry. He wouldn't turn back the clock for anything.

After speaking to a couple of his previous employees who had transferred to the new owner, Quin went with the man into a back room for a moment. 'John, has anyone come around asking about me or trying to find out where I am? Strangers I mean.' Quin tried not to sound paranoid. 'Anyone suspicious?'

'Several people have been asking questions. I couldn't tell them anything because you disappeared out of the city and I had no idea where you'd gone. It was rather annoying you know. Not to say embarrassing. People have begun to suspect me of doing away with you and taking over your business.'

John Allen laughed ruefully and continued. 'They're idiots. I've had all kinds of strange phone calls at night and my wife is beginning to think I'm having an affair. Who with I ask her, I'm too busy answering the damn phone.'

'I'm sorry John. It was out of my hands.'

'So, where were you? What if this keeps up and people want answers? Do I tell them you're back and give them your phone number? What is it by the way?'

'I'm not back. You haven't seen me and I can't give a phone number because there isn't one. Forget about me John. It's the only thing to do at the moment.'

'Well, people are asking questions but they're going away ticked off because I don't know anything. One guy tried to rough me up a little but left when I threatened to call the police. Nasty type. I'm sure he's been watching the place.'

'It's safer if you deny having seen me John. Safer for everyone.'

'Okay. I'll keep it to myself. But don't be surprised if someone sees you and tracks you down. They obviously want you real bad. You've had your picture in the papers too often not to be recognised. There's no guaranteed the people who work here will keep quiet but I'll ask them. They're a pretty loyal bunch.'

'Thanks mate,' said Quin. 'I owe you one.' Then he collected Sherry from the café and they walked outside.

Quin's dark green Jeep Cherokee was parked in the tiny customer parking area at the side of the shop. The previous day he'd gone to the long term garage and arranged to have it checked out be a mechanic and delivered there since it was easier to find parking places in Carlton than the inner city.

'I've seen wagons like that around Archer's Creek Quin. They're the kind of thing the rich farmers buy.' Sherry looked admiringly at the glossy dark green paintwork on the vehicle and the comfortable looking brown upholstery.

'It's a Jeep Cherokee,' he said, stating the obvious. 'What else could a Cherokee Indian buy.' He laughed at the confused look on her face, deeply satisfied at having his property back. 'It's my way of keeping it in the family.'

It was as they reached the Jeep that Quin felt something prickle the back of his neck. He looked around and found himself tensing as a black Mercedes sedan slowly rolled to a stop near the entrance to the car park. The windows were tinted, the occupants unidentifiable, but Quin felt sure there were eyes watching him, and watching Sherry.

Were they something to do with the warehouse robbery he'd witnessed or were they just business people looking for somewhere to park? Maybe they were well heeled shoppers looking to stop and purchase something nearby. Who could tell?

Quin had to quell the urge to throw his woman into the Jeep and drive off so fast they would have no hope of catching up, even if they wanted to.

Slowly and deliberately he got out his keys and opened the door for Sherry, helping her inside then tossing their gear onto the back seat. He walked to the driver's side and opened the door, giving the black car a sideways glance to check the number plate. Making a mental note, he climbed behind the wheel, determined not to panic and plant his foot to get away. After all, his imagination had played him tricks before and he didn't want it to run out of control before he had a chance to find out what was going on, or indeed, if anything was going on.

He started the Jeep and pulled out of the carpark without mishap and, as they left the still stationary Mercedes behind, breathed a sigh of relief. It probably wasn't anything to worry about he thought, maybe someone with plenty of credit cards was feeding the economy. They looked like they could afford it.

They spent some time going round a selection of exotic shops and even visited the Queen Victoria Market where he bought her a small silver chain bracelet with tiny silver charms dangling from it. Sherry was delighted with the gift and smiled shyly up at him. 'Thank you Quin. It's beautiful.' Her eyes became clouded with worry then and she said, 'I wish I had some money to buy something for you. It isn't fair for you to spend so much money on me. That lovely hotel cost a fortune and you've been buying me food and things. It's too much.'

'It's your birthday soon isn't it? I know you haven't had anyone give you a present or wish you happy birthday since you were ten so let me do it now. Happy birthday darling.' Then he kissed her gently making the whole noisy scene fade away like magic. Then he took her hand and they strolled on through the market, linked to each other by invisible threads of love.

She couldn't believe the excitement of it all. The variety of languages spoken and shouted across the vast expanse of stalls and the distinct earthy smell of the fruit and vegetable section of the market overwhelmed her. The trays of costume jewellery and the racks of clothes tempted her to stop and feel fabrics and to try them on. Even the jostling crowds swarming noisily along the narrow aisles like ants made her want to be a part of it all.

Firewalking

After a meal at yet another continental style café, Quin said, 'I think it's time we got going Sherry. Much as I've enjoyed today with you we're just postponing the inevitable if we stay here much longer. We need to get the situation with Ralph squared away so we can get on with out lives. Okay?'

Knowing he was right didn't make Sherry feel any better. 'So let's go then,' she said brightly, her apprehension, showing itself in the tightening of her mouth and the pulse vibrating in her throat, visible only to Quin. 'But first we have to go pick up Scrappy. He's probably pining to death right now.'

Quin negotiated the streets to his old apartment building, collecting Scrappy with many thanks to his pooch sitters. Mr. Scallini seemed to be quite recovered from his partial deafness and other minor injuries caused by the explosion of Quin's van. Mrs. Scallini told them she had fallen totally in love with Scrappy and begged Sherry to bring him back for a visit any time.

After they had made a fuss of Quin's ex cat and promised to return soon, Quin and Sherry climbed into his car and took the Western freeway flowing out of Melbourne. It was time for Sherry to go home and face her demons. Only then would she really be free.

CHAPTER SIXTEEN

Sherry felt as if she had been away from home forever. Late afternoon in Archer's Creek was just as she remembered on this bright spring day, a small mining town built on a tributary of a larger river in the gold rush days of the 1800's. The river had long since lost is power due to drought and demands for irrigation from farmers. The population was around five thousand but it serviced many outlying properties. The shopping centre was adequate but many people preferred to drive to the Rural City of Ballarat about forty five minutes away.

Quin cruised slowly down the wide main street, the blue flowered jacaranda trees lining the central strip of lawn which boasted rustic wooden picnic tables and random flower beds ripe with colour. He looked from side to side, appreciating the two story colonial style red brick buildings still fronted with balconies and wide verandahs decorated with white painted iron lace-work. The historic buildings were interspersed with a few more modern structures which seemed reassuring while still a little out of place.

'It's very peaceful,' he said. Sherry had gone strangely still and quiet. 'Even the air smells different from the city. It's clean. Are you nervous sweetheart? There's no need. I won't let anyone hurt you.'

He parked the car on a side street and turned to her, waiting for her to tell him how she felt. Her hand shook as she pushed back her fine silver hair and she took a deep breath before replying, 'I hate feeling so scared Quin. I was born in this town but I haven't felt at home here since mum and dad died. Ralph just took over everything including me. My family pioneered this whole area and mined it as well. Even now a lot of the property still belongs to us.'

'What do you mean, to us?'

'I'm not sure. I think my name was put on the deeds when my parents died but I think Ralph has something to do with it too. Dad trusted him and he has a lot of authority as to what goes on around here. I asked him one day who owned what and he told me to mind my own business.' She laughed sadly. 'I must have been feeling rebellious that day. He sure knocked that trait out of me quick smart. Maybe he's an equal partner or even more than that. I don't really know all the details. He certainly acts as though the whole place belongs to him. In his mind it probably does, after all, he is the Mayor of Archer's Creek.'

Disgusted at the control Ralph Marley exercised over the town and over Sherry particularly, Quin swore under his breath. 'Have you been to a solicitor to find out the truth of the situation?'

'Oh no. Ralph would find out.' Her fearful words brought images of punishment into Quin's mind and he reminded himself to take this thing slow. He didn't want to frighten her any more than she had been already.

Any mention of Ralph seemed to bring a terrified expression to her otherwise serene face, her eyes darting to and fro in remembered panic, perspiration forming on the fine skin of her brow.

After sitting quietly for a while Sherry calmed and turned to look at Quin, her eyes trustingly on his as she said softly, 'Anyway, the only solicitor in town is Ralph's friend Walter Slade and he wouldn't talk to me without Ralph being there.'

'That's a conflict of interest Sherry and is probably against the law.' Quin was beginning to understand quite a few things during this quiet drive through town. The place looked like a pleasant piece of history basking in the sun with nothing going on except for casual communication between friendly neighbours and the usual shopping forays of country folk on a trip to town with a game of bowls in mind or a football match. Maybe they'd throw in a visit to the local library.

Underneath the facade however, there was a seething web of resentment and lies fuelled by the ambition of one man whose corrupting power lay in controlling the life and assets of the girl he had ruthlessly subjugated both mentally and physically for the last twelve years.

'Ralph was my guardian and he was also made administrator of my estate until I turn twenty five.' Sherry sighed. 'There's nothing I can do about that.'

'What about going to the Police?' Surely he thought, someone should have been there to protect a young girl who had just tragically lost her parents, someone who didn't have self-interest at heart.

'There is a police station here but I think they're trying to phase out small local stations. Sergeant Burns is still here though. He's another of Ralph's friends. At least I think he's a friend. He always seems to be hanging around him at any rate. Does what he's told without question as far as I can see. I heard someone say once that they were joined at the hip, whatever that means. Sounds a bit uncomfortable to me.' She laughed drily.

'Ralph is also a deacon at our church and most people in town attend there as well as shop for their daily needs at the general store. He runs the store and the petrol station. It's the only one in town.' she added ruefully. 'If you don't buy from Ralph then you don't buy at all. It's that simple. Otherwise you do all your shopping in Ballarat.'

'Does he own those businesses Sherry?'

'I don't think so. They're part of the family trust handed down from my grandfather to his daughters, my mother and Aunt Jo, both of them are dead now, as well as everyone else in my family, except Ralph and me.'

'So where does Ralph Marley fit in exactly? Is he a close relative or what? I remember you've told me something about it but I can't recall.'

'He's my father's cousin's husband. Sylvia was married to Ralph and they had a daughter Susan who ran away from home about fifteen years ago. They lived in Portland in the Western District. Remember, I told you he worked on trawlers?

'I suppose Susan is alive still but I don't know where she is. I have a letter I found amongst Ralph's things saying the most terrible things about him, things he did to his daughter and to his wife. Sylvia wrote the letter. It was addressed to a woman friend of hers but then Sylvia died, obviously before she could post it, and clearly nothing was done about it. It was dated two weeks before her funeral. I think Ralph may have found it after she died and then shoved it away amongst some other papers and forgot about it, possibly not reading it but thinking it was just a letter to her friend. He probably intended to burn it later. Or maybe he doesn't even know about it at all.'

'Maybe he found the letter before she died,' said Quin with a questioning look on his face. 'How exactly did she die?'

'She took a bottle of sleeping pills. I always supposed she couldn't live without her daughter and got depressed. You don't think...?'

'Anything's possible. Ralph Marley is a dangerous character, totally ruthless and obsessive about you Sherry. I noticed that about him when I met him at the Palm Lake cabin, before we went to Queensland.'

He looked at her sharply as she gasped 'You actually spoke to him? I thought you just saw him that time and didn't speak. What did he say?'

'Nothing much. Just a lot of rubbish about you belonging to him. Seemed to think God had given him the right to control you. I set him straight then came back to you. You were asleep by then so I didn't want to disturb you about it.'

'You should have told me. I'd have explained about this religious thing he has. I think he loves the power of it all, the feeling he has that he's been chosen to direct the rest of us to his way of thinking, according to him the only way.'

'Whatever his religion, I think we're right to be suspicious of anything he does. I reckon he'd be capable of anything. Even getting rid of a wife who wrote damaging things about him in a letter, things he could go to jail for. Even taking your life over and using your inheritance for his own benefit. Yes Sherry. I believe your Ralph Marley would do anything at all to keep from being found out. Have you got the letter with you?'

'He's not my Ralph. I certainly don't want him,' she asserted.

She fished around in her bag and drew out a worn envelope shuddering as she passed it to him. 'I've had this thing in my pack for weeks. It makes my skin crawl to read it.' He took it and rapidly scanned the contents.

'Well, what do you think? Is it going to help us at all.' Sherry sounded anxious and hopeful at the same time.

'What a mongrel he is.' He looked disgusted then he grinned. 'This letter should certainly put the wind up Marley, more like a hurricane. We'd better get a photocopy of it just to be on the safe side. Would you like me to look after it?'

'Yes please Quin. I don't even want to touch it.' Sherry took a shaky breath. 'Anyway, as I was saying before, my father trusted Ralph to look after me. I guess Dad included Ralph in his will too, I don't know. They seemed to be friends. I've never actually seen the document.

'When my parents died I was only ten and considered too young to be involved in wills and such things. Ralph handled everything and Mr. Slade helped him.' In a voice filled with self loathing she added, 'I just did what I was told just like a good little girl. I was so stupid.'

'It's not your fault Sherry. Didn't you say it was your mother's father who owned this land. Surely your mother would have left it to her only daughter.'

'Yes, she would have. But she died first and everything was left to my father. Then he died too.' Tears filled her eyes when she thought of how they had died.

'I think this whole business stinks Sherry. You ought to get it investigated.'

'How? With everyone in town in Ralph's pocket, what can I do. They'd laugh at me if I made charges against him.' She said bitterly, 'He has respectability.'

'We'll see. First, we have to see what's been going on in your absence. I think it's best if we keep Sylvia's letter a secret for now. It will be an ace up our sleeve. I'll come with you to see Marley but you won't stay with him. You'd better come to your friend's place with me. Don't worry honey, we'll sort something out. I won't leave you to get through this on your own.'

Sherry smiled at him with such absolute trust in her eyes and he knew he could never leave her. And if she tried to leave him he would follow her. He'd give her time to make up her mind what she wanted and then he'd persuade her that she wanted him and that nothing else mattered. All the problems in his life and hers would be resolved one way or another but at least they would be together.

Scrappy began to whimper then and scratch at the car door. Knowing his needs must come before they began to sort out their own problems, Sherry put his lead on and took him for a walk. They stopped to buy take-away hamburgers and cokes before sitting at a picnic table in the small tree filled park at the edge of the shopping area. Several families were relaxing under the trees with their young children playing tag. Elderly folk sat on portable chairs and drank tea from flasks.

The air was becoming cooler in that peaceful spring afternoon, but Sherry felt heat crawl up her neck as several people stopped, stared and whispered, obviously recognising her. They also looked long and curiously at Quin whose tall rangy body, long dark hair and dark good looking face invited avid interest, especially from a group of three young women cruising past in a car.

They slowed to a crawl then parked before going into a hotel nearby, looking over their shoulders at Quin and beckoning with their smiles. He ignored them and they disappeared into the hotel chattering like magpies, their jeans clad hips swaying with invitation. One of them was Johnny Piedmont's girlfriend Karen.

Sherry wasn't happy to see the girl had not changed a bit. She was still gorgeous. She wondered what Karen was doing flirting like she was and obviously man hunting with her friends. Maybe Johnny was away at college or maybe the romance of the century was a non-event. She felt sorry for him if that was so because he seemed to really love Karen.

She knew the girls were talking about them and hated it. Her insecurities were rife and she wanted to run after them and say 'He's mine. Go find your own man', but she didn't. She tucked her hand in the crook of his arm and stayed by his side.

Some people said hello but hurried on without further conversation. One or two obviously welcomed her and stopped momentarily to ask how she was, their smiles cautious but genuine. Others spoke to her but left her feeling uneasy, as if they had a lot of questions but were forced to keep quiet by circumstances beyond their control. A few people, when they saw her, turned away and crossed the street, clearly unwilling to speak or be spoken to.

Sherry was left feeling hurt and confused, not knowing how she felt about the town's attitudes towards her or what some of their cryptic comments about Ralph had meant. She had no real idea as to how they felt about her return to the fold or whether they would support her in any way if she was forced to ask for help.

One elderly man said in passing, 'Your Uncle Ralph was looking everywhere for you girl. He hasn't been the same since you left.' He didn't wait for a reply.

Quin raised his eyebrows and said, 'Uncle Ralph?'

'I used to call him uncle when he first came here. I called his wife Auntie Sylvia when I was a child. Some people think he's really my uncle but he isn't even related to me at all except by marriage and that doesn't count in my opinion.'

No-one asked who her tall dark companion was and no explanation for his presence was volunteered by Sherry or Quin. They had decided earlier to keep his role in her life a mystery for now. It was a choice which seemed natural to Sherry for, as yet, she had no real idea what the future held. All she knew was that she wanted Quin in that future with her.

Maybe Ralph would get nervous and let the truth come out about his activities when he saw that she had some backup from another person, one who was not under his influence or dependent on his goodwill for an income or credit. And there was always the fact that Quin's size and strength would be a physical deterrent to Ralph's retaliatory inclinations, if he had any. After all, Sherry remembered, he'd already had a taste of defeat at Quin's hands.

As soon as they'd finished lunch they went back to the car and drove along the dusty dirt road to the north west of town, over the creek and up the hill, travelling towards Sherry's home, to a confrontation with Ralph Marley. Sherry shook with nervous tension all the way until they reached the house where she had been born and had lived for ten years with her beloved family.

Strangely, the sight of the solid timber house calmed and reassured her. She remembered the happy times and the love that had surrounded her. This was her home and she was damned if Ralph or anyone else was going to deprive her of it.

The house was empty. It had clearly been empty for days if not weeks. Dust lay over every surface, milk congealed and stank in the fridge, fruit lay rotting in a bowl on the pine kitchen table. An odour of neglect permeated every room.

Sherry's room had been torn inside out, her books ripped and strewn around, her clothes thrown on the floor, her mattress shredded. Her bible and diary she kept in her desk had been torn, obviously by someone in a tremendous rage.

Quin followed Sherry as she held Scrappy and walked through the rooms and comforted her in his arms when she cried at the destruction of her precious possessions. 'Why,' she asked him, 'Does he hate me that much?'

'I think he's a very sick man,' said Quin seriously. 'I'd better get you away from here. There's no point in staying around. Let's go to your friend Pete's place. We'll see what he has to say.' They went out onto the verandah and down the steps to the yard where an gravel path curved towards a white painted wooden gate.

'I wonder where Ralph's disappeared to? And what about Jasper, our other dog? Where's he?' Sherry looked at the large expanse of weed filled lawn in the front of the house and despaired of ever setting it right again.

Quin held her a moment longer then walked with her back to the car. He helped her in gently and closed the door having a look around at the same time.

The place was a mess, no doubt about it. The large shed which obviously doubled as a garage had a door hanging off its hinges. There was no car to be seen. The fences were half falling down, barbed wire broken and spread through the long grass, rusty spikes lying in wait. The hen house was open and a few scrawny hens pecked in the dust. 'Was it like this when you ran away Sherry?' he asked through the open car window.

Scrappy was sitting on her lap whimpering and she absently stroked him as she looked around, her eyes clearing a little. She said, 'No, of course not. Not as neglected anyway. My dad kept the place in mint condition and I tried to look after it as best I could. Ralph didn't help much. Said it was my job to keep the house and grounds clean, the grass cut. It's such an old house it needs a lot of upkeep. It's worth taking care of though. There's a lot of my family history in this house and a lot of love.' She looked around again and said, 'It's as if he's just up and gone in a hurry and not come back.'

When they reached Pete Madigan's house he came out to the car and pulled Sherry's door open. Tears were in his eyes and he pulled her out of the car and hugged her to him. 'Sherry, I'm so glad to see you safe. It feels like forever since you went away. I thought I'd never see you again.'

She hugged him back and said, 'Oh Pete, it's lovely to see you too. This is Quin Jameson. I met him while I was away. He brought me home.'

The two men shook hands and eyed each other approvingly. They silently communicated their wish to keep Sherry safe. Quin said, 'Mr. Madigan, it's a pleasure to meet you. Sherry has told me how your helped her get away. I appreciate that because it led her to me. I'll always be grateful for that.'

'The name's Pete. I was happy to help her Quin. This girl means a lot to me. Her grandfather was a very dear friend of mine as were her parents.'

They all walked inside the house and sat down in the kitchen. Pete went to the fridge and brought out a bottle of red wine and three glasses.

'You can have a drink these days can't you young Sherry. Course you can. You're almost twenty-one aren't you? Doesn't seem that long since you were a toddler racing around the place.'

'So what's been going on here? Marley appears to have taken off. Any idea where he's gone?' Quin accepted a glass from Pete.

'Yes, Pete,' appealed Sherry as she took a sip of wine with a sour look. 'This is raw,' she said, shuddering. 'So, where has Ralph gone? Where's Jasper?'

'Jasper's here with me. I found him wandering around half starved. I brought him home and if I'm not mistaken that's him yelling to be let out of the enclosure I built for him. He must know you're here.' He looked at Scrappy. 'Or he must be able to smell this little guy. They always were mighty attached to each other.'

Sure enough, they could hear the throbbing howl of a hound out the back of the house. Scrappy answered, scrabbling to free himself so Sherry put him down and he took off as fast as his tiny legs could carry him. Pete let him out the door and returned with a smile. 'I think they're glad to see each other.'

Sherry smiled and said, 'What about Ralph? Where is he?'

'He's gone.'

'What do you mean gone? Not dead, surely?' Sherry had hated Ralph but she hadn't really wished him dead, just out of her life. Quin put a gentle hand on her shoulder in comfort, not understanding her reaction. He'd thought she'd be happy to be rid of Ralph.

Pete laughed shortly. 'No Sweetheart, he's not dead. I reckon he wishes he was though.'

'What do you mean? Is he in trouble of some kind?'

'You could say that. When you ran away, then you and I left for the city, he must have fermented about your disappearance something awful. I came back to find my house ransacked. I thought at first it was teenagers mucking about but then I realised it was someone looking for something. I found a note you had written to yourself ripped up on the floor. It was about the hotel in Melbourne and Mr. Jones. Something about a job being available. I knew then he would go looking for you. Did he find you Sherry? Did you see him?'

'Yes. I saw him. He didn't see me however. He saw Quin.'

'What happened?' asked Pete.

Quin shrugged. 'He got a little bent out of shape, we had words, he banged his head on the wall and then I left. He didn't find us after that because we took off to Queensland with Jones, but that's another story.'

'That's alright then. Marley can be an ugly character when he wants to be. Anyway, getting back to what happened to him.' Pete grinned wickedly. 'He decided he needed a housekeeper.

'He couldn't find anyone who would put up with his persnickety ways or his vicious tongue so he advertised in the Ballarat paper for a live in housekeeper and cook, one who didn't know him personally or anything about him.

'The woman he hired was an excellent cook and kept the house beautifully but something he did mightily offended her and she up and left within a week. Left him a black eye and a limp in his left leg too.

'He gave up then, telling everyone that women were the devil's playground and he was having nothing to do with any of them. He was even heard in the pub one night swilling whisky neat and quoting scripture, Proverbs I think, about naughty women laying in wait for innocent men.'

Pete roared with laughter then sobered. 'It was so funny seeing his Mayorship's perfect suit and tie stained by tomato sauce from the pie he was eating at the time. I think he'd been to the footy in Ballarat. Next thing we knew he up and married. He told Slade that the cook housekeeper couldn't leave if he married her. She'd have to stay put and look after him without complaining, whining was how he put it. No doubt he thought he'd get some other advantages as well, the sort of privileges the housekeeper from Ballarat denied him.'

Pete began to laugh again, his mirth infectious. 'Think of it. That housekeeper he hired, a very large woman by the way, ripped into Marley like a bull terrier. She corralled him after church one day, right outside the gate, and told him what she thought of his hands on policy regarding the help. The whole town heard her.'

'Go on Pete,' urged Sherry, her eyes shining. 'What happened then?'

'He tried to shut her up of course but as soon as he laid a hand on her she slammed her fist into his face and kicked him in the shins. It was wonderful. I've never seen a man go down so fast and so hard.'

'Sounds like poetic justice,' said Quin, laughing at the thought of Marley being bested by a woman. 'Did she get away with it?'

'I didn't think she would at the time. When the dust settled, Ralph was calling for Burns to arrest her at the top of his lungs but strangely enough, Burns was nowhere to be seen and no-one else did anything about the woman. She just up and left town the same day and no charges were laid. No witnesses. Apparently no-one saw anything at all. They must have all had their backs turned while she was kicking and punching. Must have been deaf too 'cause they didn't hear anything either.'

'That's incredible Pete.' Sherry was laughing so hard tears poured freely down her cheeks and she had to grasp Quin by the arm and hold herself upright.'So what happened after that?'

'Well the only woman who'd have him turned out to be Molly Slade, the solicitor's older sister. She lives in Swan Hill and didn't know anything about Ralph's reputation in the town. She said yes, she'd marry him, and in a month they'd got a licence and a marriage celebrant did the job at Walter Slade's house.'

'Why not a church wedding,' asked Quin curiously.

'It seems Ralph was divorced when he was young, before he married Sylvia. The church Ralph attends has a thing about divorced people getting married. He wanted the thing over and done so he left the church and married Molly without the blessing of a minister, a funny thing for a church deacon to do.'

'Where are they now Pete,' asked Sherry.

'I think they're living in Molly's house in Swan Hill. She was a widow and had a house of her own. She'd was staying with her brother in Archer's Creek but when she and Ralph married, she decided they'd move back to the Swan Hill house and live there. He still comes back on the occasional weekend though. Usually on his own. She doesn't know what he gets up to on those weekends but you can't hide much in this town. He still has that cabin on your property in good shape.'

'Why did Ralph agree to a move to Swan Hill Pete?' asked Sherry. 'I would have thought our house would have been good enough for anyone.'

'It would have but it doesn't belong to Ralph. It belongs to you.'

'What! I thought he had a share in it too.'

'Apparently not. After Ralph married her, Molly dug through his papers, including some she found in the safe at his office. She went over all his finances and found he was living in your house and collecting rents on your properties as well as pocketing the money himself without having any right to do so.

'He'd been cheating you for years and keeping you ignorant of everything with the aid of his friend and partner in crime, Walter Slade.' Pete went to the fridge again and took out a beer, silently offering one to Quin as well.

'This talking sure is thirsty work,' he said. 'You want a lemonade Sherry. There's some in the fridge. Help yourself sweetie. This is as much your house as it is mine.' He laughed. 'Actually, that's true. I rent this place through Slade. It belonged to your parents, and now you. I don't suppose you knew about that either. I don't think Ralph does or he'd have me thrown out on my ear.'

Sherry looked stunned and Quin said, laughing gently, 'Sherry, honey, close your mouth. The flies are getting in.' He went to the fridge and found a bottle of lemonade, pouring a generous helping into a tall glass.

Taking the drink from him absently she said, 'Oh, thanks. Did you hear that Quin? I'm free. I have property of my own and Ralph's gone.' She whooped with delight and jumped up, whirling around in a circle, grabbing Quin's hand and pulling him along with her, spilling her drink down his front. 'Oh, sorry. I'm being clumsy again.' She wiped him down with a tea towel.

'I heard. It's wonderful.' Quin pulled his shirt from his chest to dry it in the air and turned to Pete who was sitting there with a silly grin on his face. 'How come Molly Slade let all this out Pete?' They seated themselves close together at the table and drank their beer and lemonade. 'There's the joke. She didn't let it out on purpose. I think she became upset one day and sobbed on the shoulder of one of her cronies from church without realising she'd just opened the district wide band broadcast channel. She's a very church minded lady, very conscious of appearances.

'I heard about the whole business on the town grapevine which, as you know is better than telephones, TV and public radio combined. I reckon there'll be a gossip page on the Internet soon.' Pete stood and went to look out the window.

He turned back to say, 'She managed to overlook his first marriage and divorce, I think because it wasn't public knowledge, but it just wasn't on for her husband to be swindling anybody, especially a relative. And it was even worse since her brother is supposed to be a respectable solicitor. She doesn't know her brother very well it seems.

'They were married by then and she took a very hard line with Ralph. Told him that since divorce was out, he'd better do what he was told or she'd make sure he had to pay back every cent to you and to all the other people he'd swindled over the years. She's good with maths and had worked it all out. She said if he refused she'd make sure the Police heard about the whole business.

'Even put his account ledgers in the bank where he couldn't get at them and told him she'd make them public if he didn't behave. A bluff of course, she wouldn't tell anyone if it meant a public scandal. She'd die before allowing that.'

Sherry said, 'I've known her for years and she loves to cook and keep house, taking care of the men in the family like they were royalty. That's why Walter Slade always looks so well fed. He's been spoilt rotten by her. I remember what a great money manager she is too. All their lives she's taken care of her brother's finances. She's one very determined woman. I would have thought Ralph would be set up for life with Molly taking care of everything.'

'He's set alright,' said Pete, deadpan. 'In concrete. She's making sure he toes the line. He has a job she found for him in the liquor department at a small locally owned supermarket in Swan Hill.

'Unfortunately for him he has to be home by six o'clock every evening. He has to eat what she cooks and like it. It's too bad vegetarian isn't his favourite food. It's doing him good though. He looks thinner and that's okay.'

Pete grinned with unashamed mischief, 'She decided he needed to go on a diet so tofu burgers and spinach souffle seem to be standard fare these days. If he wants steak he has to sneak out to the pub at lunch time. As well as that, he has only a small allowance and if he wants to buy anything larger than chewing gum he has to ask her permission. And, she makes him go to three prayer meetings in the week and two church services on Sundays. He hasn't time to swindle anyone and is learning the hard way what it means to be humble, and hungry.'

'What about the police in Archer's Creek,' asked Quin. 'Sergeant Burns isn't it? How come he didn't know about Marley's activities?' He was trying hard not to laugh at Marley's fate. He felt the man deserved everything he got for the way he'd treated Sherry and probably a lot more. Somehow it was hard to forget the fate of Sylvia and Susan, her absent daughter.

'I'm sure Burns knows most of it but even if he wanted to use it, it's all circumstantial. Slade was very clever. He managed to keep everything quiet quoting client confidentiality as his obligation. Nothing much got out at all,' said Pete. 'There's no concrete evidence. No-one can prove anything against Ralph unless Sherry forces an investigation. She'll have to be the one to file a complaint.'

'So what's happening at the moment? Is anything being done?' asked Sherry.

'Maybe something's cooking. When asked if he knew what was going on, Sergeant Burns told the Town Council he'd rather keep his job than stand by Ralph Marley who was always throwing his weight around anyway. Ralph was not a popular man. Made many an enemy in this town.'

'That sounds like Burnsie,' said Sherry. 'He was always a man who sat on the fence until he saw which side he could fall on without any danger to himself.' She was feeling more and more like this was a weird dream and that somehow she'd wake up and find herself back in her house before all this began. Her only reality was Quin who sat beside her solid as an oak, his arm around her slender shoulders silently pledging his support.

'I think there's some sort of investigation being done on the quiet concerning his activities with your property Sherry,' said Pete. 'A police detective from the city has been asking questions but up until now, no-one has known where to find you so it was difficult for anything to be done about your affairs without your consent.'

Pete shook his head sadly. 'I think many of the townspeople are a bit ashamed. They let you down by ignoring the way you've been treated, watching their own backs when they should have stood up for you, especially considering who your family are and how much they put into this town.

'They were shocked at your sudden disappearance and the speculation that Ralph may have had something to do with it made a lot of people start thinking, and talking.'

'Why didn't anyone stand up to him before,' asked Quin.

'He had ways of making people suffer. No-one was able to stand up against him without his vindictiveness coming down on them or their families.'

'I certainly couldn't.' Sherry sighed and said, 'I never want to see him again.'

'You might have to Sherry,' said Pete. 'I heard he's going to be in town this weekend. There's some sort of birthday party at the Slade's house on Saturday night. That's tomorrow.' 'If we stay at my own house I doubt if we'll see him. I don't intend to go out anywhere and there's a lot of cleaning up to do over there.'

'Well let me know if you need any help or if Marley comes around,' said Pete. 'I wouldn't mind a tangle with that rotten sod. He owes me one.'

'What do you mean?' asked Quin.

'When I got back from taking Sherry to Melbourne Ralph came around and wanted to bash my head in. He said I'd kidnapped her. Even brought Burns, that lily livered excuse for a policeman, with him.'

Pete looked disgusted. 'Wanted to arrest me on suspicion. Eventually, Burns had to concede there was no evidence so was forced to let me go. It sure did stick in Marley's teeth I can tell you. He was as green as a lizard, looked like one too.'

'I'm sorry for getting you into trouble Pete,' said Sherry as she went over and hugged her friend, remorse for his trouble making her wish she had found some other way of escaping the trap that was her life with Ralph Marley.

Then she remembered that she had met Quin by running away and, apart from Pete's trouble, couldn't find a single shred of regret for leaving.

'Don't give it a thought girl. I'd welcome the chance to go a round or two with Ralph Marley. He needs some setting down. Unfortunately, he's twice my weight so I'd probably be in way over my head. Maybe Quin could oblige, he looks tough enough to give him a run for his money?'

'I'd be delighted Pete,' said Quin with an evil grin curling his lips as he flexed his substantial muscles. 'I grew up in Sydney, on the streets most of the time. A no rules fight is what I'd go for. Last one standing is the winner.'

Pete got up from his chair and said, 'Sounds great. I hope I can watch. Right now I need to attend to a few things outside and feed the dog and the hens. I'll feed Scrappy too if you like. He's like a dog with two tails just to be back with his mate Jasper. You two make yourselves at home. Have a cup of tea.'

He looked at his watch. 'Hey, it's getting on, almost time for a meal. You must be hungry by now. There's plenty of food in the fridge. We've been yacking too long and I've forgotten about feeding you. I'll be back shortly.'

Pete went out the back door, pulled it shut it and left them alone. Quin was about to take Sherry in his arms for a hug when a commotion was heard in the back yard. Jasper was barking fiercely and Scrappy was making his own kind of noise. A yelp was heard then the back door was thrown open unceremoniously and Pete was shoved inside. Three men followed him in. The door slammed shut.

CHAPTER SEVENTEEN

Quin stepped close to Sherry's side and put his arm around her shoulders. She was trembling and he squeezed gently in reassurance. 'Steady,' he said quietly.

Pete scowled ferociously but said nothing. He shrugged his shoulders in an unaccustomed show of nerves and rubbed his elbow where it had been grasped in an iron fist. His eyes had a look of pain as he glanced toward the back door where he had left Scrappy and Jasper who were still silent, might always be silent.

One of the men was tall and thin with thick silver grey hair, thick black eyebrows and a sharp intelligent face. His nose was long and aristocratic. He wore a smile of deep satisfaction as he surveyed the scene. It was also the smile of a man with no conscience to bother him. Around forty years of age, he radiated confident purpose and to look into his grey eyes was to generate abject fear.

The second man was slightly shorter, bulky with muscle and looked capable of using his obvious strength to force his way through anyone who got in his way. A handsome young man, he had long black hair and strangely hypnotic blue eyes. Both men wore jeans, boots, black T-shirts and black leather bomber jackets.

The third man was short and stocky with longish sandy red hair fading into grey streaks and combed over a bald spot in the front. He wore a light grey suit with a white shirt and dark blue tie. He seemed reasonably sane until you looked away from the smiling lips and took in the expression in the eyes. It was the excitement of the hunt that turned him on and he had spied his prey.

Sherry went white and swayed with shock as she looked at the third man and said, 'Ralph. What are you doing here?'

'Looking for you, you little bitch. I told you there was no escape but you didn't believe me did you?' He moved closer and raised his thickly muscled arm to strike her. Quin stepped in front of him and grabbed his wrist. He squeezed tightly and Marley's face went white as he yelped and gritted his teeth in pain.

'I wouldn't,' Quin said coldly. 'You'll never touch her again Marley. I'll see to that.' He pushed Ralph away as if he was a contamination.

'And who the hell are you to tell me what to do Jameson?' Marley stepped back well out of reach of Quin's punishing grip. 'You have no say in this.'

'I'm the man who's going to put you in hospital, again, if you lay another hand on Sherry. I'm also the man who is going to take her away from you.'

Marley rubbed his wrist and snarled, 'I've been watching you two. Ever since you rolled into town you've been crawling all over each other. It's disgusting. She's nothing but a slut.' Ralph Marley was furious and it showed in his red tinged complexion and thin twisted lips. His scarred beefy hands were flexing as if he wanted to grab Quin and shake him like a rat.

Quin wished Marley would try to take him and then he'd have some excuse to beat him to a pulp. 'Don't call her that you sick bastard. I know all about you and I'm going to make sure you pay for what you've done to Sherry.'

'What I've done. You're a fool Jameson. You're the one who kidnapped her and took her away from her family.' Ralph snarled. 'I could have you arrested.'

'Try it. See how far you get. Sherry belongs to me now,' he stated baldly. 'And, you're not her family, not any more. I don't believe you ever were.'

'Interfering idiot,' fumed Ralph. 'Damn you. I'll see you in hell first.' His facade of devoted church deacon had fallen from his shoulders like shedding a skin.

'That's enough gentlemen,' said the grey haired man smoothly, his cultured tones out of place in the rough country farmhouse. Silence filled the room and Quin looked at him, wondering what was going on. 'My name is Phillips. You might not recognise me Jameson. I was wearing a police uniform the last time you saw me. We were loading a truck at a warehouse. Do you remember?'

At Quin's start of recollection he said, 'Yes, I see that you do. How encouraging. That was a rather distressing situation. The guard came to work early and had to be disposed of. Most unfortunate.' He indicated his companion. 'This is Mr. Burke. From now on I give the orders. Mr. Burke will enforce them. You will all go into the sitting room and sit down. I have a few things to say and I'd prefer to be comfortable while I say them.' Burke moved his leather jacket aside momentarily so they could see a holster and a hand gun.

'I wouldn't have known you Phillips,' snarled Quin. 'I didn't see any of your ugly faces. But now that I do know who you are I won't forget.'

Phillips just smiled sardonically and turned to Ralph who had begun shouting. He was red faced with rage. 'Look, you men have no rights here apart from what I give you. I thought you were going to help me get rid of Jameson, not interfere in my personal business. This girl is my property ..er, my ward and I intend to take her back where she belongs. If I'd known you were going to start shoving your weight around I wouldn't have allowed you to come here.'

Ralph put his coarsely made miner's hand out to poke Phillips in the chest. Burke caught him round the throat from behind with his forearm, and squeezed. Ralph went white then red and gasped tortuously. He stopped trying to speak and tried to breathe instead, clawing at the rock like arm that held his throat, his stocky legs twitching, his feet dancing as he tried to break free.

Burke hauled Ralph through the doorway into the living room and tossed him down into an armchair where he lay wheezing and pulling at his once immaculate collar and tie. Sweat poured off his face.

Pete, Quin and Sherry moved through the doorway and into the living room where they sat down on the sofa opposite Ralph and waited, Sherry as close to Quin as she could get. She grabbed hold of his hand as if, by touching him, the nightmare would end.

Pete asked belligerently, 'What are you fellas doing here? If you want money you're out of luck.'

'Forget it Pete,' said Quin, glaring at the two men. 'They don't want money. They want blood. My blood.'

Sherry squeezed his hand in a convulsive movement. 'What do you mean Quin? Why you? What have you ever done to them?'

'I was just in the wrong place at the wrong time.'

Quin looked away from her and glanced out the front window. Out the front of the house was a brown Volvo. On a hunch he asked, 'What happened to the black Mercedes?'

Phillips smiled slightly. 'It was a bit too distinctive. I thought the brown would blend in a little more. Part of the country landscape you might say.'

'Very poetic,' said Quin drily. His instincts had been right. They told him now they were all in big trouble. 'I suppose you followed us from the city?'

Phillips shrugged. 'It wasn't hard to do. We kept well behind and you weren't looking for us. I phoned some friends and we swapped cars at Deer Park.'

'You've got friends have you? I wouldn't have thought so,' taunted Quin. 'Just as a matter of interest, what did you use to blow up my van?'

'That was a pleasure to set up my friend. A timer attached to the ignition and a couple of alligator clips attaching the wires to some C4 explosive. It was all very neatly wrapped in glad-wrap and glued underneath the van. Simple yet very effective. So sorry we missed you. We did try again but you seem to have a charmed life. Not any more however. This is it.'

'What the hell is going on here,' snarled Ralph. He had recovered his breath and was almost back in fighting form. Unfortunately he hadn't gained any insight into the brutality the two strangers were capable of. He'd thought to use them but found himself used, and abused.

'Shut up,' said Burke and clipped him around the head with his closed fist. Ralph snapped back in his chair with the force of the blow, not quite unconscious.

Silence reigned for a moment, then Phillips said, 'For your enlightenment, Mr. Jameson has been an interfering busybody. He allowed himself to become over zealous in what he no doubt saw as his duty. He involved the police in my private business. I cannot allow this to go unpunished or people who once respected me will think I'm softening up. Therefore Mr. Jameson must be disposed of. The rest of you, unfortunately, will also be going with him to his final resting place.'

Sherry trembled and leaned against Quin's hard frame. He put his arm around her but remained staring silently at the two men. He had no expression on his face.

Pete said, 'You won't get away with this. People will have seen you driving through the town. You're strangers and people always notice strangers in a small place like Archer's Creek.'

Phillips smiled mockingly, 'Don't be ridiculous. We could be tourists looking at the goldfields. Anyway, by the time anyone comes looking we'll be long gone.'

'Just as a matter of interest Phillips,' asked Quin, watching the two men carefully, trying to assess their physical power, 'How did you find me? Did you have access to the police computer?'

'As a matter of fact, my brother-in-law is a police detective. He likes to keep my sister sweet and she likes to keep me sweet. It works out well all round. I have access to any information

I want and he gets to stay alive and married to my sister. It's a barter system if you like. And it works very successfully. Everyone is happy and we all make a lot of money. Including my corruptible brother-in-law.' Burke checked the watch on his wrist, took out his gun and said,

'Okay, fun's over. Get on your feet, all of you. It's time to get this show on the road.'

'Look, you don't need to involve Sherry or Pete in this,' said Quin, knowing he had to have one last try. 'I'm the one you want. Forget about them. Tie them up until we've gone and they won't be able to tell the police anything.'

'Forget it,' said Phillips. 'I've made my decision and I don't backtrack. It only gets messy and I like to keep things clean. I notice you don't plead for our friend here?' He indicated Ralph who was sitting nursing his head.

'I figure snakes stick together. Basically you're slimy cowards and there's safety in numbers. Ralph's a survivor so he'll do his little crawling routine and you'll probably figure he's not worth killing. You'll be right about that.'

Ralph perked up at this and broke into frenzied speech. 'Yes, I'm one of you. I've killed before. I can work for you. I'll do anything. You don't have to kill me. I'll help you.'

Phillips turned to him with bored interest, his voice cutting. 'Just who have you killed Ralph Marley? Some insignificant cockroach, or maybe a mosquito?'

'Well, there was ...' he gave a sideways glance at Sherry, 'there was Mike and Rose Delaney. They'd found out I was skimming money from the church building fund. I didn't want to do it but I overheard them talking. So much for loyalty to family. They were planning on turning me in. I had no choice. I doctored the brakes of their car and that was that. Kaput. Out of control, into a tree.'

At Sherry's gasp of pain Quin tightened his hold on her. 'It's okay,' he whispered. 'Hang in there Sweetheart.'

Pete made to get up and was pushed back down by Burke. 'You rotten bastard Marley. You're gonna pay for that if it's the last thing I do.'

Phillips' smile was a satisfied curl of the lips. 'Anyone else?'

Ralph was on a roll now and, exulting in his cleverness said, 'I slipped quite a few sleeping pills into a large cup of coffee. Then I laced it with Irish whisky and gave it to my wife. Waste of good liquor it was. She never appreciated the finer things in life. Anyway, she fell asleep and didn't wake up again. A nice clean job.'

He laughed. 'Stupid woman. She thought she could write to some friends of hers and tell them all about me. Said I was cruel to her and that I was doing things to my daughter that I shouldn't do. As if it was any of her business anyway. I was her father. I had the right.'

'And did you do things to your daughter you shouldn't have?' asked Phillips with every appearance of fascination in the tale.

'Might have.' Ralph shrugged as if it was nothing. 'All Sylvia ever did was complain about what I did, who my friends were and where I went at night. None of her damn business how I ran my life. An man has to have a little freedom or life's not worth living.' Ralph scowled at Phillips and asked, 'What's it got to do with you anyway? Susan was...is my daughter. I had every right to do what I liked with her.'

'I see. So you killed your two friends, you disposed of your wife and slept with your daughter. Is there any other infamous deed to which you feel compelled to confess? I'm making a list of employees qualifications so I do need to know.'

'I'm pretty good at salting away money, other people's money that is. At least, I was until my new wife found out. Molly's a hard woman. I don't mind telling you, I'm a bit scared of her. She has a fist of iron. Maybe one night I'll get rid of her too. Pity she doesn't drink.' He smiled as if in anticipation of the deed.

Phillips smiled again and said, 'I think you qualify admirably for a place on my staff Ralph. You don't mind if I call you Ralph do you? It seems friendlier. We'll discuss the job later. Now I believe it's time to go for a little walk.'

'Where are we goin'?' asked Pete as they all stood up. He looked weary with despair, his once sturdy shoulders somehow bent and shrunken and his face grey in the fading light.

Sherry had an equally grey look. Her eyes were wounded pools of hurt, her once beautiful hair a lank fall of lifelessness. She was unable to speak for fear she would cry out.

The realisation that Ralph had killed her parents had all but destroyed her and all she could think about was how she loved and missed them and how he had lied while pretending to grieve for them. If Ralph had plunged a knife into her heart right then he could not have wounded her more.

Quin just looked proud and indomitable. Not for him the pleading groans and slavish adoration of boot leather that Ralph affected. Quin would go wherever he had to go without giving Phillips or Burke the satisfaction of hearing him beg for his life. He would watch and wait and then he would make his move.

'You'll find out where we're going in a while,' replied Burke abruptly as he pressed his gun in Quin's back. 'Now you can shut up. I've heard enough bull-crap round here today to fill a quarry.'

Quin, Pete and Sherry's hands were tied with thin rope in front. Ralph was allowed to accompany them freely, after all, he had proved beyond a doubt he was as vile a creature as Phillips and Burke. He had even provided directions to a place he knew in the hills behind Pete's house, a space where bodies could be left without fear of immediate discovery. In fact it could be weeks or months before anyone came around that area.

They walked outside and up the hill. Darkness was spreading over the landscape and the air had a distinct chill which made Sherry shiver beneath her plaid western shirt. She pulled at the ropes around her wrists and wished she had some way of untying the knots.

A deep inner rage was beginning to flow through her blood at the callous way Ralph had destroyed her parent's lives. When she remembered the day he had arrived at their home and been welcomed into their family she wanted to fly at him and rip him to pieces.

Her breathing was laboured as she toiled up the hill but it was more from rage at the injustice he had perpetrated on their innocent lives than an inability to climb. Some day, she vowed, if she ever managed to escape this deadly trap, she would find a way to make Ralph pay.

The stony ground was hard to walk on but they were forced to continue over several hills which resembled barren mullock heaps. Sherry stumbled a little and asked, 'Can we go a little slower please. I've got a bad knee and it's aching like crazy in this cold wind.'

Burke scowled at her and said, 'Shut up and keep moving.' He grabbed her elbow forcing her to continue on, uncaring that she was in pain. Quin watched him touch the girl he loved with rough hands and a fierce anger came to life in his eyes. He began planning a savage retribution if he could only free himself. He continued to saw away at his rope bindings with his belt buckle which had a slightly rough edge. At the moment it was all he could do to try and find a way out of their predicament, a situation he held himself directly responsible for.

He felt anguish overtake him as he realised this could be the end of everything, of all his and Sherry's hopes and dreams for the future, the end of all their lives including Pete Madigan who had only tried to help them.

An hour later they reached a tract of land covered in trees and as the sun was finally sinking into oblivion behind the hills a cold biting breeze came to life.

After walking through the trees for a long way, they came to a gully bare of undergrowth which had miner's junk spread around. Pieces of wooden gold mining cradles and sluice boxes gave evidence of the type of prospecting that had taken place. Luckily the moon was almost full and through patches of light and shade dappling the rough path they could see where they were going.

Following a path beside the creek, they came to an abandoned mine shaft. It was covered by rough slats of timber which Burke tossed to the side like they were chopsticks.

'What do you think Marley? Is this a fitting end for the last remaining member of your family?' Phillips mocked Ralph with twisted lips, his eyes hard and vindictive.

'You're not going to get rid of the girl? Ralph snarled. 'She belongs to me, and once I've finished with her she won't have anything to say about anything. I can guarantee it.'

'I'm afraid that will be quite unsuitable Ralph. She got away from you once and she can do it again.' He laughed. 'Face it man. She's smarter than you are. Besides, she knows about her parents now and I can see in her eyes there's nothing she'd rather do than bury you.'

Ralph looked hard at Sherry's grief filled unforgiving face then shrugged. 'Yeah, I can see what you mean. Ungrateful bitch. I've spent twelve years of my life looking out for her but I should have got rid of her years ago. She's no damn use to anyone. Can't even cook worth a damn.'

Her eyes darkened with primal rage and she strained at her bonds, praying desperately for a way to make him pay for what he had done, wanting nothing more in that moment than, as Phillips said, to bury Ralph Marley.

Ralph went to the edge of the mine shaft and looked down. 'Looks like there's a decent bit of water in there. Good thing it rained last night. Should do the deed nicely for us. Won't even need to dirty our hands.' His grin faded a little as he looked back at Phillips who was smiling and looking directly at him.

Something about that smile alerted Quin who had been trying to think of a way to distract Burke. His rope was held by one remaining thread and he was poised to make his move.

Ralph shifted uneasily. 'Do you want me to shove 'em in?'

'I don't think so Ralph. I think you should go in first to check out the accommodations. It might not be suitable for our other guests.'

'But you...you said I...I could work for you. You were going to give me a job! You promised me...'

'I have given you a job. Checking out the mine shaft. Get with the program Marley. We're wasting time.'

'You can't do this to me,' Ralph spluttered. 'I thought we had a deal.'

'I might have done a lot of rotten things in my life Marley but even I draw the line at molesting my own children. I have a daughter myself and I find the idea totally nauseating. Perhaps it's a belated sense of morality, I don't know. Call it the one thing I haven't done, my salvation if you like. Enough chit chat, it's going nowhere. I suggest you climb down into that mine shaft before Mr. Burke shoots you and tosses your body down where it belongs.'

'Please Mr. Phillips. Don't do this. I'll never touch a girl again, I promise. I never touched Sherry. I wanted to but I didn't. Surely that counts for something?'

Ralph was on his hands and knees before the mine shaft, crying hideously when a streak of brown and white flashed past Phillips and flung itself upon Ralph, licking and pushing on his chest with huge soup plate paws and wagging its tail. He tried to stand up but overbalanced and fell backwards leaving Jasper to bark furiously on the edge of the hole. Ralph hit the water with a huge splash and cried out as he thrashed and tried to pull himself out. Slick rivulets of mud running down the walls refused to allow him purchase. Then another tiny body hurtled into the clearing and leapt toward Sherry as if she was the only person in the world.

'Scrappy,' she cried, going down onto her knees, tears flowing down her cheeks. 'I thought they'd hurt you. And here you are.' It was impossible to put her arms around him and pick him up as she had been tied very firmly. He had to be content with racing around her and jumping up to her legs as she crouched in the dirt. His high pitched bark was heard ringing out in ecstasy.

Burke rushed towards Sherry and tried to kick Scrappy and Jasper down into the mine shaft. 'Bloody dogs,' he snarled, totally missing Jasper. Scrappy twisted out of the way and lost his balance, rolling towards the hole.

Burke also slipped in the mud and landed on his backside, dropping his gun into the hole. In reflex he tried to retrieve it but momentum took over and he rolled over and over, covering himself in brown mud and pale wet clay.

Sherry screamed as her pet slid in the sticky ooze and it was at that moment Quin broke his bonds and leapt down to scoop up Scrappy into his arms. He was, however, unable, and unwilling, to save Burke whose ignominious slide into the mine shaft was punctuated by vivid curses and threats to any deity who bothered to listen. None answered and he sank over his head before coming to the surface coughing and spitting up muddy brackish water flavoured with lumps of yellow clay. His once clean leather jacket was now water logged and dragging him down as he struggled without success to take it off.

Phillips began cursing virulently when he saw Quin was free and spun on his heel trying to get away. He'd only taken a few steps toward the trees when a large weight hurtled into his back and threw him to the ground. Quin pushed Phillips' face into the ground and quickly tied his hands with the rope he'd taken from his own wrists.

The man was unable to speak due to the large amount of sticky mud clinging to his teeth and oozing up into his throat. His previously pristine clothes were thoroughly coated with mud as were Quin's.

Pete and Sherry turned to watch Ralph trying to keep his head above water in the mine shaft and away from the flailing arms of his unwanted companion. At that moment a voice was heard from the trees suggesting they put their hands in the air and not make any sudden moves.

In minutes the whole scene changed. Floodlights were set up. Ropes were untied. Handcuffs were put on Phillips and he was informed of his rights before being hauled away. As he went he coughed and spat on the ground, calling over his shoulder, 'You got lucky this time Jameson but things can change. The cops won't believe a thing you say, just like last time. Then we'll see who goes down.' A large hand dragging him into the trees prevented him from saying any more.

Pete, Quin and Sherry took the dogs and moved to the edge of the clearing where Sherry sat on a log out of the way holding Scrappy in her arms and Quin stood answering questions to a young police officer.

A gaunt woman with a stern countenance, her grey hair in a bun, came up behind them and said slowly and painfully, 'Sherry, my dear, I'm sorry for all the trouble you've been caused. I had no idea my husband had so many secrets and such wickedness in his soul. It seems I didn't know him at all.' A lone tear flowed down her lined cheek and she tried to smile.

Her lips trembled as she went on, 'I suspected something was going on with Ralph. He's been acting rather secretive lately. I thought he might have a woman somewhere so I followed him. He went to Mr. Madigan's place and I found, not a woman, but something much worse.

'She paused to wipe her eyes with a damp handkerchief. 'Well, I listened to what he had to say from outside the back door. It didn't come as much of a surprise. I did my best but I think I always knew there was something about him that wasn't quite right.' Ralph's wife Molly looked inexpressibly sad. 'I'd never admit it of course. Never air your dirty linen in public my mother always used to say. And this is as dirty as you can get.'

'Molly. I'm sorry it turned out this way,' said Sherry, her own eyes filled with tears, her generous spiit reaching across the barriers to the tragic woman in front of her. 'I'm sure he must have been a good person once. He just lost his way.'

'Well, I'd rather know the truth. It's less painful in the long run.' She spoke firmly, lifting her head and bringing her shoulders back with determination. 'I phoned the Ballarat Police Department from Mr Madigan's place. Then I phoned Sergeant Burns. He seems to have seen the writing on the wall and is ready and willing to help. About time too. He's spent enough time following after the wrong master, as have we all in this town, for far too long.'

'I understand,' said Sherry, putting her hand on Molly's arm in an attempt to comfort her.

'Almost everyone was afraid of him. I was too, until I ran away.'

'I know you were dear. I see now what it was like. Anyway, we followed you up here using Jasper as a guide. He's quite a dog, Sherry, and he put everything he had into hunting for Ralph. I think Jasper thought he was helping Ralph. Where is that lying rat by the way. I don't see him anywhere. Did he manage to escape?'

Sergeant Burns came up to them and, after glancing guiltily at Sherry, smiled and said,

'Come over here Molly. I'd like to show you something.'

They all walked over to the mine shaft and, looking down at Ralph, Sergeant Burns said, 'What do you think we should do with these two?'

Molly came to the edge and looked down holding on to the policeman's arm to prevent slipping. Her face as hard as stone she said, 'It's just a pair of water rats. Vermin. Leave them there. They're of no use to anyone.' She turned away.

'Molly, please, do something. I didn't mean to hurt anyone. Make them get me out of here. I'll never do it again.' Ralph whined pathetically and Burke cursed over and over again while trying ineffectually to climb up the muddy walls.

'Do what again Ralph?' asked his wife in a brittle voice.

'I won't take the car without asking. I'll stay home all the time. I'll never see her again.'

'See who again?'

'That girl in the supermarket. She led me on, tempting me with that short skirt, showing everything she had. She blinded me. But it was only one night. I'll be a model husband from now on. Just get me out of here. Please Molly. I love you, only you.' His voice was taking on the strident tones of desperation.

Firewalking

'What do you think Sherry. Shall we get him out or leave him to rot?'

'Get him out,' said Sherry in an equally hard voice, her eyes like flint but with a hint of vulnerability in the depths. 'Then he can rot in jail until he's an old man.'

'So be it.' Molly said to the policeman, 'I guess you better take him out of there. I don't want to see him again though so do it when I've gone. And, take your time, okay. You can do what you like with the other one. He seems to have such a dirty mouth on him it might do him good to have it washed out with soap.'

The sergeant grinned understandingly and said, 'Okay. It'll take a while before our guys can get out here with ropes anyway. It's not like you can drive in by road. They'll both be nice and soggy by then and easy to handle.'

Molly smiled slightly and began to walk away, then she abruptly turned back to the mine shaft and said, 'By the way Ralph. I found something in the spare room other day. You know how I like to keep things tidy. Visitors may turn up.'

Molly laughed. 'You'd hidden a flight bag in the back of the wardrobe. I thought it was laundry and I brought it out. Imagine my amazement when I found it contained money. A lot of money. I imagine it's some of the cash you've embezzled from Sherry over the last twelve years.'

'Please, Molly. It's not her money. I worked for it. It's mine. I was saving it for you. I wanted to take you on a trip to England to see your family.' Ralph was almost blubbering like a baby as he renewed thrashing about in the muddy water, knocking into Burke who turned on him, fists flying, nearly drowning them both.

'I'm sorry Ralph.' Molly waited until the turbulence in the water had died down and Ralph stopped coughing up yellow brown water.

'You're such a lousy liar. It's just a pity I didn't wake up to you sooner. I tried to believe you had some good in you but I'm afraid I was mistaken. That money, more than enough for several trips to England if I so desired, belongs to the girl you wronged. You won't be seeing any of it again, not if I have anything to say about it. Sherry can do what she likes with the money. My brother is also going to be left without a cent and I cannot bring myself to care one way or another. You both deserve everything you get.'

Her torch bobbing and weaving unsteadily, Molly began to walk away but before she passed out of the circle of lights into the trees Sherry called out to her. 'Molly, wait a moment. I have something you might like to see.'

She asked Quin to give her the photocopy of the letter Sylvia had written to her friend many years ago. Molly stopped and turned. Smiling gently, Sherry put the paper in her hand. 'I thought this might make you feel a little better. Ralph was acting like this long before he met you. His first wife and his daughter also suffered so much at his hands. You've done a wonderful thing getting the police to come out here. We can't thank you enough. I know it was hard but sometimes we have to do the right thing regardless. You made the right decision and God will bless you for it.'

The woman smiled shakily, the tears she had refused to shed earlier in front of her husband flowing freely now.

'Thank you Sherry,' she said. 'You're a very kind girl. I don't deserve you to be kind to me. Both my husband and my brother treated you and your family shamefully. I'm just glad you came back and brought your young man with you. Perhaps all will be put right at last and we can go on with our lives in peace.'

'I hope so,' agreed Sherry. 'When you've read that letter, could you pass it on to the police. I think they might find it very interesting.'

'I'll be happy to, my dear.' She turned and walked away though the trees, a solitary figure, bent slightly with the emotional pain of the past few hours. She was accompanied by Sergeant Burns who seemed determined to make up for all the years he'd spent swilling at the trough created and maintained by Ralph Marley.

A policeman handed Quin a torch and he supported Sherry over the rough ground with Pete following behind. Behind them they could hear Ralph cursing and howling his innocence. Burke was demanding to be hauled up and away from the snivelling fool who was trying to drown him and the police team were settling in to wait for ropes to be brought in. Nothing was said by the three but the release from tension was almost visible. It was time to take up their lives again and to try making some sense of it all.

CHAPTER EIGHTEEN

Late the next morning Sherry was puddling around the kitchen making breakfast. Quin was helping by cooking bacon and making toast. They'd spent the rest of the previous night curled up on the sofa together at Pete's house, exhausted but needing to be close to each other. Quin had taken their belongings out of his car the night before when they had arrived back at Pete's house. He'd brought them inside the house where they had each taken time to shower and change. Mud and clay had clung to them like a sticky film and each felt that by washing away the outer layer of grime they could wash away a portion of the inner pain as well.

Pete was outside cutting wood for the kitchen fire and throwing a ball for Jasper and Scrappy. When he came back inside he said, 'That's that then,' as they all sat down at the table. 'I reckon everything's come right for you now.'

'Looks like it,' agreed Sherry quietly. 'It's all rather weird though. I feel uninvolved, as if it all happened to someone else. Like I'm just watching a movie. I still can't get over what Ralph did to his wife and daughter, and my parents. He's truly an evil man. Maybe even insane.'

She sighed, a sad and empty sound of resignation and pain. 'I wonder if he was always like that? For a while yesterday I wanted to kill him myself but now I just feel numb, like I've been put in cold storage. Maybe I need to go away for a while. Perhaps Mrs. Scallini would let me visit with her? She's such a nice lady, kind and she doesn't ask questions, she just cooks huge meals and listens.'

'Sherry, about your parents...'

'Please Quin. I don't want to talk about it.' Tears began to gather in her eyes and she bent her head to wipe them away with her sleeve. 'It's all too much for me at the moment. I can't take any more.' She stood abruptly and walked over to the window, looking out at Pete's junk filled back yard with unseeing eyes.

'Okay Sweetheart. When you're ready. I'll be here.'

She smiled in gratitude and her heart began to lift. After all, tomorrow was a new day and she had the man she loved by her side. He had said he loved her and that was enough for now.

Later that day Pete, Sherry and Quin all went to the Ballarat Police Station to give a statement. Molly Slade was there as well. It was all rather traumatic and when they returned she told Pete she was thinking of going away for a few days, without Quin. She had rung Mrs. Scallini and was told to come anytime and welcome.

'Sounds a little drastic,' said Pete as he put the kettle on. Quin was out in the yard collecting a load of logs for the wood burning stove in the kitchen.

'I know what happened was a shock for you Sherry but it's best if you try to think about now and the future. Let the past keep its ghosts and concentrate on making a new life for yourself. Your mum and dad wouldn't want you to be sad.'

'Alright Pete,' said Sherry, a haunting fragile look to her delicate grey eyes. 'I'll try to put the whole thing in perspective. At least Ralph is where he belongs and justice might be done at last. And don't forget the heroes of the day were Jasper and Scrappy, and Molly too. They deserve a stack of credit for getting us out of trouble.'

The dogs were down on the floor eating, Jasper wolfing through his share of food and as usual hovering over his tiny companion in order to finish off Scrappy's portion too. The two dogs headed off into the living room and lay down to sleep off their meal on the sofa. Quin came back inside and sat next to Sherry at the table, pouring himself a large mug of black coffee.

Pete sat back in his chair at the table and said, 'Talking about holidays Sherry, you've just come back from getting away. What about that job you took? I want to hear all about it. Did you have a good time? Queensland wasn't it?'

Quin and Sherry grinned at each other. Sherry said, 'Yeah, Queensland. Up near Maryborough. It was interesting. The travelling was easy. The work was fairly simple, the location wonderful. Weather was great. The only point to make was the employers. They had unreal expectations of us. We decided to give it a miss and come home.'

Quin grinned at her choice of words. 'I enjoyed the trip home. It was a relief to get back to Victoria. Queensland is great but I think I'll settle for Archer's Creek. It's a lot less hazardous.' Pete's eyebrows rose. 'This is less hazardous? You really must have copped it up in Queensland. I thought you said you had a good time?'

'Yeah. I suppose we did get into a little trouble. To cut a long story short, we got involved with a bunch of guys who wanted us to make movies. Without our clothes on. We said no so things got a little rough for a bit and then we came home. At least I met Sherry and I'd go through any amount of trouble just to have her by my side.'

Pete just sat silently as he listened shaking his head and grinning. Then he said, 'Some time soon I'll need details. Not right now however. I reckon it can wait until we've all had a rest. It's been some week hasn't it?'

Quin smiled down at Sherry lovingly and said, 'Yeah Pete. It sure has.' He took her hand, stroking her fingers one by one, memorising the softness of her skin beneath the hard calluses gained in the mine.

'What about you Quin?' asked Sherry, her face becoming brighter as she looked at the man she loved and began at last to push the shadows in her mind away. She curled her fingers around his and smiled, 'You were going to tell me more about what happened in Melbourne, the reason you answered the ad? More than I learned from that monster, Phillips.'

'I saw a robbery one night at a warehouse. Some guys were loading a truck. A security guard was lying dead on the ground outside. Some of the thieves had police uniforms on.

Obviously one of them was Phillips. Remember him talking about it?'

'Yes. He was quite proud of the whole thing wasn't he?'

'Yeah. He was. Anyway, they shot at my car but I managed to escape. When I reported it they made a cursory investigation but found nothing. I was told to stop maligning the police. They said I'd better keep out of trouble or they'd arrest me for giving false evidence.'

'So why did you have to leave town. Didn't it finish there?'

'As you now know, it was Phillips and Burke and a few other charming gentlemen who reckoned I'd seen them and could identify them. They kept trying to get rid of me. Blew up my van outside my apartment, ran my car off the road. That sort of thing. After Mr. Scallini was injured, I decided it was safer to leave.

'I didn't want anyone else to be hurt because of me. I packed up my business, put the building, which I own, up for lease, and gave up my apartment. Then I took advantage of Jones' offer to disappear and here I am, with you.'

Pete spoke up then and said, 'I heard something about that warehouse robbery just recently. A couple of men were arrested and charged with theft and murder. The body of the guard was found floating in the Maribyrnong River.

'When their houses were searched the police found police uniforms and art treasures stolen several weeks before. It must have been after you two had left Melbourne. Obviously Phillips and Burke had escaped the net and were still bent on getting rid of you. Silly fools didn't know you hadn't seen them properly and couldn't recognise them in a line up or anywhere else for that matter.'

He smiled sympathetically at Quin who looked surprised at this turn of events. 'You'd probably be able to go back to Melbourne and take up your old life again. If you wanted to,' he added slyly, glancing at Sherry.

'Quin, do you see what all this means! You're free too. You can go back home and never have to worry about those people again.'

'What if I don't want to go back to Melbourne Sherry? What if I want to stay and make my home with you? Wherever you want to go I'd go.' He looked down at her sweet face searchingly. 'What would you say to that Sweetheart?'

'I'd say, let's go home. We have some cleaning up to do and a few other things to talk about.'

She turned to Pete and said, 'Would you keep Scrappy overnight Pete?. You've probably got something to feed the little guy. I don't think there's much at home. The place looks a mess.'

'What are you going to do about your business interests Sherry?' asked Pete. 'Everything belongs to you after all.

'You've been lied to and cheated out of your rightful inheritance for too many years and there has to be an accounting, especially by the people of this town who collectively if not deliberately, let you down.'

He smiled grimly, 'There's been a lot of talk lately. Ralph left town when he married Molly and moved to Swan Hill. Now, hopefully, he'll be in jail for a long time. People, your tenants, who lease business premises particularly, have been wondering what was to happen with their shops and all. With you disappearing they've been very worried. Not many knew until recently that the properties rightfully belonged to you and they've been shocked to find out how shaky their legal foundation is.

'Apparently Ralph has been acting irrationally for quite a while and the Town Council is in an uproar.' He grinned. 'That's the one thing I like about all this.'

'I'll have a talk to them tomorrow,' said Sherry, wondering what on earth she was going to say to a crowd of disenchanted shopkeepers. Thank goodness Quin was going to be there too. 'In the meantime Pete, Quin and I have some things to do. We'll see you later on. And thanks for everything. You've been a real friend to us both. We'll never forget it.'

She gave Pete a warm hug, Quin shook his hand and said, 'Thanks mate,' and they left.

When they arrived back at Sherry's house they packed away the supplies Quin had bought at the store. He had gone in alone so no questions would be asked until Sherry had a chance to talk to a new solicitor. Walter Slade had been arrested along with Ralph much to his wife's horror. She had made such a fuss when Sergeant Burns had come to her door and presented the arrest warrant but had cooled noticeably when the police offered to include her. She was even now packing her clothes for a prolonged trip to her family in Sydney and Sherry couldn't find it in her heart to blame her. The whole situation was a mess and it would probably be a long time before it was resolved, if ever. As she had found out to her cost, justice sometimes had a roundabout way of being satisfied. And sometimes the price was just too high.

Sherry and Quin cooked a simple meal of hamburgers with salad and sat on the back porch to eat them. The sun was sinking over the hills and a cool breeze had sprung up. The broken garage door was banging to and fro and the gate swung on rusty hinges, squeaking mournfully.

For a while they sat silently, admiring the freshness of the air and the peace but then Quin said, 'Let's go inside Sherry. I'd like to talk to you where I can see you. Besides, the mosquitoes are eating me alive.' He was beginning to come out in small red lumps and scratching. Every now and then a high pitched buzz zoomed overhead and then, after a moment of quiet, a slap was heard.

'Must be coming up to Summer,' she said, slapping her arms and scratching too.

They stood up and went into the sitting room where they sat on the dusty floral sofa. 'I'll have to clean this place up,' hedged Sherry, unable to look into his searching eyes.

'Look at me honey,' requested Quin, the huskiness of his voice melting her bones. He touched her face and turned her towards him. 'I know we haven't known each other very long but I feel we've been through so much together. I want you to know how much you mean to me, how much I want to look after you and love you.'

'Oh, Quin,' whispered Sherry, trying unsuccessfully to look at anything but him. 'You don't know what I'm really like. I'm not very good at talking about my feelings. Ralph used to get really antagonistic if I talked about how I felt. He said I ought to keep myself to myself and not bother anyone. He didn't talk much at all in fact. And if he did talk it was usually because I'd done something wrong and he wanted to yell at me. He preached a lot though. But I didn't consider that talking.'

'Forget him love. If he was here I'd make him sorry for all he's done to you but he's not here and he's never coming back. I want to stay here with you and spend my life with you, starting with a wedding. Mine and yours.' He gently wiped away the single tear that had begun to flow down her soft cheek. 'I want to marry you Sherry. I've been in love with you for a long, long time.'

'Oh, Quin, are you sure? I love you too and being married to you would be the most wonderful thing in the world. But this is a small town and there would be nothing for you to do here. I don't think you'd like to be a kept man. It wouldn't suit you at all.'

'Yes it would,' he asserted. 'I'm not a poor man you know. I've saved my money and invested it. I've bought some real estate as well and leased it out. My business in Melbourne was sign writing and selling art supplies but I've been painting landscapes for many years as well.' He lowered his dark eyebrows and leered cheekily at her, 'I've even done a bit of life sculpting. Maybe you would like to model for me?'

'Life sculpting. Sounds easy enough. What would I have to do?'

'Just sit still and pose for me.' He decided to break it to her later that she'd have to take her clothes off as well. It might dampen her enthusiasm a little but not his, no never his.

'Can you make much of a living at it?'

'Public art shows aren't usually very lucrative. Last year an art gallery owner in Sydney asked if I would like to have a showing. He wants to feature my work in an Art Magazine. I put it out of my mind because of the trouble I was having but I've been thinking of it again.

'It sounds wonderful,' Sherry enthused.

'I could set up a studio here and paint but if I just did that all the time I'd be bored to death. My investments would keep the wolf from the door for a long time but I'd like to set up my business again somewhere, perhaps in Ballarat. I could even help you in sorting out the mess that Ralph Marley has left. What do you think? Do you want to take a chance on me?'

'I think it's a fantastic idea. I've no idea how to start fixing things. We could do it together. But, I didn't know you were an artist. I thought you were a businessman. You give me the impression of a man who does deals and manages people. Look how well you've managed me. I'd still be up in Queensland making goodness knows what kind of movies if you hadn't come along.'

'Honey, you may be young and inexperienced but I reckon you'd have found a way out. Once you make up your mind to move, you do it without hesitation.'

'What about Marina Angelli? How did you feel about her?' Sherry looked at him with vulnerable eyes, still unsure of her own attraction. 'She was very beautiful wasn't she? Kind of sexy like a movie star. And she had that lovely black hair.'

'Yes, she was beautiful,' he agreed. 'On the outside. Inside I think she might be different, it's hard to say. As for sexy, I really didn't notice. I was too interested in you my sweet girl. You're pretty sexy yourself.' He leered at her comically and moved closer brushing his hand over her shoulder and through her long silky hair.

Then he said soberly, 'I think Marina certainly knew when to take up an opportunity. I only hope she doesn't regret the decision she made especially since that mob up at the homestead seem to have been arrested. I caught a glimpse of a newspaper in the city before we left and the story was all over the front page of the Melbourne Herald.'

He smiled grimly. 'There was even a photo of Jones and Wilson in handcuffs only their names weren't Jones and Wilson, they were Charlie Wallace, a petty criminal who was into phone tapping and burglary, and Bernard Mallinson who is a very well known British financier with underworld connections and a huge off-shore bank account. Walker was there in the background as well still looking like he wanted to kill someone. Merton too. Only his name wasn't Merton, it was John Barkley, an ex serviceman. It had some stuff about how he worked for a while as a cameraman for a television studio. Then he got into trouble dealing drugs and went to jail. When he was released he disappeared overseas. You can change your name but it takes a little more effort, and pain, to change your face. I think they felt quite secure up until now. Probably would have been okay if they'd stuck to movies.'

'Yes, well, I sure had my eyes opened in a hurry,' said Sherry ruefully. 'I don't think I'll ever forget those photos in that darkroom. You really wanted to shock me didn't you? Well, you succeeded. I was wiped out.'

A haunted look came onto her face as she said, 'We really fell into a wasp's nest didn't we? We could have ended up like that guy on the beach. All he really wanted to do was go home, poor man. His family must be devastated.'

Quin's voice was urgent as he said, 'Forget about them now. They're history as far as we're concerned. You know, I'd like an answer to my question, before I go crazy from waiting. Being patient isn't something I'm good at Sherry.'

'What question was that?' Sherry returned innocently, looking at his dark beautiful face and wanting to put her hands on it and explore.

'The one about a wedding. Ours.'

'Oh that question. Well it depends.'

'On what,' he asked, beginning to frown.

'On whether Scrappy approves.'

Quin laughed ruefully. 'That little wretch. He's still muscling in on my turf. The last time I tried to make love to you he came between us.'

'You mean in the camping trailer. He was only protecting my virtue.'

'Was he? Well perhaps he had a point. I was getting rather carried away. I seem to do that a lot around you my darling. Perhaps we'd better apply for a marriage licence tomorrow morning and show it to him. Then he'll know I mean business.'

'What about tonight?'

'How do you mean?'

'Well he's not here. He won't know what we get up to.'

'Hmm. Is that an invitation?' he asked hopefully, a feral gleam in his dark eyes.

'Well, you never know what might happen in the hours between now and morning. I love you. You love me. Like you said, when I decide to move, I don't hesitate.'

Sherry said nothing else for a moment because her mouth was occupied with Quin's invasion of it. His arms held her to his taut body and together they sank back onto the dusty couch, his warm beautiful artistic hands beginning to work a magic spell, heating the soft pliant flesh he stroked with such fertile imagination. Sherry took a breath and promptly sneezed, violently, the dust of the room rising in a cloud as they involuntarily rolled off onto the floor. Moments later Quin was sneezing too and, breathlessly, they made their way out onto the porch once more.

'I have a better idea my love,' said Quin a little while later, his arms around her shoulders as they sat on the porch swing, her head resting on his chest, her hand stroking his flat stomach and pulling at a button on his shirt. 'It's not that far to Melbourne. How about we hop in the car and drive down there.'

He grinned conspiratorially. 'We could book into a city hotel again for the night. We could have a few days holiday before we come back here. Do some sight seeing, go to the movies. That's something you seem to have missed, except for that video on the plane, what was it, oh yes, Stargate. Great movie.

'We can arrange for someone to clean up the house and it will be perfect for when we come back. The solicitor will have worked things out by then as well. We can arrange for our wedding tomorrow before we leave and that way our marriage can begin the way your parents would have wished.'

Firewalking

'It sounds perfect. But what about your family Quin. Don't you have anyone you'd like to invite to our wedding?'

He looked bleak for a moment and said, 'My parents are dead Sherry. My mother was a Cherokee from North Carolina. She was an artist and met my father when she was in Arizona painting landscapes. I have several of her pieces back in Melbourne, a beautiful desert scene and two showing the Grand Canyon. She was very talented.

'I was six when she died. Dad was a geologist but he lost his job and died when I was fifteen. So I have no-one in Australia I want to invite.' He thought for a moment. 'Except my foster family in Sydney. They were very good to me when I was a troubled teenager. Most of my so-called friends hit the road when I hit the papers. They didn't want to be associated with someone like me.'

He laughed. 'I think I scared them. Should have put on war paint and feathered head dress to complete the job. I think I've got a hatchet in the back of the jeep. They'd be so busy running away they wouldn't notice it wasn't a genuine tomahawk.'

Sherry laughed too. 'It would have served them right. The traitors. They couldn't have been real friends if a little thing like a bad newspaper report scared them away. What about your mother's family. Did she have any relatives?'

'Sure. There's my grandparents as well as aunts, uncles and a cousin or two. It's a big family. They live in North Carolina but I haven't seen them since I was small.'

'It's so far away isn't it. Maybe we could go there and visit them Quin. I'd love to see your family. Wouldn't you?'

'Yeah. It sounds great.' Quin's dark eyes lit up. 'We could go over there for our honeymoon. My aunt wrote once when my dad died. My foster mother wrote to them and told them what had happened. I remember their address was in Dad's things brought to me from the hospital. Aunt Lila told me they have a large family hotel. A resort complex I think she said. We'd only stay a few days though. While we're over there I'd like to look around, maybe check out Yosemite and the Grand Canyon. Maybe Tombstone in Arizona too. My mother loved it there. You can tell from her paintings.'

'It sounds incredible. The two of us, touring in the USA. I can't wait.'

'Neither can I,' asserted Quin. 'But we have to wait a month before we can be married. It's a nuisance but that's the law in Australia.'

'I wanted to get married straight away Quin. I don't want to wait a whole month before we can be together.'

'It takes that long for the paperwork to come through. I made some inquiries while I was in the city. Do you think you can hold out?'

'If you can, I can.' Sherry tried to sound positive but sensed she was
failing. 'Yeah, me too. If you can I can.'

'Do you suppose many people wait until they're married to sleep together these
days?' She snuggled in his arms severely undermining his willpower.

'You're becoming cynical Sherry,' said Quin. 'I thought I was the only jaded one in the family?'

She curled even closer to him and put her head under his chin. She sighed. 'Family. That sounds great Quin. I think I'll like being a part of your family.'

He looked into her eyes and smiled gently. 'I'll like being part of your family too Sweetheart. I think the role of husband and father might suit me. How does the role of wife and mother suit you?'

'Perfectly.' She sighed, a look of total concentration on her face, an iridescent gleam in her eyes and she contemplated their future, children, a home, being together, love. A dream come true.

Sherry's voice was husky with emotion as she said, 'Why are we wasting time here then. There's no way we can stay in the house with all this dust around. Let's go over to Pete's house and stay the night. You can sleep in his sofa, I'll take his spare bed.'

At her sceptical look he affirmed, grinning, 'Yes. His spare bed. I can be good if I try. It'll be hard but I can do it. We can head off to Melbourne tomorrow. I want to see Mrs. Scallini anyway and tell her what's happened. Scrappy can come too and see your ex cat. They seemed to get on really well. While I'm talking to Mrs. Scallini, you can make some phone calls to your family in America and arrange for a visit.'

Quin called his family from the Scallini's house and was overwhelmed with their response. The call took so long, almost every relative wanting to say hi. His uncle asked him about his job and when Quin told him he was a sign writer he was offered a job immediately.

We need your talents here he was told. His uncle said they were opening a new, expanded room in their hotel catering for the bingo crowd and a stack of signs were needed. Quin said he would call him back with the answer.

'Sherry, guess what? My uncle offered me a job painting signs for their hotel. What do you think? Do you want to go to America, soon. Like in the next week. We'd have to hurry with all the official details, visas, passports and all that.'

'Well, we've disappeared once already Quin, let's do it again. This time we'll choose where we go. But what about our wedding? Would we have to put it off? I don't think I can wait another six months, do you? That's pushing it too far.'

'I can't wait another day truth be told.' His dark eyes were alive with heated anticipation. 'We can always apply to the judge for a special licence. I asked about that when I was getting the papers because I wanted to marry you straight away.' He grinned ruefully, knowing his eager anticipation was there for all to see but relieved to be able to show his emotions so openly without feeling they would be used against him in any way. In a heady rush of freedom, he realised he no longer had to hide his inner self away from prying eyes. He could finally be himself. 'This hanging around is killing me.'

'What did they say Quin?' Sherry grabbed him by the arm. 'Quick, tell me what they said?'

'Be patient my darling. All good things come to those who wait, but if I'm going overseas for a job immediately, we don't have to wait. In other words, we can get married immediately.' They both smiled widely, as if they couldn't believe their good fortune, a little stunned at the speed things were moving. Sherry began thinking then, of what it would mean to be Quin's wife so soon, the pensive expression appearing on her face causing him to hold his breath, tense with the unspoken fear that she would, for some reason, change her mind. The she grinned, giving him the world once again.

'We've got things to organise Quin. Let's make a list,' she said, calling out, 'Mrs. Scallini, we're getting married. Have you a pen and paper?'

Mrs. Scallini came out from the kitchen where she was preparing lunch and said, 'I know you're getting married child. I heard you screaming.' She sat down with a biro and paper and busily began to write.

Quin let out his breath in satisfied relief and, catching Sherry tightly in his strong arms, said exultantly, 'Yeah! We're getting married. And when we've seen America and spent time with my family we'll come back here and start a new life, together. Always together.'

Sherry put Scrappy's lead on and kissed Mrs. Scallini goodbye. She grabbed the hurried list the motherly little woman had made for her, caught hold of Quin's hand and scooped up her purse. Then she towed her man and dog out to the car. Quin went willingly, knowing at last his dream of a love to last forever had come true.

EPILOGUE

The hotel at Cherokee was huge, the views of the distant mountains magnificent. It was the town where Quin's mother had been born and raised. Quin and Sherry listened at the open window for a while at the shouts of Bingo! coming from the reception rooms downstairs.

They been installed in the Bridal suite when they'd arrived at Quin's family's hotel an hour ago to a welcome from his cousins, aunts and uncles that was without compare. They were to see his Grandparents on the following afternoon. The newlyweds had discovered what it was like to have family that loved and needed them, a thing unknown to either of them for a long time.

Quin and Sherry had spent their wedding night in a Melbourne Hotel then flown to America after their hastily arranged wedding in Archer's Creek.

It was celebrated by the whole town in a joyous outpouring of delight when it was known that, upon their return from America in a few months, they were going to take up residence in the town and build their lives together there.

The Scallinis and some of Quin's friends who he had thought rejected him were there. Also his foster parents from Sydney made a special trip down. They were as proud of him a natural family would be.

Dimming the lights in the room to a soft glow, Quin then slipped an arm around Sherry's waist as she looked out the large picture window, nuzzling her ear and threading her straight silky hair through unsteady fingers.

'I wonder what Scrap's doing now?' he asked softly. 'He hates to be apart from you for long Sherry. It's embarrassing to leave him in the car he howls so much.'

She laughed. 'He's in seventh heaven right now. The woman from the Archer's Creek Post Office has a Yorkshire Terrier just like Scrap. Only it's a female. Her name is Juice. I can't imagine why. Anyway, Juice is boarding with Pete for a few weeks and sharing a kennel with Scrappy. We might have little Scrappys before long. Pete also seems to be getting on like a forest fire with Juice's owner. Maybe he's not such a crusty bachelor after all.'

Firewalking

'Lucky Pete. You know, Scrappy and Juice having a load of little ones sounds like a perfect example to me. We should follow it don't you think?' Quin pulled her closer and kissed a trail of fire down the back of her neck with great enjoyment.

She turned slowly and reached her arms around his neck, her silky halter neck dress of royal blue sliding against the bare skin of his chest. 'Yes, I think we should. You feel so hot,' she murmured, kissing and nipping at his throat, trailing her fingers along his broad shoulders. 'Like a hot fudge sundae. Absolutely delicious.'

'Keep doing that my love and I'll melt before we get to the main course.'

'I'm thinking of this as an entree.' Sherry smiled shyly up into his slumberous eyes. 'Don't forget, this is all pretty new for me. Now that I know what I was missing I don't want to miss a thing.'

'I'll never forget last night as long as I live,' Quin purred in her ear as he pulled her body close to his, sliding his large hands down her back to her thighs and back to her waist in a slow and thorough exploration, tangling their legs together as he danced her toward the satin covered bed awaiting them. 'I waited a long time for you to be mine my darling. I don't want you to miss a thing either.'

She fell onto the bed and he followed her down, their hot kisses and stroking hands desperate to touch and be touched, their bodies straining together, rolling over and over until they found a balance together, both revelling in their closeness and eager to explore the overpowering excitement of their love for each other.

He undid the buttons of her halter and bared her to the waist then pulled the rest of her clothing off in a torrent of need.

She forgot to be shy as his whispered words of encouragement flowed over her breasts, drifting through the air as he explored her delicate skin and roved with his hands and mouth over the treasures he had revealed.

Sherry was unable to stop herself touching his hot skin, helping him to peel off his jeans and exploring the untamed territory of his beautiful body, the hard muscles of his chest and his long strong legs. She gasped aloud in desperate urgency as she touched him with fingertips sensitive to every nuance of heat and texture. Burning, he came alive under her hands and she loved him with everything she had.

Quin groaned deep in his chest as she kissed his throat and threaded her hands through his luxuriant dark hair. It was like soft satin in her hands and she revelled in it. His kisses were like nothing she had ever tasted before as they burned and aroused her until she was all sensation and breathless response, totally enslaved to pleasure.

When he finally possessed her she accepted all he gave and demanded more, much more, pulsating with heat and desire. She urged him on with her hands and body, beckoning him to give in to the overwhelming hunger eating them both alive. He filled her with liquid heat and they reached the pinnacle of release together, floating back to earth in a daze of tangled arms and legs, pulsating with the shattering aftermath, unable after that moment of utter satiation to separate one from the other.

'I love you so much my darling,' he murmured as he began to make love to her all over again with total concentration. 'I'll love you forever.'

'And I you,' she agreed, 'forever,' a sated sigh of contentment crossing her lips. An imp of humour flitted through her mind as she teased, 'Did I remember to thank you last night for the best first time a girl could ever have. It was incredible and much better than a tram ride.'

Quin had to agree. 'You're right, it was much better than a tram ride. It was sensational. I should have thanked you then but I don't remember us having enough breath to talk at all last night let alone say thank you. You can say it now if you like but you better hurry. I feel another wave of breathlessness coming on and I want to be prepared.'

Sherry smiled up into his beautiful loving eyes and said softly, 'Thank you my love.' And they rode the coming wave together.

As Quin had promised so long ago, he loved her all through the night and found all the soft hidden places she had saved just for him. She gave him everything he needed and then found more to give. They found paradise together in each other's loving arms and their hearts finally beat as one.

The End.

Marguérite Turnley writes novels, short
stories, poetry and recipes. She loves to
explore the vastness of Australia in her
stories. Writing about people is her passion,
giving them life through her words.

www.ingramcontent.com/pod-product-compliance
Lightning Source LLC
Chambersburg PA
CBHW070029120726
47909CB00003B/1108